# Haunting Visions

## By

## Marie Jean (MJ) Davis

D1738492

Haunting Visions—by Marie Jean Davis
© 2015 All rights reserved—revised 2020

*Dedicated to my loving father, Leo Corbeil.*
*Your memory will forever live through my eyes, for I have not*
*forgotten you!*

# Prologue

With exhaustion taking a great toll on Jewel Seymour's youthful body, she crawled into bed. Jewel yawned, releasing most of the built-up tension from her body. As soon as her head hit the pillow however, Jewel's vivid dreams began to emerge.

Before long, a land of beauty appeared in front of her. On a tropical island, a drawn-out beach with luminous white sand stretched out before her feet. While walking down this expansive coastline, Jewel could feel the humidity with the scent of the seawater borne on the evening breeze. Despite how warm the setting sun felt on her face, her thoughts of peace and harmony quickly vanished with the approaching young lady.

Jewel recognized her as Elizabeth Nettle, but instead of being eager to see her, the girl simply alarmed Jewel further. Her smile quickly vanished, replaced by an uneasy feeling. Suddenly a thick fog eerily flowed off the ocean with a dense mist that gradually crept over her feet and within minutes it reached her knees. When the fog enveloped the entire lower half of her body, Jewel experienced a sense of fear she had not felt since childhood. The approaching girl was no more than sixteen. Once Elizabeth was about three feet away, the girl opened her mouth. A swarm of flies poured out, streaming upwards. Jewel instinctively raised her arms to avoid the teeming insects, shielding her face, an action she mimicked in her sleep.

She awoke with a start. Gasping for air as though she were drowning—with her heart racing, beads of sweat pearling across her forehead—Jewel knew this was another premonition. She sat up in bed and instinctively turned on the light. Glancing at the clock, she sighed in exasperation. Two in the morning! She immediately turned off the lamp before settling back down.

At thirty-one, Jewel thought her nightmares should be a thing of the past, but apparently, they were not. With new warning signs from the spirit world entering her psyche, Jewel was reminded that she possessed her own secret weapon of sorts—one that would undoubtedly save more lives.

Notions of impending doom still on her mind; Jewel brought her thoughts back to the peaceful beach scene before she finally surrendered to sleep once more.

# PART 1

# Chapter 1

The following morning started off like most days. Unfortunately, Jewel's calmness soon came to an abrupt end when the telephone rang. Quickly answering the phone, she discovered it was her dearest friend, Marcy Cooper.

Jewel must confess that knowing Marcy as long as she had made Jewel somewhat of an expert about her friend. Marcy had lived life to its fullest. She was an attractive woman with short-cropped sandy blonde hair. Jewel wondered why Marcy wore it so stylishly short—maybe it was an unconscious desire to be a tomboy, or merely her wish to be different—nevertheless, she wore it well. Her cute nose that curled up ever so slightly at the very tip, together with her bright blue eyes, gave her the mischievous and intriguing look that turned heads. Her outgoingness, to the point of being called a socialite, illustrated the main difference between the friends. In most respects, they were the same, although unlike Marcy, Jewel sought to stay out of the limelight. Despite this, Marcy, along with the universe, had very different ideas as to what the future held for Jewel.

Suddenly Jewel snapped out of her musing.

"Jewel, did you hear the news today?" Marcy shouted.

Jewel was about to answer her usual, "*NO, but you're going to tell me just the same,*" when Marcy began answering her own question. She frequently did this when she was excited. She was a lovely girl with very little patience. Just the same, Jewel could only grin at her. Marcy began explaining what she had just heard on the news about a girl who had gone missing last evening.

Marcy continued without hesitation. "She was supposed to arrive home after school yesterday. The broadcast mentioned that if anyone had any information on little Tina's whereabouts to immediately call the hotline that was set up at the police station." Marcy was very quick explaining all this. "You understand that you have to help…"

Jewel was not sure whether she was asking or making a statement of fact, and seriously wondered how Marcy could talk so fast without taking a breath.

"Marcy, you know I am going on vacation to Las Vegas next week and that means I won't be here," Jewel reminded her. "I really don't see how I can be of any help."

"You can't mean that! How can you think of going off to Vegas at this time, especially when you are needed here?" Marcy argued.

"Sorry, you know I can't stay. Besides for the past three months, I have worked so intensely and exhaustively that I can't possibly think straight without some time off to rest my nerves. It's absolutely draining searching for dead people." Jewel stated, hoping she would get her point across without arguing her case further.

However, Marcy was far from bowing in defeat. "But Jewel," she snapped, "Don't you feel obligated to help this girl?"

Marcy was becoming extremely upset, not to mention that she was getting on Jewel's nerves. She decided that Marcy must be in a state of shock about the whole ordeal, but she also knew her friend well enough to know she was already looking for a way to sway her into staying.

"Marcy, listen. I'll think about it and let you know later," Jewel said, desperate to find a way out of yet another difficult situation— one that could ultimately consume her. The last case nearly did.

Marcy sighed, saying, "I'll call you later to see if you could just look into her disappearance. Her name is Tina, and she lives in the old Burlington building next to the high school. I'm sure she didn't get lost since she lives far too close to the school. The police are suspecting foul play at this point. So, you do understand why you have to help!" Marcy was persistent if nothing else.

"Okay. Please calm down. I promise I will look into the case if you'll just stop fretting," Jewel retorted. "But you do know that I'm going away next week, regardless?" Jewel wanted to make absolutely sure Marcy was clear about her non-negotiable plans.

Hanging up the phone, Jewel could not help but think that Marcy most certainly knew how to get under someone's skin. On the other hand, Jewel also knew that she would be lost without her. Marcy was the one person who had the ability to ground Jewel to this world when working. She would get lost in the ethers of the far reaches of the atmosphere if it were not for Marcy's ability to bring her back to Earth.

Jewel spent the rest of the day contemplating whether she should stay or go on her well-deserved and much needed vacation. She could not help but feel exhausted and yet knowing there was a young girl out there, somewhere, who needed her assistance made the decision that much harder. It was not like her to go off relaxing in the sun whenever someone went missing. Lately though, it seemed to her that people were disappearing all too frequently!

Jewel was about to make herself a cup of tea when she heard a knock at the door. Walking down the corridor, she could hear the doorknob being rattled. Stopping dead in her tracks, Jewel felt paralyzed as she saw the knob moving back and forth as though someone wanted to break in. She stared at it, wondering who could be so bold as to push their way into her home. Tiptoeing to the end of the hall and relieved she had remembered to lock the door this time, Jewel instinctively grabbed the umbrella out of the hallway stand for added protection. She peered through the peephole to see who was so anxious to enter.

Standing there was a stout, pleasantly plump woman whom she had never seen before. What could she possibly want? Jewel called out to see whether the lady was a door-to-door salesperson but received no reply. Keeping the chain latched, not wanting her visitor to think she could simply saunter on in, Jewel opened the door a crack. To her surprise, Marcy was standing next to the woman. Jewel immediately unlatched the door, swinging it open.

"Marcy, you scared the living daylights out of me!" Jewel exclaimed as her heart continued to race—only now from exasperation.

"Oh, I'm sorry, I forgot that you always lock your door," Marcy said as though there were no other explanations needed.

"Marcy, you know very well I do." Jewel was annoyed.

Marcy continued as though she had not heard a word that was said. "I wanted to introduce you to Mrs. Helena Miles, Tina's mother. Maybe you could help find her daughter? Please Jewel, I would be forever grateful!" Marcy begged, completely disregarding Jewel's concerns; and with the missing girl's mother's eyes pleading as such, Jewel felt trapped.

At that moment Jewel wanted to strangle her best friend for suggesting this in front of Mrs. Miles; she shot Marcy a dirty look, giving her heads-up not to push it any further. At times like this, body language was the best tool to deal with the likes of Marcy, who clearly had no boundaries. What was she thinking cornering Jewel in this way, knowing full well she would either have to read the Missing Person's Report, or have Tina's distraught mother think that she was heartless? Jewel realized the only way around this situation now was to help. This only fueled more anger because once again she had been ensnared in another one of Marcy's hair-brained schemes; her exhaustion would simply have to take a backseat. With great efforts to ignore Marcy, Jewel made a gesture of civility towards the desperate woman, who had no idea of Marcy's uncanny abilities.

"I'm sorry, Mrs. Miles. My name is Jewel Seymour. Nice to meet you," Jewel said, extending her hand. "I'm very sorry to hear of your daughter's disappearance except I'm not sure how I may be of assistance. I'm sure the police will locate her in due course." Jewel half grinned.

She hoped Mrs. Miles would not pursue the matter since Jewel desperately needed some time to rest her frazzled brain. It had only been a week since the last case of a missing teen had been resolved. Extremely distraught after helping the police locate the girl's body, Jewel found it rather difficult to forget her name: Elizabeth Nettle— such a beautiful young girl. Jewel had felt helpless after realizing there was nothing she could do to change the outcome. At this point she simply felt too depleted to begin investigating another missing child's case.

Mrs. Miles asked in a strong Spanish accent. "I be grateful to sit wit' jou and try to see if anyting at all comes, si?" Evidence of desperation laced in her voice. Mrs. Miles was a short, heavyset woman. Obviously, she had been crying, her eyes red and puffy along with a raspy voice indicating she had been up all night as well: all signs, only too familiar to Jewel, now staring her in the face.

Jewel swallowed hard. "I don't want you to feel that I'm ignoring your pain in any way, Mrs. Miles, but I don't know if I could be of service at all. I just finished an extremely challenging case and I'm pretty worn out." Jewel threw a glance at Marcy that could have killed—if only she had the power to do so.

"Pleez call me Helena. I beg of jou por favor! Could jou try, si? I miss my Tina and want her home wit' me," Mrs. Miles pleaded.

Hearing the anguish in her voice with tears starting to flow down her cheeks made for an awkward situation. Jewel could detect subtle things in people, and while concentrating on Helena's aura; she instantly received a flash picture of a young girl from one of her visions. She could see this girl just as clearly as she could see Helena Miles standing before her.

"You just saw something, didn't you?" Marcy exclaimed. She was very much aware of Jewel's gift, if that is what such things were called. In Jewel's opinion, she sometimes thought she would be better off without it. For as long as she could remember, Marcy had a knack for spotting when Jewel drifted off. Jewel instinctively shook her head, indicating no, to get herself out of yet another delicate situation. Now, Marcy *and her big mouth* were the only thoughts filling Jewel's mind; she concentrated again, shifting her focus to Mrs. Miles' calloused hands, which clearly indicated she was a hard worker, possibly in agriculture.

Forming a personal profile of someone using something as obvious as his or her appearance does not require psychic ability No, to help this woman find her daughter, psychic abilities would be highly valuable in retracing the girl's last steps. *That is of course if she is still alive,* thought Jewel. Suddenly, in that moment, she completely hated the idea of being involved with this girl—she might already be dead for all she knew. What Jewel did know for certain was that once her visions began, they rarely stopped, so at this point, there was almost no turning back for her. While this plagued Jewel, she could not help but wonder if there was a serial killer at large, considering there were now two missing teens in recent weeks—a pedophile perhaps, since the girls were quite young.

Jewel knew she needed to proceed with caution, however. She showed them both into the living room. As her home was rather small, it made meeting with people somewhat difficult. Entering through the front door one could immediately see all there was at a quick glance. It was a one-bedroom suite with a small walk-in closet she had retrofitted into a tiny office. She glanced around the space seeing how disorganized her home really had become in the past few weeks.

Jewel blushed, "With all the work of late, I simply didn't have time to clean." Once more she felt highly displeased with Marcy for showing up unannounced. While Jewel thought of Marcy's exploitive behavior, she shot her a few more reproachful glances. The 'socialite' simply ignored her glares. Once she brought Mrs.

9

Miles to her front door, Marcy knew she could get her way, no matter what. This was just another way she pierced through Jewel's defenses, giving her the distinct feeling that her close friend knew her all too well.

Jewel knew Marcy had a good heart despite her extreme impulsivity. She was a very inquisitive woman who looked at life as though it were one big adventure. This is probably what drew them together initially; although at the moment, her big heart, and that overactive mind of hers were qualities that quite frankly, Jewel could do without. Being the busybody was also cause to worry—just last year Marcy found herself in handcuffs for snooping in a neighbor's backyard. Of course, Jewel had bailed her out of that situation. She tended to act first and think later, and in Jewel's mind, this was a deadly combination. At the ripe age of thirty-two, Marcy worked out every day. This kept her fit for her marathon runs. Jewel used to tease Marcy that she was just running away from things, or into them—whichever came first. And frankly no one knew for sure which.

It probably stemmed from her youth. Marcy grew up with an aunt, who raised her with lots of love, and for the most part, allowed Marcy free rein. Her aunt would tell her that she could be anything she wanted to be when she grew up, but she had to grow up first. Life had not been so easy for Marcy, however. She had lost both her parents, Ed and Gisele Cooper, to a freak accident that happened in their home while Marcy was staying with a friend. It was only when she returned home that Marcy found the police and fire trucks parked in front of her house. A neighbor had smelled a foul odor outside his back window and had notified the police. It turned out to be a deadly gas leak. They had found Marcy's parents asleep in their bed unaware of what had killed them. At the time, the whole ordeal was devastating for a nine-year-old. An older aunt, her only living relative, took Marcy in.

Aunt May lived in the same neighborhood as Jewel, and when Marcy came to live with her aunt it was fate that brought the girls together. She was enrolled the following week in Jewel's fourth grade class at Saint Vincent Elementary. At that time, Jewel secretly envied Marcy for living with her Aunt May, who religiously baked wonderful chocolate chip cookies and apple pies. The memory of walking home from school, and the powerful aroma of freshly baked cookies floating down the street still brought a smile to Jewel's face even now.

On the other hand, Jewel's father was a single parent who was working most of the time just to put food on the table and clothes on their backs. Jewel's mother had left before Jewel was old enough to remember her. She could not say that she knew her mom in the least. The only photograph Jewel had of her mother was one of her holding a baby in her arms. That photograph was still displayed in Jewel's front room. However, one simply cannot know someone through a picture. With her father being too busy with work, or with a few peculiar girlfriends, he rarely made time for them to discuss her mother. He always said they did just fine without her. Jewel could always sense sadness in his voice despite his attempts at hiding it. She was certain he said these things to avoid feeling the deep hurt he must have felt and not wanting to upset his young daughter. Truth be told, not having a mother at home did make it easier for both Marcy and Jewel to spend countless hours at Aunt May's house.

They entered the closet-office. Jewel felt quite embarrassed about the close quarters. With little room for all three to sit comfortably, Jewel shuffled some stacked papers and books around to accommodate them. The antique desk, with its weathered corners and coffee stains, was purchased that same year at a garage sale to provide some space to work on. Unfortunately, it had simply become additional shelving to pile countless books on top. Another chair from the living room was brought in and placed in the doorway, allowing Marcy to sit in on the session as well. Judging from her exasperated sigh, Jewel sensed that Marcy would have preferred to sit inside the tight confines, but she was not about to complain. Obviously, Marcy could sense her disapproval.

Mrs. Helena Miles sat directly across from Jewel, since any information received through a person's vibration, or '*vibes*' as they are known, improves greatly when the person sits directly in front of the medium. Jewel seated herself in front of Helena looking deeply into her eyes for the very first time. She could see pain and despair on the woman's face, no doubt due to her missing daughter. She obviously loved her child and was clearly very protective of her. With dark brown eyes and long lashes that painted a handsome and supple face—she had been a very pretty woman in her youth. But the years were now showing in the lines delineating her facial features. The lack of sleep likely didn't help either. After asking the routine questions regarding Helena's full name and her maiden name, Jewel began.

All at once, visions of Helena's past began to flood Jewel's senses. She glimpsed that Helena spent most of her adult life as a single mother determined to make up for becoming pregnant at a very young age. Once pregnant, her extremely religious parents had disowned her and sent her out into the world to fend for herself. Despite the burden, she did eventually marry a Mr. Miles. Upon discovering the baby could in no way be his child, he abandoned them both. Despite having many ups and downs in her life, she did very well for herself and Tina. Helena always had a smile on her face and a great love for life. She poured all her love and energy into her daughter whom she undoubtedly adored. Jewel suspected Tina's life was difficult at times, having such a protective mother. She also intuitively 'picked up' that Mrs. Miles had never regretted having her daughter, but what she did regret was not having had an extended family.

How devastated her closely-knit Mexican family had been when they learned this shocking news: an unwed daughter expecting a child was a disgrace—one that seriously affected the entire family's traditional values.

Helena wished things were different indeed. Her parents were very caring and loving people who had been raised in a very traditional background. Unfortunately, the day Helena became pregnant changed everything: she could only remember her father yelling things at her, things she would never forget, and never repeat. There were terrible words exchanged that night. So appalling, that Helena spent countless nights trying to forget them. The words that could never be unsaid echoed in her mind over and over again: 'the terrible dishonor' she had caused her family, among other choice words not repeatable. Her mother did not want her daughter to be thrown out but felt powerless to stop such disgrace her family now suffered. They had only their honor left, having suffered misfortunes of their own.

A few years earlier, the Gomez family had owned a small restaurant on the shores of Baja, California. They were prosperous people. However, when the Mexican government decided to expand into the resort business, making way for large hotels along the beach, the government seized their property. They had offered a position of busboy to Mr. Gomez in the hotel. He had held a much more respectable position as owner of his own beach restaurant, and he had refused the hotel management's offer, saving his dignity from further humiliation. Helena's parents packed up all they had and moved north with their six children in tow. They managed to enter the USA, leaving all their memories behind. Not having much by way of money, the Gomez family settled for a small shack near the ocean.

They settled in the most southern tip of California where houses were going up quickly. To make the best of their new circumstances in this new land, Mrs. Gomez found work as a housemaid while Mr. Gomez landed work as a carpenter. The fact that there were many homes going up helped a great deal. Mr. Gomez could always find work as a carpenter. It was not much at first, but they soon loved their new life. When Helena became pregnant, her father was once again reminded of the shame of losing everything and decided he would not put his family through yet another disgrace. Without further discussion, he banished Helena to a life of misery.

Mrs. Gomez had lost a daughter and missed her very much. There was nothing she could say to convince her husband to allow their beautiful daughter to return home. She never fully forgave her husband either. Regardless, she went on with life to support the other five children. Even if Mrs. Gomez had wanted to find Helena, she would not know where to begin, especially in a foreign land. But life must go on and so it did.

All these memories and Helena's suppressed feelings came flooding into Jewel's mind in an instant as she gazed into Helena's eyes. Jewel was left with an overwhelming sense of anguish. She shook her head slightly.

Once again Jewel looked deeply into Helena's eyes seeing not only despair, but also Tina. It was as if through Helena's eyes, she could see her daughter. The teenager was a bright and dedicated scholar. She had easily adopted her mother's love of life. With the passing years, Helena's bright smile expanded with appreciation for her wonderful daughter for she had brought her much joy and happiness. Sadly, the past was quite entrenched in Helena and she worried about Tina as she grew into a beautiful young lady. At sixteen, Tina looked much older. She was often mistaken for being at least eighteen. Not wishing her daughter to follow in her footsteps, Mrs. Miles had kept a watchful eye on her.

Tina had long, dark brown hair that grew thick and healthy. She had a beautiful face with eyes that could seduce any young man. Her lips were full and perfect with red that could only be found in a lipstick tube. She had blossomed into this angelic beauty—one who had most boys at school swooning at her feet. Tina knew her mother would not allow her to date, but she never knew why her mother was so overprotective, almost to the point of being overbearing.

Mrs. Miles had never shared the shame of her past with her only daughter, so any hope of Tina ever understanding her mother's protective ways seemed lost forever.

When Jewel stopped looking into Helena's eyes, she found that both Helena and Marcy were staring at her as though they were witnessing an event never seen before. She was speechless at first, not knowing what to say to either of them.

Finally, Marcy broke the silence by asking, "Did you see anything?"

Jewel shook her head and instinctively said, "I haven't seen anything that could shed light on Tina's whereabouts." Instead, she simply reassured Mrs. Miles that sometimes useful information would not always be forthcoming, but she would try again later.

Helena reluctantly rose from her chair and thanked Jewel just the same, giving the impression that she appreciated her time and for making an effort. The truth is, one cannot force such things to materialize.

Having been thrown onto this woman's path, Jewel felt compelled to assist now more than ever, and informed Mrs. Miles she would call to see whether it would be possible for her to postpone her vacation. Helena smiled for the first time, thanking Jewel for any help she could provide, "God bless jou. Jou be sent from God as an angel sent from the heavens," Helena said sincerely, while touching Jewel's hands.

Thanking her for stopping by, Jewel told Helena she would be in touch. "I'll call you tomorrow to let you know if things work out with my flight."

Jewel walked toward the front door and opened it to allow both women to leave. She had the distinct impression Marcy wanted to stay behind to interrogate her about the information she might have obtained regarding Tina's disappearance. Before Marcy got any ideas in her head, Jewel closed the door behind them. She was exhausted.

# Chapter 2

Sitting at her desk, trying to figure out just how she was going to pull off her disappearing act and head to Vegas before Marcy got to her, Jewel picked up the phone to call the airline.

A robotic recording instructed her to stay on the line as, "All customer service representatives were busy assisting other customers." Expecting to be on hold for a while, she settled in for the wait. Suddenly, Jewel received a flash of information about the missing girl. She could see Tina standing outside the school and she seemed to be waiting for someone. Jewel could not determine exactly what time of day it was, but it was definitely daytime. Before Jewel could see any other details, the mysterious image faded from view.

It was then that Jewel heard someone ask, "How may I help you?" with a distinct Texan drawl.

Snapping out of her reverie, Jewel blurted out before the agent hung up, "Yes please, I must delay my vacation plans to Vegas. Could I please rebook my flight and what flights are available…?"

After some juggling, at last the new plans were sorted out; she would be flying out a week after next Friday. This now gave Jewel an extra week to assist with Tina's mysterious disappearance.

The agent did her usual customer service routine, and with her delightful Texan accent asked, "Is there anything else I could do for y'all?"

"No, thank you," Jewel replied before hanging up. Jotting down the rescheduled trip onto her desk calendar and refocusing her attention on her new case, Jewel was suddenly overcome by a gripping sense of doom.

It seemed that lately she was extremely distracted and forgetful, which was the main reason she had planned the trip in the first place. She desperately needed a rest from the chaos of dealing with missing youths and the ensuing aftermath.

Jewel tried to pinpoint just exactly when these visions of hers had begun. How old had she been? What had triggered them? This was the part of the gift of 'knowing' or 'envisioning' certain events and situations that most people could not possibly fathom—unless they possessed the gift themselves, of course.

Jewel was only six when it first occurred to her that she might be different from other children. The fact that she had grown up on a small acreage—totally isolated from other children, with no idea the majority of people did not possess a sense of knowing as she did—likely contributed to her being so different. However, it was when she began attending school that her world as she knew it began to unravel.

At first, Jewel noticed that other children were unable to see the things she could see. This is also when she discovered that children could be very cruel. They would taunt her by calling her a liar when they could not see what she saw so crystal-clear floating beside them. But no matter how vicious the children were, Jewel found ways to amuse herself. Being an outcast, she became a loner, finding it too difficult, if not impossible to engage with, or even remotely relate to any of her classmates. So, the ghostly entourage that followed Jewel from whatever worldly place they had come from had always been her only true companions.

It was only when she reached her twenties that Jewel sought professional help for her so called '*gifts.*' Somehow the gifts felt more like an outsider looking in on other people's lives—kind of like observing people through their windows but never really being a part of their world. Although, Aunt May encouraged Jewel not to worry about what others thought of her, Jewel remained an outcast—well except for Marcy, of course.

Years later Jewel heard about a professor at the university she was attending who might be able to help with her now frowned upon 'curse.' Professor James T. Brown was remarkably good with people—a quality he needed to possess if he was going to help someone like her. With Marcy's insistence and persistence, Jewel finally agreed to schedule an appointment with him—what would turn out to be the first of many visits that were to follow.

Jewel recalled knocking on his door, feeling quite nervous about seeing someone she did not know regarding a condition that had not been well received—if not totally rejected—by the mainstream professional world.

"Come in," Jewel heard the professor announce.

"Hello, Professor Brown. Thank you for seeing me," Jewel said, doing her best to disguise how nervous she truly felt.

Professor Brown was a tall man with light brown hair, spotted with gray patches. He looked quite distinguished with his narrow, straight nose and thin lips. He smiled. "Yes, do sit down, please," pointing to the chair in front of his desk. She sat down.

Jewel glanced around the room noticing the many framed degrees and diplomas hanging on the wall facing her. There were several bookcases with stacks of books and papers everywhere. It was a wonder he could find anything at all in this mayhem. Perhaps the professor liked his desk this way, suddenly remembering that her housekeeping skills were not exactly something to brag about either.

"Professor, I've come to ask you some questions about the supernat…" Jewel's voice trailed off. She swallowed hard and restarted the statement. "I would like to know about the supernatural." *Do I sound crazy?* she wondered. She felt terribly uncomfortable. One thing she knew for certain: her facial expressions and her body language must surely be giving her away, revealing how awkward and embarrassed she felt sitting there across from him.

"Would you care to give me a description of what you mean?" He asked, showing no signs of shock, nor judgment.

Uncertain how to explain herself and almost paralyzed by an overwhelming fear; Jewel steeled herself and continued, nervously, but now determined to continue regardless of whether the professor cast a harsh "verdict" upon her or had her committed.

"What do you know about the supernatural world and people who experience visions?" Her anxiety was mounting again.

"I have done some research on the phenomenon. What would you like to know exactly?" He seemed casual, as if this type of inquiry were an everyday occurrence in his world.

Feeling slightly relieved, Jewel decided to dive headlong into the subject, whether he assessed her as crazy or not.

"Well I… I can see things that have not yet occurred," she had stammered, suddenly feeling terribly vulnerable. She had braced herself for a mental disorder diagnosis—schizophrenia maybe, where the only remedy was a pharmaceutical prescription. If he did that, she vowed only to herself, she would not take the drug. "Really? Do go on," he insisted, now sounding rather intrigued.

Jewel wondered whether he was downplaying her symptom of delusions, but she could not be sure. She shared her concerns regardless—that she could sometimes see things that others apparently could not, and it was her father who had dismissed her experiences as being the result of a wild imagination. But at the tender young age of four, she had not really understood what he meant by it.

"I would also have dreams about events that would happen the following week or so, like the time I saw the road being fixed before it was actually repaired. And another time I dreamt that the skies became heavy with clouds practically touching the rooftops of surrounding homes. Of course, seeing this stuff before it actually happened was alarming in the beginning."

Professor Brown took notes as she recounted these events. Jewel had begun to feel somewhat uncomfortable—her fears creeping up again. She wondered if he would advise the university faculty to have her expelled and locked up indefinitely in an asylum. Much to her surprise and delight, instead, he assured her that he wanted to know more, and he also wanted to start meeting on a weekly basis.

Encouraged by her first encounter, Jewel and Professor Brown developed a rapport and created a bond of trust with one another—an experience she could not recall ever having with anybody else other than Marcy and her Aunt May. The professor believed that some people may be granted some type of gift in order to help others. Having no other choice but to believe him, and not having anyone else to confide in, Jewel accepted his philosophy and began to truly appreciate their professional friendship. He had not labeled her a 'freak' and that alone had given her an incredible sense of relief.

At their last appointment, Professor Brown advised her she could always count on him to be of any assistance or comfort. As she was leaving his office that day, he had said. "Call me if you ever need anything." With that feeling of reassurance, Jewel left his office; she felt incredibly elated and blessed with her newfound life and sense of personal and emotional freedom.

She smiled as she sat at her desk. Her friendship with Professor Brown had been a special connection—as if he had been sent to her just at the right time when she needed support the most. Suddenly it occurred to her that she needed to talk to him right now—an impulse she knew she should act on.

As she sat there, she was startled when the phone began to ring, jarring her out of her deep thoughts. She picked up the receiver. "Yes?" Jewel asked.

She heard Marcy's voice on the other end. "Did you get anything concrete from Mrs. Miles' energy?"

"Marcy," Jewel sighed, feeling annoyed, "Stop pestering me, please."

With total disregard of Jewel's aggravation, her busybody friend went on. "I just thought that maybe you didn't want to say anything in front of Mrs. Miles and that's why you kept quiet." She said it quickly, as though she would explode if she did not speak out.

"You know you can be such a pain at times," Jewel retorted.

"Well don't be irritated with me. I just wanted to help," Marcy grumbled in response.

It was clear she had a way of making Jewel feel guilty for being short with her. Jewel softened her tone. "I'm sorry, Marcy. It's just that you brought her over when you knew I was planning a getaway this week. And now I feel obligated to help in yet another missing-person's case. Besides, you know how the last one turned out and how I felt so drained after such an intense search."

"I know how it turned out. It's not like you killed her yourself!" Marcy piped, striving to be on equal ground with Jewel.

"I know I wasn't responsible for her death. But this has more to do with being asked to do the difficult task of telling the family what has happened to their beloved child," Jewel countered.

"I just thought I could help as well," Marcy put in, almost whining now.

"I can't talk right now. Can you give me Mrs. Miles' phone number so I can let her know that I have changed my flight reservations for the following Friday?"

"I'll just call her and let her know myself," Marcy chirped.

Jewel felt an urge to reiterate; "You do understand that I won't be here after next Friday even if I help her out this time and, even if the case is still unresolved…"

"Yes, yes, you won't regret staying, I promise you." She did not mean to cut Jewel off, but she often did anyways.

*Right. As if Marcy can really keep her promise*, Jewel thought. She begrudgingly thanked Marcy for passing on the message and hung up the phone. Now plans needed to be put in place as to just how she was going to help find Tina in the short time remaining.

Jewel could not help but wonder if the first missing girl was in any way connected to the disappearance of Tina Miles. This would require a bit of detective work. Beginning with checking out a few things down at the police station. She decided that tomorrow morning she would pay Spence Walker a little visit. He was her one and only connection within the police department; perhaps he might be able to shed some light on this case.

Jewel had known Spence for a long time. He had been one grade behind her in school, so they had never really had the opportunity to expand their relationship. It was probably just as well: Spence had been rather headstrong during his teenage years, mellowing as he got older.

Spence had not had it very easy as a child either. Being the only mixed-race student in their school and obviously clearly exceptionally intelligent, he, too, was teased for being different: a nerd with square glasses. He kept to himself a lot and did not really develop many social skills. He believed this was one of the best ways of deterring the jokesters who made fun of him at every turn. He would sit back and observe people rather than interact with them. He had basically done what Jewel had done but for quite different reasons.

Given how extremely bright Spence was in school, he could have chosen any profession. Luckily, he made good decisions. The quality admired most in Spence Walker was his determination to make a difference in the world. Consequently, he decided that being a police officer would enable him to attain his goal. Everyone knew that Spence would soon be off to the police academy in San Diego. After graduating he returned to Imperial Beach, California.

Spence and Jewel finally met for the first time at Marcy's fundraiser soon after his return to their quaint but growing town. Later that same week, they bumped into one another at the library and began talking about their common interests. They both wanted to make a difference in the world. Also, they possessed the same type of inquisitive, forensic detective mind, although they certainly dealt with their predilection for deduction in very different ways.

Spence was tall, broad-shouldered with shiny black hair that glistened in the sun. With an athletic physique, he was extremely fit and toned, enabling him to perform his type of grueling work. He took pride in the way he dressed and paid particular attention to his grooming. Clean-shaven with striking dark eyes—any woman who captured his intense gaze would feel fortunate since he was a very handsome man. Jewel had even dated him but regrettably it had not worked out—they were too much alike—or at least that was the excuse Jewel had convinced herself. In any case, they decided to remain good friends; they had a strange bond between them that could never be entirely explained.

# Chapter 3

The next morning Jewel woke with a start, bolting upright in bed. She had been dreaming all night and felt she had not slept at all. Her dreams were so vivid that it was hard to discern them from her waking state. Last night was no different than any other night with lucid visions of the people close to her and people she had not yet met. However, she did remember having a vision of watching Tina walking down a street, almost scurrying away from a watchful eye. Unfortunately, Jewel could not see who it could be. Could someone have abducted her? Or, could Tina have run away from a stifling life where her mother kept watch over her every move, making Tina feel that she could no longer breathe? At this point one could only speculate as to her disappearance.

Jewel glanced at the clock realizing that she might be too late to catch Spence at the police station before he went on patrol. After a very quick shower, she slipped into some black slacks and a light blue fleece top as she scrambled for the front door; she grabbed her jacket, shoes, and purse seemingly all in one quick motion. She slammed the door behind her as she left.

The day was already bright and warm. These days the sunrise was so early that by 9:00 AM it was already quite muggy outside. Now Jewel wished she had worn something much lighter. No matter how hot it became, she still loved the sun. With the closeness of the sea as one's backdrop, and the green space that invited one to share in the natural beauty, this felt like heaven on Earth to her. This morning though, she desperately needed to meet up with Spence: her immediate objective now was to get to the police station on the corner of Oak and Main Street.

Driving past the ocean, she could not help but notice the swelling waves cresting upwards with white foam rolling up on the shore. She sighed. This was a particularly spectacular morning with clear blue skies, with waves pushing each other up on the seashore like an unrelenting army attacking an impenetrable wall. She may have lived here for years, but the scene still took her breath away. She imagined herself lounging on the beach with a good book; that felt much better than running around searching for missing people, but that was her occupation—her life and her livelihood.

Meeting with Spence would be the highlight of her day. They seemed to connect so well at times that Marcy wondered why they never stayed together. At times Marcy could be so pushy. Jewel insisted she was fine with being single, and she certainly did not need a man to complete her life. Jewel's mother had left when she was an infant, after all, and her father had raised her by himself. And he did just fine, Jewel maintained.

She parked, quickly plugged the meter and locked her car. Running into the station, she noticed that Steve Bronski, who usually sat at the front desk, was not there today. But he was always there, she thought. He shone by his absence, as the saying went. Jewel wondered what could possibly have kept Steve from coming in this morning. She approached the desk and spoke to an officer she had never seen before.

"Excuse me, can you help me? I was wondering if I could speak with Spence Walker, or rather Detective Walker," Jewel quickly changed tactics.

"That depends. And yes, Detective Walker is here. Can I tell him who is here to see him, Miss…?"

The young man spoke with such a low, husky voice that Jewel could barely hear him. "Yes, of course. Please tell him it's Jewel Seymour," staring past him to the window partitions, trying to catch a glimpse of Spence. She returned her attention to the officer, determined not to seem rude. "I'm so sorry. I don't believe we've met." Jewel extended her hand, hoping to find out more about him, and possibly find out why Steve was not at work.

He stood up and introduced himself as Jim Gord. He shook her hand, smiling. He had big eyes that were a shade of baby blue rarely seen in males. He sat back down, picked up the telephone and called Spence.

"Detective, there's a lovely lady here to see you."

Jewel's cheeks flushed a deep pink. "What a shame he's so young," she thought, hoping he had not noticed she was blushing like a schoolgirl. It almost seemed that the men her age were already married or divorced and not interested in getting into a serious relationship ever again. But, since she was not looking for a relationship, Jewel knew she did not have the right to complain either way. At any rate there was not enough time in the day to get serious with anyone.

Spence soon came out of his office and smiled genuinely as he spotted Jewel waiting in the lobby. "Ah, Jewel!" He shouted, "Glad you could stop by. And what brings you to my part of town? Let me guess." He gave Jewel a warm smile, while nodding at the young officer.

Was there an inside joke or some unconscious understanding that men transmitted to one another? Jewel could only wonder. As they both walked towards his office, Jewel responded. "You undoubtedly know so you can stop the pretense," Jewel said, while her cheeks went red once again. "I was hoping to speak with you before you went out on duty. Would you have time for a quick coffee down the street?" Jewel was eager to have just a few moments alone with him to find out more about the disappearance of Tina Miles.

"Sure. I think that can be arranged," Spence replied, turning back towards Jim. "I'll be out of the office for a short while. If anyone is looking for me, you've got my number." Spence cupped Jewel's back to escort her out the door.

Jewel had been extremely happy for Spence when he had been promoted to the rank of detective. It suited him to have a little more responsibility, not to mention the respect he deserved from the other officers. For Spence to have much freer rein in his new detective role was a definite plus, making it much easier for the two of them to meet up anytime.

They left the station. With Spence's long strides, they quickly walked down the street to a little café they both frequented where the best coffee was served in all of Imperial Beach—although the price of coffee was a bit of a deterrent, it was well worth it. They ordered two coffees and one cheesecake to share and sat next to the front window to get a little sunshine. The air conditioning was rather cool inside and lounging in the sun kept Jewel from freezing.

Not wasting any time with niceties, Jewel cut to the chase. "Spence, what do you know about the missing girl, Tina Miles? Her mother paid me a visit last night. Well it was more like Marcy delivered her onto my doorstep," she sighed.

Spence hesitated for a minute. "All I know is that a very hysterical mother came into the station to report her daughter's disappearance two days ago. I felt she was overreacting somewhat and suggested she wait a few more hours before getting too upset about the whole affair. You know how teenagers can lose track of time, especially when they go over to a friend's house. Mrs. Helena

Miles said that her daughter would never do such a thoughtless thing—that she just felt something was wrong. I simply filled out the paperwork at her insistence. Then I asked her to call if she still had not heard from her today. But she obviously could not wait because she called the station late evening, reporting that Tina was still missing and insisted that we start looking for her immediately. Helena was informed that there were already a couple of patrol cars dispatched in the neighborhood. I assured her that we would keep patrolling the area and we'd be broadening our search at dawn. Last night an officer dropped by her residence to get more information and to look around the place for clues. She gave us a recent photo of Tina. This morning I made copies to hand out to the rest of the men. We also faxed out copies to the nearest counties, but we've had no luck so far. I regret not beginning the search right away, but teenagers are notorious for going missing for a few hours. We are doing what we can to locate her," Spence said while sipping his coffee.

"Sounds like you've already done quite a lot. Did you get any clues as to where she may have gone?" Jewel asked.

"Nothing so far, but we did bring in a few items from her bedroom that seemed odd," Spence replied. "There was a book of matches lying on her desk that seemed out of character, especially after speaking with her mother. She thought the matches couldn't possibly belong to her daughter."

"What was on the match book? Were they from some place nearby? A phone number inside perhaps?"

"They belonged to a bar on Centre Avenue, the Picante's Bar & Grill. Her mother mentioned that Tina would never have gone there," Spence shrugged it off as though he understood teenagers.

"Perhaps someone who's been there gave it to her," Jewel suggested.

Spence's cell phone rang. He excused himself before walking towards the doorway of the café.

Jewel tried to eavesdrop on the conversation but could not make out what was being said.

When Spence returned to their table, he seemed flustered. "Sorry, I've got to run. They need me at the station. Can we talk a little later?"

"Oh sure," Jewel replied. Honestly, she wished they could have spoken a little longer to get some answers to the growing number of questions she had. Answers such as to whom the book of matches belonged to would have been helpful. Paying a little visit to the Picante's Bar & Grill herself was definitely in order. She would have to be careful when questioning the bartender; she did not want to step on anybody's toes.

"I'll catch you later, Spence!" Jewel called out as he ran out of the café, after paying the bill.

Jewel sat there alone finishing her coffee while piecing together the many clues, wondering how everything could possibly fit together. Nothing of importance came in the way of psychic information. She wondered whether the matches were just a red herring. Today was already Wednesday, leaving her only ten days to solve this case. Maybe she should pay a visit to Mrs. Miles to see if more information could be obtained from the distraught mother. Sometimes seeing the last place where a person had been before disappearing helped to connect with the missing person. Hopefully, Tina's vibes were still strong to sense what happened to her, bringing her closer to solving this mystery. Unfortunately, Jewel could never tell when a piece of information might trigger a flash of missing evidence.

Once more Jewel drove across town to see whether Mrs. Miles was home. She lived next to the high school in the same house where the retired school principal, Mrs. Claudia McCann used to reside—the same principal that Marcy and Jewel knew as teenagers. Tina's mother had bought the place a good deal cheaper than it was worth, mainly because Mrs. McCann wanted to sell quickly.

While driving past the school, Jewel looked for any signs of Tina's presence but unfortunately nothing came to mind. At times Jewel wished that one could simply summon things to happen, and perhaps then Tina would contact her. Sadly, it was not as simple as picking up the telephone.

Jewel parked across the street from the Miles' residence. While walking up the front walk, Jewel attempted to sense any activity. No such luck, however. She knocked but received no response. It seemed no one was home. She pressed an ear against the red wooden door and listened for any activity inside. Undaunted, she leaned over to peek through the large front window, not knowing what she would find, but she persisted regardless of her intrusion. She could not see any movement inside. She decided to go around to the back of the house. At first, she did not notice anything unusual, then suddenly she heard what sounded like a car engine. Rushing to the back lane, Jewel watched a blue car heading down the alley. Before she could open the gate to get a better look at the license plate, it had turned the corner and gone out of sight. All she was able to determine was that it was a medium size blue sedan. She retraced her steps to the back door of the house to peer through the window. Staring right back at her through the window was Mrs. Miles. The woman rushed to open the door, inviting Jewel to come in all the while apologizing for scaring her half to death.

Jewel felt a little guilty. "I'm so sorry, Mrs. Miles, for entering your backyard uninvited. I thought perhaps I might sense Tina's presence if I went around the property. I did knock at your front door first, but you didn't answer the door." The last thing Jewel wanted was to be arrested for a B&E! Being charged with a breaking and entering violation would be incredibly humiliating.

"No, that's all right, no need apology. Did jou get anyting new?" Mrs. Miles anxiously inquired.

"Sorry, no. Perhaps I could see her room? Maybe some useful information might be found by looking over some of her personal items," Jewel suggested.

"Ah si, do come in and sees her room, come wit' me," Mrs. Miles said while pointing towards the stairs.

The house seemed old. A fragrance of mixed cooking spices filled the air. The floorboards creaked and there were many smaller rooms that gave further indication of its age. The stairs leading to the upper level reminded Jewel of the staircase at Aunt May's old place: narrow, with a thick, handcrafted wooden rail running up one side.

Jewel followed Helena up the steps where they passed one bedroom. Judging by the contents of that room, it was likely Helena's. At the end of the hall to the right there was a bathroom, and on the left was Tina's room. Helena stood by the door of this room and with a wave of her hand, invited Jewel to go in. At first glance, it was definitely a teenager's room. There were posters of boys and what must be members of her favorite band plastered all over the walls, leaving only a few spots where the original, bright pink paint was still visible.

"This is my Tina's room. I keep it very tidy for her," Mrs. Miles offered needlessly.

No one would think that any teenager could keep his, or her room, that clean. One could only wonder whether this was a source of Tina's frustration, having her mother invading her private space all the time. Maybe Tina just could not take it anymore and wanted to vanish?

"May I have a few moments alone in here?" Jewel asked. But seeing Mrs. Miles hesitation she added, "To view Tina's personal belongings with hopes of getting some vibes from them. It really helps if I'm alone," Jewel explained.

"Ah, si, jou call me if need someting," she said before exiting the room and walking towards the stairs.

Jewel closed her eyes to see whether she could pick up anything. However, the only thing filling her thoughts were the creaks coming from the old staircase as Mrs. Miles descended.

The next moment, Jewel received a vision of a male speaking to someone unknown. She could not see Tina around and could not actually detect a connection to her either. She opened her eyes and walked towards the window, which was next to the girl's dresser. She picked up Tina's hairbrush and held it for a few minutes but still could not pick up much that would help find the lost girl. Placing the brush back where it belonged before touching her schoolbooks, Jewel sat in front of the mirror to meditate. Relieved, she finally picked up Tina's vibration. She appeared to be talking to a young man at what appeared to be her high school. Jewel watched them talking for a short while, though unfortunately, she could not hear what was being said. It was like watching a silent movie—she wished she could plug in earphones to eavesdrop on their conversation. The image soon faded in a cloud of dark smoke. Jewel sighed in exasperation with its retreat.

Receiving these vibes was similar to a bloodhound picking up the scent from a missing person by using their sloughed off dead skin cells—such as what Jewel was now doing with the person's personal belongings. She simply used a comparable method called 'Psychometry,' informally known as "object reading". And now she had captured Tina's scent, or at least the impressions left behind.

With no further details presented, Jewel quickly made her excuses to Mrs. Miles and left the premises.

# Chapter 4

No sooner had Jewel got out of bed the following morning when the phone rang again. The shrilling ring took her out of her musing of her last dream; it vanished like the morning mist. Marcy was calling for the second time this morning. This time, Jewel promptly picked up the phone. "Marcy, what do you want?" Jewel asked slightly irritated, revealing her early morning disposition: she definitely was not a morning person.

"Oh, Jewel, I've been calling. Where have you been?" Marcy sounded as though she were Jewel's mother.

"You know I was in bed *sleeping*," Jewel replied, emphasizing the word sleeping. "For the umpteenth time, Marcy… you should know I don't sleep well!"

Marcy interjected with, "You don't have to get so snarly. I was just worried, especially when you don't pick up the phone right away. Anything could have happened to you!" Marcy was now being quite short in return.

"Just don't call so early." Jewel lowered her voice, feeling bad. She was attempting to speak when Marcy interrupted.

"You can be a little nicer," obviously annoyed by then. "I'm only trying to help. You do know that, don't you?" Marcy said, offended.

Detecting Marcy's agitation, Jewel backed off. Right now, she just did not have the patience to deal with her friend—at least not until she had her first cup of coffee to perk her up for the day.

"Please. I know you just want to help. It's just that I desperately need my sleep. When I don't get proper sleep, then I need my first coffee to help me get moving, especially when I've had a lousy night—which unfortunately is most nights. I'll be more patient, all right? So why are you really calling?"

"Can I come over to see you? You know, to go over the notes of what might have happened to Tina," Marcy suggested.

"Yeah sure, but give me about an hour to get showered and dressed, all right?"

"Sure, sure, I'll be over in an hour then. See you in a wee bit," Marcy replied before hanging up.

Marcy's efforts at being helpful were commendable and she indeed meant well. It was fair to say that she tended to be a 'busybody sleuth' and 'in your face' kind of person.

"I'd better get showered because knowing Marcy, she'll be over way before the hour was up." Jewel said out loud as though someone was actually listening to her rambling on. She would be more than surprised if someone were to answer her, however.

Walking to the bathroom, it occurred to her that she really did not have much in the way of notes to go over with Marcy. She wondered why on earth she allowed Marcy to come over so early. This was why Jewel ought to have her coffee before answering any phone calls.

After showering, and now feeling awake and refreshed, Jewel sipped her first-class brew of mocha coffee, even adding a tiny bit of whipping cream on top just for added flavor. She breathed in the aroma. She sat there drinking her coffee, enjoying the smooth liquid. Twenty minutes went by. *Marcy should have been here by now. She's never late and usually arrives early so what could be keeping her?* Jewel thought.

She waited a few more minutes then decided to call Marcy's cell phone. It rang about six times before her voicemail message finally kicked in. The doorbell rang at the same time. Jewel ran to the door and opened it quickly, calling out, "Marcy! Oh!..." Jewel was totally surprised that someone other than Marcy was standing in the doorway. "I'm so sorry, Officer, I was expecting a friend of mine."

"Sorry, ma'am," he said. "I'm Officer McCoy. Are you Miss Seymour?"

Jewel wondered what she had done to warrant a visit from the police. She hoped her snooping around during a police investigation had nothing to do with it. "Yes, I am, Officer McCoy," she said with a look that was sure to betray her. She gestured for him to come in, examining him with an up and down glance.
"Ma'am, I'm very sorry to startle you like this," he apologized.

He was a young but imposing man, she thought, as he proceeded to remove his hat and nod at the same time. He sported a perfectly shaved head. Suddenly, and for no particular reason whatsoever, Jewel caught herself wondering why so many balding men, shaved their heads. Maybe it was to hide the obvious, but she was not a fan—that just did not work for her.

"I'm very sorry, Officer McCoy, do come in," she replied, feeling confused and apologetic all at once.

"Thank you, ma'am. I hate to bother you like this, but there's been an accident. May I ask you a few questions?"

Now Jewel's mind started to race. "Oh! And who's been in an accident?" She asked, feeling terribly alarmed and nervous, thinking of all the possibilities. Her first thought was—*Could it be Spence?*

"I was asked to bring you to the hospital. Can you please come with me?" McCoy asked.

"Sure, but who…? And what kind of accident was it?" Jewel asked. "Is Spence all right?" She assumed it could only be Spence with an officer at her door.

He cleared his throat before continuing. "No, ma'am, I mean…" he hesitated. "You said you were expecting a friend of yours. Is your friend Miss Marcy Cooper?"

"Why yes, but what happened?" She demanded; her voice grew ever more urgent.

"She's been in a car accident. The ambulance has taken her to North Memorial Hospital. I would like you to come along, that is, if you don't mind, ma'am?" He politely insisted.

"Why of course but is she all right?" Jewel was shaken by the news.

"We won't know until the doctor has assessed her condition," he replied. "Do you need a ride, ma'am?"

Feeling much better taking her own car, even though it was a police officer asking, Jewel declined his invitation. "I'll drive if you don't mind. I will just follow you to the hospital so that I have my car available afterwards. But thank you for offering, Officer." Jewel really did not trust herself to drive but refusing was easier. Besides, one could never tell how long the wait could be at the hospital; this way, she would have her car there in the event she had to leave.

Jewel ran to her car, climbed behind the wheel and realized her hands were trembling so much that she was having trouble inserting the key in the ignition. Maybe she should have taken the officer up on his offer.

Getting to the hospital seemed to take forever—a lifetime—with many thoughts racing through her mind. All the while she remained positive, consciously deciding to focus on her friend's current predicament instead of on what might have been. An overwhelming feeling of guilt rushed over Jewel, and to make matters worse, she had treated Marcy so poorly earlier that morning.

# Chapter 5

Jewel arrived at the hospital anxious to get some answers from the emergency doctor, but obtaining any information appeared next to impossible. The emergency department was active with incoming patients—doctors with teams of nurses were busy doing triage, and all the while Jewel sat there, patiently waiting for news about her friend. She had no choice but to accept that it might be quite some time before she received any updates on Marcy's condition. She resorted to the only thing she knew in times such as this: pray for good news.

She felt this whole ordeal was almost too surreal and after waiting for nearly an hour, Jewel rose and walked over to the front desk. "Yes, excuse me, Miss. Could you please give me a status on my friend's condition? Marcy Cooper. She came in over an hour ago and I haven't heard anything at all." Jewel stood there looking perplexedly at the nurse.

"We haven't heard anything from her doctor either," the woman replied. "As soon as we know anything, we'll be sure to let you know."

Jewel thanked the nurse and resolved to sit and wait. Time seemed to slow down to a crawl. Jewel's face fell into her hands and she struggled to hold back tears.

"I promise I won't be so hard on Marcy if only you can give me some help here," Jewel whispered, while looking up and asking for help from the heavens. As she picked through the sparse reading material, another hour rolled by and still no information came from either the doctors, or nurses that constantly seemed to avert her gaze.

Jewel got up to stretch her legs and spotted a coffee machine. Plugging it with loose change, the automated vending machine began to turn gears and eventually dispensed a steaming hot cup of God-Knows-What. But a good coffee was just what she needed to calm her nerves, so she appreciated the brew nonetheless. The only thought that came to mind while she sipped the watery disaster of a coffee was '*Could they make the coffee any worse?*'

Standing next to the machines, Jewel could not imagine what had happened for this accident to occur. Marcy was such a cautious, careful driver. Jewel knew that Marcy could be a little hyped at times, but her driving was always skillful. Maybe she had a flat tire or some other mechanical failure. She needed to get a hold of Spence—perhaps he knew something. With her luck though, it would be in that short timeframe when she went to make a call that the doctor would come to talk to her. Murphy's Law, she groaned to herself. She decided to stay put, knowing that the moment she received any news at all, she would be calling Spence right away.

Jewel wondered why it was at these critical moments just like this one, she could not use her psychic abilities. Unfortunately, her gift did not seem to work that way. Professor Brown had put it simply, claiming that when a person is too emotionally involved with someone, the psychic is unable to decipher which emotions belong to them and which belong to the other person. This was probably why Jewel could work so skillfully with strangers: she was completely detached from the emotional content and therefore able to receive 'uncontaminated' messages flowing to her with clarity.

At last, a doctor came out to the front desk and spoke with the nurse. They exchanged a few words and the nurse pointed to Jewel. As he walked toward her, Jewel sprang to her feet, praying she was the person he wanted to speak with.

"Miss," he said, looking directly at her. "Hello, I'm Dr. Green. Are you waiting to hear about Marcy Cooper?"

"For sure," Jewel replied, anxiously awaiting the news, still praying for a positive report. "How is she?" She blurted; certain he could sense her anxiety.

"She's still sedated, but she's stable," he replied.

Jewel let out a sigh of relief. "I'm sorry, Dr. Green, I'm Jewel Seymour," she said, with a hand outstretched. "May I see her?"

"Soon." He pointed to the other side of the desk, "I'll get the nurse to take you to her when she's fully awake," he continued.

He was starting to leave when Jewel shouted, "Doctor!"

He turned. "Yes?" He looked at his wristwatch, sounding pressed for time.

"Can you tell me what happened to her? I mean was she badly hurt?"

"Besides a broken leg and a fractured wrist, and judging by her test results, she does not appear to have any internal injuries, so she should be all right. We will be keeping a close eye on her tonight for any changes. She'll be required to stay an extra day or two depending on how she heals."

"Thank you. I really appreciate the information. I just need to see for myself that she's out of immediate danger," Jewel said, thankful that he took the time to explain her injuries.

"Yes, someone will be out shortly to bring you in to see her."

"Thanks again," she repeated.

Approximately a half-an-hour went by before the nurse came out to take Jewel in to see Marcy. Jewel followed her to the intensive care unit. Seeing Marcy lying on the bed, she gasped. Her first thoughts were, *Oh my God*! She was mortified to see Marcy hooked up to what seemed to be every possible life-saving machine in the intensive care unit! "I thought she was only in for more observations?" Jewel questioned the nurse.

"She is," she replied awkwardly.

"But she seems to be hooked up to so many monitors?"

"Only to better monitor her vitals while she's here. She will soon be moving upstairs to the second floor when we receive word that there's a bed available. It's easier for us to keep her monitored this way when we have more than one patient in the ICU."

"Oh, I see, thank you. May I speak to her now?"

"She should be awake so you can go on in," she answered pleasantly.

"Thanks." Jewel was pleased she was finally going to be able to talk to her friend. "Marcy? Marcy, are you awake?" Jewel whispered as she leaned in close to her ear.

"Yesss," Marcy replied, her voice barely audible.

"Are you in pain?" Jewel asked, hoping she was not.

"No," she finally squeaked.

"That's good," Jewel murmured with a lump in her throat. She swallowed before asking, "Can I get you anything?"

"No, thanks," Marcy flatly stated.

Marcy soon fell asleep. Jewel took a seat in one of the padded armchairs next to the bed and allowed her mind to reminisce on the good times they both shared over the years. She remembered how they would laugh at silly jokes, cried at their friend's funeral, and fought sometimes like they were enemies, but they mostly loved each other like sisters. Marcy had always wished for a sister, always having someone to play with, but unfortunately her childhood was generally a lonely time for her. She found it hard being an only child, although Marcy's parents doted on her and gave her everything she wanted. The only thing Marcy really wanted was a sister. But since her parents were already in their early fifties when she was born, even adoption was out of the question. She had prayed for a good friend, and now Jewel sat waiting for good news on the fate of her *best* friend.

Only briefly awake for short intervals, it made conversation between the two quite challenging, and Jewel's efforts to get information about what happened quite impossible. Once they moved Marcy to the second floor, Jewel felt comfortable enough about Marcy's stable condition to leave the hospital; she finally left around four o'clock that afternoon. Marcy was resting comfortably when she left so she decided to do her own investigation regarding the accident. Of course, Jewel went straight to the police station to see what she could unearth first. She trusted Spence would still be in at this hour. This was the first time she remembered that she had been so happy to finally get to see Marcy, that it had completely slipped her mind to call him hours ago.

After inquiring as to the whereabouts of Detective Walker, the sergeant on the evening shift said Spence had gone off duty at three o'clock. Undeterred, Jewel still attempted to obtain information concerning the car accident.

"I'm sorry, ma'am, but I'm not at liberty to release any information regarding this incident," the officer replied nonchalantly. He did not appear to be friendly or in a mood to be helpful. Jewel decided to let him stew, kindly thanked him and left the precinct.

Jewel got into her vehicle and began inching her way out of her parking spot to leave when suddenly a car rushed past, nearly side-swiping her car. "*Geez*! That was too close, he nearly ran right into me!" She released a huge breath out loud. "Holy! Didn't that IDIOT see me?" She was now shouting not only from fright, but also from rage. *And to think that this happened right in front of the police station!* She screeched. "What a jerk!" She looked at the station to see if anyone had witnessed the near miss, but no one seemed to be looking out the huge front window; it had happened so fast!

At this point, Jewel wondered if this was her sign to head home and relax. It had been a long day, after all. She drove straight home and was soon unlocking the front door, immediately locking it behind her. "Phew!" She exhaled a breath. Jewel was so tired that she climbed into bed and closed her eyes.

Jewel awoke with her heart pounding, and bolting up, she looked at the time—it was only 4:30 AM. Her dream had been so vivid and so intense that she swore she had felt the wind rushing past her. In this dream, she saw a man in a blue car, racing off as she was standing near the corner of Lincoln and Main Street. It appeared to be the same man driving the car, just like the one that had almost hit her yesterday. Fortunately, in her dream, Jewel had the opportunity to view what he looked like: he had a scar on the left side of his face beginning at his left eye that ran down past his mouth. She shivered at the thought of meeting him in a dark alley, a horrible thought indeed. Based on the creepy energy Jewel had received on this man—the same kind of feeling you get when you walk through a cemetery at night—he seemed dangerous. She shuddered and wondered if perhaps, he had something to do with Tina's disappearance as well.

Jewel must have fallen asleep again, because the next time she glanced at the clock, it was seven in the morning. This time she got up and made her way to the kitchen to make some coffee. Delighted with the idea that this morning's cup of coffee would be superior to the hospital coffee she had choked down the day before, she grinned.

She hopped into the shower, quickly slipped on some clothes and poured herself a coffee. Sipping the delicious brew, Jewel wondered how Marcy had slept last night. She knew she needed to learn what went on yesterday; perhaps, it truly had only been an unfortunate accident, yet her dreams seemed to indicate otherwise—something entirely different, but what that was exactly, remained unknown.

She arrived at the hospital and took the elevator up to the second floor. The elevator was packed with nurses, doctors, and fortunately, only a few visitors were crowded inside. She made her way to Marcy's room, but she was not there. She looked in other rooms, but she did not seem to be anywhere. Finally, Jewel stopped at the nursing station to inquire where she had been moved. Was she now on another ward?

"Excuse me, do you know which room Marcy Cooper is in? She was transferred up yesterday from the Emergency Department, but she's not in her room at the moment."

The pleasant-looking male attendant gave the impression he had been up all night. "Are you a friend, or family member of hers?" he asked.

"Her close friend, since she hasn't any family here in Imperial Beach," Jewel explained. "I'm the closest to family she has. Is she all right?" Jewel was feeling slightly anxious now.

"She was transferred back to the Intensive Care during the night," he replied.

"Oh my! Why didn't anyone call me? I left my phone number as the next of kin with the staff late yesterday afternoon. She was doing so well and resting comfortably when I left." Jewel looked around her. "Would her doctor be here by any chance?" she demanded.

The attendant gave Jewel the doctor's office number telling her, "Her doctor came by this morning, but Miss Cooper had already been moved back to the intensive care unit by then."

After thanking him, Jewel went down to the main floor. As she was hurrying down the corridor, she encountered Dr. Green.

"Ah, Doctor! Whatever happened to Marcy Cooper? I thought she was on the mend!" Jewel sounded quite distraught.

"She did have us worried last night when she began taking a turn for the worse. That's precisely why we wanted to keep her here for observation. There were some internal complications, but we got the bleeding under control. She's doing much better and resting comfortably as we speak. We're going to keep her in the intensive care for a while longer to have her closely monitored," he explained.

"So, she does have internal injuries after all? Is she awake? Can I see her?" Jewel cut in.

"Yes, other than her being out of it at the moment, she should be okay. We had her in surgery at around four this morning. Not me exactly. The surgeon on-call had to stop the bleeding."

"I see," Jewel said, swallowing hard. "What is causing the internal bleeding? Was the surgery one hundred percent successful? She felt terrible that Marcy had been alone when this crisis had played out.

Dr. Green looked Jewel straight in the eyes as he spoke. "Please understand her trauma was severe and she needs rest right now. I do not want her getting overtired," he warned.

"Of course," Jewel said with a sense of relief.

When Dr. Green left her, Jewel entered the intensive care room to find Marcy sleeping peacefully—or at least it appeared so. Jewel reached out and touched her hand. Although she understood that all the connections to every possible machine were necessary, it was disturbing, nevertheless. All Jewel wanted to do in that moment was speak with her friend—and as soon as she felt that Marcy was out of immediate danger—she would run down to the precinct to have a little chat with Spence. He was sure to be in at this time of day.

Sitting in the armchair next to the bed watching Marcy sleep, Jewel wondered whether it was Marcy who had awakened her at 4:30 AM to alert her that something was wrong. It did seem quite coincidental that she woke up at such an early hour right around the same time Marcy's health deteriorated. Or was this all a coincidence?

# Chapter 6

Later Jewel sat down at the precinct waiting for Spence to finish his conversation with a man she had not seen before. For such a relatively small town—it was closer to a mid-size town to be sure—there certainly were a lot of people here that she had never met before. But then again, they did get a fair share of transients passing through every year. It made her wonder whether she should be getting out more. She shrugged.

With the blinds open, she could see Spence through the large window into his office. Just when she thought he was going to come out, having stood up and walked to the door, he would return to his desk. Jewel observed this behavior for some time, wondering whether he would ever finish his conversation with the older gentleman in the dark gray suit. The older man resembled Sean Connery somewhat, but the probability of that happening was highly unlikely. But then again, she thought, they were in California, so anything was possible—it very well could be him.

She could not make out what they were saying either, but they did not seem to be friends. There was some hostility from the older man that seemed directed at the police or Spence, she could not be sure. They finally wrapped it up and both exited the room. They said their pleasantries to one another with a handshake before the gentleman took his leave. Spence turned around to greet Jewel.

"I'm sorry you had to wait. I was in the middle of a meeting when I saw you through the window," said Spence apologizing. "My intention was to end the meeting earlier, but I just couldn't get rid of the guy," he said with an inviting smile.

"That's all right Spence since I was really hoping to catch you before you left the office today. Can I buy you a coffee, or do you have to run off doing what detectives do?" She asked him half-mockingly, returning the smile.

"No, I don't have to run right away. Will this take long though or is the coffee just to perk you up?" he teased.

Jewel giggled. "I was hoping to ask you about the accident yesterday." She returned to the subject at the forefront of her mind.

"Ah, yes. There was an accident with Marcy," he replied rather casually.

"Yes, and she's still in the hospital. She had quite a rough night." They were walking back towards his office while speaking to one another. He did not seem too interested in Marcy's ordeal, however.

"I don't know much about what's going on with this particular incident, but I could pull-up what information there is. Do you think there's something peculiar about this particular accident then?" Spence questioned.

"I'm not sure yet. Apart from the fact that Marcy is an excellent driver, and to see her with a broken arm and leg not to mention the internal injuries she sustained yesterday. I can only wonder what went on for this to occur. I keep getting the feeling that this was no accident, but I can't explain why I feel it wasn't exactly."

"Just leave it with me and I'll see what I can find out," he said.

"Thanks. I knew I could count on you. Do you still want to go out for coffee?" Jewel asked, knowing that she should probably leave for the hospital in case Marcy woke up.

"I probably shouldn't go. I have a lot to do. Can I take a rain check this time? We can certainly go tomorrow if that works for you?" he offered.

"Not to worry. We'll catch up tomorrow for sure." As Jewel was leaving his office, she turned back towards him. "You know, Spence, you could go see Marcy at the hospital." Jewel had hoped that Spence and Marcy would have put their bad feelings to rest. Ever since they both had that falling out, it had been difficult to be friends with both of them. She never did hear exactly what caused their disagreement. Spence simply waved at Jewel somewhat dismissively.

Jewel entered the hospital, wishing Marcy had not been hurt and that she was still pestering her as usual. She made her way to the intensive care unit, stopping briefly at the nurse's station to ask if she had improved. A small nurse, named Edna informed her that Marcy was awake and other than being weak, she was doing quite well.

Thanking Edna, Jewel marched into Marcy's room. She was asleep but as Jewel approached the bed Marcy opened her eyes.

"How are you feeling?" Jewel asked out of concern. Just seeing her friend awake was the most exciting moment for Jewel.

"Hi," Marcy whispered, sounding groggy.

"Please don't talk, Marcy," Jewel protested while secretly wishing she could ask her a few questions about the accident. "I'm just glad to see you awake."

"I'm happy to see you too," she murmured. Jewel hugged her while Marcy just smiled weakly.

Jewel sat next to her bed, watching her going in and out of sleep when Marcy unexpectedly mentioned the accident. "When I woke up, I was so surprised to find myself here. I don't remember much, especially how I came to be in the hospital. Can you explain what happened to me?" Marcy asked at long last.

"Gee! I was hoping *you* could tell *me*. All I know is that you were on your way to my house…" Jewel paused. "Do you remember that?" Jewel was hoping this would jog her memory.

"Yes, I do" she said, "Vaguely."

"Good, but you don't remember getting in an accident?"

"No." She looked confused. "What happened?"

"I'm not sure but I will talk with Spence later." Jewel felt rather disappointed with Marcy's answer.

Did she sustain some kind of head injury that might explain her amnesia? Jewel remained with Marcy for another hour while she dozed on and off before quietly slipping out of the room to speak with Marcy's doctor. Perhaps he would have answers regarding her memory loss.

"Nurse, can you tell me if Dr. Green is available?"

"He was here earlier," Edna replied. "But he must have gone to the office by now."

"Would you have his telephone number by any chance?" Somehow, with everything going on, she could not remember what she had done with the piece of paper with that number.

"Yes of course, here it is." Edna handed her his card. "Is there something wrong?" She questioned, sounding somewhat concerned.

"Yes, my friend Marcy seems to be suffering from amnesia."

"Oh!" Now she appeared genuinely alarmed. "We hadn't noticed. I guess we've been pretty busy keeping her out of physical danger that we hadn't been aware of anything else. I'm sure Dr. Green would want to know," she blurted. "Would you like me to contact him?"

"That would be most helpful but if I could speak with him that would be better. Do you think that would be possible?" Jewel kindly asked if she could get the doctor on the line first, and then she would have a word with him also.

"Certainly," Edna replied, already punching the numbers on her console. "Sorry," she said. "It appears that I'm unable to get through after all." She hung up the phone.

Thanking her, Jewel left the building in order to place a call using her cell phone instead. The number Edna gave her only rang about four times before the answering machine turned on, advising that the office was now closed for lunch. Jewel looked at her watch and noticed it was a little after twelve. She reminded herself that she should get some lunch too, but she certainly did not want to eat at the hospital.

She headed for the nice Bistro on the beachfront. While driving, she thought that she would have to ground herself in order to be of assistance. As she was parking the car, she noticed that the place seemed fairly busy. After ordering some lunch, she found a quiet spot right under a palm tree. Jewel sat down and immediately devoured her ham sandwich. The fruit did not have much of a chance either, for it lasted less than a few minutes. She could not believe how hungry she was, and then it dawned that she had not eaten since yesterday.

The view was absolutely breathtaking. She could now see why everyone was crowded in the restaurant today. The Bistro was framed with a huge picture window overlooking the ocean waves rolling gently onto the white sandy beach. Jewel had a strong desire to get Marcy out of the hospital so they could both enjoy some time together. She realized that they had this beautiful scenery right off the west coast but rarely took time to admire this picturesque attraction. Instead they spent all day running around in search of lost souls. Yet, there were rewards for their tiresome investigations, such as bringing family members back together. Or, at the very least bringing closure to the families who have lost a dear one.

Glancing around she could feel the Earth's infinite healing power. She sat in quiet meditation, sending Marcy all the white light Jewel could muster, while absorbing the energy released from the surrounding flora. The light gave her a sense of elation, warmth, and a feeling of protection that surrounded her; sensing this force of goodness directed from Mother Earth, she felt euphoric.

It must have been about half-an-hour later, when Jewel felt a little chill crawling up her spine. The wind had picked up and it looked like a storm was brewing to the northwest. She could see the clouds moving in from the ocean with the sun disappearing behind it. *It certainly turned gray quickly, like an ominous event yet to occur.* She could not understand right now but knew that something just did not feel right. She raced to the car, shielding herself from the cold wind as much as possible. "Burr!" She uttered as she drove away.

On her drive back to the hospital, she thought about what she had experienced and viewed during her meditation. The sense she had was that somehow Tina had been involved in something that was way over her head; she got the distinct impression that the teenager had been dragged into something. Not clear on the details, she instinctively knew she would have to pursue it. But still Jewel could not see how Marcy was connected to the threat, if in fact, she was Approaching the hospital parking lot reminded Jewel that she needed to call Dr. Green again.

She called the number outside the hospital. "Dr. Green, please. Yes, of course, could you have him call me when he gets a chance? No, right here in the hospital in the intensive care unit with Marcy Cooper. I appreciate it. Thank you." She hung up the cell phone and went in to sit with Marcy while she waited to hear back from the doctor. While staring at Marcy, a vision appeared just above her body as she lay sleeping. At first Jewel saw her driving the car, operating with caution as usual. She then witnessed another car racing towards Marcy. It was as if looking through a thick fog. Then, just as quickly as it came, a thin veil was brought down over the vision—an indication that she was not privy to what happened next.

It was unfortunate there was not a way to pause the movie with a remote control. Jewel could only view the pictures speeding in front of her eyes—there was no way to slow them down, to freeze a frame, or replay a few clips to get more details. However, it was clear to Jewel that this was no accident, but more like a premeditated act. The big question was: Who would want to injure Marcy? And secondly, why?

At that moment, the nurse walked into the room announcing that Dr. Green was on the phone. Jewel followed her to the nurses' station.

"Yes, doctor. I was briefly able to speak with Marcy Cooper this morning. She indicated that she could not remember what happened just before and during the accident, nor anything afterwards. Is this typical with such injuries?"

He explained that it could be typical, but he would have to run more tests to see if she had sustained a head or brain injury, something they could have missed when she was initially assessed. He would refer her to a specialist who would conduct some tests to investigate her memory loss and set up a care plan for a full recovery if something did show up in her results.

"That does make me feel much better especially knowing she's in your excellent care," Jewel said before hanging up. Relieved with the doctor's response, Jewel thanked the nurse for the use of her phone. Jewel went back into Marcy's room where another nurse was changing the IV bag.

Later Jewel had driven home exhausted from yet another day of sitting and waiting. Obtaining any information on Marcy was becoming more problematic than she ever imagined. The answering machine was flashing, indicating there were messages. She heard Mrs. Miles ask whether she had any information on her Tina. Jewel knew that she really had to look into this before more time passed.

In the evening she meditated on Tina. Jewel must have been very tired because around two in the morning she awoke on the sofa, freezing as though winter had arrived early. Sluggishly she made her way to her bedroom, undressed, and with the warmth and comforts of her own sanctuary, she disappeared under the covers. After attempting to sleep for about an hour, hunger drove her to get up again. In the kitchen, she looked in the refrigerator. Not having time to pick up groceries since all this chaos began, she decided a cup of hot cocoa and a piece of toast would have to suffice.

# Chapter 7

The next morning Jewel was still lying half-awake in bed, desperately wanting to go back to sleep, when the phone rang. Not wishing to miss a call from the hospital, she immediately ran over to answer it, stubbing her toe in the process. She cried out from the excruciating pain.

"Hello! Yes, this is she," Jewel replied, holding back urges to cry out from the sheer pain. "Ah yes, Mrs. Miles, what can I do for you? I did in fact get your message when I returned from the hospital last night. No, I'm okay. And yes, I can call you Helena instead if you prefer. I'm so sorry but I don't have anything concrete on Tina yet. I've had a little emergency of my own and that's why I was at the hospital. It wasn't me but my friend Marcy. Indeed, she was doing much better when I left last evening. Thank you for asking. I would love to see you later today—after I visit Marcy, of course. I can give her your best wishes. We can meet afterwards, that is two this afternoon would be fine. I'll be there. Talk to you then." Jewel hung up the phone so relieved it was not the hospital ringing her. Though her toe was still throbbing, she glanced up at the time and saw that if she got dressed quickly, she would still be able to meet with Spence first. Jewel needed 'Intel' on both cases, and she was really hoping Spence would have some news on the accident. As it stood, Marcy would not be helpful, and Jewel had not uncovered any more clues relating to Tina's whereabouts either.

Jewel left the house around 9:30 for the precinct. While parking the car by the storefront, she glimpsed at her reflection in the glass window. It was clear that she should eat more frequently or risk fading away, which would only mean there would be yet another soul to search for. She giggled at the irony. The image made her realize that her health had to become a priority. Although she was a good-looking woman with lustrous, dark brown hair and emerald green eyes that reflected her gentle soul, Jewel was never vain about her beauty, but she truly did need to take better care of herself. Hopefully Spence would step out to eat today. Perhaps they could check out the new restaurant in town… and with that thought, she entered the precinct.

Jewel was quickly ushered to Spence's office by the sergeant.

"Are you busy right now, Spence?"

"No, why?" He questioned, looking quite suspicious as though he suspected her of a century-old murder.

"I wish you wouldn't look at me like that. You alarm me," Jewel said, rather suspicious herself, at what she saw in *his* eyes. "I was just wondering if we could get some breakfast while we talk like you mentioned yesterday. At any rate I have a very busy day seeing Mrs. Miles and such. You remember, the lady with the missing teenager. Have you had a chance to find out anything about her daughter?"

"Not yet. Though the entire force is now searching for her if that helps."

"The good news is, I don't sense that she's passed on either," Jewel offered. "I do feel she's still amongst the living."

"How do you know that Tina is still with us? Do you have some information that you're not sharing?"

"Absolutely not. Except with my psychic abilities I'm able to sense it somehow."

"Do you have any information that might help us with the case then?" His tone became insistent that she share whatever she had.

"Not exactly. Well I don't have anything concrete to use as evidence if that's what you are asking?"

"All right. Let's catch a bite. And perhaps you can tell me what you do have," Spence asked, looking rather puzzled. For the life of him he could not think what Jewel could possibly know that the force did not already have. "Just a minute. I need to let the sergeant know where I'll be and, by the way, where are we going?"

"I thought we'd try that new restaurant—you know—the one that just opened up on Sandpiper Hill."

"Okay. If you just wait here for a second, I'll be right back." He went dashing back into the station.

Before long they arrived at the restaurant. The parking lot was quite full indicating the place was likely packed with late summer tourists. Entering the restaurant with Spence holding the door for Jewel, the hostess indicated it would be about fifteen minutes or so before a table would be available.

"I hope it won't be any longer than that, Spence." Jewel had a lot of things to do today.

"We could try another restaurant down the way if you'd like?"

"No, that's all right, with any luck it'll only be a few more minutes." Jewel replied, feeling hopeful.

They sat in the front lobby, catching up while waiting.

"Have you made much progress regarding Tina's disappearance?" Jewel asked.

"Well actually there aren't any traces of her—she simply vanished. No one at the school saw anything; point in fact, no one is admitting to anything. So, we're at a dead end with no leads. I hope the case won't go cold as so many do." He paused. "On the other hand, about Marcy's accident—we've spoken with many eyewitnesses, and yes, there's a man and wife who saw a blue or greenish colored car that hit her vehicle. It looked like the car swerved, hitting Marcy's vehicle. There was a single male driver with no further details on him. It happened so fast that the witnesses didn't get a good look at his face. The man sped off immediately. So, we've sent out a "Be on the lookout—you know, a BOLO, on the hit and run, though without a license plate, it will be hard to catch this guy."

"Regrettably since her accident, Marcy hasn't been able to recall anything." Jewel mentioned.

"So, about Tina. What have you found out?" Spence asked, pulling his notebook out of his breast pocket.

"I'm now wondering if the death of Elizabeth Nettle—you know she was also sixteen—and Tina's disappearance are both connected. I was wondering whether the similarities in age were too coincidental to be ignored."

"To tell the truth, we haven't established any evidence to link anything to any other cases. Although there are rumors floating about of how the age similarities cannot be ruled out. It's hard to make connections so early in the case without more information to go on since we haven't yet established if Tina has simply run off."

"Once I see Helena today, I may obtain more details regarding her possible whereabouts," Jewel mentioned, as the waitress came to inform them that their table was ready.

As soon as they sat down, Jewel continued. "So far, all I saw in my visions was a young male speaking with Tina. No clear details to how this is linked to Tina's disappearance. Why don't you come with me to see Helena? Maybe you can help me find out new details that I may not get otherwise."

"That might not be a bad idea, but would she mind? I'm not exactly in charge of her case," Spence replied.

"No, I don't think she would mind in the least, but if you like I can call her to find out?"

They ate while talking right through breakfast, enjoying each other's company. After returning to the station, they agreed to meet at Helena's residence just after two that afternoon.

Soon thereafter, Jewel made her way to the hospital where she discovered Marcy had been moved to the second floor once again. She took the elevator up and entered her room. Since Marcy was still sleeping, Jewel made use of her time by going to the nursing station to find out if anyone had assessed Marcy's memory loss.

The nurse was quick to explain. "Actually, a psychiatrist did see her today. I'm not sure what the results were so you'll have to follow that up with him. Or possibly speak with Dr. Green for more details."

"Thank you. I'll sit with her for a while longer," Jewel offered.

Back inside Marcy's room, Jewel sat down beside her, realizing it was getting close to 1:30 PM. Jewel could not stay much longer and rushed out to meet Spence at Mrs. Miles' place. On her way out, she informed the nurse that she would be back later today.

The lack of information together with Jewel's growing preoccupation regarding both cases made meditation quite difficult. She felt that she was stretched quite thin. Pulling up to the curb, Jewel decided to wait until Spence arrived. Once his car pulled up, they both walked up together and rang the doorbell. Helena immediately opened the door, inviting them inside. During her first visit, Jewel noticed that Helena appeared to be the type that kept things quite orderly. However, today's observation of her house was that of untidiness. The dark circles around her eyes gave her the appearance of having aged at least five years since Jewel first met her.

Jewel greeted her. "I'm so sorry I couldn't get here sooner, but I have been extremely preoccupied with Marcy's accident."

No doubt Helena had the impression that no one cared about her missing teenager. "I brought Detective Walker along. The police are doing what they can to locate your daughter. If you don't mind the detective will look around for any new clues that might have been missed when your home was initially searched by the police?"

"Si, por favor. If it will help find my Tina!" Helena said.

"Thank you, ma'am," Spence replied, feeling much better knowing he was welcomed. "I'll start in here," he said, pointing in the direction of the kitchen. "Of course, if that's all right with you, Mrs. Miles?"

"Si, jou go!" Helena said with a forced grin, while motioning with her outstretched hand towards the kitchen.

"Helena, I'd like to try something unorthodox with you. I would like to sit down with you to see whether I can pick up anything useful from Tina through you. If that's alright with you?" Jewel asked.

"Ah si," Helena responded, looking quite eager at the prospect of getting closer to locating her daughter.

"I would like for us to hold hands while taking long breaths to relax. Don't worry, I will guide you through this." Jewel hoped she would be comfortable with this unusual procedure. "The reason to relax is to let go of our emotional bodies."

"Si, por favor." Helena sounded excited while thanking her.

"Now, sit directly in front of me with both feet on the floor, like so." Jewel showed her how. She offered her hands to Helena to provide a better connection with Spirit. "Now close your eyes and take three long breaths with me. Inhale one breath and hold it for the count of three, now exhale." They repeated the exercise three times while Jewel asked her to remain totally relaxed and to concentrate on Tina.

"Si," she sighed.

Both women sat there for about two minutes before Tina appeared to Jewel. Although she was running away in the woods, as though being chased by someone, Jewel could see her looking back at the person who was chasing her. The fog was thick on the ground. The scene appeared to be taking place in early evening, just before sunset. At last, Jewel had a chance to see who was chasing her. She stared so intensely at Helena that she jumped up startling her!

"Did jou see someting?" She immediately demanded.

Jewel was certain that Helena wanted to hear the best news possible while dreading the worse.

"I did but I can't explain what I saw just yet," Jewel remarked. "Can you trust me on this one?" She knew that she wanted to know what she had seen, but to tell Helena that her daughter was running for her life would not be reassuring.

"I tink so," Helena replied reluctantly.

The disappointment in her eyes was evident. It pulled at Jewel's heartstrings. Every fiber of her wanted to give Helena some hope, but drawing on her years of experience, she knew that to say too much, too early, can be very disturbing to a person—plus, she would then have to describe the whole scene to the distraught mother, which was definitely not a good approach in this case.

"I can sense that she is alive, and we will soon find her," was the only consolation Jewel could offer at that moment. Sadly, she would have to wait to get more information.

At this point Spence came out of the kitchen, breaking the focus and requesting to see Tina's room upstairs. Helena just waved him on, anxious to regain the intense concentration she and Jewel had established. Jewel asked Helena to relax once more so that she could get more vital clues. They sat there for about five more minutes when finally, Tina reappeared.

This time, however, Tina was tied up and gagged. Jewel strained to look through Tina's eyes to see if she could get any details on her location. Tina was inside a building with only one window overhead. It was quite high giving the appearance of being in an attic, or something of that sort, or even a basement or a warehouse. She could not be sure. There were bars on the window, making escape quite impossible. Having her tied up was definitely another deterrent to her escape, along with the concrete walls behind her. Tina was certainly in a terrible predicament though deducing it was likely a basement since concrete walls were not usually seen in attics.

Spence came back downstairs, breaking their connection once again. "Do you need anything else?" Jewel asked Spence as she got up from her chair.

"No, I've seen what I need," he replied, lips pressed together.

"I'm finished also," Jewel said, turning to Mrs. Miles. "We will be leaving and if I need more details, I'll call."

They both thanked her on their way out the door; Helena could not hold back any longer. Desperately, she grabbed Jewel's hand, tears coursing down her cheeks, her eyes pleading for some answers.

"Sorry, Helena, I can't reveal more right now. But I did see that your Tina is alive, though I can't tell you beyond that."

Sniveling and with a swipe of the back of her hand over her eyes, Helena thanked them both for coming and closed the door.

Once outside, Jewel told Spence about the blue sedan that she saw in the back alley, which raced off the first day she came to see Helena. He wanted to go back to the alley to see if there might be any evidence that could give him a lead in the case. Soon Spence began bagging cigarette butts present along the surrounding area behind the house. He also found tire tracks. Unfortunately, he mentioned that they could be from any vehicle driving by.

"I'll take an imprint just the same since it was farther away from the curb. Perhaps it can help shed some light on who was here on that day." He straightened up and peered into Jewel's eyes. "But I don't know why you didn't call to report this earlier?"

"I didn't know if it was relevant at the time, though I did think to mention it today. You know so much has happened in the past few days with Marcy that I simply forgot. Did you find anything in the house?"

"Not much. What about you?" Spence had the knack of turning the tables on anyone rather quickly.

"I'm not sure, but I now believe Tina may be in real danger. It appears that she is held against her will."

Although that was suspected from the start, no one had been able to determine whether Tina had run away from home or been—everyone's worse fear—molested and left for dead somewhere in the woods. However now Jewel was quite sure—Tina was still alive and held captive for unknown reasons.

"Can you get a glimpse of the person responsible?" Spence asked curiously, now showing interest in her visions.

"No clear view on the person who took her. But it was clear she was left alone in some type of basement or warehouse."

"Do you know where this warehouse is located?" He thought she might be on to something.

"Sorry to say but this was the moment you came down the stairs and broke my concentration. I will definitely look into the matter again and see if more clues can be uncovered." Jewel lingered around until Spence finished taking notes before driving off.

# Chapter 8

At last Marcy was awake and a marginal smile was detected. She and Jewel were able to talk for about two hours.

"Of course, I saw the intersection when I was on my way to your house," Marcy claimed. "I slowed down at the four-way stop. I remember stopping the car. But at that point, it was as though the sky had fallen on top of me. I assume something must have hit me from behind because I don't remember much after that. All I remember is flying in the air and everything going completely dark."

"It sounds like you do remember more details. By any chance, did you recall the driver of the other vehicle? Or, even the vehicle itself? Do you remember the color of any other vehicles that were in the vicinity at the time of the accident?" Jewel asked, hoping to jog her memory.

"No, I don't think I saw anything more."

"Remember anything at all—even if it seems trivial."

"Nothing comes to mind," Marcy finally declared.

"Not to worry. I just want you to get better. We'll get to the bottom of this while you rest and concentrate on healing your body," Jewel said before she left. She definitely felt good that Marcy was on the mend, although she was still concerned about her memory loss. The doctor had mentioned she would be going home in a few days, which had made Marcy's day, and, of course, Jewel's as well.

When Jewel arrived at her apartment, she found the front door ajar. "What the heck? What happened here?" These first questions escaped her mouth while standing in front of the opened door. She immediately called Spence, but his cell just rang and rang. In a whisper Jewel was forced to leave a message, informing him that it was extremely urgent. She hung up her cell phone and stayed outside her apartment for about five minutes, listening for anyone moving about inside.

After hearing no sounds for the next ten minutes, Jewel decided to cautiously open the door wide open. She peered inside. No one was visible, so she stepped inside on her tiptoes. She could not recall ever having felt so nervous. Her heart was pounding in her chest and every sound she heard coming from within the apartment building made her jump like a jittery cat. She walked farther inside, observing the disaster all around her. Someone sure did a number on her apartment, or maybe it had been hit by a freak tornado—but that sounded fairly improbable since her place would have been the only one hit. Stress was playing on her mind. There were books and papers and magazines strewn everywhere, furniture overturned, and everything pulled out of the cupboards and drawers. *Why would someone want to trash my place*? Jewel thought. *And, what would they be looking for?*

She was angry. Her temper was definitely rising. Suddenly, she heard some noise coming from the living room. "What was that?" Jewel murmured. The sound came from the entrance. *Oh no!* She thought. There she was all the way into the bedroom with no way out except for a small window—she was trapped! She reached for a bat from behind the bedroom door that had not been used in years. She was thankful for keeping it handy and grateful to have followed her father's advice to always have a way to protect herself.

Now she heard more footsteps. With her heart in her throat, she hid behind the bedroom door hoping the intruder would see that no one was home and leave. When she heard more steps advancing toward her bedroom, she froze with fear. She was trying not to breathe, believing any sound would surely give her away. Jewel mentally decided to strike first, hoping to scare the intruder off. She raised the bat slowly, waiting for the precise moment to swing. Her eyes could not see much in the dark. *Now!* She thought. She swung hard but the intruder caught the bat in midair, wrenched it from her which sent her flying. She hit the floor with such force it knocked the wind right out of her. Jewel's mouth flapped open, fighting for breath. When she could finally breathe again, she called out. "Damn!" She let it out with the force of a heavy sigh.

They both struggled on the floor. Now she knew it was a man … and whoever this was, he was much stronger and larger than her. Jewel fought like a tomcat and gave him his money's worth. Pinning her to the floor now, helpless, she knew she was in grave danger.

"What do you think you're doing? Are you trying to kill me?" he shouted.

"My God! Spence! What the hell are you doing here?" Jewel yelled back, but she was very relieved. "You scared the B-Jesus out of me!" She was affronted by his stealth-like entrance into her apartment. Why had he not called out to her? He could not have known it was her in the bedroom, she supposed.

"Hey, you're the one who started swinging at me, missy!" Spence angrily retorted. "Did you think you could take on someone with that bat? Why didn't you just wait for me to get here? You could have gotten yourself killed! Not to mention what you would have done to me had I not been quick," he said, slighted by her carelessness.

"You didn't return my call so how was I to know it was you out there and scaring me nearly to death as you did!" She was still furious but thanking God it was him all at the same time.

"Okay, calm down, will you. All I wanted to say is you should have stayed out of harm's way. Next time call for backup, and absolutely don't try to be a hero," he commanded.

"You didn't answer your phone, and then you didn't return my call," she repeated still struggling to catch her breath. "Why didn't you? You could have saved us both from this embarrassing—not to mention dangerous—situation," Jewel whispered, nearly in tears by then.

"Yes, I realize that now. You still ought to have waited outside for me. You could have been attacked, or worse killed if the intruders were still here. And that's why I didn't call you. I didn't want your phone to ring, giving away your position had you been close to whomever was near you. I'm going to look around so just wait here, okay?" Spence gave her a warning glare this time, except his look was likely worse than his bite, or so it seemed.

Jewel had to wonder if Spence was a little psychic to know what was going on. "Alright, but wouldn't it be much safer for me to be with you rather than by myself?" It was obvious she did not want to be left alone. He gave her a look that said to listen to him. "Alright," Jewel repeated, bowing her head in defeat.

She silently sat down on her bed, waiting for Spence to search the place. The way he glared at her was the only reason she stayed put. But she simply knew that her heart could not take another fright like the one she just experienced. When Spence returned, she felt much better having him beside her.

The tension in the air was so thick Jewel feared he would strangle her, but part of her knew better. "Did you find anything?"

"I did not, other than your place being totally trashed. You seem to be safe for the time being. I've called the station to send out a couple of our guys from the forensic department to investigate this…" he said, pointing to the disaster.

"But it's so late already," Jewel objected. "They'll probably be here all night attempting to get to the bottom of this. Finger-printing alone will take forever," she went on complaining as if it would help.

"You're probably right about that. Can I offer you a place to stay for the night? It'll be much safer in the event that someone returns—especially if it was you he was after. Or, do you have any idea what the perpetrator was after?"

"Not exactly. I definitely can't see myself sleeping here tonight either. I could just as easily get a motel room for the night," Jewel suggested.

"No, I insist. I would feel much better knowing you were safe if you stayed with me tonight. Besides, this way I won't be called out in the middle of the night to rescue you again. And particularly the way you swing at people," pointing at the bat. "I'd rather not," he protested with a smirk appearing on his lips.

"I guess it won't hurt for the night, but I really need to get a few things with me if I can find anything at all in this mess."

"You'd best not disturb the scene until the forensic team arrive to take photos."

"What?" Jewel protested to this invasion.

They both sat waiting until the police arrived, taking a few pictures before Jewel could gather up a small number of personal items. Spence and Jewel finally left, stopping briefly at a small restaurant for takeout.

Jewel was thrilled that Spence thought about having something to eat before retiring for the night. When they got to his place, they ate the Chinese food out of the boxes. Afterwards, Spence offered his room for the night while he took the couch. Jewel thanked him before closing the door for a little privacy, especially after the awkward scene at her apartment. At the very least, this gave her a little sense of dignity and normalcy.

# Chapter 9

Jewel woke up, aching all over from the extreme activity from the night before. She had not had a good sleep having tossed and turned through the night trying to get comfortable. She wondered how Spence slept on such a hard mattress!

When sleep finally did take her to the land of dreams, they were more vivid than she wanted. Jewel dreamt that Marcy's Aunt May was taking a walk with her niece. They walked over some railroad tracks towards a wooded area. Words were spoken but Jewel could not remember their content. The beauty of dreams is that one does not remember every one of them, and thank God for that, especially when dreams become nightmares. With this particular dream, she had the distinct feeling they were being followed by a man whose face she had seen before, but still did not recognize. Could he be responsible for the morbid events going on with the missing girls, as well as the person responsible for vandalizing her apartment? She was not sure what this all meant because everything in the dream was out of context. Why was Aunt May there? And why was she walking with Marcy? Nothing made sense since she could not find any connection between the dream and what was actually taking place in real life.

When Jewel got out of bed at around seven, she discovered that Spence had already gone to work. He was considerate enough to leave a note on the fridge.

> *Jewel, I couldn't sleep. I decided to run to the station to see what I can find out about who is responsible for ransacking your apartment. I didn't want to wake you so just make yourself at home. If you need anything just call the station or my cell.*
> *——Spence*

It was nice that he was looking out for her but finding coffee in his house would have to take precedence. While looking around on the counters, Jewel came across another note. The note was in Spence's handwriting again and what was written on it was most interesting:

> *- 2 PM meet with T.*

*- 5 PM take care of business.*

Jewel could not imagine what this could relate to, unless it meant that the T. was for Tina? It couldn't be, could it? Maybe the T stood for someone else, but who? Could Spence be involved? Maybe that was how he had arrived at her apartment so quickly last night. Now that she thought about it, it all appeared rather odd. Perhaps that was also why he had invited her to stay with him—so he could keep an eye on her? But why would Spence be involved? Nothing made sense anymore.

She decided it was her lack of sleep and food was affecting her sanity. She hurriedly dressed to leave the house as quickly as possible; she needed to clear her head. Jewel drove around for approximately an hour, struggling to make sense of this new information. Spence has always been a nice guy so why would he... "Oh, my God!" Jewel shrieked to herself. She thought—*You always hear about the serial killer being kind and a quiet person. If that were true, if there is an ounce of truth to it, this could be the smoking gun! An officer of the law could easily convince young girls to trust him. Perhaps that is why no one had seen anything unusual—and all the while gaining the confidence of these innocent girls. Could this be possible?* Jewel shook her head, "No, that simply couldn't be," she voiced out loud.

Realizing that today was already Sunday, which meant she had only five days left before she was to leave for Vegas, Jewel had to resolve this promptly. The drive to the hospital to see Marcy was uneventful, and yet, Jewel's concentration was all over the map. *Perhaps something important would come to her while sitting with Marcy today*, she thought, as she entered her hospital room.

"Hi, Marcy!" Jewel said, smiling. "How are you feeling today?" Her friend's condition had improved greatly in the last twenty-four hours; she was so much more alert.

"I have to say I do feel much better. It seems as though I'm definitely healing," she replied, grinning.

"It sure is nice to see you smiling again. Can I get you anything?"

"It would be nice if I had something to read."

"Oh, I'm so sorry! I should have brought you a book or something. Wait right here while I go down to the front lobby. Be right back!" Jewel said as if Marcy could go anywhere.

With the latest events bouncing around in her head, Jewel was too distracted for rational thought. She took the elevator down to the ground floor where the hospital's gift shop was tucked away in a small corner. Knowing her friend quite well made it easy to find a good magazine. While looking around the rack, Jewel spotted Spence on the other side of the bookshelf. It was a good thing that the shelves were high, creating a barrier between the two of them. Jewel ducked a little, so he would not see her. She could not imagine why he would be there. Marcy and Spence had not been friends for years, and the last time Jewel mentioned her accident, he seemed rather indifferent. So why would Spence be at the hospital now? Perhaps, he was here on police business. He proceeded to walk up to the cashier, bought two magazines, one magazine for a woman, but the other was for a teen—*yes, a teen magazine.* But why? Unless Spence had a feminine side to explain away these purchases, it sure seemed strange to her. She watched him closely as he left the gift shop and entered the elevator. Hurriedly she paid for her magazine to see which floor he would step off. She ran up to the second floor. No Spence. She decided to dash up the next flight of stairs, racing the elevator to the third floor. She ran as fast as humanly possible almost killing herself and still was too late to see who got off the elevator. She stood there long enough to catch her breath. Disappointed, she walked down to Marcy's room.

It was a shock when Jewel ran into Spence. "Ah, Spence!" She said, still a little out of breath, but not wanting to seem too surprised either.

"Jewel, I didn't know you had left the house yet. I thought I would have heard from you this morning looking for coffee," Spence replied, grinning.

"You know I almost did, but I finally found some and didn't need to bother you." Great efforts went into sounding as calm as a cucumber.

"Marcy, it looks like you have lots to read now," Jewel added, smiling and trying to sound as normal as she possibly could.

"Yes, I guess I do. Thank you both for the magazines," she replied, obviously pleased as punch.

Spence proceeded to ask Marcy a few questions regarding the accident.

"No, Spence, I tried to remember. As I told Jewel just yesterday, I simply can't remember much at all," Marcy complained, her smile disappearing quickly.

"I'll be going but if you remember anything at all, please do call. Here's my card." As Spence handed it to her, he remained quite professional. Other than feeling the strain between them, Jewel was pleased that Spence made the first move to mend this strained relationship.

"I'll see you," Jewel called out to him as he quickly left the room. She sensed he was in a rush to leave.

Laboring to catch up with him, Jewel said. "Ah, Spence, may I have a word with you first? I just need to know if the forensic team found anything at my apartment." She hesitated. "I really wouldn't mind sleeping in my own bed tonight if that's at all possible?" They continued walking to the elevator together, so Marcy was unable to hear what was being discussed further, much to her dismay. She always wanted to know everything about everybody.

"You know you're welcome to stay with me until we get to the bottom of this. And may I also point out that your apartment is in quite a state, so I'd feel much better knowing you were safe." Spence sounded rather sincere about his offer this time. "Not to mention it would be one less thing for me to worry about."

*Or, maybe to keep an eye on me?* Jewel was suspicious. "I'll think about it, but I really need to go home. I should have a look around to see if anything was stolen, don't you think?" Jewel hoped that she had given the best excuse to return to her apartment.

"Of course. The sergeant wanted a list of what's been taken from the apartment, if anything. Why don't I drive you there?" Spence offered.

Suddenly he felt too pushy for Jewel's comfort. "No, I'll be okay, really." Jewel tried sounding like she was indeed all right.

"Until we arrest someone, I just don't want another encounter with whoever ransacked your place is all."

"Really, Spence, I'll call you and promise not to enter if anything looks amiss," she conceded.

Tired of her banter, Spence said. "Sure!" He shrugged as he headed out of the hospital, giving the impression he might be somewhat disgruntled with Jewel.

Later that day Jewel arrived at her apartment to find the police tape across the door, looking more like a murder scene than a burglary. Obviously, the police did not want anybody to enter. She had to admit that walking through her living room was a little overwhelming and most disturbing with all her belongings strewn everywhere. An uncomfortable sense of vulnerability and violation flooded her that can only be empathized by those who have also experienced a home invasion. Whoever had the nerve to do this, was beyond her. She glanced around to see whether she could pick up an *essence* of the person who had done this. Receiving a picture flashing in her head would be helpful, or a view of what they were after would be useful. She kept walking around, but nothing concrete came to mind. Maybe she could make a connection with that information if she sat down and closed her eyes to do a quick meditation; she definitely felt she had an advantage in this situation.

As she stood amidst the disaster, she got a flash of a male wearing a dark fleece, hooded shirt. He wore it down over his face, making it difficult to see any of his facial features. What she could see though, was a tall, lanky male, possibly a drug user from the looks of him. When he turned, she saw that he had dark eyes with dark circles, a bit sunken in, likely the shadowing effect from the hood. She witnessed him tossing everything upside down, obviously searching for something, although she could not imagine what that could be.

It was so devastating to watch him turning her place into a disaster zone that she needed to sit down. As Jewel sat meditating on her bed, she began to hear sounds, but the noise was not originating within her vision; it seemed to be coming from the living room. Now what? Not wanting to be attacked yet again, Jewel immediately moved closer to the bedroom door to spy on any movements coming from the other room. Would he have followed her here she wondered, or could Spence be out there? Unfortunately, she could not see a thing. He could be hiding anywhere—the noise had stopped. Was it just her imagination, or did it actually come from the vision? She was not entirely sure anymore; at times it is difficult to distinguish one from the other. She could have sworn she heard something though. Perhaps it was not real after all, or hopefully, it was Spence returning. She opened the door, which began to creak before she could step out.

"Ahhh!" She screamed. It was then that he pounced! They both flew to the floor as though an animal had attacked her. Too dark to see any details—wishing she had turned on the lights—she could not fight back. The lights came on suddenly, but all she saw was someone dashing towards the fire escape by the living room window. She looked up at the front entrance where a police officer stood in the doorway. By then Jewel was sprawled on the floor, disheveled.

"Quickly!" she shouted. "He's getting away," while pointing to the fire escape. "Hurry! See who just attacked me!" she screeched.

The officer ran to the window before turning toward Jewel, shouting back, "There's no one there!"

"I was just attacked! He must still be out there," she went on yelling while struggling to sit up.

The officer called for backup on his radio, requesting the officer on the ground to keep a lookout for anyone fleeing on foot. From the fire escape, the officer kept watch from above. He finally received a message that the officer was in pursuit of someone running down the back alley. He turned to Jewel while she managed to stand up. "Are you alright?"

"Yes, I think so." After a few seconds though, Jewel felt quite dizzy, swaying back and forth.

Seeing Jewel toppling over in a heap once more, the officer rushed to her side. "You don't look alright, ma'am."

"Gee, thanks." Jewel knew she sounded sarcastic. But when she tried to stand up again, she acknowledged he was right.

He cleared his throat. "I didn't mean that you looked awful, I meant that your face is as white as a sheet and you nearly collapsed."

"Thanks for helping me," Jewel said, hanging onto the officer's arm. "I really have to get another life," she added, forcing a grin.

Jewel felt terribly sore all over. "This life is getting too much for me, if you know what I mean."

The police radio came back on, informing the officer that a suspect had been apprehended.

"You'll have to come to the station to identify the intruder," he told her. "Do you need a ride there?"

"No, I'll manage to drive myself there, just give me a few minutes first."

Before leaving her apartment, he glanced back at Jewel out of concern, wondering if he should have insisted.

"I don't know if I can identify the intruder," she told him. But she was not sure whether he heard a word. He had already left the apartment by then.

Jewel quickly shoved a few clothes into a carry-on bag. This time she was adamant that she was going to get herself a room. It was obvious that Spence may be right: it was no longer safe here. In any event she was too exhausted tonight. The last thing she required right now was Spence hassling her, arguing his point. The thought of being uncomfortable again on that hard mattress two nights in a row was not tempting in the least either. Feeling a bit more stable and centered, she quickly drove to the station and marched in.

Spence was there to greet her. "Hey! I just heard about your assault. Did I not tell you to stay at my house?" He scolded her as though she were a schoolgirl.

"I know, Spence. But I sleep better in my own bed. I don't want to impose, so I'm staying at a motel for the night. If someone has targeted me for some reason or another, no one will know where I am. But for the life of me I cannot figure out why they would! Maybe if I get some sleep I'll be able to piece this puzzle together, but right now, nothing is making sense. It's so sweet of you to offer though." Jewel hoped that the rejection would not be received as ingratitude.

"The intruder is in a line up and we're hoping you can identify him," Spence went on, ignoring Jewel's words. Now it felt as though he was giving her the cold shoulder, or perhaps just getting down to business. At any rate, he was always more business-like than anything else.

"Thanks, but you know I didn't see a whole lot. It was dark in the apartment. In retrospect, I should have turned the lights on. Instead I only had the last of the daylight streaming through the window, which created more shadows than anything else. Hopefully I can still identify his body type and the clothes he was wearing."

"Yes, with any luck," Spence said coldly.

Jewel felt a freezing gush of air between the two of them. She wondered whether she had seriously offended him, or a bad spirit had just passed between them.

Jewel was ushered into a room where there were six men lined up along a white wall. She looked at the first man to her left—number one. She stared at the second man and quickly moved on to the third. Still she was not able to identify anyone. She certainly did not sense anything from any of them either. She hoped they caught the right man. Looking at the fourth man though, she did notice some similarities in body type. The fifth was not a match at all and was immediately eliminated. The sixth man was close to the right size, except his clothes were totally wrong. From where she stood behind the two-way mirror, the texture of the material did not look like a match. She also felt quite certain it was not number one or two either. That left number three and four. So, which one? She pointed to number four, feeling pretty confident he was her attacker. He definitely had the right body shape and it looked as though he was wearing the same hoody she had felt when he flung her to the floor. His eyes were sunken, and he peered through a gaunt face, the same face she had caught a glimpse of earlier when fighting him off.

Spence called out: "Number four, take a step forward." Number four was clearly uncomfortable but he complied.

"Yes, I really do believe he's the man who attacked me tonight."

Spence turned towards Jewel informing her that he was indeed the man who had been picked up running from the apartment building directly in the alley behind the complex.

"What now?" She asked, feeling exhausted and lost with this whole business. Police work was not her forte, although she had to admit that she had certainly had her fair share of detective work in the past few days. Perhaps she had underestimated herself and her abilities.

"We'll interrogate and fingerprint him to find out whether he is the same person who destroyed your apartment. We'll ensure that he is charged with something."

"Spence, could he be connected with the disappearance of the teens as well, do you think?"

"There's no way of knowing that," he replied.

With the seed planted in Spence's mind, Jewel felt quite confident that he would pursue this line of inquiry to determine the man's guilt on both accounts.

"Well if you don't mind, I'm going to get a room to clean myself up so I can get some rest. Would you mind if I left now?"

"No, of course not, but leave a contact number with the officer. Are you sure you don't want to stay at the house?" Spence asked again but knew Jewel well enough not to overreact.

"I'm sure. Besides, I don't want to take your bed again. I'm perfectly fine in a motel. Being in a motel almost makes me feel like I'm on holidays!" she said, amused.

Jewel drove off to a motel as fast as the speed limit would allow. While driving she wondered whether it would be wise to see Professor Brown, who could explain away her trust issues with Spence. Once she had arrived at the motel, Jewel took an overdue shower before crawling between clean sheets where she fell fast asleep.

# Chapter 10

Monday morning came far too quickly. Somehow Jewel had a nagging feeling that the day would not go the way she had hoped. The fact that she finally had a good night sleep was a positive sign, so she was determined to stay optimistic.

Growing up, Jewel had suffered from night terrors, which she believed would automatically stop once she reached adulthood—as her father had told her. Yet, here she was in her thirties, still suffering from nightmares at least a couple of times each week. She so badly wished they would stop once and for all, but for some reason, that just did not seem possible.

It was right about then that a flash of last night's dream rushed into her brain like a runaway train. Jewel remembered Marcy entering her dream. Marcy had kissed Jewel's cheek as though she was leaving, but to where? The dream absolutely made no sense. Perhaps she was seeking to help Jewel in locating Tina, showing Jewel the way to find her. The fact that Jewel could not recall more details from last night, gave her very little to go on.

Jewel trusted the professor's conclusion that her night terrors were likely premonitions of some sort. Then again, the professor was not always around to interpret them for her. Looking in the mirror now and seeing a much older woman staring back at her, she knew two things: it was a much younger woman who began meeting with that professor on a weekly basis all those years ago, and she also realized how skinny she had become. Determined to nourish her depleting body, she quickly got dressed and went on a hunt for food. She drove to an all-night breakfast place and ate like a bear would have after a long winter's hibernation.

Leaving the restaurant, she decided to first head over to the police station in order to get some answers regarding the unexpected visitor last evening. With all their expertise in the field of interrogation, she trusted they would have obtained some information from the intruder by now. Upon arrival, she soon discovered that Spence was nowhere to be found.

"Do you know where he might be?" Jewel asked.

"No, ma'am, but I'm sure he'll return before long," the desk sergeant suggested with assurance.

Jewel wondered what happened to Steve Bronski. She decided to visit Marcy at the hospital rather than wait for Spence's return. Perhaps, her friend had remembered something new about the accident. The doctor advised Jewel that her memory would come back in fragments. Arriving at the nurses' station, the head nurse greeted her and told her that she wanted to speak with her. Jewel was puzzled. She followed her to the family sitting room, wondering if they were ready to discharge Marcy.

The nurse asked Jewel to have a seat before saying, "We're very sorry to have to inform you that Marcy Cooper didn't make it through the night." Her tone was sympathetic.

Jewel's mind went blank. She started to stammer. "What? But, I… I don't understand. I… I just left her yesterday and she was on the mend and… saying that she was bored." Jewel hesitated. "But the doctor was preparing to release her. What went wrong? I don't understand," Jewel repeated. She obviously was in shock for she was nearly shouting at the woman.

"I'm truly sorry. The doctor would like to speak with you, of course," she said, desperate to calm a very confused woman.

"Why didn't anyone call me last night?" Jewel asked, anger surfacing in her tone.

"The doctor tried to reach you but couldn't get through. Did you not get our messages?" she inquired.

"No, I didn't. What number were you calling?" Jewel demanded.

"I believe it was the phone number you left with us," the nurse replied, remaining calm.

"I… oh, my God! You were calling my home phone number, weren't you? With what happened to me last night, I had to stay in a motel," Jewel explained, and feeling as though she was going to faint. Her stomach churned. Suddenly she felt nauseated and the room started to spin. Her last thoughts were, *why didn't I see this coming*, just before she collapsed to the floor.

Opening her eyes, Jewel found that she was in a hospital bed. She became conscious that she must have hit her head when she went down, and it now throbbed something fierce. At that very second it also hit Jewel that Marcy was gone. Or could this be someone's sick joke? Or was this one of her nightmares? "*No, this can't possibly be happening! How could it be so? Marcy was doing so well. Truly I must get to the bottom of this tragedy,"* as Jewel sighed deeply, and her stomach churned once more.

Jewel swallowed hard and rang for a nurse. Once the female nurse entered the room, Jewel immediately went into private sleuth mode. "Please tell me. What happened?" Even though she knew why she was lying in this bed, she needed some answers; yet she was unable to accept this horrific news about Marcy all at the same time.

"Even if you feel better, do not get up." The nurse warned her. "The doctor will be here to look at that nasty bruise on your head," she stated while holding Jewel's shoulder down on the bed. It was clear to her that she did not want Jewel fainting again.

"Really… I'm fine… just a nasty bruise that's all. I'm sure it will go away with some ice. Do you think you could get me some?"

"Yes, I'll be right back if you promise not to get up."

"I promise to stay put. Could you please tell me when the doctor will be in?"

"He said as soon as he's finished with the patient he's currently seeing," she replied before walking out of the room.

It looked as if Jewel was in the ER with only a curtain separating her from others. Of course, they could hear what was going on. The nurse soon reappeared with a small ice pack. At this point Jewel's head felt like it was deformed with agonizing pain.

"Ouch!" She let out when the ice was placed on her head. The nurse looked at Jewel and winced. If she only knew the half of it, and how many bruises she had received during her altercation with Spence, which now covered her entire body, she thought. There simply was too much chaos in her life.

The nurse left her alone to absorb the news of Marcy being in the spirit world. Being alone like this, Jewel could not help but think about Marcy dying alone. Being a psychic was really beginning to bother her. Why on earth was she unable to see her own life? And when it came to her own affairs, she was blind as a bat. Professor Brown made compelling arguments about this topic. But still Jewel questioned why she had not seen Marcy dying, or even just before she passed so as to stop her passing somehow? Shouldn't she have received a clue? Then she remembered having the dream where Marcy had kissed her cheek, and Aunt May had been there as well. Could this have been the premonition she received last night? Right about then, the doctor entered her room and began to ask questions.

"How are you feeling?" he asked.

"Like a bad hang over without the alcohol," Jewel admitted.

"I see you like us so much you want to stay here." He was likely endeavoring to lessen the blow regarding Marcy. "We're very sorry about your friend, Miss Cooper, especially when she went so quickly. It was rather unexpected. One of the night shift nurses walked into her room and discovered she was not breathing—she called Code Blue immediately, but we were unable to resuscitate her." He paused. "Let me have a look at that nasty bump on your forehead. We'll have to take a scan of your skull and if everything checks out, we can discharge you then."

"Sure. But is there any explanation for Marcy's unexpected death?" Jewel asked him with a lump in her throat. She needed some clarification but realized that he may not know himself.

"Whenever someone has an unexpected death like that, we are legally required to perform a postmortem to rule out foul play," he informed her. "Not that we suspect any inappropriate conduct amongst the staff. We hope to have some answers in a few days. Again, my deepest sympathies."

"Thank you," she whispered, closing her eyes, not wanting to cry in front of him. A few tears escaped. The doctor must have felt her pain; he patted her shoulder with a compassionate tap with just the right amount of pressure, such that only a doctor with many years of experience would do. Although he had to leave, he reassured her that he would get some answers for her.

Jewel was immediately wheeled to the CT scan department. When a concussion or any other kind of injury had been ruled out, she was discharged.

She climbed into her vehicle but knowing there was no way she could deal with going back to her apartment, she drove to the police station to talk to Spence instead. She desperately needed a shoulder to lean on before the tears began to flow uncontrollably. When she arrived in front of the station, she realized that if Spence was involved, perhaps he was the last person she should talk to. She turned the car around and went back to the motel to gather her thoughts. Perhaps the bump really did affect her in such a way that she was now suspecting, of all people—Spence, of wrongdoing. Before lying down, she called to book another appointment with the professor for Tuesday evening. Jewel then thought about calling Aunt May, Marcy's only living relative, but did not have the courage to give her the dreadful news just yet. Instead she rested on the bed for a couple of minutes before she heard someone at the door.

She got up to answer the door, knowing her face was a mess from not only the bump but also her puffy eyes. At this point she just did not care. It was a young girl who said she had a message. She handed Jewel a note:

> *Meet me at the bridge next to the railway tracks at 7:00 PM,*
> *——Helena.*

Jewel glanced at the time and realized it was now 6:20 PM. She barely had time to jump into the car and drive there to meet her, let alone fix a little make-up so as not to scare anyone. Once she arrived at the location, she must have waited for about forty-five minutes with no one in sight. It was cool for this time of year, and every sound made her jump, from the eagle above to the vehicles driving past. When she was about to leave, Jewel saw a car pull up. Helena got out, pointed down the railway tracks, walked right back to her car, and drove off. *"What the heck?"* Why would Helena just leave without so much as a word? *"And what was she pointing at?"*

Jewel walked towards the railroad tracks and saw a man who had come up the tracks towards her. *"Who is that??"* She had never seen him before. He looked like he had not shaved for quite some time and was quite filthy.

Getting closer, Jewel could now see deeply into his eyes. Fear gripped her. She turned to run but she could not. It was as if she was running in water with little progress being made to safety.

# Chapter 11

Jewel woke up with her heart racing and her body soaked to the bone as though she had just run a marathon. At first, she was delighted to find that it was just another nightmare, and then she remembered that her best friend was gone forever—the searing pain in her heart returned.

She must have fallen asleep—or cried herself to sleep in all likelihood. If only she knew what that dream was trying to reveal; she was certain there was a message there, trying to get through to her.

"Ouch!" Her head still throbbed, and she knew that part was not a dream, unfortunately. She glanced at the clock—it registered 5:30, and by now it was already Tuesday morning. She knew she would have to cancel all her vacation plans, so that was one thing she would need to deal with today, for sure. Solving these growing, and possibly connected mysteries that were shrouding her life were the only things she needed to focus upon; this was imperative.

The sickening sense of loss returned all over again as soon as she thought of Marcy. Unfortunately, that part was also real. How she wished it had only been a dream. Right then, a flash from the night before came to her.

Jewel realized that she had, in fact, been given a sign. She had dreamt of Marcy kissing her goodbye, and only then did it become clear what it was that Marcy had sought to tell her.

Jewel felt the full effects of losing her—she had been as close to her as a sister. Jewel missed Marcy terribly and wished she had not left like this. If only she could simply lie back down to sleep, none of this would be so. Or would it?

All the unwanted feelings rushed back through her like a thunderbolt with more tears trickling down her cheeks. They had been friends so long and the only time they had disagreed was in the past year when it seemed to Jewel that Marcy was behaving quite oddly; she had not been her usual self. They simply could not see eye to eye, and especially of late. Then she wondered if it might actually be the other way around: maybe it was she who had been behaving differently, and totally blaming Marcy. Well, she thought, now most certainly was not the time to figure it out: she had to make funeral arrangements and start phoning Marcy's loved ones. She realized that with Marcy's parents both deceased, and being an only child, the only person she could think of, at least at the moment, was Marcy's Aunt May Applebee.

Aunt May was Marcy's mother's sister, never married. Nevertheless, May always declared that she had plenty of children at school: she was a great teacher, who retired not long after the accident that took Marcy's parents' lives. It probably was the teacher in her that allowed her to be firm but fair with Marcy. Aunt May was grateful to have someone in the house to dote on, filling a void. Once Jewel was introduced into May's world, she helped Jewel develop her own talents. May was not judgmental, but instead she would always reassure both girls to use their God-given talents no matter what. If it were not for Aunt May, Jewel would have never harnessed her psychic abilities—she preferred calling them 'powers'—to assist countless people over the years. Today, Aunt May lived too far away to visit often and her health had declined as such. Jewel had to admit that she missed her much more than her own mother. In a way, Aunt May had stepped into the role of mother for both Jewel and Marcy. Jewel had a lot to be grateful for when it came to May. Now, the thought of having to call an elderly woman with such dreadful news made her extremely anxious, although, she knew she had no choice but to make the dreadful call.

"Hello, Aunt May? It's Jewel. How are you? That's good that you are feeling much better now." Jewel hesitated before she proceeded with the alarming news. "I'm afraid my call is not one of pleasure. Yes, I'm fine… sort of… but no, not really. It's about Marcy." Jewel hesitated again. "Umm, there's been a car accident. And I apologize for not calling sooner. In truth I should have called, except Marcy was actually doing so well and I didn't want to bother you. I planned on calling you once she was out of the hospital. However, yesterday Marcy took a turn for the worst. I'm so sorry, but she didn't make it." Jewel managed to say.

"Oh my!" Aunt May let out. "Are you certain? I… I don't know what to say, child. Perhaps they've made an error? You know these things do occur," she clearly had reservations about this shocking news.

Jewel knew May was attempting to process the dreadful news and was not ready to accept her niece's early and unpredictable death. "The doctors still aren't sure why she didn't make it.

Certainly, they'll perform an autopsy and will get back to me with the results. Yes, just like 'CSI.' I'm truly sorry to have to relay this, Aunt May." Jewel found it heartbreaking to have to deliver such painful news. It took every ounce of courage for her not to fall apart. She was too choked up to continue speaking about Marcy, desperate to get off the phone before falling to pieces. The lump in her throat was preventing her from pronouncing her words properly.

However, Jewel was forced to continue speaking, regardless of her constricted throat. "Aunt May," she rasped, "I wish I had another answer for you. I'm still in a state of shock myself, so I apologize for being direct. You should not be alone at a time like this. Is there anybody who could be by your side?" Jewel knew she should have asked this question before delivering the upsetting news.

Aunt May began to take over the situation. "No, no that's alright, I'm fine. You don't worry about me. Marcy's mother had already given me clear instructions as to what she wanted done should anything tragic occur to her daughter. I had made a promise to Gisele, years ago that I would look after things should the unthinkable happen," she spoke with a self-assurance that surprised Jewel.

"Yes, Aunt May, but she was my best friend also, and I don't mind arranging the funeral. It's the least I can do, and you live too far away to arrange a service." Jewel protested, knowing that Aunt May must be in her seventies by now. She believed the winding roads around lakes and mountain passes, while grieving would prove to be too difficult for her—it would be a challenge for most.

"No, no," Aunt May protested again with more determination to keep her promise. "I am quite capable of dealing with the arrangements. Don't you trust me to do so? I have outlived many of my own friends and know exactly what needs to be done."

Jewel was surprised by May's resilience. *Why is the older generation so strong?* Jewel thought. More than likely they lived through tougher times and knew their own inner strength from years of conditioning.

"No, I didn't mean to offend you, Aunt May. I just thought being so far away might be overwhelming. I simply wanted to save you a trip coming out here so quickly to deal with Marcy's death. The coroner must do a postmortem on her first. It's mandatory to have it done in unusual situations, and I was told that her body won't be ready for at least another few days…" Jewel wanted to explain herself.

Aunt May cut in. "That's alright…" and added, "I already made some arrangements for her, thinking that I would die long before her and didn't want to burden the state with my own duties. Just leave everything to me and I will contact you with the details. Can you give me the doctor's name and number so I can contact him for the legal papers?"

Jewel was astonished to hear how calm Aunt May seemed to be. "Yes, of course, I have them right here." She proceeded to give her the details. "Will you be coming soon then?"

"Yes, as soon as I can book a flight, most likely tomorrow."

Jewel choked back her tears. "I'll call you later to get the details of your flight." When Jewel hung up the phone, she still had a huge lump in her throat. She did not want to cry so she decided to keep her mind busy by getting in touch with Helena. Perhaps she would survive this a lot better by helping others. In any event, it would be what Marcy wanted her to do.

Jewel poured herself a glass of water, wishing it were stronger; alcohol might take her anxiety levels down a notch or two. Possibly? She drank the glass empty before calling to cancel her Vegas trip. Although she had no intensions of crying any longer, the tears were more stubborn than she was. At the very least the tearful sobs released the tightening feeling in her chest.

Perhaps later today, when she met with the professor, he would know what all the dreams symbolized. It would be beneficial to decipher last night's dream to get a better understanding of why Helena had arrived on the scene the way she had.

But first Jewel had to get out of her motel room. Hastily, she washed her face, put on a bit of make-up to conceal the dark circles under her eyes, then she drove over to Helena's house, parking directly in front of her residence. Jewel walked up to the front door and suddenly heard someone yelling. Jewel froze, standing by the front door unable to move. She could hear Helena shouting at someone. Maybe she did not know Helena as well as she thought she did initially. Jewel stood there listening intently to hear what was being said.

"Si, I know what jou said, but I want to ask jou…" How unfortunate that Jewel could not make out the rest of the conversation. Helena had either lowered her voice or moved to another room. Darn, perhaps her dreams were relevant after all. Jewel kept listening but could only hear slight movements inside.

Jewel began knocking at the door, with more intensity than usual, hoping to see the person Helena had been shouting at. The door opened almost immediately.

"Ah, Jewel, I be so pleez jou come. Si, come in," she said politely and seemingly very calm.

Jewel could not help but think that perhaps Helena was a two-faced actress—a very good one. Maybe it was time to look into who Helena really was because what she had just experienced certainly did not align with the first impressions that she had received the other day during her initial meeting with Helena. "Thank you," Jewel replied, as she followed her inside. She glanced around the room, doing her best not to appear too nosy. "How are you?" She asked, making small talk while they walked into the kitchen. Jewel kept her eyes peeled to see who might be inside. Not seeing anyone was rather disappointing. The window overlooked the backyard. "I just thought we should keep making efforts to receive information on Tina. I had a dream last night and wanted to see how it ties into Tina's disappearance." Jewel offered by way of explanation.

"Si! Please help my Tina!" Helena pleaded. "You see someting in your dreams to help find her?" She asked with anticipation.

"Yes, I did actually. Unfortunately, I'm not sure how it helps. Do you know of some railroad tracks that cross an overpass, or perhaps a bridge?"

"Si! There be a place where's my Tina went wit' me on holiday last jear. We travel by train to Otay Mesa. It be only about fifty miles from 'ere," she excitedly gushed. "Do you tink my Tina goes dere?"

Helena seemed more energetic today than she had been yesterday. "I'm still not sure, but it may be our only clue thus far. Did you meet anyone there?" Jewel hoped to connect the dots before long, especially now that she had far more pressing things to deal with—the reminder hurt.

"We always meet people whereas we go. Oh, si! We did meet a man on the train going to Otay Mesa. I believe 'is name was William. I don't remember 'is last name. It start wit' an 'S' I tink?" She looked like she was recalling something. "Si, an 'S t, but I no remember his last name. So very sorry," Helena said, seemingly stressed she could not recall more especially with her daughter's life weighing in. "Do you tink he took my Tina? Oh, my goodness!" She put her hands up to her mouth in panic.

"I'm not sure, but it may be important. If you do remember anything else, could you call me straightaway? I'm going to take a trip to Otay Mesa County. It would be very helpful if you could remember where you went once you got off the train."

"Si, let me see!" She looked very intent on remembering. Even in the face of misfortune and as distraught as Helena must be feeling with the whole idea that a casual stranger may have abducted her child, she was doing her best to assist.

Helena announced, "Oh! We get off train and took taxi to park. We stay out dere for I tink two hours before we goes to town to pay for our room. Only dere for two days, si."

"But who did you meet other than the man on the train? Was it William, you said?" Jewel asked, wishing that she would recall something, anything really, that could quickly solve this case. "Where did you stay?"

"We stays at a little hotel called…. Oh my! I can't remember. I keep receipt some place 'ere," Helena said, crossing the kitchen floor at a trot. She opened a drawer and began sifting through quite a lot of papers. "It be 'ere with this," she pulled out a handful of receipts. At least, she had them all in one drawer, thought Jewel gratefully—unlike her place at the moment.

"Not to worry, but if you can find the receipt it would be a starting point to the search in Otay Mesa County," Jewel replied.

"I keep looking. Si, I do remember the next day we goes for breakfast at the hotel's dining room. Dere be only a couple dere, dining and, oh, si dere be another man. He sat by 'imself and stare at us when we eat. Not polite to stare at jou! Maybe he took my Tina?" She asked, more eager than ever and with her excitement her English faltered. "We no speak to anyone dere, just waitress who bring food. We ate meal and left. Dat's all. We took taxi to museum. Very nice museum in Otay Mesa so we spend lots of time dere… maybe two or tree 'ours in dere."

"I definitely will go to the museum also. You've been most helpful, but I must be going now. You keep remembering—I must get a lot done before I leave for Otay Mesa County."

"Do you tink you find my Tina?" Helena started to let a few tears roll down her cheeks.

The sight of her tears just tore at Jewel's heart; she was grieving her friend's death and it hit her hard. That realization brought it home for Jewel; she decided she would not tell Helena about Marcy's death just yet. "I'm going to leave so keep positive and strong for Tina's sake," Jewel told her, knowing full well that the loss of her own best friend could not possibly compare to the devastating loss of a child. Yet, somehow, she *did* know how it felt. Jewel patted Helena's shoulder before she headed towards the doorway. A lump formed in her throat preventing her from speaking further.

Helena followed Jewel to the door and while stepping outside, Jewel asked with great difficulty. "I really can see how courageous you are. Oh! Before I go; is there…" she hesitated. "If I could have a picture of Tina to take with me, it would be helpful."

Helena turned around, crossed the floor in a rush and disappeared somewhere inside. She returned minutes later with a picture in hand.

"Si! Jou take tis and find my Tina." Helena brushed away a few tears from her face.

After some thought, Jewel had to ask, "You know, I thought I heard you speaking with someone just before I knocked." Jewel was cautious, but she *was* attempting to locate her daughter after all and there was a chance this information might be useful.

"Si, I be talkin' with police. I don't tink dey be doing everyting dey could to find Tina."

"Ah, I see! Did they say they were going to do more?"

"Si! Dey say yes," she stated, somewhat triumphantly.

"That's good. I'll be leaving then. I look forward to your phone call regarding the name and address of the hotel," Jewel reiterated while rushing back towards her vehicle.

While driving away, Jewel watched Helena standing outside her front door wiping her swollen eyes with her apron. Jewel knew Helena would most certainly lose her mind if Tina was murdered, just like she might go crazy herself as she struggled to come to terms with losing Marcy.

Jewel's thoughts started deviating—*I must give this my all in order to find her little girl to bring a smile to her face and hopefully to Marcy as well—she had been so adamant about me assisting in locating this girl.* Continuing to work on this missing-person case was a welcomed diversion that would likely help her keep it all together. If Jewel could help it, she would prevent another person from going through the pain of losing someone very dear to them. Perhaps Aunt May would also be a nice diversion. Jewel reminded herself that she still needed to call May to find out her arrival time. Running to Otay Mesa, the next county over, and making it back before Marcy's funeral service could be a tricky feat to pull off, but it was certainly necessary. For some unknown reason, she had the distinct sense that her world was about to get more complicated in the very near future

~

Not long afterwards Jewel arrived at the university to find Professor Brown seated at his desk. She sighed heavily. "I'm so grateful you could fit me in this evening," Jewel mentioned while sitting across from her favorite professor. She looked quite downhearted.

"Not at all," he reassured her. "So, what can I help you with?"

"I've been having many dreams of late, but not knowing how to interpret them, I'm at a crossroads. For instance, Marcy appeared to me the night before last, and yesterday, she was found dead!" Jewel explained, once again choking back tears that threatened her composure.

"First of all, I'm terribly sorry for your loss. And next, I'm not sure what I can tell you about this particular dream except that perhaps she was letting you know of her passing."

"Thank you." Jewel replied, still choking back her tears. "I realize that now, but at the time, I didn't connect the dots. How does one do that? That is, to know the dream is a premonition and not just a random dream?" She swallowed hard before the lump could escape into tears.

"Again, I'm afraid I'm not an expert in the interpretation of dreams, so you may not know until the event occurs. I can see whether there is any literature on the subject if you like?" he offered.

"That would be kind of you. The other area I'm really struggling with is trust. Could you help me understand from a soul's point of view why that is?" Jewel felt that Professor Brown might be able to shed some light on this particular topic, as it was more up his alley. "Not just a soul's point of view but also a personal one."

"Of course. From my extensive research, I have read that the soul is on a quest to experience all that there is. One probability is that your soul has either experienced betrayal and now wants to experience the opposite through your personal viewpoint. Therefore, it will find people whom you can trust. Or on the flip side, the soul may have experienced trust and now wants to experience mistrust. It could all be experienced simultaneously as well, for the soul learns—I mean experiences—all there is right in the now."

He seemed to have answers for this subject. "That is truly amazing! How does the soul experience all in the now?"

"Well of course that discussion has been countered by many theologians and a few scientists. But neither group has come to any agreements as of yet, despite the fact that this has been an ongoing research topic debated through the years. Theologians are currently researching many different religions to see what they have on this subject of course." He peered at Jewel but looked triumphant at his response, yet, knew she needed more than a few words of wisdom.

"Fascinating. Could you keep me informed? And could you read more on this subject matter?"

"Most certainly," Professor Brown agreed with a broad smile. He was always happy when one of his former students called on him to work on one hypothesis or another.

They said their goodbyes and Jewel left the university practically running, as if being chased by a fire. Surely tomorrow would be an early start. And there still remained a few things to be done before her departure for Otay Mesa County.

On her way home Jewel had a good cry. She then made plans to stop at her apartment to grab a few more clothes—especially a warmer sweater. Once at the apartment, while looking around, she found the note regarding the matchbook Spence had discovered in Tina's bedroom. It reminded her that she must have a chat with the owners of the club—maybe they would recall meeting Tina.

Consequently, she decided to drop in at the bar before returning to the motel. She drove to the Picante's Bar and Grill to ask a few questions of the staff. After showing Tina's picture to the bartender, he claimed to have never seen her before. He also mentioned something about her not being of age to be at his establishment. Jewel had to admit that it was odd for him to mention Tina being underage, especially since he had supposedly never seen her before! She wondered how he knew this from her photograph. Additionally, his answers did not account for the matches being in her possession either.

Back at the motel, Jewel called Aunt May to see when she would be arriving. "Aunt May, it's Jewel. Sorry I seem to be having trouble hearing you tonight. We might have a bad connection." Jewel raised her voice a decibel. "Can you speak up? Yes, that's better. I just called to see when you are arriving in Imperial Beach. At 9:30 in the evening on Thursday. That's wonderful! I'm sure they'll have completed the autopsy by then. And, call me on my cell phone if you need to talk to me before you arrive. I'm going to go out of town for a day or two, but I will be back by the time you arrive on Thursday evening. I'm looking forward to seeing you too. Yes, I wished it was under better circumstances also."

Jewel hung up the phone after jotting down the arrival time and flight number. It did not take her long to pack a light bag of the few items she had retrieved from her apartment. She decided to do this task right away instead of scrambling to do so first thing in the morning before she left for her trip. It was now 7:30. Even though it had begun to rain—a serious storm had erupted—Jewel knew she had to venture out. It would either be the restaurant at the motel, which had a sparse menu, or go to the amazing Chinese restaurant that had the best soup in town. She put on a warm sweater with a raincoat and headed over to the Chinese place. No matter what was going on, she had to keep her strength up.

On her way there, she could have sworn she saw Spence drive past her in a police car. He would have been off duty by now so why was he heading in the wrong direction? He lived on the other side of town. Where was he going at this late hour, and why was he using a police cruiser if he was off duty? She had more questions than answers. She made an illegal U-turn to follow him.

Spence drove out of town towards East County. It started to rain harder with lightning illuminating a very ominous dark sky. Maybe Jewel should have stayed at the motel after all, remembering that she was still quite tired. She was also worried that he may spot her following him with the lightning illuminating her car, however briefly.

"Where is Spence headed to?" Jewel called out perplexedly. She watched him turn right. She had to go straight through the intersection so he would not see her tailing him.

For the second time tonight, Jewel made a U-turn. How would that look making yet another illegal turn following a cop? Her father would not have approved of her unlawful moves. The rain was coming down in a downpour and it became impossible to see more than a few feet in front of the windshield. She turned left into the side road Spence took, which was especially muddy. Her tires kept hitting large puddles of water. Finally, she accepted that she would have to turn back because of the bad weather conditions, but she was still determined to find another way to find out where Spence had been going.

She drove directly back to the restaurant, picked up the soup, and headed back to the warmth of her motel room. She was terribly cold and in need of a hot bath. As she ate the hot soup, she sighed with satisfaction thinking the soup alone had made the trip worthwhile. Jewel had brought in her road map to look up where the side road would lead. It appeared to go down an old abandoned mineshaft, but Jewel could not imagine what Spence would be doing down there.

She needed to get some rest and maybe if she ate more regularly, her psychic abilities would return stronger and more accurately than they seemed to be lately, making her efforts more productive. The soup may have warmed her up, but a bath would soothe her aches and pains. Looking at her badly bruised legs was discouraging to say the least. She sunk into the tub to avoid seeing them. This soon followed by crawling under the covers while praying that she would fall asleep quickly. She would gladly exchange all this chaos, especially preparing for a funeral for her beloved friend, to regain some sense of balance. With a heavy heart and with emotions welling up in her chest—threatening to spill its deluge once more—Jewel knew that she could not possibly have enjoyed herself if she had taken a trip to Vegas at this time. She also knew in her heart, that using her time effectively to find Tina alive in order to avoid yet another heartbreaking incident, was vital.

It felt nice to be in bed alone, thinking of Marcy, and privately shedding a few tears.

Jewel decided to meditate before taking off on the wild goose chase in the morning. She lay there taking extended breaths to clear her anxious thoughts. Now that she felt cleansed and relaxed, she could open up to her source from the universe to catch a glimpse at whatever had to be seen.

With her eyes closed, she saw the overpass again where the tracks crossed. No sooner than a blink of an eye a train came barreling down the railway tracks. It was traveling at such a speed that the train rushed past her. And yet Jewel could distinctly see a man in the window who was staring out in her direction. It was disturbing to see his eyes looking right through her. She shivered with fright—not knowing how or if this was connected to Tina's disappearance was irritating. Perhaps the train was a way this man found his victims? It could definitely be an effective method of meeting many young girls, or boys for that matter. A sickening feeling came over her.

She quickly opened her eyes to pick up a note pad sitting on the nightstand. Jewel started drawing the man's face, capturing the image while it was fresh in her mind. While sketching the rest of his face, she went back to his eyes making them even darker and deeper as they had appeared to her. "There, that resembles him somewhat," she said out loud, feeling quite confident with the image that now stared back at her. Jewel found the image most eerie to look at. It now seemed imperative to visit the small county to get a better look at the railroad, and of course, who she might find there. She placed her head down and fell into some type of slumber, or was it?

Jewel suddenly found herself in a large tunnel, or room at the front of an immense open space with many stone benches surrounding her. She was facing individuals in long robes, and in front of her was a stone pillar from which she was reading its inscriptions. The symbols were circular in nature. The audience started to chant while she continued to recite the words in a language that was beyond her comprehension. The room became very dark with a few candles remaining, most blown out by a wind that emanated from all directions. It was creepy to the point that when Jewel awoke from what appeared to be another nightmare, she gasped for air. After regaining her senses, Jewel sighed and once again fell asleep.

# Chapter 12

The alarm sent her senses into high alert and her body into action. The fact that today was perhaps one day closer to finding Tina, gave Jewel the energy to spring out of bed. No sooner, the memory of her terrible loss of Marcy resurfaced and she had to lie back down, then her trip to Otay Mesa came back to the forefront. She glanced at the clock—5:35 AM. It was getting late! She had finally slept peacefully and sighed in relief. The beauty of this dream was that she had not felt as though she had been running all night, which she always found so exhausting. While remembering a few details of her dream, Jewel admitted that she could not understand what a priestess would have to do with Tina's disappearance.

Once more she hurried with only enough time to grab her packed bag, purse and raincoat to catch the early train to Otay Mesa County. Jewel quickly turned to lock the motel door and felt frustrated when the key would not lock the door easily. But when she turned around to go to the car, she saw something she was not expecting and screamed automatically. "Ahhh!!! What the hell are you doing? Why are you right here like that, Spence?" She felt chilled and overheated all at once and realized she was yelling. She thanked God she had not used a lot of profanity. He was standing only inches away from her.

"I was just paying you a visit." He shrugged. "I went to your apartment last evening, but you hadn't returned. So, I inquired at the precinct to get your location."

But he sounded too calm about how he turned up at her motel room at this hour of the morning. He had really freaked her out. Could he be up to something? Could he be monitoring her? She could not be sure, but she wondered why he was behaving in a strange way. "Spence, you know you could have called instead of scaring me half to death yet again?" Jewel blurted, sounding extremely annoyed with him, which of course, she was.

"I just wanted to see if you were alright. I've been worried about you since Marcy passed away. And, I thought you would have stopped by to see me," he added, looking hurt about her reaction.

Jewel had switched tactics and now was pretty certain he was merely making efforts to remain calm and offering his condolences.

"Where are you headed off in such a hurry?" he asked, suspiciously looking down at Jewel's luggage.

Feeling like her actions were suspicious, she replied. "I thought I would get away for a day or two. Too many memories of Marcy here, so I thought getting away was the right thing to do. Besides, focusing on her death isn't healthy right now." All the while she wondered why she felt the urge to explain herself to Spence. She gazed straight into his eyes, assuring him that she was quite fine.

They had been an item for just over six months, but not for a few years now. Back then, Jewel was not ready to commit entirely to a relationship with him, believing that she needed more time to assess what it would be like to be in a relationship with a detective. Now, in the present, she hoped he was still at peace with the decision he had made to break it off. She certainly was fine with it. Jewel definitely did not want him thinking they were anything but friends now. And unquestionably, she did not want him to know that she was suspecting him of possibly being involved in this case in a sinister way—but of course, she was not yet entirely sure. Perhaps her mind was overreacting to his seemingly strange actions of late?

She wondered if she should say something to him, even though she was in a hurry. Judging by the expression on his face, Jewel concluded that he was probably also feeling sad about Marcy's sudden death. And yet, she still felt slighted that he had turned up unexpectedly like this. They may be friends, but that did not give him permission to spy on her every move. And, for some reason, she still felt she had to tread lightly with their relationship.

"Oh, I understand," he said. "Very sorry about…" He hesitated. "Are you sure you want to leave now? You know I'm here for you."

"Yes, I really feel that getting away will be good for me. But thanks, I appreciate your concern."

"Okay then, I'll see you in a few days, alright?" He immediately turned on his heels and at a quick march went back to his patrol car.

"Bye, Spence," Jewel shouted across the parking lot. He sped away while she was still struggling to place her luggage in the trunk. The least he could have done was help with her suitcase even though it was small. If it were not for her body aching everywhere, which made the job a little more delicate than usual, she would not have given Spence's hasty departure a second thought.

Jewel promptly parked at the train station. She looked upwards at the heavens. The sky was still gray and heavy with dark clouds, threatening to release their moisture once again. She swiftly purchased a return ticket to Otay Mesa County. The roads were already soaked to capacity with muddy puddles, looking more like little lagoons. More water than road was visible on the streets. She skipped over the worst area and boarded the train. It had been quite some time since she had gone on a train and she was excited about riding one again. She sat down comfortably in her seat. It felt strange to sit and do nothing. Perhaps she could read a little for the hour that it would take to get there. She took out her book to start reading when she noticed a couple walking past her down the aisle. They seemed to be arguing about something. They eventually sat down. There was another man sitting two rows in front of her.

The train whistled to announce its departure. It was a treat to ride such a relic of a train—they prided themselves of owning and operating such a historical railway. It reminded her of the Old West as depicted on television. She thought it might even be the only historic railway still in service. The smoke rose from the bottom of the train appearing more like fog than smoke, but it only obscured their view of the outdoors.

At last, they were finally leaving. Jewel settled in to read but found that the side-to-side rocking motion caused her stomach to feel queasy. She decided to close her eyes to catch some needed rest. With eyes closed, she thought she could sense someone right in her face. When she opened her eyes to check, the very same man she envisioned last evening—the same one she had drawn his image on paper—was staring right at her.

"Gees!" She jumped with fright and demanded: "What are you doing? And what do you want with me?" She desperately wanted him to explain his rude behavior. This was the second scare this morning, and at this rate her poor heart might not make it to the end of the week!

"I was just wondering what you think you are doing here, all by yourself?" He asked it in the most intimidating way—by turning the question back on her.

"It's none of your business," Jewel protested, feeling quite out of sorts by his redirected question. "I asked you first," she shouted right back at him. "You know that you're the one in my face."

He stood there for a moment not saying a word. Jewel blinked for no more than a second when he simply vanished in thin air.

"What the…!" She looked around to see if anyone else had seen him. But no one seemed to be looking her way. *Didn't anyone see anything? How could they not have seen, or heard anything?* It was then that Jewel felt someone grabbing her shoulder. She nearly jumped out of her skin. "Gees Louise!" This startled her so much that she opened her eyes, only to witness the conductor staring right at her as though he had seen a ghost. Talk about a déjà-vu. Maybe he had seen something.

"Pardon me, ma'am. Are you alright?" He asked out of concern.

"Oh, yes, yes, I'm fine. Did you not see a man walking right past here a second ago?" she asked, hoping he had seen the man speaking to her.

"No, I just heard you yell and thought something was wrong." He seemed genuinely concerned as he bent down to face her.

"I must have had a bad dream, that's all." She was desperate to downplay the whole outburst, turning red from embarrassment.

"I'm sorry to have woken you then, ma'am!"

"No, that's quite alright. I think I needed someone to get me out of that nightmare, so I thank you." In fact, she wanted him to leave while she still had a little dignity left. She felt quite mortified at her public display. He must have thought she had completely lost her mind, and no doubt, he would not have been the first to ever think so.

"Good day, ma'am," he said, resuming his walk down the aisle toward the front of the train.

Soon they arrived at Otay Mesa County station, where everyone got off on the platform which now seemed to come right out of a 19th century storybook. Everything was made of wood and the platform was more than likely used for many western movie sets. But, instead of horse and buggy, Jewel took a 'real' cab to the Eastside Inn where she had reserved a room for one night.

She looked around the front lobby, wondering if this was the place where Helena had stayed with her daughter. Jewel sat down to see if she could sense anything. The place did feel like it was where Helena and Tina had stayed, even though Helena had never called her back with the actual hotel name. Jewel inquired with the desk clerk if there were other inns thereabouts. He indicated that there were only two other ones in town: the Portal Inn and the Otay Mesa Inn. "Do you recall if this girl was here lately or perhaps last summer?" Jewel held up Tina's picture.

"Umm… no, I don't remember, but we do get a lot of tourists through here so I wouldn't necessarily remember anyone in particular. Though she is pretty," he smiled.

"Thank you." Jewel turned to take the stairs to the second floor. Her room number was 251. She quickly dropped off the luggage, freshened up a bit, and went out to find something to eat. Afterward, she decided a visit to the museum would be her first stop.

The cab ride to the museum was noticeably short—after all, the entire town was pretty small with only thirty-five hundred residents occupying the entire valley. Jewel saw many interesting artifacts but was not sensing any connection with Tina or her mother. The trail went cold. So, Jewel decided to head for the park where Helena had indicated they had spent considerable time. Perhaps Tina enjoyed it more than what Helena had mentioned.

The driver had dropped her off at a bakery so she could buy herself a muffin before heading out to the park. Crossbow Park was endowed with beautiful sceneries, the trees showing off their spectacular colors. Trails led to the interior of the park, welcoming visitors to the lushness that could be seen from the roadway. Although Jewel was not sure where the trails led and what she might find there, she paid the cab fare, got out and began looking around. Birds flew to the ground in search of the remaining crumbs left by the tourists who frequented the park. The birds did not seem to be alarmed by her presence. She walked towards the trees and instantly connected with an energy she sensed as Tina's presence.

Tina had definitely been here at some point; Jewel was certain of that. Now, if she could only pick up a time frame, it would prove beneficial to this case. She would need to sit down on the ground and close her eyes to see if that would help. She scanned her immediate area quickly to see if anyone was near that might frighten her as she placed her raincoat on the ground. No one could be seen down the paths either. The solitude would give her ample time to meditate.

She closed her eyes and breathed deeply. She felt relaxed and waited to see what images would appear. There was something hypnotic about being in the park. Jewel could hear the wind blowing and heard the whispers left from previous visitors. It was then that Jewel saw Tina. This must be where she had been last year, looking much younger than her most recent picture.

Jewel then began receiving glimpses of what Tina had observed last summer. She seemed quite happy being here with her mother. Next, Jewel saw the same man who kept invading her thoughts. He was sitting at the picnic table to the far right of her. She saw him gaze at Tina and could not help but think that his motives appeared rather sinister. She shivered with the thought. "Was this the man who took you, Tina?" Jewel asked her as though Tina was sitting right next to her. Judging from Tina's bodily reactions, Jewel sensed that Tina was frightened as well. This gave Jewel a strong sense that the man had something to do with her disappearance. As the vision receded, Jewel opened her eyes. Her first glance was toward the woods with the trees, which still seemed to be creating an inviting atmosphere. Enticed, Jewel rose to take a walk down the first path.

The perfect scenery generously provided for a serene, relaxing walk, taking a little while for Jewel to check out the energy around it. The park smelled of large redwood cedars, pine, sequoia and palm trees, as though one was walking deep into a dense forest. She walked no more than ten minutes down the path, obviously used many times by tourists. When she arrived at a stream on her left, Jewel stopped. It was beautiful at this time of year with the foliage turning into a spectacular array of colors from crimson reds, brown, pale green and yellows, with the sun blazing on their outstretched branches and the river running through the forest. Autumn is typically a dreary season with lots of rain due to the cooler winter months approaching. Standing there, with the foliage from the low-lying shrubs displaying such a spectacle, Jewel noted that such a fantastic setting was indeed memorable.

She kept walking down farther when a young girl appeared. Jewel watched the girl approach and when she was less than a hundred feet away, the girl spoke.

"Can you help me?" She asked with a hopeful plea.

Jewel felt that she had seen her before, or knew her from somewhere, although at the moment, she could not remember where.

"What seems to be the matter?" Jewel called out to her.

"I need your help," the girl pleaded once again.

"Of course, I can help. Are you lost? This path leads to the road," Jewel offered, pointing in the direction of one pathway. There were plenty of paths yet to search so Jewel hoped that was all she required from her. "Do you have someone who will take you back to town?" Jewel asked.

"No, I need your help. Please help me," the striking girl insisted.

By then Jewel felt perplexed as to how she could possibly be of assistance out here. "But I'm not sure what I can do to help." Jewel felt utterly confused as to why she was not telling her what she needed. "I'm sorry. Are you hurt? I could call for help."

"I need your help," the girl repeated in an eerie voice.

In the end, Jewel turned around, pointing in the direction of the path behind her, clearly showing the exact direction for her to take to get out of the woods. "This way will only take you about ten minutes to the roadside." Yet, when Jewel turned back towards the young girl, she had vanished. Jewel wondered if she had gone back down the path just around the bend. She decided to follow the path to see if the young lady had rounded the corner. Perhaps she required help for someone else and wanted Jewel to follow her.

When she reached the bend, the girl was still not visible. Jewel continued to walk another five minutes before spotting her walking up ahead. It was obvious, especially after calling out to stop, that the young lady did not require help after all. Reluctantly Jewel returned to the roadside before she, too, would become lost. She reached the picnic area, relieved to leave the park. The appearance of the girl had distracted her from her original mission. She called a cab to return into town.

Once there, Jewel walked into the first restaurant she saw in order to sate her hunger—she was famished. She could not believe she had not eaten much before leaving—just that muffin on the way to the park—which, besides the long walk into the woods, had certainly given her the right to a veritable feast. Jewel brought along Tina's picture to show around town, effectively killing two birds with one stone. After ordering, Jewel produced the photograph to show the waitress—she had not seen the girl before. Jewel asked how long she had been working there.

"Let me see. I guess I started in April, so about six or seven months now," she replied, before disappearing into the kitchen.

A few minutes later with lunch in hand, she returned. The chicken salad looked scrumptious and was received with a warm smile. "It looks divine," Jewel said before returning her smile.

"You know, Flo usually works here. She's been here for more than five years. You should show the girl's picture to her," the waitress suggested.

Jewel wondered if the girl could sense her desperation. "Is Flo here then?" She asked feeling encouraged by her search. "And what is your name? I'm Jewel by the way."

"I'm Dee. And no, Flo is not in right now, but she usually comes in for the evening shift," she offered.

"Okay, then. What time would that be exactly?"

"She'll be here at six tonight." Dee added almost shouting as she hurried to clear more plates from other tables.

"Thank you for your help," Jewel called out to her as she vanished through the kitchen doors. She finished her late lunch knowing she would return after six for a light dinner to question Flo.

The next course of action was to go over to the Portal Inn to present Tina's photo there. After making her way to the hotel, Jewel noticed several guests registering. She would have to wait her turn to speak with the front desk clerk. While waiting, however, Jewel began to sense a weird presence. She felt like it was ominously evil, as well as having a very heavy weight to it. Feeling as though a cold breeze had sailed behind her, Jewel shivered with fear and goose bumps covered her body. She looked around her to see if anything was amiss. She wondered whether the evil presence came from one of the guests, yet she was unable to detect any malevolent presence from the people in the room. She continued to wait in line. When the guests finally left, Jewel approached the counter. She stood waiting until the male clerk finished speaking on the phone before she could be served.

He hung up and said. "Yes, what can I do for you?"

Smiling, Jewel said, "I am hoping you have seen this girl." She placed Tina's photograph in front of him.

From his body language, Jewel was almost certain the young man recognized the image. Nevertheless, he shook his head. "No, I don't believe I have seen her before."

"Do you know if there are other employees working here who may have seen her?" Jewel asked, while intensely observing what he would say or do next.

"No, why do you ask?" he answered with a question.

Jewel was very well aware of this little trick people play when trying to evade a question. Or better still, they hope the interlocutor will leave. "I was hoping you may have seen her, or perhaps know someone who may have?" Jewel pressed on, definitely not wanting to play his game.

"Sorry, but I don't," he replied, putting in another attempt to dismiss her.

"I thank you for your time, sir," she finally said with a smile. She left giving the impression she was untroubled by his dismissal. She decided to exit without making enemies. She stood by the entrance, appearing to leave by looking both ways, but intending to observe the clerk instead. Just as she thought, he picked up the phone and placed a call. Unfortunately, Jewel was unable to overhear what was being said. She set off to check out the last hotel down the street. She made a point of walking slowly in front of the hotel's front window to watch the clerk's reactions as he put down the phone. It was disappointing not to know who had been on the other end of the line or what had been disclosed. Perhaps, she would have better luck at the next hotel.

While she was walking, Jewel still sensed someone was either watching her, or following her since having left the Portal Inn. As she entered the Otay Mesa Inn, an older man stood at the front desk asking about checkout time tomorrow. When he obtained an answer, he turned and disappeared into the elevator. Jewel approached the counter, and again, smiled at the front desk clerk, who, in turn, smiled back at her.

"Excuse me, could I ask you to take a look at a photograph to see whether you've seen a certain person before?" Jewel questioned, aiming at a friendlier approach.

"Yes sure, can I see the picture?"

"Thank you, here it is." Jewel pulled it out and showed the photo to the clerk while glancing at her nametag—Tanya.

"She's lovely and does look familiar, but I really couldn't tell you where I saw her. Is she in some kind of trouble?" The woman asked.

"Not at all, but do you remember if you have seen her recently or some time ago?"

"Let me see. I thought I saw her here, but in truth I can't tell you when. Sorry, I can't be more helpful. We do see so many come through here especially during our peak season," Tanya said.

"That's alright, you've been more than helpful," Jewel said, feeling good with the knowledge that she had been quite obliging. "Thanks for your time, and if you do remember anything at all, here's my card. You can reach me either at Eastside Inn, or better still at this other number. Thanks again." And with a warm smile, Jewel turned to leave.

"You're welcome, but I haven't really done much," Tanya said.

"No, that's alright, you've been very kind," Jewel replied before she left the inn.

Glancing at her watch, she realized that it was already 6:25 PM. She had to get back to the restaurant to see Flo. Perhaps, she would be more cooperative. Jewel walked as quickly as she could. When she reached the bistro-like eatery, she took a quick look around to see if she could spot her. Jewel soon spotted the only waitress and so presumed the woman was Flo.

"Excuse me. Are you Flo?"

"Yah, who's asking?" She glared at Jewel.

"Pardon me, my name is Jewel Seymour. I was wondering if I could ask you a few questions regarding a young girl." She was hopeful that Flo would remember seeing Tina.

"Sure," Flo said, now with a smile on her face.

Jewel pulled out Tina's picture from her purse and handed it to Flo. "Have you seen her, or do you recognize her at all?" She definitely needed some good news, as time was running out for Tina.

"You know she does look kinda familiar, but I haven't seen her for some time. If I remember correctly, I think she was here with an older person, her mom maybe?"

"Yes! Do you remember anything else about her, maybe seeing her lately even with someone other than her mother?"

"Why? What's the kid done?" Flo went on, thinking that Jewel was attempting to get the dirt on a runaway teen. It must be human nature to be curious, even suspicious regarding horrific news.

"No, she's not in any trouble, at least not that I'm aware of," Jewel replied, a slight smile crossing her lips.

"You know she looks like a good kid, and she was pretty polite to me when she was last here. Let me see, yes, I think it was the summer before if my memory serves me correctly. You know I do have a good memory. Well, at least, all my friends tell me so."

"That's a good quality to have," Jewel expressed. "I wish my memory was as good as yours. It sure would come in handy at times, particularly when looking for my keys. But seriously, Flo, if you do recall anything more, would you be so kind as to call me on my cell? It is very important that I locate this girl," Jewel said.

"Oh sure, I could do that, Miss Seymour."

"It's Jewel—just call me Jewel," she offered her card.

"Yah, sure I'll call you if I think of anything else," she assured Jewel. "You know, I believe I saw her picture on the tube the other night on the news. She's that missing girl they're looking for, isn't she?" Flo asked rather looking pleased with her memory.

"You do have a remarkable memory. And, she is the girl who disappeared, so, yes, it's vital should you remember anything at all."

Jewel thanked Flo again before she ordered some takeout and left the restaurant. She decided to walk the few blocks back to her hotel. It turned out to be a beautiful evening with the clouds clearing and leaving a clear patch of blue sky over to the west where the sun was soon to set. However as beautiful as the sky was, the peacefulness did not last long.

While walking, Jewel noticed a car tailing her. It was following about a block behind her, so she decided to stop as if window-shopping. She wished the car would quickly pass her. Sadly, it did not. Instead the car came to a stop, which made her quite nervous. Rather than loitering, she hurried back to the hotel. In the meantime, she hoped to catch a good look at the driver. Relieved to reach the Eastside Inn, Jewel went inside and immediately peeked through the front window to watch the car drive by. They both stared at one another. Jewel got a sense of impending doom and shivered from fright. *What was that all about? Perhaps she was stirring things up?* Unfortunately, it was getting dark, and she could not get any details from his face because the shadows around his features made them indistinguishable. She turned to go up to her room, anxious to lock the door behind her. She definitely needed something to calm her nerves.

Jewel ordered a chamomile tea to help calm her growing tension. As she sat thinking about the day's events from the early start with Spence terrifying her, the conductor frightening her, and the late evening drive by—it had proven to be quite an adventuresome day.

After her tea arrived, Jewel ate her supper, took a soothing hot bath, and crawled under the covers. At least the day had not been a total loss, but she wished she had obtained more conclusive information. Perhaps tomorrow would produce a few more helpful clues toward elucidating Tina's disappearing act. Being in this town, she somehow felt closer to Tina. But could she be wrong?

Exhausted, Jewel fell asleep without thinking of Marcy for once. She felt frustrated when she awoke a few hours later. Another fleeting dream of something that had startled her awake and she immediately sensed that Tina was in big trouble, but she was not clear how she could help her. Jewel plopped her head back on the pillow, hoping for more sleep, and with any luck, more information would surface about the girl. Admittedly, the last dream had not made much sense. What Jewel had seen was Tina sitting on a bench at a bus stop, or at least it appeared to be one. Next, she observed that she was no longer sitting there, but instead, she was sitting on a bench in a room, staring blankly at a stone wall. The room appeared to be in a basement with someone walking past the window. It seemed as though a dark shadow with the power to freeze everything in its path had walked past. Jewel was not sure what that meant exactly.

While the dreams were supposed to help, Jewel found that the interpretation could be quite disconcerting. Even though Professor Brown had informed her that he could not interpret dreams, maybe he could simply explain the content of the dream itself. Jewel decided that she just might have to pay him another visit in the very near future—although she was not sure when that would be.

The next instant it was now Jewel herself, who was fleeing away from someone or something. She kept darting from tree to tree in the woods, dodging a black shadow. It would move ever so close to her, as though they were engaged in a cat and mouse game—and she was the mouse! She was terrified and felt helpless. With her heart pounding in her chest, she made a run for the side road where she could see lights from an approaching vehicle. If she could only get to the road, flag the driver down to help before the dark shadow caught up to her, and then to safety. *Oh my!* She looked behind her and realized the shadow was getting closer, but the road was not near enough for her to escape the shadowy grip. Fear froze her in such a way that her legs became stiff. Petrified with fear, her heart in her throat unable to scream, Jewel struggled to get away. But the shadow was too powerful for her. Subsequently, she slipped on a pile of wet leaves before rolling around on the ground. She must have rolled down a small embankment at the edge of the woods adjacent to the ditch. Now being so close to the road, Jewel prayed for a car to drive past. The dark shadow was currently on top of her and she was unable to move. It started laughing a hideous laugh, piercing her ears so that she instinctively cupped her hands over them. It grabbed her and with little effort, it pulled her to her feet, dragging her back towards the forest. What will it do with her? Jewel was so weak from struggling that her arms and legs ached all over. If only she could get a look at its face to see who he was. The next thing she knew, he shoved her forward. At that moment she made her move. Dodging in front of a tree, she raced around and pulled off its hood.

It was then that she woke up. *"Damn!"* Jewel cursed.

Now she could not see who had been chasing her. It was disappointing not knowing who was responsible for chasing her down like a scared animal during a foxhunt with hounds closing in on its prey. It seemed like this was the same person who had been murdering young girls, like Elizabeth and perhaps Tina as well if she was not found soon.

Jewel's dream was so surreal. She wondered if Professor Brown could explain what she had just experienced. She needed to get to the bottom of this mystery before it got the best of her. These premonitions originating through her dreams usually came as forewarnings of impending doom, or accidents. Dreams could also give her clues to solving mysteries, although lately it appeared she had been a little off her mark. Lately, the clues needed deciphering and interpreting—they were complex and too elusive. This was the reason people paid her big bucks for her skills.

Early on, Jewel had learned from life's experiences to trust the information she received. Everyone is born with a sixth sense, often referred to as intuition or a notion. Whatever it was called, Jewel had been trained that trusting it proved to be instrumental in helping others. She honestly believed that she had tapped into her Higher Self and had been able to apply the information to her everyday work. Admittedly, she found it easier to get information for strangers than for herself. For example, obtaining information for a dear friend such as Marcy should have been easy, but lately she had to resort to visiting Professor Brown for assistance with the interpretation of the information she was receiving. She wondered whether Marcy's death had put her off her game.

Regardless, she intended to solve this puzzle quickly since Tina was relying on her to help. And that was exactly what she was going to do. Unless of course, it was already too late!

# Chapter 13

Getting up in the morning was more difficult than yesterday. With the looming funeral, not to mention rushing about before Aunt May's arrival, Jewel forced herself out of bed. Life would be easier if she trusted Spence to crosscheck the police database to search for similar arrest charges. In doing so, they could potentially discover that both cases were connected somehow. Jewel had to find a way to get that information—with or without Spence's assistance or anyone else's. But who could she trust?

Jewel finished packing to return later today to pick Aunt May up at the airport. This meant she had six hours to locate Tina Miles and return to Imperial Beach. Jewel grabbed a quick muffin with a coffee-to-go and took a cab to the park. She was hoping she might receive a little more information through her psychic senses, but this time she would really concentrate and open up enough to Source to receive pertinent details as to Tina's whereabouts.

Jewel was determined to go a little deeper than she had yesterday. Closing her eyes helped her receive prophetic information. But keeping her eyes closed in this situation would essentially be like walking blindfolded, especially with the many turns and steep edges along the pathways, could prove disastrous. So, she was forced to stay alert, not just because of the terrain either, but also being out in the open without knowing who might be dangerous. With eyes peeled on the path, she carefully proceeded forward, although this method proved difficult to go into psychic mode.

If only she had a bodyguard! Jewel simply could not figure Spence out. What could have changed him? His behavior was suspicious and quite out of character—even for a detective.

Jewel would pause if she felt her senses receiving information. Getting psychic information this way was like wearing a radio headset. Turning down certain pathways, one could experience sudden disruptions in communication, picking up static noise with nothing clearly emanating. Yet, suddenly on another stretch of the path, the music may actually transmit loud and clear like a strong radio signal. In a way, she could be called a portable radio on legs.

She simply picked up the signal from someone in the vicinity. Others have described it as being like a bloodhound picking up a person's scent to track them down. Every psychic develops their own specific skill or craft in the manner that best suits them—based on their wiring, if you will. So, whichever method works best for that individual is the one they use to detect and locate someone or something.

Jewel walked a little farther, suddenly pausing to see if she could tune into Tina's frequency. Nothing! She moved beyond the path to repeat the process for another half-an-hour. Finally, Jewel stopped. She could feel something. She picked up Tina's vibration, sensing she was once happy here with her mother. But then Jewel felt her mood shifting: now she was feeling scared, frightened of something… or someone. Jewel was not clear what it was that had terrified Tina, except it was clear that she had been afraid.

Jewel must be on the right track, so she decided to go a few more yards to see whether she could pick up a clearer image. Perhaps she might see buildings in the area, but nothing concrete came through. Knowing she still had to make her way back to the main road, she resigned herself to the fact that she would have to be finished for the day. However, when she turned to leave, she distinctly felt she had walked into a vortex of some kind. *What is this?* Jewel felt as though she just walked into an IMAX theater where everything was huge and directly in 3-D. Wow! She proceeded to walk past this point, and the vision, or impression disappeared as quickly as it came in. Wary to stay there at this point, especially without someone watching her back, Jewel felt a strong urge to get out of the park without necessarily knowing why—she just knew. She started to run down the path towards the main road until her side hurt. Finally arriving at the roadside, she anxiously called the cab company.

"Hurry! Answer the phone, won't you?" She said out loud, desperate to be as far away from this strange place as she could. She had never felt such a weird phenomenon before today, and never in a park. She could only wonder what it was. The cab finally arrived and not a minute too soon either. As Jewel climbed into the cab though, she saw the same girl emerging from around the bend on the path.

"Wait!" Jewel yelled at the driver and jumped out. "Just wait here one minute," she told him.

Yet when she turned back the young girl had vanished. Jewel did not know what to think. Maybe she was not really there after all. "Did you see a girl over there?" Jewel asked the driver.

"No, lady. Do you still want a ride or what?" He snapped at her.

"Yes, sorry, let's go," Jewel replied, although she felt reluctant to leave the young girl yet again.

He sped off while Jewel stared down the path, seeking another glimpse of the girl. Jewel did not like the thought of the driver not having seen her, however. Was he blind? Maybe he saw her too, but was in a hurry to leave, eager for his fare. She had seen this girl twice now, but why would the girl be hanging around this park?

They pulled up in front of her hotel. Jewel got out, paid the driver, and then asked if he could pick her up at six to catch the six-thirty train back to Imperial Beach.

Upon returning into town, she immediately went over to the restaurant, hoping for a word with Flo. She entered the bistro-style eatery where the pleasant warmth was a welcomed relief. After being outside in the cool air for part of the morning, Jewel found the atmosphere comfortable. She sat next to the fireplace situated in the centre of the room. She thanked the waitress, instantly feeling the heat from the fire soothing her aching body. The outdoor air had seemed especially damp in the past few days, but then, they were approaching the rainy season. She ordered the same—the delicious homemade soup. The waitress brought the soup along with a small loaf of warm, homemade bread. With the buttery spread melting on top of it, Jewel was quite content to eat. Sitting next to the fire, enjoying good food was more to her liking than traipsing through a forest searching for lost girls like a bloodhound. What was she thinking? But Jewel felt compelled to continue just the same. Moreover, Marcy would have wanted her to pursue her investigation—even in death—her friend remained her driving force.

While enjoying her meal, Jewel observed an older man who entered and sat three tables over. As soon as the waitress left to retrieve his drink, he nodded at Jewel. Somehow, she recognized him, but from where? If only she had Flo's remarkable memory. She believed he was the man who had been following her yesterday. She now wondered if he was attempting to unnerve her by shadowing her. Or worse yet, he might want to hurt her because she was searching for Tina. Perhaps he was responsible for her disappearance? Jewel sat watching him from the corner of her eye, not wanting to alert him that she recognized his face. Jewel closed her eyes to see whether she could pick up any information from him. She saw that he was involved with some aspects of this investigation but not sure to what extent. For all she knew, he could be on the law enforcement side. But why follow her? However so, she simply would have to keep an eye on him. He had average features with dark brown hair, graying at the temples with a receding hairline. He was perhaps in his forties with a round, clean-shaven face. She could not see the color of his eyes from where she sat. He was wearing a light, tan raincoat. The waitress brought his drink. She chatted with him for a minute. While they conversed, the young waitress, who worked yesterday, entered the restaurant to start her shift.

The waitress, Dee, according to her nametag, came over to Jewel's table. "How are you today?" She asked with a cheerful smile

"I'm just fine thank you, and how about you?" Jewel replied while not wanting to lose her target.

"I'm good, thanks. Just wondering if you got to speak with Flo?"

"Indeed, I did—last night, and I thank you for your help. I was wondering if you've seen this man before, the one seated over there?" Jewel asked, nodding in the man's direction.

"He has been here before, but I don't know much about him. I don't think he lives around here. We're a small town so we would know who's a resident or not. He's probably just passing through town and will most likely be moving on soon. Tourists are our main revenue," Dee explained.

Jewel was surprised that Dee knew so much about the town's business concerns. "Thanks, I just wish I could get his name somehow," Jewel said without thinking.

"I could find out for you," Dee had jumped on the request before Jewel could stop her.

"No, maybe that would be too personal, and I wouldn't want him to know I inquired," Jewel protested in a low tone. She had to try before she was too far from Jewel's table. "Psst," Jewel whispered.

Dee walked back to Jewel's table, whispering, "I could get the information without giving it away. Just watch," she said as she walked off.

"Well no!" Jewel snapped, struggling to stop her once more. But it was too late. Dee was already halfway across the room. *Shoot! What have I done?* She was bewildered. Just what she did not need right then! She could see Dee talking to the staff inside the kitchen.

Dee soon came out to offer some coffee to the man, and seamlessly struck up a conversation with him. They talked for a few moments and she then came over to offer coffee to Jewel. She wondered whether this would attract unwanted attention.

"Would you like some more coffee, ma'am?" Dee carried on as though Jewel was just another customer. Dee must have missed her first calling. Perhaps it was not too late for her to audition for a movie part in Hollywood.

"Yes, I would love some coffee, thanks," Jewel responded, carrying on with the whole charade.

Dee poured the coffee while whispering, "He's just passing through," keeping her words to a minimum.

"Thank you and could I bother you for a glass of water?" Jewel was now working the part.

"I'll be right back," Dee said, giving Jewel a wink as she turned to leave. Next, she approached the other customer, asking if he would like some water also. Dee then disappeared through the kitchen door. Amazingly, she looked all too comfortable in her new role—Dee was a natural. A moment later, she came out of the kitchen with two glasses of water, handing one to the gentleman seated closer to the kitchen. She had a few more words with him and proceeded to Jewel's table.

"Here's your water, ma'am," and placed it on the table. "Is there anything else I could get you?"

She was too good to be true. "No thanks," Jewel replied.

Dee whispered yet again, letting Jewel know that she was lining him up to ask the question. Before long she marched to the front counter where she grabbed two dessert menus and offered one to each of her patrons.

The desserts did look quite tempting. Jewel went ahead and ordered the banana custard pie. Meanwhile, she heard the gentleman ask for his bill, and Dee graciously handed it to him. He got up to leave, first paying the tab with his credit card. No sooner did he leave than Dee waltzed over to her table.

"Mission accomplished. His name is Philip Denver," she added, looking pretty smug.

*She definitely got the job done and she should feel proud of herself,* Jewel thought. She sincerely thanked her for all her efforts and made sure to give her a generous tip. She was certainly a very sweet girl with an obvious talent for the big screen. Jewel offered to give her a recommendation should she require it in Hollywood. They both laughed at the idea.

Jewel left the restaurant with an air of victory even though she was not entirely responsible for it. Yet, the need to know who was following her was crucial. Her pessimistic father had continually harped about knowing who your enemies were before planning your next move. She did feel somewhat uneasy when Mr. Denver had looked her way. She would not go as far as to call it creepy, but it was a close second in any case.

She went back to the hotel to rest for a short while before departing. But instead of resting, she concluded that meditating on Mr. Philip Denver might prove beneficial. Having his name would certainly help focus on his personality.

Walking into the Eastside Inn, she passed the front desk clerk who handed her a note. She quickly opened the note. It stated—*Meet me at the train station at 6:30 tonight.*

*Now what?* Jewel wondered. She was not sure who had sent the note. Perhaps it was Philip Denver himself. Honestly, she thought that a little guidance would be necessary, hinting to the Gods, or whoever might be listening to her prayers. A feeling of alarm like red flags flashed in front of her mind's eye. She sighed heavily.

Jewel went up to her room to meditate in private. It was nice to shut the door from all the excitement of the day. She relaxed, deeply breathing. With eyes closed during the meditation, she hoped for a vision. By her third breath, she started to release all her thoughts and emotional body. It was then that she received her first vision in colored pictures. At first, she saw the girl at the park. The young lady was mumbling something or other, except it was too muffled so Jewel could not make it out. Jewel asked if she could repeat it a little louder.

"I'm waiting for you," came through loud and clear, even though she had only whispered.

With shivers going up and down Jewel's spine, she asked, "Waiting for what? Can you tell me who you are?" She was getting quite anxious for answers, although she was ready to end the session.

"I'm Claire," she whispered in response like the wind blowing down Jewel's neck.

"But I don't know you, Claire. Can you tell me why you need my help?"

The telephone rang and Claire vanished in one quick instant. Reluctantly Jewel got up to answer the phone.

"Hello, yes this is she," Jewel replied to the girl. "Yes, thank you." She hung up the phone and wondered what on earth was transpiring. She had been summoned to go down to the front desk. It was already passed 4:30 so Jewel decided to take her luggage with her, not wanting to return at this late hour.

The police greeted her downstairs.

"Are you Jewel Seymour?" the officer asked.

"Well yes, why do you want to know?" she replied, feeling a bit nervous.

"Could you come with us, ma'am?" the second officer said. Jewel had reservations but felt she did not really have any options. It was more of a command than a question.

"Am I under arrest?" she asked.

"No, ma'am, we would like to ask you some questions," the officer replied.

After paying her bill, they left the hotel with her carry-on. The drive to the station was very brief. She informed the officers that she had a ticket to leave on the 6:30 train for Imperial Beach this very evening. She simply could not be late to meet Aunt May.

They all entered the station and were greeted by a Detective Stanley. He introduced himself before asking Jewel to sit down, gesturing toward an empty chair across from his desk. He was rather average-looking, but a tad rugged, unshaven with his hair grown out a bit too long. She guessed him to be in his late thirties.

"I'm sorry, but I'm not sure why I'm here?" Jewel mentioned.

"Sorry to detain you, ma'am. Your name is Jewel Seymour?" Detective Stanley asked without revealing his intent.

"Yes," she replied, more than frustrated by the inconvenience they were causing.

"I know you're leaving town tonight; however, I was wondering whether we could ask you a couple of questions, ma'am?"

"Well, of course. I'm clearly at a loss to know what this is about, Detective Stanley." No matter how upset she seemed, she sat patiently waiting for his questions while striving to relax. It was not easy.

"Did you see a girl today when you were in the park?" he began.

Now this distressed her since she could not imagine how or why he would have known what she saw. Now she considered whether she was not the only psychic in town.

"How could you know about what I have or have not seen in the park?" Jewel flared, showing her annoyance at the line of questioning.

"Let's just say that I have my sources," he replied, a smirk of satisfaction drawing on his lips.

"I would like to know the reason for your inquiry?" Jewel demanded.

"I've got my reasons. I just need you to answer the question, ma'am," he retorted, making sure Jewel understood that he was in charge.

"I don't know about you, but it appears we're going around in circles, do you not agree?" Jewel asked.

"You're right, but I would prefer you to trust me on this," he replied, feeling as though he had switched tactics on her.

"I would like to trust you, Detective, but I'm not sure I have enough time invested in our relationship to do so." Once again, she showed him the lighter side of things. "Now if you can cut to the chase and tell me why, maybe we can get this cleared up so I can be on my way."

"I guess having my reasons is not satisfactory to you. I must tell you that it's an ongoing investigation, and you guessed it, I'm not at liberty to say more than that." he said smoothly.

"If I can end this interrogation sooner by telling you, then I will—yes, I did see a girl on the pathway. Unfortunately, I don't know who she is or where she went." Jewel knew she could not inform this detective how she obtained the lone girl's first name. He would probably never understand.

"Could you give me her description at any rate?"

"Yes, I guess I can," she said reluctantly.

"Would you be able to describe her to our sketch artist?" he asked, being a little gentler with his questions.

"I could try, yes. But it's getting rather late and I would appreciate being on time for the train ride back to Imperial Beach."

"Yes, yes of course."

"Thank you," she felt relieved that Detective Stanley would allow her to catch the train.

"Come with me, will you?" he waved his hand. "I'll introduce you to the sketch artist," he said, while walking towards another office down the hall.

Jewel had to ask, "Who told you I saw someone at the park?"

"Sorry, I'm not at liberty to say, as I mentioned," was the only explanation he provided.

Feeling defeated, Jewel followed. They arrived at a closed door. The nameplate on the door indicated that it was the office of Alice Connelly. They entered her office where Detective Stanley introduced Jewel and left immediately thereafter.

"I hope I can provide you with the correct details of the girl I saw at the park," Jewel said to Alice. "Does Detective Stanley usually have such nice manners?" she asked while smiling.

"Oh, you must have caught him on a good day then," she replied, returning the smile. "You shouldn't worry about the description. I'm used to drawing with whatever information I receive."

"All right. I'll start with her face then. She was quite fair. You could say she was pale. She had a heart-shaped face with fine features. I couldn't tell what color her eyes were as she was too far away, but they were probably blue since she had such a fair complexion. Her hair was a light blond, a little longer than shoulder length and straight as a pin. She was about five feet, maybe seven inches tall. She looked skinny like she could use a few extra meals. I would guess she was about twenty years old. Perhaps a little younger than that." Jewel shook her head. "Sorry, that's about all I remember." Jewel wished she had more to add.

"Good, but did you remember what she was wearing?" Alice prompted.

"Ah yes, she had on a white dress, just down over her knees, with small pink frills at the hem. I must admit that the dress seemed out of place in the park. I found that part quite odd to say the least."

"That's great. Anything else, even if you think it might not be relevant?" the artist questioned.

"I don't think I've forgotten anything. Wait! I do recall something. She was wearing a gold chain around her neck with a gold medallion that was about the size of a silver dollar."

"That's excellent." Alice finished drawing, turning the drawing around to show Jewel. "Does this look like our mystery girl?" she asked.

"Yes, that does have an uncanny resemblance to her. Her dress however was more sheer-like in texture. You know like curtain sheers."

Alice returned to drawing the dress and quickly showed the picture once more. "How about that?"

"You have captured the girl as though you've taken her picture. That's so incredible! I guess the only other relevant piece of information is that I did see her twice. The first time I saw her she was asking for help and I told her to continue down the path towards the road, thinking she was simply lost. However, for no apparent reason, she vanished farther up the path. I thought that it was silly of her, but then again who can understand teenagers. I just couldn't see how I could have helped her otherwise. The second time I saw her, was just after the cab arrived to take me into town."

Alice scribbled this latest information into her logbook. "Thank you for helping us with the details," she said while she escorted Jewel out of her office.

"What do I need to do next?" Jewel asked, not knowing if she was free to leave.

"You are free to go now, but we will need your phone number in case we need to contact you," Alice informed Jewel.

"Yes, of course. It's on my card, here," Jewel replied, handing her business card. "This is my cell number and my home number. I'm currently not staying at home."

Alice thought it was already implied since Jewel was obviously not staying at home currently. But not wishing to insult her she thanked Jewel for her cooperation. "And feel free to stay in touch," she offered.

They shook hands and Jewel was relieved to leave the police station. She walked to the front entrance where one of the officers offered her a ride to the train station.

"Thank you, but I have already arranged a ride with the cab company, although I could catch a ride to the Eastside Inn where the cab is likely waiting." Jewel was anxious to get home. She looked forward to meeting Aunt May tonight.

"Sure," the first officer smiled, as he opened the door of his cruiser. He drove to the hotel. Jewel got out, but no signs of the cab. She dashed inside to see why. The clerk advised her that the cab driver had been waiting, but the clerk told the driver she had already checked out.

"I see," Jewel said, obviously feeling frustrated. "Thanks," she forced herself to say while she rushed back out to see whether the officer was still there. She was in luck.

"Excuse me, Officer?" she called out to him. "I'm afraid I will require that ride after all. Do you mind?" Jewel looked like a lost puppy with no home to go to and no ride to get there either.

"No, not at all, ma'am," he assured her.

"Thanks so much, I do appreciate the ride."

While they were driving, Jewel asked for his name.

"It's William, but most people call me Bill Casey," he replied.

"Thanks, I'm Jewel, but then you already know that, don't you? It feels weird when someone knows your name, but you do not know theirs—it makes for an awkward introduction."

They soon arrived at the station. As they pulled up to the platform, she remembered the note asking for a meeting at 6:30. She hurried to catch the train while the officer brought her luggage to the platform. It was then that she saw the man from the restaurant walking past her. She assumed he was the one that sent the note to her hotel. Nervously, she looked at the officer, then back at Philip, but he kept on walking instead. Bill saw that Jewel was suddenly anxious. He stared at Philip Denver and seemed to instinctively know something was up.

"Are you going to be all right?" he asked.

She took a deep breath. "I'm not sure. I've been followed since arriving in town yesterday."

"Oh really!" Officer Casey replied. "I can stay with you until the train leaves if you would like?" he offered kindly.

"But what happens if he embarks with me?" Jewel asked, now feeling quite unnerved.

"Let me see if I can take the trip with you to provide a safe ride home," the officer was quick to offer.

She found Bill quite manly looking with a square jaw line. To have him escort her home would not be too unpleasant. "Only if you don't mind, Officer?"

Officer Casey quickly radioed the station, asking permission for this unexpected and rather unusual police assistance. They boarded the train together, sitting next to one another for the ride back. Jewel assumed that approval had been granted to the officer to escort her home given that young women had been disappearing at an alarming rate.

107

"I have to thank you for staying with me. I hope you don't get into trouble on my account?" Jewel smiled.

Bill returned her smile. "No, all is good. Detective Stanley prefers that I escort you rather than have another woman go missing. It doesn't help tourism," he chortled.

"How many women are missing then?" she asked. "It could be important to Tina Miles' case."

"Let me see, I believe there are four missing. Well no, that's not quite right either because one girl was found dead. Wasn't her name Elizabeth?" he asked Jewel directly.

"So, you do know who I am then?" She peered into his eyes, and yet, he averted her eyes. Strange! Frankly, she felt a little weird about the new revelation he mentioned.

"Yes, I do, ma'am. We do know you helped find Elizabeth Nettle's body. You're quite the psychic, aren't you?"

Did he want to know, or was he simply stating a fact. She was not quite sure. "I've been called other things, but yes, I'm a psychic. You probably don't believe in this line of work." Jewel hoped to get his view on the subject.

"I never did believe in psychics. I believed they basically lived off the desperate, and the misery of the unfortunate, who really only require police assistance. Then again, I met you, and after hearing what you've done to assist, I've had a change of heart. I must confess that I'm not sure what I feel about psychics in general..." He trailed off.

"What have I done?" Jewel asked so he could explain himself.

"Please don't be offended. I'm just explaining how I used to feel about psychics. And now seeing and meeting you, alters the image I had of what psychics actually do. I don't believe that all psychics are good. I'm just saying that you shouldn't judge a book by its cover."

Jewel had to smile. "Spoken like a true believer," she joked. "If I didn't see with my own eyes the results that I've seen, I probably wouldn't believe it either. I still see some people who claim to be psychics, but really aren't. In this world, there are all kinds."

Bill was now smiling with her. He was definitely the type of man Jewel could see herself dating. With deep blue eyes through which his soul was reflected, and a handsome, robust build, he could be a catch, she reasoned. One only need stare into the depths of the eyes to see what a person's soul is made of, although frankly, she simply could not get a true fix on his eyes—he never once peered directly into hers. She wondered why. Perhaps he was shy? He had a five o'clock shadow, which to Jewel, made him even more alluring. His hair was thick and dark—it was very uncommon for someone with such dark complexion to have such blue eyes. Bill also sported broad shoulders. *Phew! Nowadays, what more can a girl ask for?* Notwithstanding of all his great qualities, she had some serious reservations about him. For the life of her, she could not put her finger on what her reluctance might be, however.

With that last thought, the train pulled up to the station platform. It seemed incredible that they had already arrived at her stop. It was tempting to continue the ride just to mull over Officer Casey. Perhaps she would discover why she received two very different perceptions of him—she just could not quite put her finger on what was bothering her. Somehow he was stirring feelings within her that had not been stirred in a long time and making sense of it was too confusing right now. The train came to a full stop. Officer Casey promptly stood up and, regrettably, it was time to leave him behind.

"It was nice speaking with you and getting to know you," Bill said, while grabbing her luggage. "I'll help you with this," he added, being a perfect gentleman—unlike Spence.

"Why, thank you so much for all your help, Bill," she replied, knowing that she may never see him again.

They both got off the train together. Bill stood there waiting until Jewel got into her vehicle. They said their goodbyes, but it felt as if he wanted to be invited to stay, yet she could not imagine herself asking him. She would be too embarrassed even suggesting such a thing. The moment felt long with neither of them saying a word. Awkward moments like these did not happen often since Jewel usually had plenty to say. Now she found herself speechless. They just stared at one another.

She rolled down her window. "Thank you, again," Jewel repeated, relieved to break the awkwardness. She could not make herself ask him for a coffee before heading back to her motel. At any rate, she had to rush off to the airport in due course. Though the thought of spending her evening with a nice man was rather appealing.

Bill started to leave when he stopped, turned around and said, "Would you mind if I called you sometime?"

His request startled Jewel. She smiled and nodded, but she was still speechless. It had been so long since she had had someone in her life, that she had forgotten what to do or say! Bill must have sensed this. God! She hoped he had not gotten the wrong impression as to why she was so dumbstruck, but by the smirk on his face, he seemed to know. She watched as he took the next train back to Otay Mesa County.

Jewel continued watching the train as it disappeared down the tracks. She had to admit she was definitely getting different vibes from Bill. At any rate she could not possibly be thinking of dating at a time like this. What was she thinking? She had a funeral to prepare, and even though Marcy continually harped about dating, she would appreciate Jewel putting her funeral first.

No sooner did the train disappear from sight, Jewel immediately spotted Philip Denver! Her eyes grew large, her pupils even bigger, shivers running up and down her spine again. She promptly started her car to escape, watching Philip in the rearview mirror.

She sped away, wanting to put as much distance between the two of them. Now with the knowledge that he was in the same city was extremely disconcerting.

It was far too early to pick up Aunt May, but she had enough time to call Professor Brown. With his invitingly easy manner, Jewel called him. He answered the phone and suggested she come over right away because he was available. She headed to his house to go over the ever-growing dilemma that plagued her dreams.

Professor Brown cordially invited her in. It felt quite strange somehow—maybe even a little invasive—to enter his home, his sanctuary, even though the professor was quite amicable. They went into his office. Judging by the appearance of the room, it looked as if he saw other students or patients here also. She found it quite inviting and comfortable sitting on his oversized leather couch.

"Yes, Professor, I have so many questions that I'm at a loss as to which one to address first. As you probably know, I'm working on another case, and since then a good friend of mine has passed away. Ah, yes, I've already mentioned that," she choked down the lump threatening to resurface and wiped her eyes with the back of her hand.

"Again, I'm truly sorry about your friend," Professor Brown sincerely expressed.

"Thank you for your sympathy," Jewel said. "Of late I've had multiple disturbing dreams, and although you mentioned that you don't interpret them, I wondered if you could help me make sense of it. At least this latest one."

"So, tell me more about your latest dream, will you?" he asked, as he easily reclined in his high-back chair.

"On one occasion, I dreamt of some type of black shadow, perhaps an entity of sort, pursuing me like a cat and mouse game. I ran like the devil across the forest, and yet, I could not outrun it. Could you tell me if this is a premonition, or what it could possibly mean?" She then shivered from the memory of her recent fright.

"Yes…, hum, usually black signifies evil, but also danger and I believe you've been warned of what you must be dealing with in this new case. Do you believe it is related as well?"

"I do, somehow, but I wanted some confirmation of its presence. Do you mind looking at one more?" He nodded. "I also saw my friend, Marcy, kiss me goodbye the night before she died in the hospital. Do you believe she knew she was dying?"

"Souls know everything there is to know. Therefore, they have the advantage of seeing the future. They can send the spirit to where it's required to go in order to say their goodbyes, such as what Marcy had done, so it seems."

They spoke briefly about Marcy's untimely death, but soon it was time for Jewel to leave.

# Chapter 14

Realizing it was too late to go back to her apartment to fetch anything, Jewel checked into a motel once again. She really had to clean her apartment tomorrow. Living in a motel was nice for a short while, but not having her personal items, nor being able to invite Aunt May to stay with her, was very upsetting.

With Aunt May due to arrive soon, therefore not leaving much time to rush out, Jewel just threw on some warm clothes. The evening promised to be chilly.

The drive to the airport was quick so it gave her a little time to reflect on the case at hand, and how she could tie all the little bits of information together. At this point, she did not have enough information to arrive at a final conclusion.

Jewel parked close to the nearest entrance. The airport was small compared to the one in San Diego or Los Angeles. She plugged the meter and ran in to find Aunt May. Thank goodness the plane had not arrived early. Relieved, Jewel sat in the front row of the large picture window to watch May's plane land. It was not long before she spotted the plane flying over the horizon. After landing, they taxied a short distance from the runway before they came to a full stop.

Almost immediately the passengers disembarked and entered the airport. Jewel spotted May coming out of the crowd. She sure looked good for someone her age. She was a handsome woman with short, curly, gray hair. She was tall and slim, and it was clear that she took care of herself. She wore thick-rimmed glasses that gave her a certain allure of respect.

May finally spotted Jewel through the crowd.

"Hi, Aunt May. Can I help you carry your bag?" Jewel offered.

"Why, thank you," she said, setting her suitcase down.

Jewel hugged Aunt May to welcome her properly and sighed with relief. "It's so nice to see you again. Do you have any other luggage to pick up?"

"No, I travel light. Don't need much, you know, just a change of clothes. And you are aware that we wear black at funerals? So how hard is it to pack? I won't be staying long either. As soon as the funeral is over, I plan on flying back," she stated matter-of-factly.

"I see," Jewel said, as she lifted the case. May could have fooled Jewel about her packing light, however. *What on earth did she pack in her suitcase?* she thought. It definitely weighed a ton more than an overnight bag. If there could be anyone more military-like, it had to be Aunt May. Not saying she had no heart—it was actually the opposite. Jewel knew all too well that May was simply very focused on the matter at hand, but unquestionably had a loving heart.

"How are you holding up, Aunt May? I hope this isn't too much for you?" Jewel asked, as she was honestly worried about her well-being.

"As well as can be, apart from the fact that my only niece has passed away before me. How are you holding up, my dear? You and Marcy had been so close for countless years—you must miss her dreadfully," Aunt May said, turning to Jewel.

"I think I'm okay. I've been trying not to think about death. I'm afraid I'll start to cry and might not be able to stop if I reflect right now. I know where people go after death, and so, the knowledge helps me deal with bereavement. That doesn't mean I don't miss her, but I've also been really busy. Which brings me to the other thing I wanted to mention. I won't be able to spend a lot of time with you either," Jewel sheepishly confessed.

"That's all right, dear, I have quite a busy day tomorrow. You know the funeral is the day after. I'll finalize those details in the morning, and then call you about the time of the funeral. Is that all right with you?" She asked, knowing that even if Jewel were to disagree, she would feel it was her duty to attend. Jewel dropped May off at the same hotel she had booked for herself.

"I'm sorry we had to get together under these circumstances, Aunt May," Jewel said ruefully.

"Yes, I know. Did you ever get the report from the coroner's office?" she asked.

"No, but we could look into that tomorrow afternoon, if you'd like. Say around 3:30. Would that work for you?" Jewel hoped May would agree on the timing because she already had a busy day planned for tomorrow.

"That would be quite fine. It gives me all morning to get the funeral arrangements completed. Will you be picking me up afterwards?"

"Of course, I could pick you up at 3:15. Will you be at the hotel?"

"Yes, and if not, I will call your cell. If that's okay with you?" May questioned. Jewel nodded. "And thank you for picking me up. I'll see you then." As May disappeared into the lobby, the bellboy assisted her with her luggage.

*She sure had kept her wits about her,* Jewel thought in amazement. To think she was in her late seventies and still quite active. Jewel knew a lot of people her age who were in nursing homes for various reasons, but mainly because they had lost their wits from some form of dementia. She just hoped that she, too, would take after May.

Jewel drove back to the motel so she could get something to eat, along with a hot drink. Under the overcast skies, and with the fog rolling in and rising during the evening sunset, it was quite cool outside.

Jewel parked. Walking towards her room, she inexplicably bumped into Spence. "What are you doing here, Spence?" she demanded abruptly, a little miffed at him. All she wanted was a nice, quiet night by herself—one that involved enjoying the meatball sub she had just picked up, followed by a long, hot bath. She sighed.

"I thought I saw you drive up, so I wanted to check to see if everything was alright. That's all. Why do you ask?" he questioned, sounding annoyed with her. His eyebrow rose showing his contempt.

"I'm sorry, Spence, I didn't mean to sound upset. I just wanted to relax tonight. There's been too much going on lately. I told you what I was supposed to be doing, but Marcy had a very different idea and drew me into this mayhem with Tina Miles. And now Marcy is gone, Spence, she's actually gone!" Jewel exclaimed, choking on her last words. She started to tear up and quickly wiped her eyes.

"Are you sure you're going to be all right?" Spence asked, now looking like he regretted checking up on her.

"I guess I am. But right now wouldn't be a good time to talk," Jewel dismissed him with a wave of the hand.

"I see that. I thought you went to Otay Mesa County to relax?" He questioned, now wondering what she had been up to during her stay.

"Yes, that was my intention, initially, but that's not quite what happened," Jewel confessed.

"Can I call you tomorrow?" he asked.

"Well tomorrow I must go over to the apartment to straighten things out—I'm getting really tired of living in motels, and it's starting to get on my nerves." As soon as she pronounced the words, Jewel regretted opening her big mouth. She pressed her lips together.

"I asked you to stay with me, but no, you didn't want to. So, let me help you with the cleanup, at the very least, alright?" Spence offered. He genuinely looked like he sincerely wanted to help her out, but as usual, he came across too assertively with his offer.

Jewel had known Spence for many years and saying no to him would only make him insist all the more.

"You know what? I really could use the help. Thanks. I'll meet you at my place tomorrow at around ten, and I'll bring the coffee. Agreed?" He nodded and left rather quickly.

It felt wonderful to see Marcy once again—even if only in her dreams—so waking up that morning was a great disappointment for Jewel as Marcy, who was now appearing as a phantom to Jewel in their communications, slowly began to vanish. She awoke abruptly, mainly because the hotel guests in the next room kept slamming their door. It was too early to be doing that—why were they not more respectful of the other guests in the hotel? Looking at the clock however, Jewel suddenly realized it was time to go. "Almost 9:30!" She shouted while jumping out of bed. It was a good thing she had taken that hot bath last night since she had no time to do anything but leave. Having a shower later after the cleanup of her destroyed apartment meant she would appreciate it even more.

Recognizing the amount of work involved today—her home resembled a condemned disaster zone—Jewel dressed quickly to get there on time, and hopefully before Spence got there. She reached the lobby by 9:45. If she were late, Spence would simply have to wait for her, but hopefully he had been detained. Even with all this chaos going on, Jewel still smiled as she recalled the dream she had experienced last night about Marcy—it gave Jewel a profound sense of tranquility.

She grabbed two coffees and bagels after checking out, grateful for the continental breakfast, and raced out of the motel with the bellboy on her heels. Spence could already be waiting for her at the apartment and she did not want to keep him waiting.

As she arrived, Jewel observed Spence talking on his cell phone while sitting in his patrol car. "Are you working, Spence?" she yelled from the rolled down window. "Because if you are and must leave, I do understand," she offered, knowing that she could manage without him. Although it would be much easier if he helped put her apartment back in order, she did realize his work came first.

"No, I'm fine. I'll be right up in a minute," he called out before returning to his conversation.

She took the elevator and walked to her apartment. But then as she glanced around, the mess was almost more than she could bear. A complete overwhelming feeling consumed Jewel as she entered her residence. She felt like turning around to leave, but that would mean another night in a noisy motel, so she braced herself for the task at hand.

When she thought of someone rummaging through her personal belongings, a powerful sense of invasion and violation overtook her. Whoever did this, had destroyed all her property—even pilfered through her underwear drawer. Mortified with that thought, she shook her head, and then worse, she noticed that the remaining pairs had been strewn about like discarded rubbish. *And, all for what?* she wondered. It instantly put her in a bad frame of mind.

Where would she begin? Probably the kitchen would be the best place to start. Jewel put the coffees down on a clean spot on the counter that she cleared with her elbow. After clearing the debris covering the floor and returning the kitchen chairs to their proper location, she would now have somewhere to sit down while they drank their coffees and ate their meager breakfasts.

 Now for the table, and voila! the kitchen already looked much better. Before she could enjoy her coffee though, she decided to pick up what was left of her undergarments before Spence arrived on the scene. It was bad enough the other officers had been required to sift through her personal effects, but there was no need to have Spence subjected to the same embarrassment. After gathering the underwear, she sat down with coffee and bagel in hand and waited for Spence. Jewel prioritized the cleanup and judging by their progress, she would likely be able to sleep in her own bed this evening. This was definitely her motivation of undertaking the grueling task of tidying her apartment.

Jewel could not help but think how one-minute Spence was not to be trusted—at least in her eyes—and then he would surprise her by coming out to assist. Not knowing whether Spence was involved in this case, other than as a police detective, unnerved her, however.

Perhaps she simply had it all wrong. She sat meditating on Spence to see what she could pick up. *Could it truly be Spence?* At this point she had no clear idea. Determined to find out, Jewel would keep a watchful eye on him to see if any further details would be revealed. Jewel wondered whether the emotional trauma surrounding Marcy's death had created too much tension within her. Somehow it appeared to have disturbed her search for the people involved in Tina Miles' disappearance. Frustrated, she moaned.

"Spence! Yes, come in," she yelled at the door for him to enter. By now Jewel had the kitchen partly back to some semblance of its original state. They both finished their coffees before tackling the living room and her bedroom.

"Do you think Marcy's death had anything to do with Tina's disappearance?" She finally asked him. "Perhaps, she knew something since she mentioned she was coming over to go over our notes. It made me wonder what she knew exactly."

"I'm not sure but anything is certainly possible," he replied.

In the end, the clean-up had not been as bad as Jewel had expected. They had been cleaning for approximately three hours when Spence received a phone call. He did not say what was so pressing as he rushed off.

In the meantime, Jewel took a shower in her own bathroom. She felt secure again knowing that the landlord had fixed the broken window and had changed the locks. She stripped off her dirty clothes, walked into the shower, and then her phone began to ring.

She immediately jumped out, dripping wet. "Yes!" She answered a little more tersely than she planned to.

It was Helena. "No, it's all right," Jewel said. "Yes, sure I can. Could you meet me in about an hour? Yes, that's right." She hung up.

Wondering what was happening, Jewel stepped back into the shower to finish washing up—thankfully, without any further interruptions. Putting on some fresh, clean clothes felt awfully nice, but she certainly did plan on washing everything thoroughly when time permitted. She left the apartment in a much better mood now that her home was back to its original condition, so to speak. In a few weeks, it would be more so.

Jewel mused on the meeting with Tina's mother. Not being able to find her daughter was disappointing. What could she tell the mother that she did not already know? Maybe Helena could shed some light concerning the trip to the park to get to the bottom of her daughter's disappearance.

The drive was short, uneventful. They had prearranged a meeting for a coffee at the local coffee shop. Jewel entered to find Helena seated at the far corner of the room beside a large fireplace. She crossed the room saying hello to Helena before she made her way to the counter to order two coffees. Jewel brought them to the table, setting one down in front of Helena.

"Nice to see you out and about, Helena. I know it must be terribly hard on you, but getting out can be healing," Jewel said as she sat down across the distraught mother.

"Thank jou," she replied while giving a half grin. "Have jou heard anyting on where my daughter be?" she asked, looking as desperate as ever.

"Not exactly. I'm sorry… and truly wish I could offer you more right now. On the one hand I am making progress, but I'm sorry to say that I'm unable to give you the details. I do have some questions I'd like to ask you if you don't mind." Jewel felt like the detective yesterday at the Otay Mesa station.

*Her heart must be breaking*, Jewel thought. She was sure Helena was aware that as more time elapses from the moment a person goes missing, the less likely they are to be found alive. It must be terrifying for Helena. This was the main reason Jewel had never wanted children.

A television hanging in the upper right corner of the coffee shop was broadcasting news when Jewel noticed that the station was just then, running a news clip about Tina's disappearance. The police were asking people for information. Jewel glanced at Helena, and to her dismay, she was also watching the newscast.

"I'm so sorry we haven't found her yet, save for the fact that we are getting closer, plus, my sixth sense is telling me that she's still alive." Jewel watched Helena's face change to being alert. "I usually can feel when someone has passed on, but I'm certainly not feeling this in Tina's case. So far I've been pretty accurate in that regard."

Helena tapped Jewel's hand lightly, saying, "Don't jou worry. I know jou be doing your best to find my Tina. I be grateful."

Jewel wanted to give her more positive news but returned to their conversation. "Helena, I must ask you more questions about your visit to Otay Mesa County last year. Do you remember what you both did there? Can we go over the details, even if you think it may not be important?" Jewel asked.

"Si, it be a long time since we be dere. We went to park for picnic. Next we take walk over by path to river and to de falls."

"I didn't see any falls, but then again I didn't go too far down the path either. Did you meet anyone there?" Jewel asked, probing further to link Tina with the mystery girl in the park.

"Si, how jou know? We did meet young girl dere," she said, nodding, eyes growing wider.

"I see, can you describe her?"

"Si, she be tall, taller than my Tina. She blond wit' long hair and si, she wearing a very pretty dress. She stop, said hello to us. Tina asked girl what was down path. She says waterfall. Tina was excited to see them. I tanked her for helping us. Girl go back to de road and we go find waterfall in park." Helena's English got remarkably worse in her excitement.

Pressing on, Jewel asked, "Did the girl tell you her name?"

"Si, she say Claire, or someting like that," Helena replied.

"Did you also get her last name?"

"Si! Someting like Doson."

"Are you sure it was Dawson, or could it be close to that name?" With that request, Helena scribbled her name on a napkin.

"Ah, Dobson, thank you, that's very helpful," Jewel smiled. She was obviously pleased with the new information. "Now that we have a name, I'll go down to the police station to search the database and maybe this girl will provide us with another lead to locate Tina. You were most helpful." She paused. "I simply have one more question. Have you received any phone calls from the abductors—if that is what has happened here, asking for ransom—you know, money for Tina's release?"

"Not so, si. Do jou tink they call?" she inquired.

Perhaps Jewel should not have asked. "No, that's alright. I just wanted to eliminate any possibility of a ransom but I'm sure the police must have asked this question. I must go so I can get over to the police station," Jewel said, getting to her feet.

"Do jou tink Claire know where my Tina be?" Helena asked.

"I'm not sure, but maybe she's somehow connected," Jewel replied. "I really need to find out, though."

"Si, por favor, jou go."

119

It must be quite frustrating to be unable to find your missing child. Jewel sighed before leaving the coffee shop.

Driving over to the police station, Marcy invaded Jewel's thoughts. She appeared so real last night that Jewel could have sworn she was warning her of something. But what could that be? Jewel parked and ran into Spence. He was on his way out.

"Spence! Where are you off to?"

"I've been called out. Do you need something?" he asked.

"Yes, I was hoping to get some information on a girl named Claire. Can I use the database computer to get the information on her?" Jewel was nearly pleading with him for some assistance.

"I'm afraid I would have to be present. You know we have policies and procedures, and the ones governing access to our databases are especially enforced. There are strict rules regarding passwords. If you can wait until later, I'll be back to help. Right now, I must go, sorry!" he shouted, as he rushed to his unmarked cruiser.

"Of course, Spence," she yelled back. She thought it best to go to the library for the information.

She watched Spence drive off in a mad rush and wondered where he could be off to. Back to the problem at hand, Jewel hoped there was something written about a Claire Dobson in the newspapers. It was a long shot, but then it was all she had to go on. However, glancing at the time—it was almost 3:20 PM—there was no time for the library. Aunt May was likely waiting.

Jewel had to turn the car around to race to May's hotel. As she pulled up in front of the hotel, she saw Aunt May waiting for her. *Blast it! It's now 3:35 so hopefully May hasn't been waiting too long, but she will probably say something nonetheless,* Jewel presumed.

"Aunt May, I'm sorry for being a tad late. I lost track of time," Jewel said as she opened the passenger door for her.

"Yes, that's alright, dear. I'm sure you have lots to do," May simply replied.

Maybe Jewel had her wrong after all.

Not long after May sat down, she started with, "In my day, we wouldn't think of being late."

And with that statement, May succeeded in making Jewel feel guilty. Jewel simply smiled in response.

May came back with, "We must see the coroner. Maybe he can give us an explanation for her sudden death."

Jewel could see that May was choked with those last few words. "Yes, that's an excellent idea," Jewel agreed. She was glad that May did not harp on her about her tardiness any longer.

They pulled up at the coroner's office. Aunt May had made the appointment and Jewel was thankful to have her support. Jewel's world appeared to be fraught with random incidents. "I'm still not able to comprehend Marcy's departure," Jewel blurted to May. Honestly, Jewel was not sure how she was going to cope once this whole mess simmered down. In a way, Tina's disappearance was a saving grace, because without the distraction, Jewel could never get through the funeral process.

They both got out of the car to enter the office. The coroner's name was Dr. Frank Cobb. After introductions, they were offered a seat. Jewel assisted May to her seat first before she took hers.

"So, you want to know what happened to Marcy Cooper?" Dr. Cobb asked directly and without preamble.

"Yes, that would be kind," May said firstly. "I don't understand how my niece passed away in the first place. Apparently, she was doing so well from what Jewel expressed to me."

"Let me see. Since she was a healthy, young woman, I had to examine everything. I did find some unusual drugs in her system that couldn't be accounted for, at least according to her medical chart."

"What kind of drugs? I don't believe my niece to be a drug user." May made her feelings quite known on this particular subject.

"Like I've mentioned, it's not something that could be explained. In fact, it wasn't a drug the hospital used, and I take it that she wasn't using any street drugs that you know of. We will therefore sign off the death certificate as a suspicious death," the coroner concluded.

May looked surprised with that verdict. "I was hoping to know what really happened. It appears that there are more questions than answers," May grumbled, obviously displeased with his conclusion. "Could someone have given her this drug by mistake?"

"At the moment, we don't know the answer to that, ma'am. I believe the police will be asking further questions about Marcy's habits and lifestyle choices. Maybe they will be able to find out something before long." Dr. Cobb seemed to be falling awfully short of his goal.

"Thank you," Jewel cut in, attempting to sooth the abrasive nature of their conversation.

"But I wanted to know why anyone would want to see Marcy dead," May cut in. She was looking for answers of which the coroner was in short supply. After all, he was a medical examiner and not a detective.

Dr. Cobb shrugged his shoulders. Jewel rose to leave, offering to help May to her feet. She refused to take her hand. Instead she simply hoisted herself out of the chair, looking proud, though one could see that she was not happy. It was clear she was not going to take this whole affair lying down. In a way, who could blame her? Jewel knew that the doctor could not speculate beyond the cause of death. He could not elaborate on the perpetrator either. There would be no point in carrying on with this line of questioning with him. Glancing at one another, the women departed, taking along the paperwork. The death certificate indicated the cause of death as suspicious. Jewel made great efforts not to shed any tears. Aunt May had noticed that Jewel was wiping the corner of one eye. She put her arm around the younger woman's shoulder. They silently walked back to the car park.

"I'm sorry, Aunt May. The reality is too harsh," Jewel admitted. After choking back more tears, she drove to the funeral home where Marcy's body would be delivered by the time they arrived.

They both walked into the funeral parlor to complete the dreadful ordeal that neither would wish on their worst enemy. Jewel sat at the pew with her head hung low, making efforts not to fall apart. May was the pillar of strength as she forged ahead with the final arrangements so that they could put Marcy's body to rest the following day. They both left, heavy hearted, to return to their own little space and grieve.

With the knowledge that Jewel could not do any more today, she dropped Aunt May off at her hotel. As sad as this was, Jewel drove towards her own place. At this point she was just too emotionally drained. It was as though someone had kicked her in the stomach.

She walked into the apartment, only too happy that her home had been restored to its original state. She longed to sleep in her own bed so that slumber could take her to another space and time. Jewel felt better just knowing that she could cry herself to sleep without worrying, who by proximity, would be forced to listen to her sobs. She decided to make an herbal tea before bed. Afterwards she slipped under her covers, closed her eyes, breathing a sigh of relief that she was alone. It was too early to sleep, but Jewel felt exhausted beyond anything she had ever felt before. Her limbs felt numb. Her whole body seemed to sink into the mattress as if it wanted to disappear in the arms of Orpheus.

Tomorrow would be a tough one with the funeral. It was next that tears began to flow, and unable to contain them any longer, Jewel allowed herself to mourn. She must have fallen asleep sometime later with relief that twilight had finally overtaken her grief-stricken heart.

# Chapter 15

Awakening around 3:35 AM and not wanting to get up, but also unable to sleep either, Jewel decided to meditate on Marcy. With any luck, something would appear to explain her sudden death. She relaxed her body first to remain in a calm state. Marcy finally appeared. She was talking to Claire. *How odd?* Why would Marcy be speaking to Claire? Besides, did Marcy even know her? Taking a deep breath, she decided to see if anything else would come to light from her meditative state.

The next thing she knew, someone appeared in Marcy's hospital room. *Who was with her?* Jewel had been under the impression that only she and Spence had visited Marcy, yet in this state, Jewel could distinctly see a man standing over Marcy's bed. He was dressed in a light trench coat, and wore a cap, which was out of place. He finally turned around to leave, giving Jewel the opportunity to see his face. No luck—he was wearing sunglasses along with his cap pulled low over his brow, and a surgical mask over his mouth, masking his face entirely. Very suspicious. If only she could see something distinguishable about him other than being about six feet tall and medium build. The image soon vanished and, immediately, Jewel found herself back at the park with Claire. She watched words being exchanged with Tina. *Could this be last year?* Then again, sometimes there are no distinct timelines in which to place these visions—the preceding scene of Marcy at the hospital, was one of those exceptions.

The phone rang with Jewel nearly jumping right out of her skin! She glanced at the time. It was now 7:30. What had happened to the last few hours since she awoke in the middle of the night?

"Hello?" Her rasping voice gave away the fact that she had just woken up. "Yes, I'm up," she fibbed. "Yes, I can be there soon. I'll be getting something to eat first. No, you don't have to buy me breakfast, Aunt May. Alright, I won't argue with you," Jewel said, knowing full well she would not win any arguments. Yet Jewel was not sure whether she could eat anything. She showered quickly, and looking in the mirror, she was pleased with what she had chosen to wear. Aunt May would have disapproved of her wearing anything but black to the funeral. Choosing her only black outfit was the right choice—it was an evening dress she had yanked on and pulled the hem lower to try to hide her legs. Shrugging on her long black sweater and a pair of pumps, she grabbed her purse to leave.

Looking up at the sky, the cloudy day matched her mood perfectly. Jewel dashed towards the car, jumping over puddles to reach it. Not wanting to be late—Aunt May did not approve of tardiness—Jewel drove a little faster than usual. It was not long before she pulled up in front of the hotel and only forty-five minutes after receiving May's call. It must have been a record. Nonetheless, Aunt May was waiting in the lobby. Jewel wondered whether she had ever been late for anything in her entire life—*and that's a very long time*—she thought and inwardly chuckled.

"Hi, Aunt May," Jewel said, as she pulled up to the entrance.

May opened the car door and got in before it came to a full stop. "You're on time, thank you," she said, as a matter of fact.

A compliment no less. Jewel smiled pleasantly. "Where would you like to have breakfast?"

"Do you have any good breakfast places in town?" May asked.

"As a matter of fact, we do. I know a good place not too far from here and they serve good English tea," Jewel replied.

They drove over to the *Pancake House*, an all-you-can-eat where the best pancakes and waffles in all the state were made and served with a popular East Coast maple syrup. Jewel's mouth watered at the thought of the pancakes with lots of butter and syrup dripping over the edges. Perhaps, she could attempt to eat something if only to settle her uneasy stomach.

Aunt May must have sensed Jewel's downcast spirits.

Concentration was most difficult on anything other than the funeral. Without many words spoken, they both quietly finished breakfast, leaving a good portion on their plates. They left for the funeral home, where they would stay until the end of the service.

People came and went for the most part. Before long, the morning flowed into the early afternoon. The guests, comprised of a few friends, former and current co-workers, and other people Jewel had known briefly, offered their condolences and gave their support. Both women thanked them for attending. It all felt so mechanical that Jewel wondered whether she was having an out of body experience. The funeral service was about to begin and would be followed by the interment service at the cemetery shortly thereafter.

Jewel was pleased that Spence had shown up. To be honest she was not sure he would attend. She walked over and opened the conversation with, "I was beginning to think you wouldn't make it. Thank you for coming. It was kind of you." But in the end, she wished she had remained silent. It was as though when she spoke, she distinctly heard herself speaking but she was literally disconnected from her body since the words seemed to come from beyond.

"You know I would have come regardless of what was going on," Spence stated firmly.

When the service began Spence stood at the back, whereas May and Jewel stood in the front near the coffin. Jewel wished he had come for moral support only, but she was quite certain the reason for his presence was two-fold—he was also there to monitor who attended Marcy's funeral. Now she realized she should be grateful rather than being disgruntled.

Soon the funeral service came to an end with the singing of Marcy's favorite hymns. Thoughts of younger years gone by surfaced—the two of them playing at the park in the beautiful sunshine, long nights spent giggling—now flooded Jewel's senses. Tears escaped and she sniveled, dabbed at her eyes before turning to leave. Spence came over to see them and placed his arm around Jewel's shoulder.

"Are you going to be all right driving back after the cemetery service?" He posed the question in such a way that Jewel was not sure if it was the cop in him coming out, or genuine concern.

"You know I could easily drive you both back to town afterwards," he insisted.

"If you don't mind, Spence, that would be really nice of you," Jewel replied automatically. She knew that she would probably not be able to drive in her emotional state, sighing with relief. Both May and Jewel rode to the cemetery in his vehicle just behind the hearse.

Watching the coffin being lowered into its final resting spot was almost too much to bear. As the coffin descended, the local clergy said a few words, and it settled at the bottom of the freshly excavated grave. The skies were threatening to drizzle over the few people remaining at the gravesite, so they left, traveling back with Spence.

While they were driving back Jewel noticed that Spence looked terribly sad and very tired. Although he did not say much regarding

Marcy, Jewel was certain he was feeling the effects of Marcy's death, nonetheless. They did not get along very well in the latter years, but surely, he did not want her dead. Jewel had always wondered what went on between the two of them. They both refused to speak about their friendship breaking up suddenly. Right now, however, there were more urgent matters to address. Fully aware that Spence had more than likely seen the autopsy report, Jewel desperately wanted to pose some questions concerning Marcy's suspicious death. She would pursue this later when things were calmer.

When she drove Aunt May back to her hotel, Jewel walked her back to her room. They sat down for a few minutes and cried. Jewel wiped away her tears before saying goodbye. Aunt May wanted to rest and said as much for Jewel to do the same.

"Are you sure you'll be all right, Aunt May?"

"Yes, and you should get some sleep dear," she replied, looking concerned. Knowing she was the one looking rather disheveled instead of the robust one, Jewel agreed. "No doubt about it—that would be really nice. I think I'll go home, have some tea and relax for the rest of the day."

"You just do that, my dear and we'll speak later."

Jewel was about to leave when they suddenly heard a knock at the door.

May spoke. "Ah, Spence! Good you came. Would you mind following Jewel back to her house? I think she feels poorly." Aunt May informed him as soon as she opened the door for him. She seemed to enjoy being in charge.

"Yes, by all means," Spence agreed with her.

Jewel turned back to Aunt May saying, "Are you sure you don't want to come over later?"

"No, no. I just need a little time to myself, that's all. I hope you understand." May responded kindly.

"Yes, of course. No problem," Jewel assured her.

Spence walked her to the apartment, ensuring she was all right before he left. While closing the door, Jewel mentioned that she would be fine once she had a little time to herself. Immediately she kicked off her heels and went to the kitchen sink to put some water in to the kettle. The kitchen was situated at the back of the apartment with a window that overlooked the parking lot. She watched Spence get into his car, when suddenly she noticed a man waiting nearby. To her horror, it appeared to be Philip Denver!

"Ouch!" Jewel yelled when she had accidentally poured hot water over her hand. By the time she lifted her gaze to look out the window again, Mr. Denver had vanished. She hoped the stranger was not in her building and on his way to her apartment! She reached for the phone and called Spence. It rang several times, but he did not answer.

"Now what? Spence had no sooner left," Jewel shouted and redialed. "Come on, Spence, please pick up," she pleaded.

When she heard a knock at the door, her heart skipped a beat. Peeking through the peephole, she could see Philip Denver on the other side of the door. Maybe if he did not find anyone at home, he would simply go away. She kept quiet, but he knocked again. He was quite persistent. What was she to do? Ever so quietly, she tucked a chair up against the door. Her heart was racing, and it was hard to listen through the door. She heard footsteps. Holding her breath, she wondered whether he had left. She peered out again. He was still standing there. The doorknob began to move. Jewel almost screamed from fright and it took all she had to not shriek from panic. What on earth could he want? She must have stood there for a long time without moving a muscle. It was almost as though she was frozen on the spot. She heard more footsteps, and just when she thought he would never leave, she heard him walking away down the corridor. She sighed heavily.

This time she dialed the police station. She needed help. Looping around in her mind was how badly she wanted to believe that Spence was not connected to this incident. She dearly wanted to be wrong about Spence's possible involvement in any of this.

"Hello, yes, can I speak with Spence, please? I mean Detective Walker. He's not there?" Jewel complained to the Sergeant who answered. The officer stated that Spence had the day off to attend to personal business.

"I've tried his cell, but he still didn't pick up. Of course, this is an emergency! Do you think you could call him for me?" She insisted, desperately struggling to calm down with little success. "Yes, that will be good of you, thank you." Jewel hung up the phone. "Gees! What next?" She called out and knew she truly could not take much more. At that point in time the phone rang, startling her further.

Jewel reached for the phone, "Yes! It's you, Spence. I'm so glad you called back!" She must have sounded desperate because Spence asked what was wrong before she could explain herself.

"I think someone's following me," she finally admitted.

"What do you mean? And, do you know who?"

"I was followed from Otay Mesa County, and now the same man that followed me was here at my apartment. He just left. I'm not sure how he knew where I lived though. It's possible he followed me from the cemetery. I'm not quite sure. Can you please come by to have a look around? I'm afraid I might be attacked again!" Jewel claimed, while feeling out of breath and sounding quite rattled. She felt better after telling Spence of her ongoing episodes with Denver. Jewel refused to believe that Spence could be involved—but if he were, she had just placed herself in harm's way. After her longwinded explanation, she took a deep breath to calm herself.

"Why didn't you tell me earlier?" he asked, sounding annoyed.

"With all that's been going on, I thought it might not be anything at all—part of an overactive mind. But now that he came knocking on my door, I know for sure that he is following me. I'm not sure why, though." Jewel felt compelled to come clean. Besides, other than Spence, whom could she truly count on?

"Do you know who this man is?" he repeated.

She was not only frustrated, but also scared to death. Jewel answered. "No, not really. Well… maybe. It's a long story, but a waitress got his name for me." She paused. "His name is Philip Denver, but it's probably an alias. I don't know for sure, of course."

"Alright!" Spence said, sounding impatient. "I will do a quick check on him before I arrive. Just stay inside, and don't open your door for anybody, okay?" Spence ordered.

"But, Spence, could you not get someone else to do the checking and come over straight away?" She was trembling with fear by now, desperate to regain her composure. At this point she would most certainly feel safer if the police were guarding her door. "And yes, I don't think I'll be venturing out right now, but thanks for the warning," Jewel said.

She looked out the window to see whether she could spot anyone in the parking lot. Nobody. She walked to the door to see if there was anyone lurking about the hall. Once she was satisfied with her security check, she decided to change her clothes to some slacks and a t-shirt and threw on a sweater. She sat quietly until Spence arrived.

It was not long before Jewel heard another knock at the door. She froze! Did Philip return?

She stealthily walked to the door, spying through the peephole for her intruder. "Thank goodness!" She exclaimed when she saw Spence standing in front of her door. She breathed out a sigh of relief and opened it for him. "Did you see anyone lurking around?" She asked in a hurry.

"No, I didn't. Maybe he got scared and took off. Are you alright?" he asked, appearing terribly concerned.

"I think so. I was going to make a cup of tea before my stalker appeared. Do you have time for one?" she asked.

"Not right now. I'm going to take another look around the place to ensure he hasn't returned. Just stay in for the rest of the day and if he returns, call me directly. I'll keep my phone with me at all times, alright?" His tone warned her to listen to him this time.

"I will, of course. Thanks again."

She was sure he had picked up on how disappointed she was that he could not stay. She locked the door behind him and only too happy the locks had been recently changed. Spence likely thought he could do more on the outside than sitting with her, but she felt the opposite. She wondered whether her imagination had gotten the better of her and she was misinterpreting his actions with her foolish notions. Why was she so worried about Spence since he had been a real friend to her for many years? Was it Spence's recent odd behavior that was causing her to think all these crazy things about him? Being so suspicious? The shock of Marcy's untimely departure could very well be the root cause of his odd activities. Yes, that must be it, she reasoned.

Jewel sat up drinking her tea, worrying about the new intruder, when a thought occurred. '*Perhaps he's the same burglar that broke in last week. Or, was it a ring of thieves? Could he do it again?*' Now she was even more apprehensive. She also wondered why Spence had not put a police officer at her door. She should have asked. Another question arose about the fingerprints the forensic may have lifted from her furniture. *How did life get so complicated?* she wondered. All she was asked to do was to find a young girl and bring her back to her mother. A seemingly easy task had somehow grown completely out of control. She decided to make sense of all the details that were obvious. Perhaps writing those down would help connect the dots.

First, Elizabeth went missing only to turn up dead. Her death was suspicious also, but then how could it not be? Secondly, Tina goes missing, and her trail led Jewel to Otay Mesa County, where she saw another young girl named Claire. She is the third young girl that might be missing. Could all of them be connected somehow? Does Claire know something regarding the two other girls?

While forcing back tears, she simply could not forget about Marcy. She, too, ended up in the cemetery. Now that made four girls, either missing or dead. There must be some connection. Perhaps there was only one conclusion to draw at this juncture— everything pointed to a serial killer targeting young women in their late teens or early twenties, notwithstanding Marcy.

*Was she the next victim to add to his growing list?* Jewel thought. Although Jewel was older than the other girls, it was a possibility she should not dismiss. It could explain Spence's nervousness about Jewel venturing out. Did he know more than he was letting on?

Jewel must have sat up for quite some time looking at the same piece of paper, when she realized it was 5:45 PM. She was pretty worn out by the ongoing activities; not forgetting the funeral itself had been exhausting. She wondered why Spence had not called yet. He was probably busy. Since he had commanded her to stay in for the night, she decided to take a nice bath. After drawing it, she lit some candles around the tub. She undressed and stepped into the foamy water. It felt good to relax. Now if only she had a glass of wine. But that would mean leaving the apartment and that was not an option. Having no intensions of disobeying Spence's orders, she basically would relax and enjoy the bubbles popping happily around her. After her soak in the warm water, it was off to bed for an early night. She knew she ought to meditate on the four girls first. Maybe she could see how they were all connected.

As she lay down quietly, breathing, relaxing for about five minutes, she started to receive images. First Elizabeth came into view. She was a beautiful girl, but nothing seemed significant, however. Following this image came Claire who was also beautiful and tall. She had to confess that there was an uncanny resemblance between the two girls. Claire was walking in the park, but she did not say anything to her either. Next came Marcy, and Jewel was delighted to see her.

While the others had not spoken, Marcy did. "I'm okay you know. I got in over my head. I'm still here just not in body."

Jewel smiled at her presence. Just as quickly as Marcy appeared, she disappeared from sight before she could ask her friend what she meant by '*getting in over her hea*d'. Tina appeared immediately as Marcy's image vanished.

Tina also spoke. "Can you help me?"

Jewel answered with a big emphatic "Yes. But where are you?" She then heard a knock. Maybe Tina was endeavoring to give her a clue as to her whereabouts. Jewel heard the knock again, but this time she knew it was not from her visions. There was someone at the door.

Initially, Jewel could not move. She dearly hoped that whoever it was at the door would simply leave or disappear just like in her visions. The knock was persistent, however. Before she could answer the door, she would first have to come out of her trance and out of the tub. Finally reoriented, she threw on a thick robe and braved going to the door to see who had the nerve to be at her door at this hour.

Instinctively, she tiptoed across the floor to look through the peephole. It was Philip again. Now she wanted him arrested. Jewel reached for the phone to call right away before Philip left the premises.

'*Come on, Spence, please answer the blasted phone,*' Jewel whispered under her breath. "Spence," Jewel murmured as low as she could, not wishing to be heard on the other side of the door. "He's back once more and I'm frightened!"

Spence yelled back, "I'll be right there."

Jewel must have waited for what seemed eternity before she saw Spence pull up to the building. He got out of his SUV. She saw him draw his gun before entering the building. She could not see him after that.

Jewel then heard some noise in the hall. She hoped Spence had apprehended this vile man before she became number five. Although she could not tell what was happening on the other side of her door, she wondered whether Spence would arrest him. Worse yet, what if he attacked Spence and broke in? What would she do then? She decided to lock herself in her room with the chair pushed up against the bedroom door. Then she sat down, drawing White Light to and all around herself, and then also filled the room for extra protection. Next, she pushed it all down the hall where Spence was, in hopes it would help him catch Philip before it was too late. Jewel would have preferred to assist Spence, but she knew he would not want her to risk her life.

Once again, she heard someone at her door. Now what was she to do? Should she risk leaving the sanctuary of her bedroom to answer it? Hastily, she threw on some clothes.

# Chapter 16

Aunt May had packed to leave for home and looked forward to leaving. The trip had been extremely tiring, the funeral in particular. But apart from her sincere concern for what she considered the only remaining family member—as she thought of Jewel—she had no other business in town. And it was this uneasiness that was at the root of why she might prolong her stay. May would check on her pseudo niece right now.

The telephone rang until it went to voicemail. May Applebee despised leaving messages on those contraptions. At any rate she was ready to leave on the late flight tomorrow and since she had no other plans during her last night in town, she would check up on Jewel.

However, before stepping out, she remembered that there was one more thing to do before leaving town: she wanted a word with Spence.

May had known Spence for quite a long time. He used to hang out at her place with Marcy. She smiled when recalling her statement, 'If you see one, you see the other.' That was when the two were very young, and before Jewel came on the scene. Not that the same sentiment hadn't applied to Marcy and Jewel—it most certainly did—but she never did see the three of them together. When Marcy left for college, Spence and Marcy rekindled their friendship, becoming close once more. *At least Jewel had Spence as a friend since Marcy passed to the Otherworld,* she thought. And now with both her sister and niece gone, May was left with the distinct feeling that she was living on borrowed time. Especially since seeing her doctor back home—he had given her approximately six to twelve months before she 'cashed in her chips'.

May had no relatives to bequeath what was left of her legacy. Being a single person with no children to spend her money on, May kept investing the bulk. She originally thought of leaving it all to charity, whereby her money would benefit many of her favorite charities, but now it dawned on her that she could instead leave some of her fortune to Jewel. Doing so would provide this special young woman the financial backing to enable her to continue helping young girls find their way home. She knew that Jewel was extremely busy helping others, struggling as she was, and perhaps it was time to help her in the same manner. In doing so May would in turn help so many.

Unfortunately, Spence was not at the police station when she phoned, so May decided to head to Jewel's apartment right away via taxi. But hunger drove her to get a small bite to eat, and she would pick something up for Jewel to eat also. Just because she was dying didn't mean she should starve herself! So, putting on her wool sweater to go in search of a tasty meal was the first order of business.

Knowing she would soon be joining her niece and sister, was the only consolation that assisted May to shake off her distress. This reason alone helped May hold her composure together. It was her coping mechanism that helped her through this gruesome ordeal surrounding Marcy and her mysterious death. Admittedly, May truly understood Jewel's feelings of loss and was not unsympathetic to them at all. Upon reflection, however, May should have insisted on returning with Jewel so she could take care of her, or at the very least support her through this trauma. How selfish of her not to think about this earlier. She quickly redialed Jewel and it went straight to voicemail again, so she chose to head out immediately. In her haste, she totally forgot to call Spence back as intended.

~

Hearing a loud sound emanating within the living room, paralyzed with fear, heart ready to explode, nerves beyond frayed, Jewel gasped for air. It was incredibly ironic that she was not afraid of the supernatural world but horrified when it came to every little sound originating from within her apartment. And yet with Jewel's world in turmoil one could understand her panic. Not long after that disturbing sound, with hands shaking, Jewel managed to place a call to Spence from the safety of her bedroom.

"Spence, answer the bloody phone, won't you?" She whispered before redialing yet again. "Come on please answer your phone!" No response. But before she left a voice message, she stopped herself—doing so might give away her location. Instinctively, she dialed the police station instead.

"Yes, officer, I do need help, immediately. There's an intruder in my building. Yes, likely forced his way into my apartment door. Please send someone straight away to 44 Copeland Avenue,

Apartment 4B. And please hurry," she whispered to the officer. She held the door firmly shut by pressing her back against it just after securing the chair under the doorknob. Her heart was racing at such a quick pace; she wondered whether a heart attack was imminent.

Then, shockingly, Jewel heard a voice. A female voice? It sounded like Aunt May. *No! It couldn't be. Could it?* Jewel thought. She feared the intruder would attack her also. But then again where were Spence and the intruder?

"Dearie! Jewel?" May shouted again through the door.

"Aunt May, I'm in here," Jewel screamed. She hurriedly removed the chair from her bedroom doorway. "Did you not see Spence out there in the hall?" Jewel shouted while making her way to the apartment door. "I didn't know you were out there," Jewel sheepishly answered back, while quickly unlocking and swinging the front door wide open. It was at that moment that it dawned on her—how exactly did Aunt May get into her apartment building?

"I certainly did see Spence. He seemed to be in a rush though. He raced off even after I waved. I shouted, but he was being quite rude for some odd reason. He just drove off. It was so unlike him. I'm at a loss to understand you youngsters," May grumbled. "And yes, I did call first, but of course no one answered. So, I thought I would come right over to see if you were alright," Aunt May went on as though no other explanation was needed. "And it's a good thing I did by the looks of things." May peered around the apartment.

"I'm so happy it was you out there. I was scared out of my mind. That's why I locked myself in my bedroom," Jewel confessed. Though honestly, Jewel pondered whether Aunt May had the distinct impression that she had completely gone over the edge.

"Whatever do you mean?" May asked.

"Well there's been a lot going on lately, aside from the funeral, but it's rather a long story." Jewel brushed it off. "Aunt May, how did you get into the building?" Jewel asked to divert her attention since she did not feel it necessary to alarm May further.

May waved her hand, "I got in by pushing my way in."

"I don't understand why the building door is not locked," Jewel protested. She did appreciate her arrival, nevertheless.

"You probably need something to eat," Aunt May suggested, lifting the bag of drive-through goodies she had stopped to pick up on her way.

"Maybe. You know I did hear someone out there. Didn't you see someone in the hall? Spence was likely chasing the intruder off when you last saw him. I tried contacting him, but he didn't pick up… he's more than likely chasing the fiend," Jewel admitted. "Oh, my goodness! I called the police for them to send an officer out because I heard a loud noise. I thought the intruder had somehow entered my apartment." Jewel attempted to clarify things for Aunt May, but instead she simply confused matters worse.

Suspicious of Jewel's frame of mind, May tried to rationalize her strange behavior. "You know that young people have such vivid imaginations. Maybe you watch too much television?" May suggested, as though she herself raised children, making her an expert.

"I must call the police back to inform them of what went down," Jewel insisted. Too late. They could hear police car sirens blaring as they approached the building. Or, were they actually at her building?

She placed the call to avoid the police thinking she'd completely gone raving mad. "Yes, it's Jewel again. I know. I'm calling to update my situation, and yes, I'm aware you've likely dispatched someone already. Detective Walker was here not long ago. He must be in pursuit of the same intruder. Could you radio the officer on his way here to assist Spence instead? Sorry for the confusion but there was indeed a prowler here earlier. I fear Spence is in danger." Jewel continued, rubbing her brow. "Yes, thank you." Jewel immediately hung up the phone.

She turned toward Aunt May who was now busy in the kitchen. She had marched to the fridge to find something to put in her tea. May turned around and fixed Jewel with a wary gaze. "You haven't anything to eat?" May did not look happy with the discovery.

As if Jewel concerned herself with her refrigerator status. "There are pickles in the fridge," Jewel responded. "I'm sorry but there wasn't a lot of time to go shopping to get much else."

"It's a good thing I brought some coffee and muffins for you then. We'll order out. What would you like for supper?" she asked. At this point May wished she had brought more food with her.

Jewel felt she could get out of this situation by telling May that she was not hungry. Once Jewel dressed in warmer clothing, she went back to the kitchen and found May had set the table with her tea, coffee, and a few muffins neatly placed.

"Well I guess a little something wouldn't hurt," she agreed.

It was then that Jewel heard another knock at the door. It was probably the officer that was sent out. With a mouthful of muffin, Jewel walked over to the door to let him in. She had presumed that another explanation was in order. She swallowed and opened the door saying, "Yes!" *What... the...? He wasn't the officer unless he's in plain clothes?* "What can I do for you?" Jewel asked. It appeared that the building doors were left open for anyone to come right in.

"Let me see! How about coming with me?" He ordered while pointing a gun to her chest.

Jewel's heart sank and began skipping a few beats with her new predicament. "What's going on?" She demanded, her voiced lowered. She had not seen this man before. Not wanting to alarm Aunt May, she left with him without another word spoken. She also did not want him to know that there was someone else in the apartment with her.

The man had extremely dark and sinister-looking eyes. *Who is he?* Her assumption was... if *he's not with the police force then who could he be?*

They both exited the building with him pointing a gun in her back. Jewel pinned her hopes that May's eagle eyes would notice them from the kitchen window and call the police again.

She had just called them back to say she did not need their assistance, but now wished she had not done so—she should have paid attention to her little voice within. Years ago, she had understood that lesson well—when she was taught to go with the flow—and she now understood that calling the police in the first place was for a good reason. *Why had she not listened to her instincts this time?*

Aunt May turned around after setting the table. "Now where did she get to?" she mumbled. "I'll never understand young folks," she complained yet again. She called out to Jewel, but no reply came forth. She first checked the bedroom to see whether Jewel had retreated to her room, then she checked the bathroom. No Jewel anywhere. Casting an eye out the window, she caught a glimpse of Jewel climbing into a car with a strange man. "Maybe she went to the police station after all, but why wouldn't she tell me?" She wondered out loud. "You know she did mention an officer stopping by," Aunt May kept chatting out loud as though someone was listening to her.

Perhaps she did suffer from the onset of dementia. She looked around the apartment for any phone numbers that might help her investigate the odd disappearance of her niece. She recalled Jewel calling the police just after her arrival. Immediately she pressed the redial button and someone answered saying, "This is Officer Gord, can I help you?"

"You most certainly can," Aunt May replied. "Did one of your officers take my niece to the station? I know she cancelled the requested officer, but why would they take her at this point?"

"Slow down, ma'am. First of all, who is your niece, and I also need your name, ma'am?"

"Yes of course, my niece is Jewel Seymour and my name is May Applebee," she informed Officer Gord.

"I'm not sure if an officer did take your niece, ma'am, but can I look into this for you."

"Certainly. Will that take long?" Aunt May inquired.

"I'm not sure, Miss Applebee, but we will return your call as soon as we are able."

"You know, Detective Spence Walker raced out of here not long before the officer arrived here to take Jewel. Could someone let me know what's going on with him as well?"

"I'm not sure, ma'am, but we will call you back after we check into both incidents. Would that be all, ma'am?"

Feeling slighted May answered. "Yes, yes, that would be fine." She hung up. "Oh my! I forgot to give the officer my phone number," she groaned. Redialing again, she gave them Jewel's telephone number before adding, "Please call as soon as you can. I hope you get to the bottom of this so I can return home tomorrow," May said. Suddenly realizing she missed her quiet life back home— *just too much excitement going on for the likes of me,* May thought.

Aunt May went over to the kitchen to make another cup of tea. Perhaps she could calm her nerves while she anticipated the officer ringing shortly. She could not imagine why Jewel had not taken the time to inform her as to where she was going.

May had noticed that Jewel had been acting quite strange since the funeral and wondered whether her niece was headed for a nervous breakdown. It would not hurt for her to stay a little while longer to ensure Jewel was well. She decided to call the airline to cancel her return trip until she was convinced Jewel's frame of mind was stable. Maybe Spence knew something, but then he had not exactly been friendly lately either. She could only speculate that he, too, was not dealing with Marcy's death in the way he should have. *If only she knew of a good psychiatrist out here who offered group rates—since this town was in need of serious help by the looks of things,* she mused. This assumption only fueled her concern further to stick around for a while longer.

# Chapter 17

They drove for what felt like hours, probably not more than one hour, but then she had no way of knowing for sure. Her abductor forced her to drive the car while he aimed the gun at her side. It was obvious they were headed for Otay Mesa County. She was not sure why he wanted her company, however. She suspected he was somehow connected to Tina's disappearance, and in all likelihood linked to the other missing girls as well. But why would he kidnap her? And, should this be obvious to her?

While driving, Jewel glanced at him several times to see whether she could pick up anything psychically. She saw a middle-aged man with furrows set deep on his forehead that were well marked, as well as a few too many pockmarks populating his face. His eyes were dark and deep set, which, along with his angry expression, gave him a sinister look. Unfortunately, she could not pick up much regarding his personality.

Jewel had watched a program once about abductions. The overall message was that a person's chance of survival could greatly increase if he or she made an emotional connection with their abductor. Right now, she was willing to try anything—she needed all the help she could get.

"You know, people will be looking for me," she said, striving to establish a dialogue. Any dialogue.

"Keep quiet!" he ordered coldly.

"If I'm going to have an eternity of silence," glaring at his gun pointed to her side, "I'd rather talk now while I'm still alive," she told him, keeping some kind of control over her dire situation. All the while, Jewel was ever mindful not to push him past his breaking point or he would surely discharge a bullet. She was only too aware that she was treading in very dangerous waters with this man.

"You'd better be quiet or you'll soon find yourself in the trunk for the rest of the trip," he warned.

Not the response she was looking for. Regardless, she decided another question was in order. "Where are we going exactly?" No answer this time. "Do we keep driving until we run out of gas? And by the way, we are quite low." Jewel thought that perhaps communicating something vital would evoke a response.

"We'll stop at the next gas station to fill up," he commented.

"Yes, of course," she said, only too happy with the unscheduled stop. She decided to ask a different question. "So, what are you going to do with me?" After blurting it out though, she sighed with regret.

"You'll soon see!" He replied, smirking a devious grin.

Jewel shivered but pressed on anyways. "What exactly does that mean? Think me crazy but I need to know."

"What's it to you? You'll soon see that we're going to use you," he informed her, all the while sneering.

"What do you mean?" Jewel wondered what she had jumped into. Not like she had volunteered for this, obviously, but sometimes the nature of her work brought all kinds of characters across her path. If she truly had to go to the spirit world, she dearly prayed for a painless passing since she would not do well under torture.

"Just be quiet, or I'll gag you!" he barked back.

"I gather that you enjoy seeing my reaction to your intimidation," Jewel said. It was one thing to know you are going to meet your maker, and frankly, she had never been afraid to meet hers, but to think that someone may torture you first was another matter entirely. She truly wondered where her courage was coming from as she communicated with this loathsome individual.

"Here, pull over," he ordered, pointing to the right towards the gas station. "We'll get gas at this place," he commanded. His facial expression told Jewel that it wasn't the first time he had captured someone or held a hostage at gunpoint.

"All right," Jewel replied, desperate for any kind of relief. Perhaps, she would have the opportunity to get help, or better still, flee from this ruthless man. For the first time, she felt there was a glimmer of hope at escaping this crazy predicament in which she found herself.

"Now if you try anything, I'll fire, so don't you get any ideas," he warned, while poking his gun into her back.

She knew he meant business. Her optimistic outlook evaporated. "I will, but I really need to use the ladies' room." Jewel hoped he would allow her that break at the very least.

"You'll get to use the washroom, after I get gas. We'll both go in together to pay. I'll then ask for the washroom key. Got it?" He instructed, looking like he would use his gun with no questions asked.

"Sure, that sounds alright. Can I have your name?" Jewel hesitated. "Of course, it will sound better if I call you something instead of 'hey you'." She pointed out.

"Just call me Jeff," he answered, irritated by her constant chatter.

"Okay, thanks Jeff." He probably was not Jeff, but at least she could call him something while she continued to close the gap between them.

They came to a stop in front of the gas pumps. Before Jeff got out, he yanked the keys out of the ignition. Impatiently, Jewel strummed her thumbs on the steering wheel while Jeff refilled the gas tank. When he finished, he ordered her out of the vehicle and to walk ahead of him toward the station. Jewel wondered how she could write a note for the owner. They stepped into the store.

Jeff paid for the gas with cash. Jewel attempted to use her eyes to get the cashier's attention but fell short when the girl failed to acknowledge her signals. She had brown eyes and dark brown hair but wore no nametag. She was a pretty girl, who probably worked there after school. Jewel wished there was an older person around that could assist her, perhaps someone who had seen more of life than this lovely but young woman.

While Jeff was waiting for his change, she heard him ask if they could have the key to the washroom.

"Ya, sure! Here you go," the girl said, passing her the key.

"Thank you," Jewel said.

She entered the woman's washroom, took a paper towel, and began writing a note asking for help with the pen she had snuck from the front counter. Now if she could only give the note to the girl at the counter without being noticed. Jewel immediately tucked the note in her shirt and walked out of the washroom. There was Jeff waiting right outside the bathroom door. She was startled. His face was not a pleasant sight to behold and she shivered.

"Now let's get on the road!" he demanded.

"Yeah, sure, but could we get something to eat, like a bag of chips or something light? You wouldn't want me fainting from starvation while driving, would you?" She was intentionally delaying their departure using anything she could think of—pleading for his understanding, although she knew he had none. Jewel knew that every minute she detained him added precious time to any rescue efforts underway. She dearly hoped that Aunt May had called to report her disappearance.

"Fine! Get yourself a bloody bag of chips, and hurry!" Jeff barked, sounding positively annoyed with Jewel.

Jewel walked to the cooler, picked out a pop, and grabbed a bag of chips from the rack in front of the cashier's counter, leaving the note for the cashier to find. With any luck at all, she would spot the note right after they got back on the road. Jeff was watching her every move. His eyes riveted on her back; Jewel could not take the chance of handing the note to the young woman directly.

"Here," Jeff said while offering her three dollars for what Jewel hoped was not her last meal.

They soon left the station. Jewel's heart sank with the knowledge that she may be driving to her own doomsday. Her only hope was the attendant at the cash register. She decided to push white light to the cashier, so she would instinctively and immediately want to help Jewel when she found the note. Jewel could still see her bright brown eyes in her mind's eye, and this helped her to push white light around her, knowing full well that it would protect the girl also.

Jeff was next. Jewel began to surround him with white light hoping to redirect his intentions, but once she zoomed in on Jeff to get a better sense of what she was up against, she gasped. Jewel began feeling sick to her stomach. Something was definitely wrong. She got the strong sense that he had been ordered to abduct her—if only she could see who was forcing him. Jewel had to stop looking into Jeff's psyche so that she could eat something before they got into an accident, which could result in her even-earlier demise.

~

May Applebee was now feeling terrible—first the death of her niece, and now Jewel's disappearance. What next? She moaned. May patiently waited for nearly two hours before placing another call to the police station.

Determined not to lose another niece this week, she pressed the redial. "May I speak with the detective in charge, please?"

"And your name, ma'am?" the officer inquired.

"Yes. It's May Applebee, thank you," she said firmly.

"I'll put you through to the detective who is currently here."

"Hello, ma'am. I'm Detective Stone, relieving Detective Walker. What can I do for you?"

"Do you know where Detective Walker is?" May questioned.

"He's not here right now. I'm afraid he's out chasing bad guys, ma'am." He went on sarcastically, implying that people had no understanding of what they truly did all day. He was also playing down the fact that Spence was on a top priority case without knowing Spence's whereabouts currently. Notwithstanding his lack of knowledge, he was also not at liberty to inform the public of their every tactical move.

"Don't be using that tone of voice with me, young man!" May retorted. "I do know that! But I left a message nearly two hours ago regarding my niece, Jewel Seymour, who disappeared without a trace during the early part of the evening. Is anyone looking for her?" She was annoyed with the detective.

"Yes, ma'am, we are aware of your niece's disappearance. I do believe Detective Walker is personally looking into the matter. I take it you haven't heard from her this evening either?" As soon as the words left his mouth, he knew he should not have asked.

"Of course, I haven't. Do you think I would be calling if I heard from her, Mr. Stone?" Aunt May had never been treated so poorly. "Will someone please tell me what's going on? I'm staying at Jewel's apartment waiting for her call, or yours at any rate."

"Yes, ma'am, I'll relay the information to the detective as soon as he calls in." He did not want to alarm Aunt May, especially with Spence not answering his cell phone either, but there was no getting around this. "Is there anything else I can do for you, ma'am?"

"No, thank you, Detective Stone." Aunt May had the distinct feeling she had disturbed his coffee break.

After hanging up the phone, May wished there were more she could do besides hanging around by the telephone. It was like watching a kettle boil.

She made herself comfortable with the expectation '*this is going to be a very long night*.' She poured herself another cup of tea and sat in the chair, expecting the phone to ring at any moment. She drank a sip to relax her nerves, which felt like they were about to unravel. At that same moment, the telephone rang. She practically jumped to answer it. The caller turned out to be an undesirable telemarketer. She told him that she was not interested in whatever he was selling. Upset, she slammed the phone down. With a heavy sigh, she sat down again, thinking of what she could do next. If she had only brought her knitting with her or a good book—either one would have made for an excellent distraction.

"If only Jewel would call," she uttered to herself. "What could have possibly happened that Jewel couldn't pick up the phone? She must know how worried I am. Young people have no idea what we go through." She spoke as though someone would answer her. Was she speaking to Marcy in the afterlife?

This whole affair absolutely upset her, and she was, without a doubt, getting angrier by the minute. The one thing that kept her from completely losing her mind was that Jewel had recently lost her best friend and was more than likely too distressed to bother calling. Perhaps she had gone out to have a few pints at the local pub— seriously, without telling her? May knew that was highly unlikely— Jewel was never inconsiderate. Considering the number of highly stressful events Jewel had been through—and all one after the other—who would not crumble under such circumstances? May reminded herself that people often did things that were completely out of character for them when under duress. Now she debated whether she should go out to look for Jewel, or just stay put.

# Chapter 18

Jewel and her abductor drove for another ten minutes before turning left down a gravel road. Another five minutes elapsed before they pulled up to a two-storey house. Jewel was convinced the abandon building had been condemned a century ago. After parking in the back of the house, Jeff ordered her to get out of the car. His vicious tone had not mellowed. He proceeded by shoving her up four steps to a deserted porch that had probably been begging for paint years ago. The wood was stripped with signs of decay. She took each step cautiously, not wanting to fall through the rotting boards. After opening the door for them, Jeff pushed her into the living room and the pungent, moldy smell assaulted her. The opened door in the room led to a basement. From what Jewel could see, she imagined that it was dark, damp and foreboding—much worse than what she was currently witnessing upstairs. He shoved her towards the open door.

She certainly did not want to walk another step toward a basement that probably harbored a variety of insects, especially spiders. And God only knew what other creatures crawled down there. Rodents probably inhabited every inch of the walls—likely inside every crack in the beams above—her worst imaginable thoughts were being played out. Now faced with her worst fears, she was horrified.

Jewel was not too happy to be put through some test at this exact moment in time. She was much more comfortable speaking to the dead than to be surrounded by little creatures that crawl in the dark. She had to laugh at herself though—despite knowing her situation was not funny in the least—but her nervousness came out in peculiar ways. Even with a gun pointed in her back, she summoned all her strength and resisted the temptation to step down the steep stairs that descended to what she felt might ultimately be her death.

"You know we could simply stay up here," she suggested, "I could just sit in that old chair by the kitchen if you'd like?" Pointing to the half decaying chair that rested next to the sofa that was beyond any salvation. Jewel had to attempt anything to stay upstairs, believing she would have a better chance of escaping this God-forsaken hole that way than if she was locked up in a basement. She told herself that no matter what, she was not going down that basement even if it meant taking a bullet in the back—she just had to convince Jeff of that.

"You'll do what you're told," Jeff barked.

Apparently, he was not in the mood for negotiations. But still she did not want to go down to that uninviting dungeon. Jewel was now experiencing fear like no other time in her life! With a greater fear of the living than of any ghosts—and her current situation had not changed her mind in the least—Jewel hesitated to put one foot in front of the other.

"You know I won't try anything, or I would have probably tried by now. It would be much warmer and much more comfortable for both of us up here, don't you agree?" she pleaded.

"That won't work and besides, I have strict orders to follow."

With that bit of information, Jeff confirmed what Jewel had suspected: he was being forced to do someone else's dirty work. Or, perhaps he did not mind doing someone else's bidding as much as she first thought he would.

"So, who gave you orders? I can't believe someone has that much control over a strong guy like you." Stroking his ego might keep her away from her day of reckoning, or at least delay it. Being on the main floor, she had at least a fighting chance of escaping her captor.

"I was ordered to take you downstairs. Now for both our sakes, we'd best be going down." After barking these orders, he took a deep breath. "Now move it!" He shouted these last few words with the gun shoved in her face.

"Alright! Alright! But I need to use the washroom before we go down." She pretended by pushing her knees together.

"Not long ago you used it at the gas station," Jeff argued.

"I know, but I also had that soft drink which goes right through me. Besides, I don't imagine this house has a washroom in the cellar, do you?" She asked with a final attempt to remain upstairs.

"Over there then." Jeff pointed to the hallway leading to a closed door at the very end of the hall.

She walked down the hallway, observing her surroundings to see whether she could find a way out. Nothing so far! She opened the bathroom door with hopes of escaping through an open window, but her first impression was one of disgust. It was so dirty that she felt she would certainly contract some deadly disease just standing in the room. She closed the door for privacy. Glancing around the room,

Jewel found no openings either. *Damn! Who would build a bathroom without so much as a vent?* She skipped using the washroom, leaving it as fast as she could. Now she felt certain the cellar would be most dreadful.

She was still wondering what on earth she had gotten herself into, and how in the heck she was going to get out of such a deadly fix? While descending the stairs, both she and Jeff did so with a great deal of caution so as not to fall. There was no railing, nothing to hold onto. It crossed her mind that falling to her death would not be so bad if her only fate was to be killed anyways—or worse tortured—something that had not necessarily been ruled out yet. They continued downwards, as each step was twisted and uneven, squeaking an incredibly eerie sound that resonated in her brain like alarm bells. There was only one small light bulb in the centre of the room dangling from its cord. With the room so poorly illuminated, Jewel could barely see one foot ahead of her.

Once at the bottom, the sand floor reminded her of her grandmother's basement, which Nana D called the root cellar. They had dug out the basement after the house had been built. Living up north, Nana D would store her vegetables such as potatoes and carrots below ground, so that they remained cool while winter raged outside. All winter long her vegetables were just like they were freshly plucked out of the garden. Nowadays there are large shopping centers, importing fruit and vegetables for people to buy— food that has lost its nutritional value during transportation. To avoid losing total control of her wits right there and then, Jewel elicited various memories of how she had been surrounded by love at her grandmother's place—the only relative her father had taken his family to visit.

They finally reached the wall nearest the stairs, and to Jewel's disappointment, she discovered chains attached to the wall. Jeff shoved her against the wall, fumbled as he attached the chains around her wrists and ankles, and grinned at his handiwork before turning to leave. In her present state, she simply could not imagine how escaping from this dungeon could even be remotely possible. The spiders were now the least of her concerns.

"That should keep you from escaping. Now I won't have to worry about you after all," he gloated just before going upstairs.

With the poor lighting, Jewel watched Jeff cross the room, but could only see him go so far before he was completely out of sight.

She heard him kick something with a loud *umph* before he went up, making as much noise as he could. Jewel wished he would fall down the old stairs, landing on his head.

She was left alone to think about what she had done to attract this whole scenario—which in turn reminded her of being a small child. The whole trip utterly brought too many unwanted memories and feelings back into her mind. Was she supposed to learn something from this? If so, what was it? What could it be?

Once her eyes adjusted to the poor lighting, Jewel was able to see another body on the other side of the room. She shivered at the chilling discovery. With the light so dim, she could not make out who was there. Much to her alarm, the person lying on the damp floor was not moving. She could not tell if the person was still alive or dead. Was she next to meet with the same fate? To her horror more unpleasant thoughts crept up about a dead body rotting not far from her. Putting those repulsive thoughts aside, Jewel forced her thoughts to more immediate work, using her psychic abilities to zero in on the body.

She received confirmation that the person was not deceased—not yet anyways. "Thank God!" She whispered with a sigh of relief. She was very thankful since the predominant thought was of teaming insects running rampant over the corpse. Jewel sat there, psychically looking at what came to her in a vision. She jumped when the person moved! Turning toward her, she now knew it was a man and she could finally see the faint silhouette of his face.

"Spence? Is that you?" Jewel let out a shriek.

"Mmm, not sure," he rasped, his voice barely audible.

"Are you okay?" Jewel was now whispering.

"I think so."

"Do you know where you are?" She wanted to keep him awake, afraid he may have had a head injury. And to think that the cruel man upstairs had kicked him was quite appalling. She prayed Spence was not too badly hurt.

"Not really," he replied softly.

Jewel felt he wanted to sleep it off, but if Spence had sustained a head injury, it could be serious. "Are you tied up?" She asked, knowing her abductor probably was not that sloppy.

"No," he replied, "I'm not."

"You've got to get us out of this place!" Jewel demanded, even though she was even quieter now to not alert Jeff of Spence's status.

Spence pulled himself to a sitting position but fell right back down. If not for their dire circumstances thrust upon them, Jewel would have laughed. He soon forced himself up, staggering to his feet only to fall over yet again.

"Are you alright?" Jewel called out, wondering whether he really had hit his head, and was once more unconscious.

"I think I'm okay," he responded. "They must have drugged me—I can't seem to get up. And the room is spinning, a wicked feeling like I'm a drunken sailor on sea legs," he whispered.

As Jewel watched Spence attempting to stand, she was tempted to make a joke but could not utter the words. It was not a laughing matter and he was probably not in the mood for one of her jokes. How could she even conceive of being comical at a time like this?

"What do you propose since I'm tied up over here, and you're clearly over there? Can you think of something?" Jewel asked, knowing that she must escape before she started to feel the he-bee-gee-bees. If only she could wake up from this nightmare?

Spence broke her thoughts by suggesting something practical. "I will crawl over there so I can free you," he said, but he did not sound particularly convincing.

"Yes! That would be great." She felt she owed Spence an apology for doubting his involvement in the case, although being down here with her did not necessarily rule out his participation either.

"Do you know why we're here?" He mumbled while crawling on the filthy ground.

"Not exactly, but I did hear the guy upstairs say they wanted to use me, except I'm at a loss to know how or why."

Spence finally reached Jewel. "Well, we're going to find out if we don't break out of here," he whispered in her ear.

She was sure it was his way of reassuring her. "Here, let me see how these chains are hooked up." He moved over to her right side and attempted to release the shackles. Struggling with the chains, he discovered he could not pry them apart. He would need a crowbar, or at the very least, a hammer.

They both heard some noise coming from upstairs and froze instantly. Not wanting to get caught, they did not move a muscle and hardly dared to breathe as they listened to what was going on above.

They heard more footsteps overhead. "He might be returning so we should resume our previous positions." Spence was already crawling back as quickly as he could.

They heard a series of footsteps and both immediately thought there was now another person upstairs—one assailant was more than enough to contend with. They both stayed put for about five minutes before Spence crawled back towards Jewel. He held a metal object that he must have found lying on the surface.

"Excellent that you found something to free me?" Jewel was delighted with his efforts.

"Turn around," Spence ordered. She felt a little pain but within seconds her hands were free and before long, so was her legs.

"Thanks! That feels much better. But now what?"

"We'll have to go up to get out of here. I didn't see any windows except a small vent. Do you know where we are?"

"I know we're in Otay Mesa County, down a country road off Interstate 68."

"Excellent," he said. "I think I might know where we are then," now more excited about their grand escape.

They began their ascent. The staircase creaked and moaned with every move and they were certain they would be discovered. Miraculously, there did not seem to be anyone in the house. Arriving at the top step, Spence stopped to listen intently at the door. "What are you doing?" Jewel whispered, wondering why they had stopped.

"Shush," Spence whispered almost inaudibly.

Jewel crouched quietly.

Finally, Spence whispered. "The coast looks clear. We'll open the door and when we get up, I want you to follow me. Do not get all daring on me," Spence warned, fully aware that Jewel might attempt something foolish.

"I wasn't exactly thinking of going solo," she murmured.

Spence's mouth was so close to hers that Jewel felt uncomfortable. And this time it was not fear gripping her.

"Shush," Spence puffed out. He was not a man with a lot of words.

Jewel answered with a nod.

Spence opened the door a crack to look out. Nothing! There was nobody around. Once assured, he stood up to take a better look around. He was still moving as if he had drunk the entire bar down to the last drop the night before. He steadied himself before saying, "Now we'll make our way to the door, alright, so follow behind?"

"Okay," Jewel responded to his command.

Jewel was scared but also excited to put this disgusting place behind them. At this point she would be grateful to get off her knees, she thought, but then again standing was almost unbearable so she crouched instead. They both made for the front door. Spence opened it a crack and glanced around. There was no one lurking about, and with no sounds emanating from within, they scrambled out of the house. Spence pointed to the far side of the woods. It was now dusk, and the conditions outside could not have been better for their escape. They both began to dash towards the woods to the left, closest to the road, which Jewel believed led to the highway. With Spence in the lead, she ran right behind him. When Spence suddenly stopped, she, of course, ran right into his backside. Spence turned, catching her in his arms before they toppled over one another. Jewel landed right on top of him.

"Sorry, Spence," she blurted out, embarrassed. The sheer closeness made her feel quite uncomfortable yet again.

He whispered in her ear, "That's alright."

While his mouth was brushing her earlobe, Jewel could feel his breath. It was sensual and her heart raced uncontrollably, as if his near presence had moved her in some way. Her breathing quickened from pure fright that someone could still have this effect on her. Yet, knowing Spence for so many years, she could not describe the feelings that ran through her body. It was definitely betraying her. With her confused feelings, Jewel struggled to regain her emotions, doubting he felt the same way. She needed a diversion.

They stumbled in the dark for a long while before Jewel wondered whether they were going in circles. "Spence, I think we're lost!" she finally said to him.

"Just keep following me," he whispered with both scrambling to their feet having just tripped over something yet again.

Suddenly, she tripped over a log. Falling to her knees, again, Jewel started to feel around. She had not tripped over a log; she had tripped over a body! She let out a shriek, "Oh my God! Spence!"

Spence immediately grabbed her mouth. "Shush!"

"Spence?" She tried saying, but with his hand covering her mouth it came out as a mumble.

"What is the matter?" Spence whispered so softly that Jewel could barely hear him.

"I think I just stumbled over a body," she said, appalled.

"Where?"

"Right over here! Can't you feel something?"

Spence felt around the area as well. "I think you're right."

"Wait, I'm getting an image of her," Jewel whispered. "She looks like the girl from the park. I wonder if she had a sister who went missing. That would explain why she was at the park, perhaps looking for her sister. Just a second while I ask the spirits to give me her name." Jewel was stalling for the answer, but Spence insisted that they push on regardless.

"It's too dangerous to stay here," Spence said, bringing Jewel back to the present.

"But I was hoping for a name."

"Name be damned!" he said abruptly. "We've got to get out of here before they start looking for us, or we'll end up like this poor girl." Spence knew they only had precious moments to get as far as they could from that place. He placed an upright stick to mark it.

Jewel followed him to the side of the road—not that she had a choice in the matter—Spence had tightly gripped her hand. It felt nice to have someone next to her especially after feeling so frightened in the last while. They hid in the ditch while waiting for a vehicle to come down the road.

"But what if it's the person who kidnapped us in the first place?" Jewel questioned. "We can't be recaptured," she voiced.

"We're going to have to apply your psychic abilities to keep us out of danger, now won't we?" Spence insisted.

*As if that helped me before,* Jewel thought. Knowing that she had to be psychic while their lives were in danger, added pressure on to her powers. With this last thought, Jewel calmed herself so she would be able to access the gifts everyone seemed to want to possess. *Relax, breathe, calm down, think of the beach,* she thought. "It doesn't work that well when I'm frightened to death!" she pointed out. "All I want to do is be somewhere else, anywhere other than here."

"Will you just try?" he insisted again.

"It doesn't leave me a lot of time to zoom in on the driver before he reaches us. It's not something that you can will all on its own," she remarked. The driver's energy would be shown to her and either an enemy or an ally and Jewel should be able to detect it. Then again, she had to have enough time to do so before they cruised past them. "I'm not sure whether I can zoom in before the car drives past us," she complained once more. They had been in the forest for hours and exhaustion was taking a toll.

"Do your best since it's too dark to walk through the woods without the full moon, and…" pointing to her feet, "you can't possibly walk much farther with those shoes of yours," he commented. The pair of indoor loafers she had on were now soaking wet. At any rate he knew the full moon would guide them to safety if they stayed out of the woods.

"I would have put on the appropriate footwear had I known. You know I don't get the privilege of seeing my own affairs." *Had she already informed him how this process worked,* she wondered? "Otherwise, do you think I would have allowed this to happen? I certainly wouldn't find myself here in the woods with you, fleeing for our lives. And if I could see my own fate, I would have been rich by now! God gave me a gift, but also wanted me to experience the physical world. At least that's what I've been told."

"Sorry I mentioned it. I didn't mean to sound like I was criticizing you," he said. The pressure was also getting to him.

"I shouldn't be so sensitive either. It's been a frightening long day and night and we're both tired," Jewel admitted.

"So which way do we go?" Spence asked, looking on either side of him. The twilight had been upon them for some time, and even with the moonlight's assistance, light was in short supply once the clouds passed over them.

Jewel felt the vibrations from the road leading away from the building they had just escaped from—at least she thought it was in that direction. Then she turned around facing the other direction to feel the energy of the road on which she had driven earlier today.

"Spence, I believe we have to go down the road that gets us towards Otay Mesa County," she finally advised.

To Jewel's astonishment, she heard, "Alright then, let's go."

She was not used to Spence agreeing so readily with her suggestions. Jewel followed him as closely as she could, stumbling now and again. It was not long before they were making progress, ducking whenever they saw vehicles approaching that Jewel could sense were not friendly. When Spence felt they were far enough, he flagged down the first vehicle. They desperately had to do something before the clouds prevented them from doing anything more than wait out the night in the forest.

# Chapter 19

Aunt May was sleeping in a cozy chair next to the television, when, startled by the strident ringing of the phone, she awoke with a start. She glanced up at the clock and saw it was 12:30 in the morning. Quickly she picked up the receiver with expectations that they had found her niece. "Hello?" she said with a croaky voice.

"Is this Miss May Applebee?" the caller asked.

"Yes, it is. Who is this?" She asked suspiciously, after all he had been the one who startled her awake.

"Sorry to disturb you, ma'am. This is Detective Stone returning your call. I apologize for taking so long and the late hour."

"Did you find my niece?" she asked with renewed hope.

"No, ma'am, not exactly. I gather you haven't heard from your niece either, have you?"

"I have not heard a word at all from her, nor from Spence." Aunt May replied with a hint of disappointment in her voice.

"I was just checking, ma'am. We haven't been able to get through to Detective Walker either. We're sending out more officers to see what we can find."

"That's good. I'm still sitting here waiting for a call, Detective," she added.

"If you should hear from them, could you please call us immediately?" Stone asked. Now it sounded like alarms had gone off. Honestly, Aunt May would have been much happier to receive better news.

"Sure will, Detective." May was pleased to hear that the police were finally investigating both disappearances. With great satisfaction that the police had finally taken her seriously, she bid him goodnight and hung up the phone.

May glanced around the apartment, looking for something to do but feeling too tired to clean. Although cleaning was a good pastime, at this hour she pushed the impulse away, preferring to get some additional sleep. A little while later she crawled into Jewel's bed—even though it was not her own—she reckoned she might as well get a comfortable sleep. Who knew what tomorrow would bring? If the past day were any indication of what was to come, it could very well be a busy one. She double-checked that one of the house phones was placed in the bedroom before she slipped under the covers. To her it felt rather nice to be able to lie down after sitting for so long. She could not sleep at first, so she decided to pick up a magazine that was lying on the nightstand.

*This looks interesting*, she thought while leafing through the first few pages of the magazine. She must have fallen asleep shortly thereafter because she soon began to dream of happier times. Waking at 5:30 AM, she realized no one had bothered to call her. Her concern for her niece's safety was becoming unnerving indeed. She could not imagine what kind of trouble Jewel had encountered that she could not simply call her. She just could not understand. *Nowadays, everyone seemed to have cell phones,* she mused. Her nerves were beginning to unravel. Suddenly the phone rang.

With a trembling hand, May picked up the receiver. "Hello! No, I'm sorry she's not in right now. Can I help you Mr…?" she asked, seeking to uncover the caller's identity. "I'm sorry but I don't know when she will be home. Can I tell her who called?" she questioned. After hearing a loud click on the other end of the line, May hung up. "Well the nerve of him hanging up on me like that! Sometimes I wonder about people—all in a rush to get to wherever."

While shaking her head, she got up. She went to the kitchen to put the kettle on to brew a cup of tea before having a shower. She was thinking a fine brew might calm her apprehension regarding the nightmare she had unwittingly stumbled into. If only her niece would call. What could have happened to her? She really did not want to go down that same road with the numerous possibilities that might befall someone. May reminded herself that Jewel seemed to have a special knack for attracting calamities, though she would keep a positive outlook on this unfolding state of affairs.

"I'm not going to lose two nieces in one week," she vowed. She wondered if this whole grieving process was causing her to lose her mind. Glancing at the clock, which displayed a little after six in the morning, she decided to grab a cab back to her hotel room to check out first. It would not take long—the only thing she needed to do was grab her suitcase, which thankfully, was already packed and ready to go. She would then return to the apartment and stay there until she decided to go home to Canterbury.

Upon her return from the hotel and with luggage in hand, May strolled down the hallway towards Jewel's modest suite. While struggling to unlock the door, she could hear the telephone ringing inside. Hurriedly she unlocked the door, but unfortunately, she could not pick up the phone in time before it went silent.

"Blast it all!" she let out. Why is it always so? Sitting for hours with no callers and the second you step out you miss your important call. *Who could it have been?* She wondered before scrolling the caller ID. Interestingly, the last number was a blocked number. Her only hope was that whoever it was would soon call back. She instantly noticed the answering machine light flashing. Maybe it was the police, or better still, Jewel herself? With renewed optimism, she began to search for a way to operate the answering machine. If only she knew how to run this contraption, she would have heard the message by now. No matter, she instinctively called the police station.

"Hello, hello?" Aunt May repeated once the phone was answered.

"Yes, ma'am, what is your emergency?" the officer immediately asked.

"I've been waiting for you to tell me if you've found my niece. Did someone call with news?"

"Sorry, I don't know who your niece is, ma'am," he stated.

"Oh, I'm sorry, Officer. This is May Applebee and my niece is Jewel Seymour. Did someone call to say she's been found?" Aunt May was now more than anxious.

"I certainly didn't call, but do you know which detective was working on the case?"

"Not exactly. I've spoken to... let me see, a detective, I believe his name was Stone. Would he be in?"

"No, ma'am. Can I tell him to call you when he returns?" the officer said politely.

"That would be fine, thank you," she said and hung up the phone. *Stone likely burnt the midnight oil last night*, she thought.

After breakfast she sat drinking her tea while she sat next to the telephone. Luckily, she managed to pick up a few supplies like milk when traveling back from her hotel room. With time on her hands, she began to reminisce. She recalled what her sister, Giselle, had said regarding her stubbornness. 'May, if you weren't so dang stubborn, you would have found a man by now.' She smiled at the memory of her late sister. She missed her more than she would have thought possible, especially since she had joined the retiree league. She would miss her beautiful niece, who had recently joined her mother. May strongly believed there was a heaven and that she would meet up with her relatives once she departed this life. She was not too sure where this heaven was, however, other than it brought her joy to believe in such a place. And at this moment, she needed happy thoughts to help her through this rough patch.

May had long since known that Jewel connected with the dead and that her sister, along with Marcy, would certainly connect with her adopted niece some day. Jewel had always been close to May's heart and she regarded Jewel as her own. Jewel not only resembled May, but her mannerisms were strikingly similar to her own as well. At this point in May's life she reflected on her decision not to have children—a painful chapter—and particularly now that she felt so lonely. May had come to acknowledge that she was a stubborn old fool, a state of mind that had become more evident with the passing years. After the death of Giselle's only child, May had no other soul to worry about, except Jewel, of course.

Once again, the phone rang, bringing her out of her musing. May quickly picked up the phone. "Can I help you?" Without realizing it, her former schoolteacher persona had been summoned as she answered the phone.

"Yes, ma'am," he replied.

"Can I ask who's calling, please?" She requested. With the hesitation that came from her caller, she continued with, "You know you can't be too careful these days."

"I'm Officer McBride, ma'am. Have you heard from Jewel?"

"I haven't heard from my niece all night, Officer," May replied, somewhat annoyed with him.

"Do you have any suspicions as to where your niece may have gone?" He pressed on.

"I'm sorry, Officer. I haven't the foggiest notion where she went. Do you know anything about her?" She turned the questioned back to the officer.

"No, but we are looking into the matter," he reassured her. "Well thank you," he said, and promptly hung up the phone.

*Well that's one more officer asking questions, but who's actually looking for her?* May wondered as though someone would answer. She glanced at the time again and decided to make something to eat.

Seeing that the police were not any closer to finding her niece, she knew that she would have to remain at Jewel's apartment for the foreseeable future—especially since there were no vital reasons to race home. Besides, it was not all that inconvenient. In an odd way, given the current circumstances, she was grateful for the diversion because life at home was becoming a little dull. Lately she found her bridge club, along with Bingo Night with her friends were becoming less exciting. Besides, the old girls seemed to have run out of things to talk about and man-bashing had become boring many years ago. More to the point, Jewel's life seemed much more interesting than her own dull existence. Now she wondered why she should not simply move back here. But then she would miss her little cottage and her garden. Plus, she had been living at the same address for over ten years; she questioned whether she truly could move back without missing everything she had grown accustomed to. Well maybe moving was not such a good idea after all. She decided she would need to think about it at length before making any hasty decisions.

A few more hours slipped by and Aunt May placed another call to the police station.

"Hello, this is May Applebee calling. I was wondering whether you've heard from my niece, Jewel Seymour?"

"No, ma'am, but who were you speaking to concerning this issue?" he queried.

"Well I've spoken to a few of them. Let me see, I spoke to Detective Stone and I believe, Officer McBride," she informed him.

"I know Detective Stone, but I'm not aware of an Officer McBride working here," he replied.

"What do you mean?" May began to wonder who she had spoken with earlier. She was getting old, but always prided herself on her excellent memory.

"I received a call from one of your officers earlier today asking questions about Jewel's whereabouts."

"No, ma'am. We don't have an officer with that name. Are you sure it was McBride, ma'am?" he continued to question her.

"Pretty certain, Officer. I may be old but not senile, at least not yet."

"I'm afraid we haven't heard anything regarding your niece, but I will get Detective Stone to call you back." He said this as if making great efforts to appease her.

"That would be just fine, Officer." She hung up. May could only wonder who had called and was more concerned than ever as to what kind of trouble Jewel had run into.

# Chapter 20

Spence and Jewel were dropped off at the nearest gas station just outside of Otay Mesa County, approximately ten miles from where they had been picked up. The timing could not have been better because as certain as the sun would rise this morning, Jewel knew her legs could not have held up much longer. Knowing they had put sufficient distance from their abductor gave them temporary peace of mind, but they could not help but wonder if they had yet reached safety. Immediately upon arrival Spence asked the owner to use their phone. It was dawn by the time Spence placed his call to the Imperial Beach police station.

Jewel went into the lady's washroom to clean up while Spence placed the call. The image she saw in the mirror was positively frightful, not at all flattering.

She could not imagine what the poor clerk thought of her dreadful appearance. It was no wonder the store attendant had—ever so reluctantly—passed the washroom key over like she was afraid of catching a disease. They had been out all night long, running through the woods, stumbling in and out of ditches, splashing in mud puddles in those trenches, and falling over tree stumps. Jewel's whole body felt like it had been run over by a semi with more bruises on her legs than she could ever remember having had as a child. Coupled with the chills she could not shake off, Jewel thought for a moment that perhaps death would not be a terrible option. Regardless of her condition, it seemed God had another plan for her—she was still among the living, and to her relief, so was Spence.

Ambling out of the washroom—still extremely sore on every inch of her body—she glanced around for Spence. She was surprised when he was nowhere to be found. Without delay, Jewel walked right up to the counter to speak with the cashier. She was a slender girl who wore braces and had rosy, high cheekbones.

"Excuse me, did you see the man that came in with me?"

"Yes, ma'am. He went out with the owner, Mr. Wright," she explained and pointed towards the entrance.

"Thank you. Did he indicate he'd be back?" Jewel asked, not wanting to stray too far from Spence. Despite such a dreadful night, she secretly acknowledged to herself that it had been nice to be within reach of him, giving her a sense of security—hopefully not a false one.

"Not sure, ma'am," she replied.

Jewel decided to go out in search of him. "Spence…?" she shouted.

"Yes, what's up?" He replied, while sticking his head around the corner of the building. He wore a five o'clock shadow.

"I was just looking for you," she answered, "that's all!" She did not know she could feel so insecure, but after their last experience she decided she had a right to feel that way. "I'd like to see what I can find to eat. I've only got some loose change with me. Do you have anything?" She shouted back at him. She knew she needed to stabilize her blood sugar as soon as possible.

"I'll be right in," he said, cracking a tired but gentle smile.

"Thanks," she called out before going back inside where it was a lot warmer. She looked around and found some snacks. Spence walked in just in time to pay for their breakfast. He grabbed a muffin and a coffee. The owner agreed to allow them in the staff lunchroom located in the rear of the building while they sat waiting for help. Looking totally disheveled, they sat eating their breakfast, grateful for the owner's hospitality.

As Jewel stuffed her face with a chocolate muffin, she commented on how nice it was to sit down and eat. The knowledge of going home soon was also a relief. "Did you get through to the police station in Imperial Beach?" she asked between bites of muffin.

"Yes, I did. They're teaming up with the local police to investigate the abandoned house where we were kept hostage. I'll be going back to the old relic when they arrive so you will be alone for a short while. Is that all right with you? I've also mentioned the body we found while darting through the woods. They're bringing search dogs with them to locate the body." Spence brought her up to speed between drinking large gulps of warm coffee and eating his muffin.

Jewel wrapped her frozen fingers around her coffee mug. "Do you think the body is our missing teen?" she asked. Her suspicions were on high alert.

"Can't be sure," he replied. "Looks like you've handled yourself quite well," he remarked.

"Thanks, but what on earth will I be doing while you go off to the old house, which in all honesty, I never want to see again?"

163

"We're going to be here for quite some time so would you prefer to get a room at a motel to rest?"

He must have been reading her mind. He knew just what she needed. Sometimes Jewel wondered if Spence was psychic too. "In all honesty, I don't really want to stay here at all, especially while this Jeff guy remains at large," she complained.

"I can understand how you feel," Spence said. "How about if we have an officer guard your door while you sleep? I'll probably need you later today to give a statement and a positive ID—that is, should we apprehend this Jeff guy if that's his name. Regardless, we'll still require a statement."

"It's not necessary to place a guard at my door. And yes, of course, I'll do whatever it takes to get that man off the streets. I don't understand why, but I've been drawn back to Otay Mesa County twice now, so I have a strong sense that I'm supposed to look for Tina while I'm here. Coincidence? Maybe. But all I know is that I do believe she's somehow connected to this place. If you do find Jeff, please promise you'll check that information out for me."

"You might be right about that," Spence agreed. "But didn't you tell me that you think there's somebody else behind all of this that forced Jeff to abduct you?"

"Yes, I did. So, if you catch this guy, you need to question him on that also." Jewel hesitated. "Could we also go to the park to see if we can find the girl I was talking about when we stumbled across that body in the woods?" Jewel requested, even though returning to the woods was the very last thing she wanted to do. "I did tell you her name was Claire, didn't I? With all the excitement I might not have mentioned it." She wondered whether he would be upset for holding back vital information.

"I'm not making any promises," Spence replied, "but I would like to go with you, so don't go traipsing through the woods without me. I don't want you falling into the wrong hands again, okay?" He knew full well that Jewel would go off to the park alone if he did not agree to go with her.

"Don't worry. I don't think I'm strong enough to go right now." She glanced down at her disheveled state. "Sleep would be lovely. You might want to get some rest yourself." She knew Spence must be exhausted as well. Then she reminded herself that he had been unconscious for God-Only-Knows how long while down in that horrid cellar.

"I won't be able to rest until we get this guy in custody. Time is crucial. I don't want anyone else getting hurt. There's really no telling what this guy is capable of," Spence stated.

"You're quite right about that," Jewel admitted.

~

The first thing Jewel did when she walked into the hotel room was climb into the shower. It felt nice to wash the mud off, but she could not help feeling a bit guilty that Spence would be returning to that God-forsaken house—that very idea felt overwhelming. Officer Casey had joined Spence, along with a member from the local police force, to stake out the place. They hoped to catch Jeff and anyone else involved in the kidnappings. Spence felt quite confident they would apprehend him, although their ultimate goal was to get to the mastermind of the whole operation—this was critical. The police suspected a serial killer in their midst, and they would not rest until he was caught.

Still shivering, Jewel decided to get under the covers after her shower. Sleep would give her a new lease on life.

*Oh my God! I completely forgot about poor Aunt May. She must be beside herself with worry,* Jewel remembered. She had to contact May before falling asleep. She dialed the house but there was no answer. She hoped May had been all right during all this time while waiting to hear from her. Maybe she had already left for her hotel room. Jewel dialed the hotel hoping to catch May before she left for the airport, and for the life of her, Jewel could not remember what time May's flight was to leave.

The desk clerk answered. "Yes, may I help you?" he asked.

"Indeed. Do you still have a guest registered there by the name of May Applebee?"

"Just one moment," he replied, but before long came back with, "No, I'm afraid she's already checked out, ma'am."

She thanked him and hung up the phone, wishing she could connect with May. Jewel assumed May had already left for home—so desperately needing sleep—she made a mental note to call her later at her residence. Thankfully, the hotel sold various items in their kiosk and Jewel had been able to purchase some over-the-counter medication to reduce the inflammation in easing her pain. Sleep came quickly even though her body still ached all over. She had been asleep for approximately three hours when she woke with a fright.

While lucid dreaming she finally caught a glimpse of the person likely responsible for their abduction. Marcy had come to warn her that the rogue was extremely dangerous and enormously powerful. Jewel simply could not believe that he was responsible for the kidnappings, and possibly the murders. She shivered violently.

Feeling compelled to warn Spence; she wondered whether returning to the stakeout immediately was best. Hastily, she dressed to catch a ride out to the very place she swore she would never return. She would have to relay Marcy's message to Spence in person, somehow.

The cab driver pulled up in front of the motel and Jewel jumped in, handing the driver the address. It was not long before the cab driver dropped her off as close as possible without being seen. Cautiously, Jewel walked up to the driveway, wondering where Spence might be. How peculiar—there seem to be no one about. She was now becoming quite distraught and confused at the desolate place. Could she have mistaken this house for another one? The old buildings looked similar, but she was certain she would never forget the horrific dungeon.

It was at this point that Jewel woke up. *What the heck?* she thought. She honestly believed she was at the old house! Now she had a gripping sick feeling in her stomach. Now what was she to do? Should she risk going back to that abandoned house that kept its prisoners without hope of survival? Or, would it be better if she remained behind? Based on what her dream had shown her, she could not be certain that Spence was even there. And yet, she felt obligated to warn him one way or another.

Convinced that she could not wait while his life was in danger, Jewel called for a taxicab. There was no way she would allow something terrible to happen to Spence.

She dressed in a hurry and ran out the door to catch the cab. Fortunately, it was waiting out front. During the ride—after pinching her thigh—she knew she had to have a plan, a good one. They arrived at the intersection where the gravel road began near the old homestead. Jewel got out. The cab driver could not wait. Regrettably, she did not have money to get him to stay and wait for her—Spence's money had finally run out.

As she stood on the side of the road, a terrifying feeling flooded her senses. Was she stupid to return? She could not see anyone around, although at stakeouts she knew there would be officers in the undergrowth. She kept walking towards the house but stayed close to the edge of the tree line, not wanting to be seen by the wrong party. It was unfortunate that her dream had ended about then—now she had no guidance to work with.

"Psst, Jewel," she heard. "Over here, come over here," someone whispered. She could not see anyone about. "Right here! Over here!" She heard again. Then she spotted someone near the tree line motioning her to get down. She crouched down so that she did not give her position away. It was Officer Bill Casey, not Spence. '*Awkward*,' she thought, as she half-crouched, half-crawled toward him.

"Hi, Bill! Where's Spence?" she asked in a whisper.

"He's giving a statement. He will be setting up on the other side of the property afterward," Bill replied, also in a whisper. "What was so urgent that you had to come over here, risking your life?" Bill continued being quite inquisitive, but Jewel could distinctly feel his annoyance.

"Ah, just needed to have a word with Spence." She had to downplay it not wanting to alarm Officer Casey.

"So, you thought you would come running down here? You should remember that it's not safe for *anyone* to be trespassing," Bill scolded.

Perhaps he was right. Jewel knew that she should have stayed away. Yet, she was all too aware that she could not take the chance of phoning Spence either. If his cell phone rang, it could have made matters worse. She was also aware that she was digging a huge hole in which she would inevitably fall.

"I hear you," she whispered, striving to get Bill off her case. Jewel had to confess that she really hadn't thought this through—it was more like going by the seat of her pants. "I'm sorry. Do you think I could speak with Spence?"

"Not really. He's kind of busy right now, and the fact that he's on the other side doesn't help. It's too risky. It will have to wait," Bill said, obviously not pleased with Jewel. He had been much more patient with her when he had escorted her home on the train the other day.

"What about radioing him?" Jewel asked. But Bill shook his head. "I could simply go back to town," she then suggested. She felt it necessary to get away from Bill to make her way to Spence.

"You'll do nothing of the sort," Bill ordered.

"All right then. What can I do?" she asked, feeling frustrated. Why didn't she see this coming? Damn, this is why she woke up in the first place. If only she had finished her dream instead of being startled out of it.

"You'll sit tight where you won't be getting yourself killed," he informed her.

It was clear that she would have to do what she was told. Spence would have to wait until she could get herself out of this new imbroglio.

They sat there for several hours, as the sun slowly began receding below the top of the trees, and the temperature dipping incrementally. As the air became increasingly cooler, Jewel regretted her decision to play the part of the heroine. If only there was a way to slip away to warn Spence.

Bill started to look more intent just then.

"Did you see anything?"

"Shush," he whispered. "Once we catch this guy, we should be able to clear out."

~

At long last Jeff showed up with someone in his vehicle. He stepped out of the car while glancing around as though he knew he had been observed. Jewel felt as though he might spot them in the woods. To her relief Jeff turned towards the house instead. The second man, sporting a beard and a long, straggly, head of brown hair covered by a hat, remained seated in the car. As Jeff entered the deserted dwelling, Jewel started to wonder if the bearded person was the leader, and therefore, the one in charge of the whole kidnapping ring. She also felt he had a strong hold over Jeff. The bearded man finally stepped out of the vehicle. His hat masked most of his facial features. He was quite tall compared to Jeff, almost lanky, and wore some type of overcoat. He stood there gazing towards the woods. For some odd reason Jewel felt as though he could see right through her. To her relief, he finally moved towards the house. She picked up a very strange, weird sensation from him. He carefully entered the house. Jewel and Bill could now hear a whole lot of shouting.

They had obviously discovered Spence and Jewel had escaped the repulsive dungeon.

Bill stood up to move closer to the house before he turned towards Jewel, shouting. "Don't move. We don't need you captured again," he ordered before leaving.

"Yes, I know," was Jewel's simple response.

Bill inched his way towards the house as though he had done so many times before. Jewel witnessed Spence and another deputy closing in on the house. They were very professional. It was fascinating to see real police work in action. Following orders, she did not move a muscle, but did what she did so well—she enveloped Spence and his team in white light to protect them in their mission.

She sat as comfortably as possible leaning against a tree trunk. As she concentrated on sending white light around Spence, she had the distinct feeling that something was dreadfully wrong. Jewel was not clear what it could be, and therefore continued sending white light to him. She was in the middle of this process when she heard cracking sounds emanating from behind, breaking her deep concentration. Turning her attention towards the source of the noise, to her horror it was not human. Without a doubt something much fiercer than any criminal she had ever known.

Standing on its hind legs was a large brown bear. She did not know what to do. She searched her mind desperately trying to recall anything she had ever read about what to do when you encounter an angry bear? Her thoughts were frantic; her nerves were jumping all over the place.

It gave out a warning—a very low-toned growl. Jewel's instincts told her to run for her life. Trying to ignore this heightened sense of fight or flight was next to impossible, but luckily her saving grace was delivered—she was frozen in place, which was the answer to her prayers. Being frozen was her only hope if there was any at all at this point. Jewel sat there, praying the bear had just finished a big lunch, and a skinny white woman was not what it fancied for dessert. She stared at him wondering if this was the protocol, or was she supposed to avoid eye contact? *What was she to do? I need some help down here!* She pleaded to her guides, knowing they were always with her. In times of stress—and this was certainly one of those times—she valued and considered her spiritual guides her rescue team.

Meanwhile the officers were already in place around the house. When the two men came out, they found themselves surrounded by cops. It looked as though the entire operation had been executed flawlessly as they were being handcuffed. With perfect synchronicity, a police cruiser approached the house, came to a stop, and Jeff was placed in the backseat. The arrest seemed almost too effortless. Another cruiser drove up and then words were exchanged between the officers. The first cruiser drove off with the drivers of both cruisers, leaving the scene with Jeff and the third officer. While the second police car remained behind with Bill, Spence, and the bearded man, who had been placed in the backseat.

This all seemed too smooth to Jewel who was dealing with her new circumstance. What followed next completely shocked her: Bill hit Spence over the head!

With the brown bear staring at her she was dismayed at what she could possibly do next. Sensing it did not appear to be feeling up for the chase, she took a quick look at it to see if she could get a connection to confirm. Visions of Bill attacking Spence kept flashing in her mind, distracting her from being able to focus on the bear. Clearly, it was too late to warn Spence—the reason she had gone there in the first place. *If Spence is down, then what will happen to my sorry ass if I even escape the bear attack?* Jewel wondered.

She was startled out of her assessment when a gunshot rang out, sending the bear running off in the opposite direction—not a second too soon. "Thank God!" she erupted.

But now a more serious situation presented itself. To not be detected, Jewel would have to slowly tread through the woods along the tree line. She stumbled more times than she could count, giving her bruised knees more color than a rainbow, and each time she fell she desperately struggled not to cry out in agony. Finally, she made it over to the roadside to call the cab company. Badly timed, the police cruiser pulled up alongside with Bill Casey driving. She made a feeble attempt to hide behind a large tree, but she heard Bill call out.

"Where do you think you're going?" Bill stared at her like she had disobeyed his orders.

She noticed Spence was sitting next to Bill, and the other bearded man was in the backseat. She felt as though she was about to find out what they had been up to all along. She just wished it were on her terms.

# Chapter 21

They drove towards the eastside of town just past the railroad tracks, where traffic was sparse, to a small town called Mayers. When Bill pulled up to the side of a hill and stopped the car, they were all ordered out of the vehicle. Bill Casey suddenly pulled out his gun, ensuring their full cooperation. He pointed the gun at Spence who was bleeding down his left pant leg. Jewel presumed he had sustained a gunshot wound while fighting his attackers, and no doubt it was the shot she had heard. Hopefully, it was a simple grazing.

Bill looked at Jewel with his gun pointed at Spence's skull, saying, "If you try anything—and I mean anything—he gets it. Understood?" There was no mistaking that Bill meant business.

Jewel swallowed hard. To avoid any more bloodshed, all she could do was follow Bill's orders, and those of their mystery man, into what looked like the entrance to a cave. They all entered it, following this tall, bearded man, who Bill now called Brock.

The smell of damp litter scattered over the main opening to the cave was putrid. It was cold and dark, with little light coming in from the outside, making it extremely hazardous to move forward. With focus and determination, Jewel calmly pushed white light around her and Spence. They were escorted all the way into a long, winding tunnel, which was likely an old mineshaft.

After arriving at the end of the tunnel, it was difficult to see past one's hand. There was a mist that traveled along the floor, enveloping them as they moved farther into the depths of the cave. The mist seemed to swirl all around their legs making walking increasingly more treacherous with each step. Not knowing whether a hole would suddenly appear, with extreme caution Jewel reluctantly moved forward, sliding her feet along the ground to avoid a catastrophic ending.

At the back of the cavern, she saw a table of immense proportions. On it, lay an ancient opened book. Jewel immediately observed the opening to an even larger room with an altar. It was rudimentary, but likely effective. The light from Bill's flashlight was quite dim, so it was with great difficulty that they could see anything at all. Finally, Brock grabbed a torch from one of the sconces punctuating the cave's walls and lit it. The entire cave resembled a type of worship grotto. '*What on earth have we been thrust into and had become involved with?*' Jewel wondered with an anxious sense of awe.

Bill shoved Spence down on the ground, falling quite hard. When Spence did not get back up, Jewel became terribly worried. It was apparent he had lost a lot of blood. She grasped the seriousness of the situation and realized she would have to be the one to get them out of this mess—but not having a clue how that could be accomplished with a gun pointed at them.

"Can you tell me why you've brought us here?" Jewel braved asking. She knew that she probably would not receive an answer. "I think Spence needs a doctor."

"Not to worry. In fact, you should be more concerned about what we're planning to do to you!" Bill said in such a sinister voice that it sent goose bumps up and down her spine. It was as though he derived immense pleasure at another's suffering, or was it the *fear* he instilled in them that brought him such enjoyment?

"What are you planning to do with me?" Jewel asked, not wanting to wonder any longer, but at the same time dreading the answer. She felt as though she was a sacrificial lamb being dragged to the altar, which would likely be followed by a feast. Her throat began to tighten its grip over her airway, as though someone had wrapped their bestial hands around her neck, and squeezed ever so tightly, making speech that much more strenuous if not impossible. Swallowing did not seem to help either.

"You'll soon see," he retorted.

Jewel distinctly observed a tiny crooked smile at the corner of his mouth, giving her another spine-chilling feeling. She was certain her task to save them both would be quite challenging, maybe impossible. He was far too pleased with himself and while his laughter rang out, inwardly, Jewel shuddered with the thought of what was to follow. They escorted her to the altar and forced her to lie down on the top of it. She had to comply since Spence's life depended on it.

Brock was now donning his black robe, which he had taken out from a half hidden wooden chest on the far side of the altar. Jewel started to shiver while lying there atop a freezing block of slate— one that was especially cold being in a damp cave with swirling vapors rising from the floor. The cave had likely never seen daylight since the beginning of time. Therefore, heat was never an essential element to its inhabitants—whatever they might be.

Brock approached Jewel with a chalice, insisting she drink from it. With him so near, Jewel noticed a scar under his one eye. She shook with fright.

"I'm not thirsty," she replied. She refused by shaking her head while keeping her teeth clenched and her lips tightly pursed. He forced the silver cup to her mouth once more.

She turned her head away. "No, I can't drink that vile stuff. I don't even know what's in it." *Besides it rank of something the cat dragged home*, Jewel thought.

"If you don't drink, your friend here will get a bullet between the eyes right in front of you," he threatened, while forcing the chalice to her mouth and nearly breaking her front teeth in the process. He had a strong grip on her hair at the back of her head. He tore at her hair so severely that it was more than a powerful persuasion—it was vicious, a sadistic act. As soon as the liquid hit her tongue, Jewel could plainly taste metal and salt in her mouth, and this did not surprise her since she was now bleeding from her lip. Any attempts to resist were futile, but for some reason she knew that every second she hesitated ensured her survival.

As for Spence, frankly she was not too sure he would survive much longer. While he lay bleeding and now unconscious, Jewel knew it was dangerous to carry on with Brock. This predicament seemed too uncertain to continue refusing the concoction that would likely have her surrender to an involuntary act of mysterious making by Brock himself.

But fearing the worst for Spence, she finally yielded. She dearly wanted Spence alive because not only was he her friend, but he may be the only one to save their sorry souls from this brute. Plus, what choice did she truly have? Obediently, but under duress, she took a sip. It did not taste as bad as she thought it would, but the stench made her choke. Brock forced her to drink again. She thanked God for the small favor, before the room began to spin. "Now what?" was the last thing she managed to utter before the room went completely dark!

~

Hovering above the table, Jewel could see herself lying on the cold surface. She was having an out-of-body-experience. Watching her body below felt as though the lines between reality and fantasy were blurred. She witnessed herself—at least it seemed to be her—walking towards an altar that looked very ancient in a time she had no recollection of having ever lived. The altar was constructed out of what appeared to be some type of stone marble, though not a marble that she had ever seen before. Even though the room felt empty, she could still sense 'beings' all around her. When the altar appeared directly in front of her, Jewel turned around. She saw a procession of monks, or at least that is how they appeared, all dressed in long, brown robes tied with a cord wrapped around the waist. They approached the altar from the far-left side and came towards her, where she was now kneeling. The monks came forward and laid their hands on her head. It was then that she felt a powerful surge of energy —some type of vibration—enter the crown of her head where their hands rested. The sensation was so strong that Jewel awoke with a start. The dream left her unable to put words to it, yet she could still feel the vibration coursing throughout her body, as though a small current of electricity was passing through her. She felt incredibly energized but unable to speak.

It was certainly something out of this world, but Jewel wondered what this had to do with her current predicament—she became aware again that she was still lying on top of the cold surface of the altar. A chill came over her—a blast of air whooshed over her entire body as if someone had just opened a window on a cold, wintry day. She feared that winter had arrived well before its time, bringing with it a dampness that penetrated right through to her bones. Jewel continued to shiver uncontrollably. She had to focus on something other than her current condition or she would succumb to hypothermia. She imagined and concentrated on a roaring fire to keep her body warm.

Lying there also gave her time for reflection—thoughts ran through her mind regarding what actually occurs after a person expels their last breath. Did one continue to have thoughts, or did everything cease to be at that very moment of expiration? Or, did we simply rise to find ourselves in the spiritual realm? If not, was there merely eternal darkness surrounded by a void?

How could she be thinking in this fashion? She knew she was too spiritual to wonder about the existence of an afterlife. Had the process of hypothermia begun? Something was adversely affecting her thinking. Presently, the end would be a welcome relief and just as quickly as that thought crossed her mind, her will to live took over. Her innate survival instincts would not permit her to give up.

Does a belief in a higher-power help in such a quandary? She honestly had nothing to lose by hanging onto her strong belief in a Creator God, and a prayer would not hurt either. She had to do something, but what else could she do?

Jewel decided to open her eyes to peek at her surroundings. She first looked down at her own body to see why she could not feel warm. To her horror, she lay there nearly naked with only a sheer gown over her skinny frame. With no indication as to how she became attired with such a thin, translucent garment, she looked around the room. Jewel looked for Spence, but he had disappeared. Scanning her surroundings, it appeared she was alone, though it was difficult to discern with the rising mist. Where was Spence? Where had they taken him? With only one small candle illuminating the area around the altar, it was too difficult to see anything much beyond that point. Then Jewel heard voices approaching and knew they were coming for her. She struggled to remain as still as possible with hopes that they would not discover she had regained consciousness. It was likely her only chance of survival. As her memory came back, she wondered what hallucinogen had been in the drink Brock had given her.

She heard Brock yell, "Move it!"

Not wanting to give up her state of consciousness, she was forced to keep her eyes closed. She presumed they were shouting at Spence. She heard someone fall to the ground next to the altar, and moan. This person was not male, so it was not Spence after all. She was relieved yet began to wonder all over again what they had done with him, especially in his condition. What on earth was going on, and more importantly who was in the cave with her? Who was crying as though weeping for a long-lost world? The girl sounded terrified. Jewel could not blame her, knowing the frightening circumstances into which they had been both thrown—like the far reaches of someone's sick playbook.

With eyes closed, Jewel could hear a man approach breathing heavily, and now she could feel his breath on her face which made her skin crawl. He was probably checking to see if she was awake. Lying still was problematic with the incessant shivering Jewel was experiencing. Her body betrayed her at every turn. Fear gripped her once more, though she knew to keep her head together and literally on her shoulders. Instead Jewel prayed for a miracle that he would become distracted and leave her alone.

Then Jewel heard Brock say, "She ought to be waking soon. I thought the drug would have worn off by now. Maybe I gave her too much. By the looks of her skinny body she's much thinner than what I first thought."

It was clear that he was not happy with the results. It was also a good thing Jewel could not respond to his remarks since she was biting her tongue not to set him straight about his rude comments.

Meanwhile the girl continued sobbing, although Jewel did not believe her efforts would prove sympathetic to the likes of their captors. With limited energy, Jewel surrounded her with white light; hoping doing so would calm her. If they were going to survive, they would need their wits and strength about them. Jewel pushed the white light all around the weeping girl until she stopped.

Jewel could hear Brock say, "Why are you crying? You should be excited because it's show time. I'll be right back to begin our entertainment. And if you so much as move a muscle, you'll not get to watch the show, at least not alive!" he threatened before leaving.

Jewel could hear him laugh another of his sinister chuckles. When she did not hear sounds coming from Brock any longer, Jewel opened one eye ever so gently, just a slit to get a view of her surroundings. She had to see who was out there. Through the mist, Jewel could not believe that it was Tina. Well thank the Lord for bringing them together and, of course, for all assistance in finding her. At least now she knew who had kidnapped the girl. She peered around the room to see if there were other girls here as well. Fortunately, there was only the two of them. They would have to make a move before the spectators returned to watch the performance. Jewel had a sneaking suspicion that she was the star attraction in tonight's show. *But, what of the girl?* Jewel wondered. She could not be sure what they planned to do with Tina.

She got up from the altar to escape before Brock returned. However, while standing, she nearly fell over. She shook it off and grabbed Tina by the arm with one hand before placing the other over her mouth so she would not cry out from fright. Whispering to her, "Stay calm and quiet," Jewel indicated the exit. They had to get out despite not knowing which direction they should take. Anxious to free themselves and to put great distances between them and their deranged captors, Jewel quickly peered around the room. Once her eyes had adjusted to the darkness within the dim light of the dying candle flame, she could see another smaller tunnel that she prayed would lead to the outside. They both crouched down into the mist so they would not be detected. She did not know what Brock was capable of—although she feared she was about to be his sacrificial lamb. Could it be that he had done the very same thing with the other missing girls? The sheer gowns had been a growing theme.

It was slow going as they felt their way down a tunnel. They were about halfway down when two tunnels appeared in front of them. Jewel was at a loss as to which one to choose, or which direction to take when, at a short distance away a female appeared through the vapors. Jewel's first thought was—*not another lost female in trouble.* It seemed they were coming out of the woodwork tonight! About five feet away from her, the young girl pointed for them to keep going to the right tunnel. Jewel said as low as possible, "Thank you, though you must follow us. We must all get as far away from this place of horror as quickly as we can because there's no telling what they will do to us." Tina just gazed at Jewel as though she had lost her mind. Jewel ignored her puzzled look, assuming she was likely suffering from too much trauma.

Jewel quickly turned to look for the girl, but she was no longer there. "Now what?" She hoped she had not gone to play the heroine by leading Brock and his goon down the opposite tunnel. Jewel was convinced they needed police protection with so many of them running for their lives. She also thought that she should have asked the young girl in the tunnel whether she had seen Spence. Hopefully, he had not met with foul play, though she could not fathom why they would want him alive. If it had been to guarantee her cooperation, this escape would be his death sentence. A sharp pain pierced her heart at the thought.

Even with all this anxiety, Jewel had a strong urge to go back for the other young woman. Recognizing that doing so would most certainly place Tina's life at risk, she hurried out of the tunnel, knowing the mystery girl knew her way out since her directions had been accurate. Feeling daylight on their faces, Jewel and Tina sighed with relief and ventured out further. They must have been inside that wretched cave all night long. At this point, Jewel could not be sure which direction to take. Tina was clinging onto her arm like a young child clings to her own mother for security. Jewel could certainly understand her fears, especially after having been gone for such a long time.

They both heard gunshots! Panic gripped them both and they ducked. Jewel prayed that they had not just killed Spence since he no longer served a purpose given their escape. What rang in Jewel's ears was Brock's warning that he would kill Spence should she try anything. She knew he had meant it. She also knew Spence was a strong man and could easily take care of himself even with his injuries. He was a brilliant detective and if anyone could make it out alive, it was him. She whispered a prayer for his safety, nonetheless.

Right now, she needed to focus on getting Tina and herself to safety beginning with putting as much distance as possible between them and the crazed men. They chose to run down the road—the woods were too thick with lots of short underbrush making it impossible to make a run for it. The fog persisted, rising from the ground so they could easily escape into the mist and hope that it would provide them with enough cover to go undetected.

"Hurry Tina! You must run, please do!" Jewel yelled at her. "Run for your life!" Jewel continued to push her. She felt her limbs in agony. She wanted so desperately to stop and rest but was propelled to continue by her unwillingness to face the dire consequences that doing so would likely bring. The fact that Tina had been gone for so long and probably suffering from malnutrition and dehydration, made it difficult for her to have any strength to run. If not for her will to live, she would have surely collapsed—she was so weak.

They heard a vehicle approaching. Grabbing Tina rather roughly, Jewel jumped into the thick woods before they were spotted. It was not Bill or Brock, but they simply could not take any chances.

They finally rested for a minute and breathed in deeply. With her sides hurting, Jewel took a moment to consider what they should do next. How she wished Spence were there with them! He would know what to do. Jewel had to release all her erratic emotions to concentrate on her higher power. With eyes closed, Jewel saw which way they should go, as the path was shown to her as being illuminated. They were to follow a river, which was to their left, behind the thick woods they would have to traverse. They were heading through a gorge towards a wide region of forest, where the thick vegetation grew lushly. She sensed they were close to the river.

"Follow me, Tina. I think I know the way out!" Jewel exclaimed to her. They continued to run through the thick forest, falling, stumbling, yet somehow making progress no matter how little it was. They would fall and assist each other up, then run some more before falling yet again.

At last they reached the river. The location looked like a wall of trees and riverbanks of bedrock, which rose on both sides of the river. While the river looked inviting and refreshing, both knew it would be very cold—too cold to cross—so Jewel could not decide which way to take for their escape. Should they walk along the river upstream or downstream? Then something caught her eye. Up ahead, Jewel spotted the other female from the tunnel simply standing there by the riverbank looking straight at them. She was not wearing much, only a sheer gown like the one Jewel had seen herself wearing during her out-of-body experience.

"You made it!" Jewel yelled to her, "I wanted to thank you for helping us out of the tunnel. Let's hurry, we'll all make it out together. Do you know which way we should take from here?" The female pointed upriver. Jewel was so disoriented that left to her own devices; she would have probably chosen to go downstream instead. "Thank you! Now let's get out of here."

They turned to run up stream by the river's bank for only a short while until they reached a bridge. Concluding it had to be the overpass into the town center, which must be only minutes away since they could hear sounds of traffic overhead, Jewel turned to thank their guide once again. But only Tina was standing there. "Now where in heaven's name did she go this time? No matter," Jewel could not keep worrying about this girl—she was obviously capable of escaping since she made it this far. "We must find a safe place to hide," Jewel said to Tina.

"Who are you talking to?" Tina finally questioned. Her voice was hoarse like it had not been used in a long while, notwithstanding her sobs of course.

"Could you not see? You must be so tired and traumatized that you didn't see the girl," Jewel said, shaking her head.

"See who?" Tina repeated.

"My point exactly! I simply don't have the time to explain right now." Instead they dashed through the park, passed the fire station and found a payphone to call for help. They both needed to feel safe again. They did not have a dime between them. Instead Jewel dialed

911 to connect to the police station in Imperial Beach, fully aware that the police in Otay Mesa County were corrupt—well at least one officer was. She simply could not take the chance at Bill's place of work.

"Is this Detective Stone?" Jewel asked.

"No, ma'am. What is your emergency?" the officer asked.

"Yes, it's Jewel. Jewel Seymour. Can I please talk with Detective Stone?" Jewel requested.

"I'll transfer the call right away," he told her.

"This is Detective Stone speaking. What can I do for you?" he asked.

"It's Jewel Seymour here, and I have been running for my life since the day before. And I have Tina Miles with me. She is frightened to death and it looks as if our abductors still have Spence. He is in danger of losing his life, that is, if he hasn't already succumbed," she explained.

"Wait a minute, where are you? Who's chasing you?" he demanded.

"We're really scared that our abductor, umm…" Jewel hesitated. "That somebody named Brock will find us. There is also a matter of one corrupt officer with the Otay Mesa police force. He is also involved with this whole murder ring, so we can't go to the police station here in Otay Mesa County. We really need your help, detective." Jewel rambled on so he got the message of the seriousness of their situation. Their lives were in imminent danger.

"Okay, slow down. Where are you now?" Stone asked.

"We're near Otay Mesa in the town of Mayers I believe, according to the sign next to the fire station. Can someone help us right away?" she pleaded. "I don't know where Spence is, but I do know he's injured with a gunshot wound to his leg."

"Alright, I'll call the fire station to inform them of what's going on. They can protect you until we get some officers over there?"

"But can we trust them?" Jewel questioned with raised concerns that were clearly justified at this point.

He was clearly angry at the situation. "I'll ensure that. I know the chief, so don't worry!" Stone reassured her.

"Thank you. We'll knock on the door. Could you call straight away? We don't know how much time we have before they come looking for us," Jewel went on, obviously sounding frightened and shivering from the frigid weather. She again looked at her apparel and knew why she was shivering. She was mortified.

Although grateful for Stone's assistance—even though she remained gripped with fear, as Tina stayed clamped to her arm as though Jewel were her lifeline—she was extremely apprehensive about trusting anyone.

# Chapter 22

Once inside the Fire Station, Tina and Jewel sat for a little while, waiting for Detective Stone to arrive. Seeing that Jewel was clad in next to nothing, the firemen gave them some oversized coats to wear. Both women were only too happy for the extra warmth. The firemen did not seem too put out to help a half-naked woman and a teenager either. They were extremely sensitive without any derogatory words spoken. Given their line of work and training, they possessed the compassion to navigate the awkward situation professionally.

While warming up with a hot cup of coffee in hand, Tina began to open up, revealing how she got mixed up with her captors. She stated that one of her school mates, Carlos had known Jeff who eventually betrayed her. Carlos, being a bit older than Tina, had met Jeff at the Picante's Bar and Grill. He told her that Jeff could help her make some extra money. Apparently, Jeff had connections to arrange an interview with a famous movie director. The director was specifically looking for a Spanish girl to star in a new movie, and it was a stark coincidence that she just happened to fit the description to a tee. Jeff was to meet with her after school to discuss what she would earn to act in a small part in the upcoming thriller. Tina was extremely excited to be able to make some extra money to surprise her mother. She had not considered any possible consequences, but instead focused on what she had recently overheard her mother complaining to a friend.

Apparently, her mother needed to come up with the back taxes owed on her property or risk losing their home. Tina had been wondering how she could help, suggesting that she get a weekend job. However, her mother had flatly refused to allow her daughter to work, pointing out that Tina was everything to her, and that no daughter would ever have to work at such a young age. From her mother's perspective, Tina's job was to concentrate on her studies to ensure she would not have to work as hard as her mother did, once she completed her education. Tina was still determined to lend a hand, so she decided not to tell her mother about the acting job to surprise her mom with the money for the back taxes.

Nonetheless once Tina had agreed to sit in Jeff's car, he drove off, claiming that they would need to meet with the director himself. It was only then that she would see that he was legit. After driving away however, Tina knew she had made a grave error in judgment. Worse, she had no idea how to escape to return home.

Jeff initially brought her to a damp, cold basement, where she was kept for a few weeks before moving her to the cave—eventually meeting up with Jewel. It seemed there may be more to the story than what Tina was willing to share presently, but Jewel was certain more would be revealed in time.

When Detective Stone arrived at the fire station, Jewel thought she had never been so happy to see somebody in all her life. She told the detective where she had last seen Spence, and several patrol cars were dispatched immediately to locate him. At long last, both women were brought to the hospital where Tina received medical attention for dehydration, and finally was reunited with her mother. Jewel was so grateful she had been found alive. The doctors concluded that Tina would completely recover physically, but psychologically, she would likely suffer from trauma for quite some time.

Jewel was given a good bill of health except for minor cuts and far too many bruises. They were taken by ambulance to Imperial Beach hospital, where Tina would stay for a couple of days longer for observation. She would also receive some much-needed counseling. The doctor promised that Jewel would be released later that day.

Detective Stone came to visit and informed Jewel about Spence's condition. They had found him lying close to the cave's entrance. He managed to stumble out of the tunnel somehow, perhaps during the timeframe when Tina and Jewel had made their escape. Brock had likely went searching for the women thereby allowing Spence the opportunity to flee. They believed Spence had been drugged and his dosage was likely underestimated, but this was not yet ascertained. In any event, Spence had made a run for it. He was hospitalized and in critical condition.

Later that same day Jewel went to visit him. She sat with him, watching over his lifeless body. She felt overwhelmingly guilty for leaving him behind. If she had not been so frightened, perhaps she would have gone back for him. Then again, she knew that Tina had to be taken back to safety, which had played heavily on her decision. Jewel sat there beside Spence, wondering if he would pull through this time. She could not leave the hospital, so she spent another night watching over him. The doctor informed her that he had lost a lot of blood, and he was not sure Spence would pull through. They had done all they could by removing the bullet and "It was now up to him," were the doctor's exact words. They also mentioned that it was a miracle he had survived given his critical condition.

Jewel sat beside him, pushing as much white light around him as she humanly could, but she knew he had already been unconscious far too long, and with no apparent signs of him waking up soon, she was terribly worried.

Aunt May quietly entered the room while carrying a cup of coffee and a sandwich.

"You didn't have to but thanks just the same," Jewel whispered to May while taking the sandwich. She truly did not feel like eating with Spence hanging onto life by a thread, but she knew that she had to regain her strength if she was going to be of any assistance to him.

"Don't mention anything to me about not doing something for you. I have lost one niece, and I'm not about to have you starve to death while I stand around doing nothing," May stated firmly.

Although Jewel saw it more bordering on scolding, she could not help but smile at her Aunt May.

"You're absolutely right, of course," Jewel said. Resigned to defeat rather than losing more energy arguing with her, Jewel gladly took the coffee but sat the sandwich down on the nightstand. Through this whole ordeal, May had been a doll. Once this was over, Jewel would do something special for her. "Thank you so much for staying to help, Aunt May. I appreciate everything you've done for me," Jewel grinned.

May smiled like a proud mother.

Jewel patted her hand. She felt relieved. The fact that her hands were finally beginning to warm up also felt wonderful, especially after being so cold while lying on that glacial altar. Nestled between her cold and clammy hands, the coffee cup felt comfortable. Jewel drank it like it was her last cup as they both sat looking at Spence lying motionless.

Jewel sighed. "Will he be alright?" she asked May.

"You know he's a strong man. Don't you remember when you both were much younger, and he had fallen off that steep embankment? He made it all right back then. I think he's too strong to let go now," May continued reassuring Jewel.

"But I didn't know Spence when we were younger. I think you might have me confused with Marcy." Jewel forced herself to remember the first time she met Spence.

However, May soon interrupted her thoughts, saying, "Ah, yes. You are right about that, though you ought to get some rest, you know," she repeated, endeavoring to convince Jewel to take a break.

"I'm sorry, Aunt May, what did you say?" Jewel clearly had not heard her.

"I wanted you to take a break. It would do you some good," May said. "This also reminds me that," she hesitated. "I was thinking about you needing someone around, you know, to look after you?"

"No, I'm really all right," Jewel said, knowing full well where May was headed with her line of thinking.

"I really believe you could use some help to prepare meals and clean the house. Besides, I could…"

Jewel cut her off, saying, "I'm perfectly fine. Besides, I don't need anyone in my life." Jewel could not ask her to stay with her, especially since her freedom would undoubtedly be compromised. Furthermore, Jewel most certainly did not want May laboring over her, especially at her age. What was she thinking?

"Please, let me finish," May insisted, a little frustrated.

"Sorry, go ahead," Jewel conceded, accepting the fact that she would not allow May to change her mind either.

"As I was saying, you should get someone to help out around the house. Maybe you would get some meat on your bones. You should eat more." May started sounding like a mother hen. She carried on like she wanted to move right in with Jewel.

*Please help…*, were Jewel's dismal thoughts. "I know you mean well however I do look after myself much better than what you have seen in the past few days. I have just been under so much pressure, helping the police find these missing girls. Now that it's all over, I expect to eat like a glutton again." Jewel smiled to reinforce her declaration.

But May continued with her supportive comments at any rate. "I'm afraid you don't understand. You are aware that I have quite a lot of money. And now with Marcy gone, I've no one to give it to. So, I'm proposing that I pay to have someone come over to cook and clean for you. This way, I would feel good about leaving you.

Truthfully, it would make an old lady feel so much better. Would you allow me to do this for you?" May asked with such a sincere expression on her face.

Jewel felt choked and somewhat guilty. Aunt May always had a way of making someone see it her way. "I really don't think it's necessary for you to do that. Perhaps you can give some money to charity?" Jewel offered.

"I already donate lots to charity. Please, Jewel, allow me to do this for you so when I leave this world, I can go without worrying about you, alright Dear?" she continued. "You help so many, and this would be my gift to you, along with the many missing children out there that would benefit from your services."

Knowing Aunt May, Jewel would never hear the end of it unless she agreed. *Determined as always*, thought Jewel, *but being good-hearted really was her best quality*. "Only if you think it will help…"

"Thank you. I already know whom I can hire," May stated with a devious smile on her face before Jewel could finish what she was about to say.

"I knew you were up to something," Jewel replied, returning the smile. "What are you thinking? I'm quite capable of hiring someone myself, although I still have some serious reservations about your need to help."

"I was just thinking about the Spanish lady, Mrs. Miles, and her young daughter, Tina. Apparently, she could use the extra money, and you could use the help," May said before Jewel could protest. Then, pausing to consider the idea, Jewel had to admit that she was absolutely correct. "You are a crafty one, Aunt May! You're also very thoughtful and your idea doesn't sound too bad either."

"So, it's all set then?" Glancing toward Jewel for approval while grinning like a cat that just swallowed the canary.

"Did you ask her already, Aunt May?"

"I was thinking that if she was all right with the idea first, that you might be more willing to allow me to help you out in this way."

"Do you know that you are too much?"

Aunt May rose to her feet, and quickly winked before exiting the room, leaving Jewel wondering where she was off to next. But May was not gone but a few minutes when she reappeared with Helena and Tina not far behind. They said greetings before Helena offered her sincere thanks and apologies regarding Spence's condition.

Jewel reassured Helena that she had not caused this and should not feel terrible about what had gone down.

~

Two days passed. The four women were gathered in a vigil surrounding Spence, waiting for any signs of improvement. Detective Stone entered the room, pulling Jewel out of her reverie.

He removed his police cap. "Hello, ladies," Stone said.

"How are you, Detective?" Jewel asked.

"Fine, thank you. How is Spence doing? I have to admit that he has been sorely missed at the precinct. Have you heard any news on his condition?" Stone asked.

Jewel responded. "Unfortunately, no. In fact, the doctors have done all they can and now we're just waiting to see whether Spence will improve. He's been in a coma for almost two days, most likely due to the severe blood loss from his wound along with the blow to his head. The doctor has ordered an analysis of his blood to see what kind of drugs those scoundrels gave him, but I personally haven't been informed of what they might be. We're still hopeful that he will wake up very soon," Jewel shared with Stone.

"I see," the detective answered. "Well maybe a little update will be encouraging. Brock and Bill have not been seen thus far. The police have bulletins out for their arrests. We don't believe they could have gotten far. The officers are looking far and wide, in addition, all the airports are on high alert. Both criminals are probably laying low for now. But we will be there when they resurface, I can promise you that," Stone firmly added. "While I have all of you in the same room, perhaps I could get a full statement from Tina?" he asked.

Tina answered with—"I don't really know much. I was mostly kept in a basement, where I was questioned about knowing something about the supernatural world. But I couldn't give them anything. I think they had me confused with someone else, or maybe they were mistaken about what I knew? I'm not sure. I was so scared. I thought I would never see my mother." A tear escaped the corner of her eye.

"Perhaps they were mistaken." Stone repeated. "But why did you get in a vehicle with someone you didn't know?" he asked.

"Thinking I could make some extra money, but I was deceived. I was told that I would be able to act for a famous film director. I vow never to get into a vehicle without my mother again." She stated to Detective Stone with obvious tears flowing down her lovely cheeks.

All the while Tina recounted her story, Mrs. Miles held her daughter in her arms.

Stone said, "I would hope not. Perhaps they had other motives to kidnap you. We're not sure of their motives yet, as the investigation is ongoing." Just then his phone rang. The detective excused himself and turned away to take the call. "Yes, what's up?" he questioned within earshot, his voice trailing as he walked out of the room. But with his boisterous sounding Irish accent he could still be heard in the next room.

"You're kidding? That's great! Yes, I'll see you at the station in five." With one quick motion he hung up his cell phone. He returned to the room, saying, "It looks as though we've apprehended one of the guys responsible for the kidnapping. I'll know more once I get back to the station. Miss Seymour, we'll likely need you to come down to identify him in a lineup, if you don't mind leaving Spence for a short while?" He hesitated as he glanced at Tina. He seemed to have reservations about asking her to come to the station as well since she had not been discharged. Detective Stone exited the room.

A while later Jewel turned to Aunt May and said with a degree of satisfaction, "That would be great if they've captured one of them before anyone else gets hurt."

Aunt May had already given Helena the good news about working for Jewel. Before Helena left the room, she thanked them both. They decided to connect next week to put together a schedule. Aunt May stood up to leave the room, and determined to put weight on Jewel's small frame, May made a big deal of announcing that she was going to buy some delicious desserts in the cafeteria for her niece, as she escorted Helena out of the room.

In May's absence, Jewel prayed. "*I know that I've not always done what I'm supposed to do, but if you could do me just this little favor by returning Spence back to us, I would be eternally grateful to you. Thank you.*" Jewel glanced at Spence and wondered what more she could do to bring him back to the living.

It was time she went into spirit form to see what she could find out. As Jewel closed her eyes and took a few deep breaths, she inexplicably saw Spence in a ghostly form. He was in a long bright tunnel looking rather lost.

"Spence!" Jewel called. His spiritual form turned around staring right at her. He smiled in recognition, but instead turned towards the bright light for a second look. Recognizing the woman who stood at the entrance of this brilliant light appearing like the sun, he smiled.

Jewel shouted, frantically trying to persuade him. "Spence you must come back." Then Jewel heard another voice from beyond the light.

"Spence, my boy, listen to your Grand Mammy! You will come to see us, but not yet, my boy. You'll have to go back now!" She firmly stated. Spence waved at his grandmother.

To Jewel's relief, Spence turned back towards her. "Spence, you must know that I care deeply for you. You're my only remaining friend so I would be lost without you. Please quickly return," Jewel pleaded. "You can't possibly realize how many times I wished to call you but chose not to. I believed I would be showing signs of weakness. Although in my weakened state I did cry out to you. After our breakup and feeling extremely hurt, I held a cold heart. I refused to fall prey to yet another person's calloused heart. I was tainted with despair and a begrudging temperament." Honestly, Jewel had no idea where these expressive words had surfaced from. All she knew was that they must have come from the deep reaches of her soul.

At this point Aunt May returned to the room with desserts in hand. She peered at Jewel while she was in spirit, and seemingly, totally out of it. May bid Jewel back to Earth by uttering, "Ugh!"

It most certainly worked because Jewel immediately and forcibly was frightened out of her wits. "Ahhh!" Jewel shrieked out loud. "What the..., Aunt May? You could have shocked me to death!" Jewel complained.

"But you looked rather dead just then. I had to see if you were also going to leave me all alone," May voiced a little irritated.

At that very moment, May seemed so uncharacteristically fragile that Jewel felt distressed and guilty for her sudden outburst. "I'm so sorry, but yes, you are quite right," Jewel said, not wanting to explain what she was up to. "Aunt May, did you see that?" She stared at Spence's arm. "He moved! Did you not see that movement?" Jewel jumped up. Promptly she approached the bed and watched for another sign. "Spence, can you hear me?" Jewel asked him rather loudly.

"Yes," he replied feebly.

"Ah, Spence! That's wonderful!" She was so elated to hear a response from him that Jewel thought she would blurt out in laughter. "Are you in any pain?" She shouted again, forgetting herself in her excitement.

"Stop shouting," he grimaced. "You're hurting my ears, and my head hurts something fierce," came his whispered response.

"Sorry, I just lost myself. Aunt May, could you please call for the nurse?"

"Yes, I'll be right back." She left the room.

"I'm so happy that you woke up," Jewel expressed.

"Did they get the two guys?" Spence asked in a very gruff voice. He began to rub his head, as though he had a headache. He groaned.

He was weak but his recollection was precise. Perhaps capturing these hoodlums was the only thing that had kept him going through his heroic defiance and his near brush with death.

"Spence, you shouldn't worry yourself about these things. By the same token," she whispered, "I do believe they have captured one of them. I'm just not sure which one."

"Good! The bastards need to be behind bars," Spence angrily stated.

Aunt May entered the room with nurse in tow. "See, he is awake," she let out, sounding quite pleased with herself.

The nurse who approached Spence's bed, saying, "Are you in any pain?"

"Yes, of course," he stated. "But if I could just get some water..." Spence managed to say, too parched to swallow.

"Here are some ice chips. I can't give you much more until the doctor assesses you. We've already called him, and he's on his way," she informed him.

Spence thanked her though appeared to be out of breath. He painfully swallowed his ice chips.

"What's wrong with him?" Jewel asked the nurse.

As she examined the monitors, she replied, "He'll need more oxygen, that's all," and placed the oxygen mask over his mouth.

"Do you know how long before the doctor arrives?"

"He's already on is way so he should be on the scene any minute now."

The doctor arrived not long after the nurse did her assessments, then she left the room.

"We're so pleased to hear from you, Spence. You gave everyone quite the scare," the surgeon said, while continuing his examination. "It appears that you're out of immediate danger. Your heart sounds strong, but we're going to have to keep you here for a while to monitor your vitals, especially with that gunshot wound. People don't necessarily die from the wound once the bullet is removed, but secondary causes such as infection. I don't want to take any chances. Anyhow you are quite the celebrity, saving that young girl from who knows what fate she might have met with," the doctor cheerfully stated.

While the doctor conducted his assessment, the women stood outside the room, and when he left, Spence was in good humor.

Both women sat for about an hour talking to Spence, as he drifted in and out of sleep. Soon Aunt May was exhausted, so they decided to leave, informing Spence they would be returning first thing in the morning. Spence was so drowsy that he did not mind in the least.

"It's so nice to see Spence, alive. He's going to be all right just like I said," Aunt May put in.

"Yes, you sure were right."

"You know, I always wondered why the two of you didn't get married when you were seeing one another."

"Aunt May, please don't start matchmaking."

Arriving home was a very pleasant experience for Jewel. They soon began preparing some soup for dinner. Jewel had not eaten much in the past four days. She had not been able to stop for any groceries either. They sat around talking for the remainder of what was left of the evening. Jewel could not help but appreciate what a wonderful person May was. She would surely be missed when she left to go home. Never married, but always so caring. Jewel wondered whether May had ever regretted her choice to remain a spinster and not having any children of her own. Jewel knew May would have made a good mother, and perhaps now she was stepping up as the mother Jewel never had.

Aunt May had already informed Jewel that she would be leaving tomorrow for her hometown of Canterbury. Jewel knew May had to return, but she had dearly hoped she would stay for a while longer. They agreed to go see Spence in the morning and then Jewel would drop her off at the airport. Jewel felt odd for some reason.

Before forgetting to do so, Jewel booked an appointment with Professor Brown at the university for the following day. It was time to obtain answers regarding the girl Jewel had unwittingly encountered during her harrowing escape. Moreover, she wished to get more information about Claire, the young girl in the park.

# Chapter 23

The following morning, May and Jewel prepared to visit Spence at the hospital. May was ready with suitcase in hand not long after her tea. They left with plenty of time to visit before May's flight.

Spence was doing so much better than the doctor's initial prognosis. The man of the hour explained that he was relieved that the gruesome nightmare was over. At the onset, he was held in the basement of the old abandoned house for several hours—perhaps even longer. He received more bumps on his head than one could count and wondered why they kept him alive. He was happy when he saw Jewel, but then upset about her capture, knowing that death may soon come to them both. He was perplexed as to why she had followed him, however. "You know I care deeply about you, don't you?" His tone was now softer, tender.

"Of course, I know that, but it wasn't like I asked to be kidnapped," Jewel responded, more defensively than expected. Although those latter words rang in her ears, he actually 'cared deeply' for her. Uncertain what to reply she simply said, "Indeed."

Spence continued. "I know you didn't plan your abduction. It just made our situation that much more dangerous, and of course, more difficult to rescue both of us."

"I know what you're saying. I felt the same way while in the cave with Tina. I wanted so much to go back for you, but I knew it was an impossible feat without risking our capture once again. I'm terribly sorry that I wasn't there for you," Jewel admitted ruefully. She reached over to touch Spence's hand. They held hands for the rest of the visit. The energy flowing between them was palpable.

Being this intimately close to one another in the moment presented an optimal time to address the concerns Jewel needed to reconcile for herself. She could not suppress her uneasy feelings any longer. "Where were you headed the night of the terrible storm?" Jewel asked. "I saw you turn down the old trunk road."

"I was checking out an abandoned mineshaft, wondering if Tina had been held captive there," he explained.

Jewel was happy with his answer. "But what about the note I found in your kitchen. The one about a meeting with T?"

Jewel needed to know everything before she would finally be able to put her suspicions to rest. Perhaps she should not have pressed so hard, but her intense desire for honesty was driving her onward.

Spence's brow rose. "It wasn't meant to be Tina, if that's what you're thinking. If only I could have found her earlier, I could have saved that poor girl a lot of anguish. It was Ted Howard, a detective in Canterbury. I wanted to compare notes with him to see if he had any missing young girls. Why do you ask?"

"I have to admit that I was really perplexed by that," Jewel answered sheepishly. "And what about 'taking care of business'? Whatever did you mean by that?" She continued probing, undeterred.

"I had to see whether I could make more room in the house for you to stay without worrying about you. Is that why you didn't want to stay with me?" he asked, looking rather offended.

"It was only a small part of why, but I truly didn't want to impose." That was the best explanation she could come up with right there and then, making every effort not to hurt his feelings any more than she had already.

"I see," he answered somewhat coldly, releasing her hand.

"Please, Spence. Let's not talk about this right now. We can talk about it another time," Jewel pleaded. *You, silly woman, you've gone too far with your 'inquisition.'*

To break the tension, Aunt May rose out of her chair and walked over to the bedside to say her goodbyes.

While also standing to leave, Jewel said, "I must get Aunt May to the airport." Jewel sighed with relief, most appreciative of May's quick thinking.

At the airport, Jewel reluctantly said goodbye to Aunt May with a lump in her throat that threatened to surface into uncontrollable sobs.

May seemed relieved to be going home. The excitement of the past few days had been a little too much for her. She was looking forward to relaxing in her own home where she would finally begin to grieve Marcy's death. She admitted that her life could sometimes be quite boring, so despite the circumstances, she had dearly enjoyed spending time with Jewel—no matter how little. If only Marcy were still alive—she had always been a source of joy and a wonderful distraction from May's otherwise mundane existence.

Jewel was going to miss her aunt but promised to visit sometime next month. She also assured her that she would be all right without Marcy once she accepted the whole matter on a more conscious level and navigated the grieving process herself.

With sad, heavy thoughts roaming her mind, Jewel departed the airport immediately driving to the police station to make a statement.

While there, Detective Stone gave her an update on Bill Casey and Brock. Apparently, they had been apprehended at the airport attempting to flee—they had been wearing disguises, hoping to go unnoticed. Jewel was incredibly relieved that they were finally in custody. To think that she had once fancied Bill was a frightful thought indeed. *What does* that *say about* me? She promised herself she would discuss this fully with Professor Brown at their next appointment.

Jewel was also asked to pick Brock out of a lineup. When viewing the lineup, she spotted him instantly. His name was Brock Simms, among a few other aliases. Detective Stone suspected that Brock and Bill had likely been after her all along. This disturbed Jewel further. All the terrible emotions returned, flooding her senses with unpleasant thoughts and intense feelings. Shivers ran down her spine at the thought of what they may have been scheming. Had they planned to use her on a long-term basis, or was she to be executed in a demented sacrificial ceremony? She shuddered and everyone in the room felt it.

Looking into Brock's eyes, Jewel swore that she recognized him from somewhere, though for the love of her she could not remember where. It was like having a déjà-vu. But nothing clear came to mind. This task completed, she thanked the detective, apologizing for needing to leave early. She was anxious to get to the university to meet with Professor Brown.

She had visited the professor, and it did not take long for Jewel to describe her harrowing experience and Spence's close call. Though aside from the basic information he helped her with, she had left quite disappointed. He had rescheduled for the following week so they could proceed with another method.

~

After their last meeting, just over a week since her harrowing escape, she had rebooked to proceed with a different method to obtain valuable information. The week had crawled by very slowly.

The professor had been waiting for Jewel in his office. She immediately sat down in front of his large desk. She impressed upon him how eager and desperately she needed insight and explanations for all her unanswered questions. She asked him to help her understand what was going on during her terrifying ordeal, which ultimately led her to Tina Miles.

The professor explained that hypnosis would probably give her access to the details she was seeking, but that possibility rested on her—he could not force her to do anything, as this would interfere with the process. In no way, would he ask leading questions, as doing so would diminish the quality of her session and call into question whether he was filtering information from his own psyche. This would negate any information that surfaced and presented itself for observation. He asked Jewel to read and sign the form he had prepared specific to this process. Jewel asked a few more questions before signing it.

Satisfied that Jewel understood the process and each of their roles, he verbally asked for her full permission to hypnotize her, as a written consent, in his mind, was still not quite enough, he also wanted verbal authorization. They began.

First, Professor Brown informed Jewel that he was familiar with the 'Akashic Records,' which was a soul's life history. He added that he was quite fascinated by this concept and had conducted extensive research. If appropriate, he suggested that perhaps he could take her to the Hall of Records, or The Library, as it was sometimes referred, as doing so could be most beneficial. Here, she would have access to the information she was seeking. He gave her an opportunity to indicate she understood, while also giving her the opportunity to change her mind entirely about undergoing the process. Jewel trusted Professor Brown completely, she stated emphatically, and they continued.

He explained: "Okay. You will be going under hypnosis to ask your questions, the ones concealed in your subconscious. So, if you are sure you want to do this...." He trailed off but Jewel showed no signs of changing her mind, instead adjusted herself to ensure she would be comfortable during the entire process, no matter how long she remained 'under.'

"Alright. We will see what information comes up on Claire, and the other girl—the one in the tunnel—what was her name, again?" the professor asked.

"We were so busy struggling to stay alive that I kept forgetting to ask. We all ran together and the next minute, she was gone, vanished into thin air. I also forgot to mention this to Detective Stone. If we can establish her full name, and perhaps, why she vanished the way she did, it would be of tremendous help to me and to the case. Maybe she's another missing girl?" Jewel suggested.

"I will do my best to get her name from you through hypnosis. It's very tricky to do that, for reasons I will share another time, but I will certainly do my best." Professor Brown's voice had taken on a profoundly serious tone to impress upon her that he did not take this process lightly. "Now you will be guided under my watchful eye to go deep into your subconscious for any hidden information, bringing us closer to the truth. Remember also that you will only go as deep as you permit yourself to go. You are always in control; I am only your guide. I cannot force you to do anything." He knew Jewel had faith in his abilities as stated, and he did not want her to be disappointed in the results, especially in view of how she had suffered of late.

"Yes, I do understand, and I am comfortable with it," she offered, recognizing that he seemed to need a bit of reassurance himself. Then, somewhat sheepishly, she added, "Oh … and I'm also wondering if we could ask a few questions about my love life. Well it's nonexistent, you see, and I was wondering whether you could shed some light on that area of my life. Is it possible to access this information using this method? Perhaps this could help me understand it a bit better?" In her mind, she was visualizing her recent experience with Spence while in spirit.

"We can most certainly go deeper in order to help you on that subject," he gladly offered. He hoped for a fascinating session—for both of them!

Jewel felt somewhat apprehensive at the idea that someone would become familiar with her most intimate thoughts, but she felt a sense of excitement as well. She decided to ignore her discomfort around that. *Qualms be damned*, she chuckled inwardly.

"Don't worry. It's not like you will be unconscious. You'll be in a wakeful, alert state of attention, so as to zero in on anything you may have missed consciously, thereby shedding new light on the missing girls, and with some luck on your love life as well," the professor added, a tentative smile crossing his lips. "Now let's begin. I want you to relax in your chair. Are you sitting comfortably?" he asked.

"Indeed," she simply replied with a grin.

"You're going to relax, and we'll slow your brain wave patterns to alpha, and finally to theta, which is the level just before the deepest level. Now I want you to stare at this crystal pendant while I move it from side to side." The pendant hung from a gold chain. He knew this method was old-school, and yet, he wanted to employ it to see whether it would work on Jewel and her susceptibility to hypnosis.

The crystal moved in a slow rhythmic pendulum pattern, as Jewel's eyes focused on its motion. The professor gently guided her with slow calculated words. "You are getting sleepy. You are so tired that your eyelids are extremely heavy. It's beginning to be too difficult to keep them open. You are so relaxed, so calm. At this point you are feeling happy and very light. Now your eyes are much too heavy, and you no longer can keep them open. Your eyes are now closed. You are now at the top of a flight of stairs. There is a landing at the very bottom. You will descend these ten steps to the landing below. With each step downward, you will become more and more relaxed, and with each step, you will fall ever so deeper into your subconscious mind. Now step down, descending down the first step, then the second, getting more relaxed, third, fourth, and fifth steps," he slowly counted each. "You are extremely relaxed now. You are descending down to the sixth, seventh, eighth, and finally the ninth step. Onto the tenth step, you are in another time in space. You will now go back to when you first saw Claire. Where are you?"

"Here," was Jewel's simple reply.

"Where is here? Where are you when you first see Claire?"

"At the park in Otay Mesa County," Jewel heard herself respond to the professor's command.

"Well done. Now do you see Claire?"

"No, not really, I first walked down a winding path before spotting her." Jewel spoke softly.

"Excellent, now go ahead and start walking towards where you see this girl," he coached. "Do you see Claire now?"

"Yes, there she is. I spoke with her, but she is only asking for help. I'm not sure why."

"Ask Claire who she is," the professor directed.

"Claire says that she was taken from the park by a man named Brock. He took her to an old abandoned house. She tried desperately to get away, but he eventually killed her and left her body in the woods." As Jewel heard her own response, she swallowed hard. Her latest predicament was not unlike Claire's situation. Jewel's body language began to demonstrate tension and nervousness, as her hands were covering her eyes as though she did not want to see.

"Alright, I want you to relax once more. Breathe slowly," Professor Brown encouraged before continuing. "Can you continue?"

Jewel nodded.

"Now you'll be outside this particular situation where you will simply observe the actions. Do you understand?"

"Yes," she said in a relaxed state.

"Good, now we'll continue when you first saw Claire's body. Are you there?" he prompted.

"Yes. Spence and I are in the woods when we accidentally stumble over a body. At first, I thought it must be Claire's sister because the resemblance was so uncanny, but it turns out that it is Claire's body lying in the woods. Now I am back in the woods by myself. I see Claire! She looks as alive as you and me."

Professor Brown made a series of notes on his pad while Jewel's face was making confused and contorted expressions as she tried to make sense of it all. Her eyes were physically squinting as she attempted to focus in on Claire, despite being very physically present in the room in her now-regressed state.

"Now relax and take long slow breaths once again. What was Claire's last name?" He needed her to remain at the scene, not consciously return to her body.

"Dobson," Jewel instantly responded to the professor's query.

"Good. Now we will go find the other girl you saw in the cave. We are going to the cave. You are safe. You are now at the cave. Nothing can hurt you. What are you seeing? What is happening?"

"Back inside the cave but I really don't want to be here," Jewel anxiously protested.

"Just relax. Remember that you are no longer scared. You are safe. You are here only to observe—like you are watching a movie. Do you see the girl now?"

"Yes! Tina and I are dashing out of the cave when a young woman appears to us. She is guiding us to find our way out by giving directions."

"That's good. Now can you ask her who she is."

Jewel nodded. "She says her name is Andrea. Yes, it's Andrea Gilbert. She is telling me that she was held at this cave for over a year. She was a psychic that Bill Casey befriended. Then he brought her to the cave because he wanted to convert her to get control over her, using her like a lab rat. Oh my! They are involved in demonic worship and black magic. Andrea wanted nothing to do with the dark arts. She refused and was consequently killed for refusing to cooperate." This revelation sent shivers down Jewel's spine. Her body began to tremble uncontrollably.

The professor tried to control the situation. "Now I would like you to relax once more. Take a long, deep breath." The professor coached Jewel back to a state of relaxation.

Instead, unexpectedly, Jewel entered a small convulsive state with involuntary tremors and twitching. Her eyes flew open while her head jerked back, and her legs and arms jerked wildly. The Professor looked as though he were about to have a heart attack!

# PART 2

# Chapter 24

"Wake up, Jewel! On my command, wake up! You are in the present time," Professor ordered, quite frightened at what he had just witnessed.

"I'm here," Jewel said in a barely audible, monotone voice.

"You were becoming increasingly upset at what you were seeing, so I had to bring you back. I'm pretty sure your blood pressure was increasing very rapidly, and I could not risk continuing with the session. Honestly, I have never had a patient do this before. This would be considered a very serious reaction." He asserted, calming down somewhat.

"I see," Jewel remarked, obviously disappointed. Regardless of the professor's concerns—and while she knew he had taken precautionary measures—she was also upset with the way he brought her back to reality so abruptly. The intense sharpness of her return was puzzling to say the least. "I'd like to complete this session if possible," she maintained, disregarding any signs that the professor was at his wits' end. "I know it seems madness…"

Professor interrupted, "Perhaps," but shook his head indicating no. "For the first time being under hypnosis, you were there far too long. I wonder whether you somehow took on the death of Andrea as perhaps your own that caused such spasms? Just a thought," he continued while handing her a glass of water. "You need to drink something to fully integrate you back into your body. It will also help stabilize your blood pressure, which I believe went through the roof!" Professor Brown looked rather disheveled himself. "Here. And eat one of these," passing her a plate of cookies. "Nothing grounds a person faster than having something to eat or drink. It sends a message to your body-mind-spirit connection to return fully to the 3D physical dimension."

"I see, yes, of course. That makes sense. Thank you," choosing from one of her favorite delicacies. "Did we get the information required in order to put to rest the girls' demise?"

"I believe we did, so we can perhaps reconvene at a later date." He opened his calendar on his computer. "Let me see…," Professor paused. "I'm quite busy until next week. How does next Thursday work, as in Thursday of the following week? Same time?"

"That should work for me. I must finish a few matters as well," Jewel said, rising from her seat. She felt quite stiff in her neck and limbs, so she stretched like a cat.

"I will email you a copy of your session, or do you want me to just give it to you next week? Every patient should listen to their session at least three times. There is always imbedded information that one can only hear after listening to the recording a few times— three at least." He said in a way that she would know he was giving her instructions, not just suggestions.

"Next week will be fine. I won't have time to listen to it anyway," and she truly would be too busy.

Curious, Jewel decided to ask just how long she had been under, to which the professor replied, 'Too long.' But that did not seem possible since it felt as though she had been *away* for just a few minutes. "I guess time flies when you're having fun, hey?" she commented, tongue-in-cheek, attempting to lighten the energy in the room. "Until next week then," she announced, as she walked out the door.

On the way home Jewel felt exhausted. She thought of how gracious it was of Aunt May to come to her assistance—these sessions were beginning to consume a great deal of her time. Passing the local grocery store, she stopped to pick up some much-needed supplies. She was now absolutely famished as well, so a spaghetti supper would hit the mark.

When she arrived at her apartment, the phones were flashing indicating she had messages. After preparing the sauce for dinner and allowing it to simmer, Jewel finally checked her messages. Aunt May had called. The next message was from Spence. Regrettably, he had missed her last call and was now returning hers. Still feeling quite drained, she decided she would call him back tomorrow— especially given that he would have gone home by now and since it had been more than a few weeks since his harrowing ordeal.

In retrospect, Jewel suspected he would be putting extra hours in at the precinct. The investigation involving Bill Casey and Brock Simms was ongoing. They had been remanded into custody pending an official arrest warrant. The thought of these criminals taking possession of her body—while lying half naked on the cold altar—had been haunting her every moment.

This was difficult to put behind her, especially since the trial had not commenced and may not be set for a long time. It would only be when they were securely behind bars and posing no threat to the public that Jewel would feel safe again. She would do anything to facilitate the process, even if that meant Jewel would have to testify under oath about her experience. She sighed at the thought of having to dredge up the unfortunate young girls' fates—reliving this would be nerve-racking and unsettling. Shivers crept up and down her spine and her stomach was queasy. Better to block all memories of this case lest she lose her appetite.

Redirecting her thoughts, Jewel finished preparing her dinner, enjoying the sounds of easy music. To her delight, the spaghetti had been delicious. Relaxing now, after a good meal, she thought this was the perfect time to call Aunt May.

As usual, May's flight had been short and uneventful. She was glad to be home. Jewel promised to call her again next week to provide an update on Spence's progress, as well as that of the investigation.

~

A couple of weeks passed before Jewel called Aunt May again. She had not done much besides tying loose ends and getting Mrs. Miles working on a schedule they both agreed upon. It was truly a relief for Jewel to have someone attending to the household chores and preparing meals while she was attending to more important matters.

"Hello, Aunt May. How are you? Perhaps I should come for a visit sooner rather than later then?" Jewel suggested. Naturally, May protested, but with a little insistence on Jewel's part, she informed her aunt that she would look at flight availability. May conceded that it would be nice to have a social call, and Jewel admitted that having company might help her escape from the ongoing nightmares she was now experiencing with increasing frequency and intensity.

Upon hanging up, Jewel was troubled at the thought that May might spend her last few years alone.

After searching the Internet for last-minute flights—little in the way of seat sales, nor any available seats—Jewel was disappointed. She decided to have a shower and get a good night's rest. Yawning, Jewel felt there was plenty of time in the morning to check for available flights.

Not long after her head hit the pillow, dreams of Marcy began. Marcy had come to inform Jewel that Aunt May was indeed leaving her world to join the spirit world. Jewel had desperately tried to find out when May would pass, but regrettably Marcy turned to leave. This earth-shattering information was disturbing, but Jewel hoped it would not be too late to visit her. To her relief the dream soon faded into oblivion. The rest of the night passed without incident.

When Jewel awoke, the first thing she did was check for flights. How fortuitous that a seat was available that afternoon—except she had to get packed much sooner than she had anticipated. Marcy's forewarning had been a blessing, indeed.

Afterwards she called Spence, but his voicemail picked up so she left him a message advising him that she would be out of town visiting May. She had hoped to tell Spence that May was ill, but one does not leave such news in voicemail messages. She had hoped to meet up with him before her flight, but now resigned herself to accept that they would have to connect again when she returned.

~

The flight to Canterbury was pleasantly relaxing and quite short. Jewel was not far into reading the magazine she had brought with her and they were already landing. Somewhere in that time, however, she had managed to reflect on what Spence might be in the process of doing. She almost felt guilty she had chosen to fly there rather than drive. But time was of the essence, so she justified her decision. The roads were too difficult at the best of times to travel alone—and since her terrifying capture by Bill Casey and the whole harrowing Brock event—she found the whole idea of a road trip by herself very unnerving, and therefore, completely out of the question.

After landing, Jewel caught a cab over to Aunt May's residence. She lived just on the outskirts of town in a small cottage. After paying the fare, Jewel rushed up and knocked somewhat impatiently. She was so excited to be there, and yet after the third knock, Jewel began to worry. May was aware of Jewel's arrival so this alarmed her. After peering in the front window and seeing no signs of Aunt

May, Jewel went around the back. There was still no sign of her anywhere. Her next option was to go over to May's neighbor's house in the hopes that they would know where May had gone—perhaps she had given them a message expecting Jewel to do exactly what she had done. It was quite possible May did not want to leave notes placed in her door advising that 'no one was home.'

No sooner after knocking, the door flew open. Startled Jewel said, "Hello! Umm, I'm so sorry to bother you. I was wondering whether you knew where May Applebee was?"

The woman who answered the door wiped her hands on her apron and nodded. "Yes."

Jewel came back with, "And that would be?"

"And you'd be?" the lady of the house asked.

"I'm sorry, I should have introduced myself. I'm Jewel Seymour, Aunt May's niece."

Giving Jewel a quick once over, "She was taken by ambulance during the night. Are you here to visit her?" she queried.

Considering her disturbing dream last night, Jewel felt an immense sense of panic urging her to reach the hospital, quickly. She found herself speaking rapid-fire. "Oh, my word!"

"Yes, of course you are. May spoke highly of you. She was taken to Charles Memorial Hospital. Are you able to get there?" she asked. "By the way, I'm Rose Timber and my husband, still watching his program, is Stan. He's a sports fanatic and can't be interrupted during the games. You would think he used to coach or play for all his enthusiasm," Rose thoughtlessly continued.

Jewel smiled. She did not need to know any of her husband's TV habits, but she was pleased that Aunt May had a friendly neighbor. "Yes, thank you," Jewel said while extending her hand for Rose to shake. "And, I don't have a ride. I can call a cab, so not to worry."

"No, not at all. Come in," Rose said, opening the door wide and rushing to the living room. "Stan, this is Jewel, you remember May's niece. She spoke highly of her, remember?" She shouted over the program applause.

"I'm watching the golf tournament. Why don't you both have a nice time?" he said rather nonchalantly.

Affronted by this, Rose turned to Jewel. "Why don't you allow me to drive you since Stan is involved with the game?"

"That won't be necessary, Mrs. Timber. I can easily call a cab," Jewel protested anxiously, secretly hoping she would not have to make a call to arrange for a cab. Thankfully, Rose simply waved Jewel off and began searching for her purse.

"I'll only be a minute. It would take longer for the cab to reach the house. I'll grab my sweater too, put on a little lipstick and we'll be off. Stan, we'll be gone in a moment," she shouted over the television and with renewed hopes of doing something productive.

Once they arrived at the hospital, the Intensive Care nurse, appearing extremely busy, greeted them. They were versed that only family would be allowed in. Jewel informed the nurse that she was the only living relative and Rose was her dearest friend and neighbor. She understood and allowed both to enter the ICU, though reminded them of the importance to not upset the patient. Upon entering the room, May looked terrible. She was so thin, frail, and unrecognizable. How could she not have called to let Jewel know of her condition? And more importantly what was her condition? Jewel took a second look at Rose before approaching May's bed. How, and when did this all happen? Jewel wondered why she had not sensed or dreamt that May's health was deteriorating at such an alarming rate. Jewel stood there feeling completely helpless and, truth be told, annoyed.

Not wanting to wake her, Jewel quietly asked. "Aunt May, are you awake?"

"Yes, I am. Is that you, Jewel?" May asked before opening her eyes to see who it was.

"It's so good to see you, Aunt May," Jewel replied. But after she saw how May's eyes appeared glazed over, she concealed a gasp.

"Yes, it's delightful to see you too, and you as well, Rose. I'm surprised they allowed you to enter my room. It appears I have the German Gestapo as nurses, and they usually turn away everyone who is kind enough to visit. Mind you there weren't many remaining alive to trouble themselves to pay me a social call."

Jewel said with a slight grin, hiding her concern. "Please don't upset yourself, Aunt May. I wouldn't want you to leave before I had a chance to speak with you." She realized that this visit could be the last one she had with her aunt, and then that thought gripped her chest.

"Of course. So good of you to come all the way to see me, and now knowing you will be visiting me in a hospital." And almost reading Jewel's mind, May added, "And yes, I do know I ought to have told you sooner. I just didn't want to upset you. It hadn't been long since Marcy's passing so I hope you understand."

"I do, although I would have come sooner had I known the severity of your condition," Jewel protested.

"I'll not live forever, my dear. Besides life can become quite boring, especially when you don't feel well. One can only read so many books and watch so many programs on the tele before the walls begin to close in on you. After visiting you in Imperial Beach, I hadn't felt well enough to visit my friends. If not for Rose, I would not have any visitors of late whatsoever. It appears I've outlived most of my good friends since there has been an epidemic of deaths, almost a mass exodus of sorts. It's been quite upsetting, and to be frank,"—May leaned closer to Jewel, whispering—"I seriously suspect the food at the nursing homes to be the culprit. But no one will listen to me. Perhaps you could look into the matter?" May sparked to life with that last request.

"Yes, of course I can if this is what you wish. Where would you like me to begin?" Jewel asked with a little sarcasm in her voice. She immediately felt terrible for her tone and quickly retracted her last words before May would think the worst of her. "I mean, who do you think is doing these murders? Causing the food to be, what, poisoned, you suspect?" She was more concerned about May's condition than these suspicions. How wonderful that May's first thoughts were altruistic. Why would Jewel not want to help? *For the moment, and perhaps for the first time in her eighty years, May ought to be a little selfish*, Jewel thought.

"Now let me see. I have two of my friends pass in the Canterbury Nursing Home, and another at the Lodge. Only one passed at home. Her name was Gladys. She passed from a heart attack and I feel quite confident she went from natural causes. For the other three, I couldn't be too sure it wasn't '*murder*.'" Emphasizing the last word. "The first thing I would do is question the cook at the nursing home."

After a little grin at this last statement, Jewel composed herself and replied, "Indeed. Do you have names? I'll see what I can do. Perhaps my anonymity will serve us well. You know—they will not suspect me. I will do this under the pretense of looking for a great nursing home for my dear old aunt. I will not give them your name, of course. This is a small town where everybody knows everybody," Jewel nicely offered.

"I dare say, I will never go into one of those dreadful places, especially in light of these disturbing deaths," Aunt May made this declaration with an air of defiance.

"No, no, of course not. I don't mean for *you* to live there—I mean that this is the way I will go about obtaining information without anyone suspecting my motives. I'll work discreetly. No one will be the wiser," Jewel countered.

"I'll be ever so grateful to stop these murders. To think, someone preying on the elderly!" May scoffed. "I cannot fathom someone being so despicable!" An expression of horror crossed her face briefly.

"I will help you only to reassure you that nothing is amiss. But other than that, what is troubling you? I mean what have the doctors told you about your condition?" Jewel asked, suppressing her deepest fears.

"Besides them taking too many precautions," May responded, nonchalantly, "I have cancer, dear, but no one lives forever. So, I'm quite all right with it, you see." Her demeanor had not changed for one second while she relayed this most dreadful news.

"How long have you known then?"

"Let me see, although my memory is not quite what it used to be—a little less than a year, I believe." May knew full well that Jewel would be truly upset with her for not disclosing her condition to her sooner.

"Aunt May! You should have said something at the funeral. Why didn't you tell me?"

"With all the commotion about Marcy's funeral, and what followed afterwards—you know with your harrowing escape from those beastly men—I plum forgot to give you more 'disturbing' news," she sheepishly admitted.

Rose glanced up while the women discussed Jewel's concerns regarding May's unexpected news. "Alright then, I do understand." Jewel paused. "Though, from now on we must be honest with one another. I dearly want to be near you. Did the doctors say how long you would be in hospital?"

"Not exactly, I think the doctor is quite upset with me. According to him, I should have come in sooner, and now he's making a fuss. I feel weak, but other than that, I'm quite capable of dying without their intervention," she added. "Maybe you could speak with the doctor and tell him that you will be staying with me. That way he'll be persuaded to let me go home," she pleaded.

All this time, Rose remained seated just across May's room, reading a magazine she had found in the lounge area.

Jewel had suspected May's exit plan from the outset. And possessing traits one would attribute to a Pointer dog—or were her senses keener, like those of a Bloodhound—she had already sniffed out May's plot long ago.

"We'll see. For now, I'm going to book a room at the nearest motel to this hospital so I can keep an eye on you," Jewel said, cracking a smile.

"I won't hear of it. You simply must stay at the house. That's the only way the doctor will be more inclined to release me so that I can leave this dreary place. I don't need the Gestapo running my life." May was seriously annoyed by then.

"Of course not. But you live too far from the hospital and I don't have my car with me, remember? I decided to fly here instead of driving," Jewel protested.

"That's alright, Rose can take you home with her." May turned to see her neighbor's head nod. "And my car is parked in the garage. The keys are on the hook by the back door. Now let's not argue, please," May said firmly.

Jewel finally agreed that having a car would be much better than cabbing it, especially with May's suspicion regarding the deaths of her friends. She would have to park May's car somewhere where it would not be noticed since everyone in this town would recognize her vehicle. It would be a pointless exercise if they saw a young woman driving May's vehicle going around town asking questions at the retirement homes.

May provided a list of the names of the individuals she suspected of having been murdered. The first one was Iris McDonald, then Ginger Ferris and the last name was Cybil Lancaster, the only one at the Lodge. With Cybil living in a different retirement home, one could not help but wonder '*How could it be possible for one person to pull off murders in two separate locations?*' There had to be a common denominator, May had voiced.

Jewel had a private conversation with May's nurse and then she and Rose headed back. On their return trip, Jewel had a recurring thought. Why was it that May's energy levels had increased, and she became 'spunky'—while in ICU no less—when she began discussing her suspicions of her friends having been murdered. It seemed so strange to her.

After thanking Rose for her generosity of her time and energy, Jewel entered May's residence. The house seemed very eerie without May's presence. Jewel still could not get over the smell of antique furniture polish, lemon scented, and how the furniture was polished to a brilliant shine. Each piece was easily hundreds of years old, not to mention all the valuable china and silverware which were all strategically placed in the best locations for maximum exposure and appreciation. Altogether, her collection was probably worth a small fortune.

On her first night there, Jewel did not get a decent night sleep in the spare bedroom. Her mind constantly traveled to May, whom she envisioned lying in a hospital bed without a soul to monitor her care—the Gestapo staff notwithstanding. May had complained highly about the staff, when in fact, she knew it was not possible that the nursing staff could treat their patients as poorly as she described. Could they? It was more likely a case of 'continual nursing regimen'.

Moreover, Jewel realized that she had no clue how May wanted to dispose of her property, should the worse come to pass—which was inevitable. *It was probably time to have that discussion,* she thought. May appeared quite frail but her stamina was remarkably intact, despite her diagnosis and prognosis. Jewel knew she would have to speak to May 'soon' regarding her final wishes. Despite her reservations—these conversations were always so awkward—yes, Jewel knew it was time to broach the delicate subject. It had to happen—and sooner rather than later.

Tomorrow Jewel would visit the Lodge, and if time permitted between visits to the hospital, she would also try to make it over to the Canterbury Nursing home as well.

# Chapter 25

The morning materialized too early, especially after having tossed and turned throughout the night. After a quick shower, Jewel decided to call Spence before she left for the day.

"Spence, I've been trying to reach you. Yes, of course you've been extremely busy. I wanted to inform you about Aunt May's condition. No, Spence, she's actually dying of cancer." Pausing, then swallowing the lump that threatened to choke her. "Indeed, that *is* horrible. I can't tell you how long she has. Yes, that would be nice. No, I do understand your situation. Maybe next week you could get a little time to fly out here?" Jewel asked then paused. "That would be considerate of you to take the time." After saying goodbye, Jewel hung up. Seconds later she wondered whether saying something to Spence regarding May's suspicions would have been wise.

She finished preparing herself for the day, and Jewel locked all the doors before leaving through the garage. She would not want to encourage thieves and burglars—they would no doubt think they had discovered Ali Baba's cave.

The drive into town was brief. It looked more like a desert town than a small metropolitan, but who knows why people choose to live in such places. Jewel felt a pang of longing just thinking about how she already missed her hometown.

She spotted the Lodge to her left and drove into the parking lot. It was a small, quaint nursing home with very few residents sitting out in wheelchairs, soaking up a little sun before it became too hot. Jewel casually greeted them before entering the home. The entrance was spacious, having a western theme, propped with a cactus in the far corner for added measure. The building looked like a large Victorian home that had been converted into a nursing home. She envisioned how at one time the many bedrooms had housed numerous children, back in the Victorian days. Nowadays, it had become quite fashionable to adapt existing homes to current-day needs.

Approaching the front desk, she asked for the person in charge. The young clerk informed Jewel that the administrator would not be in today but offered to schedule an appointment for tomorrow. Thanking her, Jewel immediately left to visit May.

Entering the hospital seemed even grimmer than the nursing home. The ambulance had suddenly pulled up to the emergency bay and the attendants were unloading a patient. He was an elderly man, who looked too gaunt to even be alive. Undeterred, Jewel went in to visit May. She was asleep so Jewel went to speak with the nurse regarding her precious aunt's condition. The unit clerk recommended for Jewel to speak with May's doctor instead, who was scheduled to come on shift shortly.

Jewel sat next to May's bed, observing her aunt for a few minutes. She looked so peaceful lying there. Jewel was tempted to wake May.

In the event of her death, Jewel reasoned that May would not want to be resuscitated. She likely had a Do Not Resuscitate (DNR) in place—*she should definitely ask the doctor about that*, she thought. Jewel began to browse through a magazine to pass the time while waiting for the doctor's arrival.

Not long afterwards the doctor arrived. After a formal introduction from the nursing staff, they briefly stepped out of the room. He seemed happy to speak to one of May's relatives.

Without further small talk, Jewel went straight to the matter. "Could you explain to me what has happened so far?"

"Of course. Why don't you sit down?" Dr. Ford said, pointing to a few chairs in the hallway. Jewel immediately took this as a sign that things were not good. Dr. Ford was a fine-looking older man. He had thick graying hair with no sign of receding. His thin lips pressed together, and his small nose highlighted the deep gray-blue eyes that reflected a compassionate soul. His tall and thin body, although healthy, looked as though it could use a good meal.

Dr. Ford spoke. "May is in the late stages of cancer but she is a tough old bird. Thank God her pain tolerance is high because she would likely be quite sedated at this point. She refuses most drugs, swears that they would alter her state of mind, and so of course, she will have none of that." He appeared to be quite concerned with May's welfare and shrugged as if saying, 'not sure what to do.' Finally, he said, "She ought to remain in hospital—we can take better care of her here. But I do know your aunt and she has a very strong will."

Jewel thought he almost felt sorry for her and shook her head. "I do know what you mean. But May has voiced her opinion about going home. I presume she wants to die at home in the comfort of her quiet life and with her family. I could stay with her this week, although I have an appointment next week with the professor at the university in my hometown. Perhaps I could rebook for the following week," Jewel suggested so that Dr. Ford would release May into her care.

"I would be happy to discharge her as long as I know someone is staying with her 24/7. She shouldn't be living alone at a time like this. We could discharge her as soon as her vitals looks good and the staff can arrange it," he explained.

"Yes, that would be nice. I could care for her, but frankly I don't have any nursing skills," Jewel confessed.

"You would only need the phone number for the hospital. We do have nurses on call for such situations. Right now, all you truly need is compassion and a desire to help," he stated while gently smiling.

"How long does May have, do you suppose?" Jewel knew it had to be asked.

"Not long, perhaps a few weeks, at best a month or two," he sadly replied.

"But she seems so alert and full of spunk. She doesn't appear to have signs of…" Jewel trailed off. "Although she is a little frail compared to what she was a few weeks ago."

"Like I said, she has a very high pain tolerance so we may not be aware of how gravely ill she truly is," he reiterated.

"Of course, you would know best in these circumstances," Jewel said before standing up. They shook hands and said their goodbyes before he repeated that he would be in at the same time tomorrow unless things drastically changed. Jewel sat with May, who slept for another half-an-hour before the nurse came in to check on her vitals.

As soon as May opened her eyes Jewel said with optimism, "Hello, Aunt May. How are you feeling today?"

"Not too shabby, my dear. Can't get proper sleep in this place from the constant nursing around the clock, but other than that I'm holding up well." She said before throwing a little smile at the nurse. Her "room" was a stall with curtains all around, so the constant commotion was extremely bothersome.

"The doctor said you can come home as soon as your vitals are more stable, and the staff can arrange it. Isn't that good news?" Jewel asked as enthusiastically as she could, hoping to cheer May up a bit. She did give a warm smile with the latest remark.

After exchanging warm pleasantries, Jewel informed May that the only way she could speak with the administrator of the nursing home was to schedule an appointment. Her plan today was to pay a visit to the other nursing home on her way back. She also mentioned that Spence was hoping to come up next week, time permitting, and providing all the 'dust settled' enough that he would be able to get away for a few days. This seemed to cheer May even more, and it was this reaction that made Jewel wonder if May's real issue was that she was dying of loneliness. They said goodbye for now, as Jewel would be returning later in the evening.

Driving over to the Canterbury nursing home Jewel noticed a small restaurant, which seemed so inviting that she decided to stop to have a quick bite before her next stop. She ordered the breakfast special, which was *Eggs Benedict*, served with coffee. *What a great way to start her day,* she thought. This was most agreeable.

Once at the nursing home, Jewel asked to see the person in charge. Mrs. Boucher, the administrator was in, but apparently Jewel would have to wait about an hour before she could see her.

"I'll gladly wait," Jewel said and added, "It will give me some time to look around to get a better feel for the home, seeing that my aunt is seeking a nice place to stay." Satisfied that the clerk did not suspect her intentions to snoop, she strolled freely about the place.

She looked around the residents' rooms. But besides many residents being either quite frail or bedridden, there was not much to report. The hour passed rather quickly.

Mrs. Lisa Boucher came to greet her and guided Jewel to her private office. She was an odd-looking woman with eyes that protruded out of their sockets. She had a small mole next to her mouth that did not help in the looks department, but she seemed agreeable enough. She asked Jewel to step into her office. Jewel readily accepted.

"Thank you. I'm currently searching for a home for my aunt. She will soon require a nursing home, and I thought perhaps I would get some information from you. I hope this is all right?"

"Of course. Did anyone recommend us?" Mrs. Boucher asked.

"Not exactly but my aunt did mention she had a friend staying here," Jewel replied.

"And since we have one of the busiest homes in town, you might have to act quickly. Fortunately, we've had a few openings just recently. I could show you the rooms that are available if you have time."

"Yes, by all means let's," Jewel responded.

Lisa rose from her chair and grabbed a couple of keys from the hook behind her desk.

"Please come with me," she said, walking out of the office.

"How much does a room cost these days?" Jewel queried as they headed for the first room. She wanted to appear as genuine as possible.

"That depends on whether you rent the one bedroom with two beds per room, or the single-bed room. Which one does your aunt prefer? Has she told you?"

"I'm not sure, but what would the cost be for the single-bed room, as my aunt dearly loves her privacy?"

"A single-bed room costs twenty-two hundred a month, and a two-bed room is sixteen hundred."

"I see, perhaps the shared room would be more reasonable, although I'll have to speak with my aunt first."

"Naturally."

As Mrs. Boucher opened the door to one of the double-bed rooms, Jewel asked, "How long has this room been available?"

"Not long, less than a month actually."

"Who occupied it?" Jewel knew she was pushing her luck. But how would she ever know unless the questions were asked? She was watching Mrs. Boucher keenly, for any signs of awkwardness or discomfort as she posed her questions.

"It was Mrs. Ginger Ferris. Her husband had passed away last year, and she moved in not long afterwards. Poor thing, she just couldn't cope after losing her husband of forty years. We can only do so much."

"What was her cause of death, if you don't mind me asking? I would think she might have died of a broken heart?"

"I have it on good authority that she died of a bad case of influenza. You know these flu bugs take so many of our elderly each year. How is your aunt's health? Does she have any health issues?"

Jewel knew that Mrs. Boucher was throwing the questions right back at her, probably hoping to change the topic. Her sixth-sense detector was sounding off alarms.

"She's not too good and that's why I am putting arrangements in place to have her looked after and I only want the best for her. I live out of town, so unfortunately, I won't always be at hand for her."

"I do understand," Mrs. Boucher said, nodding. "This would make a lovely home for your aunt."

She looked a little *too* happy as far as Jewel was concerned. She had sensed that Lisa would fall for that disclosure. "You said you had yet another room. Could we also see that one, just in case?"

"By all means. It's down this corridor." She led them around the corner. It was a square shaped floor plan with rooms on both sides of the circular hallway. The one-bed rooms were on the inside of the square while the shared rooms were on the outer side. Made perfect sense, except that the inner square residents did not have much of a view. It seemed wrong to her that it would cost them more for such a poor view, but the upside was that they did not have to share their space with strangers. Jewel also wondered whether husbands and wives typically rented a single room with a queen bed.

"The rooms are very nice, and I did notice a skylight in the smaller rooms. This must at least provide some sun light?"

"It does. We've had many residents feel quite cozy in those rooms."

"I don't know how to ask this question without coming across as... cold or harsh... but do...vacancies come up often? You know... what I mean..." Jewel stammered awkwardly, yet intentionally.

"Yes, unfortunately, we do. But then the majority come to us with many serious preexisting health issues. We operate a very resident-comfort focused facility, but even with all our best intentions, we cannot stop nature and its course. We do what we can."

"I do understand. Well I must be leaving. I can't keep my aunt waiting too long, or she'll be wondering what I'm up to. I just couldn't tell her about my visit here, not yet. I will mention it to her once she recovers a bit more."

"I'd like to give you a brochure about the Canterbury homes, should you decide this is the way to go for her."

"Thank you. I'm grateful for your time today. I can see myself out. Again, thank you very much for showing me around."

"Until we meet again," Mrs. Boucher replied, cracking a smile.

Jewel was leaving the building when a resident stopped her.

"Psst," was all she could hear from his low voice.

"Can I help you?" Jewel whispered back, not knowing what to expect from the gentleman. She dearly hoped he was sane and did not want to talk about his hallucinations or the likes.

"If you're thinking of having someone join this place, think twice," he whispered to her.

"Why do you say that?" Jewel whispered back.

The man looked around before continuing his conversation. "No one lasts very long here," he stated flatly and as quietly as possible.

"I understand. But can we speak discreetly regarding this concern? You name the place," Jewel voiced.

"Sure, dear! Best you name the place and time. I've got nowhere else to be, and time is all I have left," he said with sadness in his eyes.

"We could meet tomorrow if you'd like. I've got to be somewhere tonight, but tomorrow morning around eleven would work for me. I could pick you up, or you could meet me? We could go for brunch if that appeals to you. Would that be all right with you?" Jewel asked.

"That sounds like a date. By the way my name is Fred Fisher." He offered his hand for her to shake.

"And I'm Jewel Seymour. I'll be here at eleven. Will you meet me in the circle out front of the building then?"

"Affirmative, until the morning then." He said before he was off to wherever it was that appealed to him. Jewel was not too sure whether they had any planned activities such as card games, or crafts that one would expect at a nursing home. Mrs. Boucher had not mentioned anything like that while giving her a tour of the premises. Perhaps the brochure would enlighten her.

Jewel drove over to the hospital to visit Aunt May before it was too late in the day to do so. If May had a good day, perhaps she would be able to return home. Jewel could only hope so. She immediately checked with the head nurse on May's progress. Jewel was informed that May was doing fine and if they saw the same, or an improvement tomorrow, she would be discharged. Jewel smiled at the good news.

"Hi, Aunt May." Jewel cheerfully announced after peeking through the curtains.

"There you are. I'd hope you'd stop by," she replied. "Did you get a chance to check out the Canterbury Nursing Home?" May asked, looking optimistic.

"As a matter of fact, I did. And I have to say, you just may have stumbled onto something here, Aunt May. I met an elderly man, Fred Fisher. Do you know him?"

"I believe I met him once, but I don't know him well. What did he have to say?" She was enthused, her face glimmering with hope.

"I'm not sure, but he thinks there is something very strange and troublesome going on in that place. I have a date with him tomorrow for brunch," she giggled knowing Aunt May would get a kick out of that. "He wants to tell me what he knows. He said people don't live long in that place, but that was all he said."

May looked positively delighted. "I knew it! That's good, Jewel. That's really, really good. Excellent work, my Dear!" She seemed lost in her thoughts now.

Jewel took this opportunity to zoom in on the nursing home, Fred in particular, to see what she could pick up. Nothing significant came to mind. She was likely too distracted to get a good fix on the place.

It was getting rather late when Jewel left May—she was sleepy but content. Once back at the house she attempted to call Spence but unfortunately, he did not answer so Jewel was forced to leave him another voicemail. To get to the bottom of this new investigation, she was going to require help.

Exhausted, she quickly undressed for bed, crawled under the covers, and slept.

# Chapter 26

After oversleeping Jewel found herself hurrying out the door. It was unusual for her to sleep through the night without waking, but this whole murder business was beginning to take its toll on her. Meeting with Fred this morning meant she would have to miss her meeting with May's doctor. She knew which meeting Aunt May would prefer she attend, so she carried out with her plans with Fred.

As soon as Jewel pulled up to the entrance of the nursing home, she could see Fred standing outside. The moment the car stopped, the door swung open and Fred jumped in. It was as though he was making a getaway. "Drive, drive, for goodness' sake!" he shouted, looking out the passenger window as though being shadowed.

She grinned at his role-playing—if that was a role—thinking it was just in good humor, something from his glory days. Yet something told her he was not playing games, so she acted on that impulse. Slowing down to merge into traffic, Jewel turned to him. "Look, I'm not your getaway car. I hope you plan on returning." Jewel said, wondering once again what she had just opened the door to—and to her world also.

"I'd rather not, but if I must, I don't expect to live long—not at this place anyway. You'll be reading my life story in the obituaries."

"Do you have family you could call then?"

"Not in town. Though in all honesty, they really think I've lost my marbles. They think I've fallen off my rocker and gone raving mad. It's a damned thing getting old. It seems that all your life you work hard to earn some respect and believability. But as soon as old age creeps in, everything you built gets all washed away like the tide carrying away the rubbish along the beach to a distant shore never to be seen again. How can this happen to an old person? It's not right. It's just not right." Fred raised his arms, exasperated.

"I'm not sure, Fred, but I can definitely relate." If anyone knew what it was like to not be believed, it was Jewel. "For what it's worth, I don't think you're insane so let's get some breakfast in you. We can talk freely about your anxieties once there. Is there a place you have in mind?"

"Why yes. Let's stop at that breakfast place a block or so away from here. They have great pancakes and I have a hankering for some good old fashion food," he replied, gleefully.

Jewel's first observation of Fred was that he seemed a delightful man. He had a prominent straight nose, graying hair and ears that showed his age—long and droopy. He was, by all accounts, a rather good-looking man, and in good shape too for someone his age. "How long have you been staying at the nursing home?"

"Not long, but I'm quite alert for eighty-two, and besides I've been keeping my eye on that place. Couldn't trust anyone right from the start. They need to earn my trust. I have to admit the staff haven't succeeded in that quest yet."

Jewel's concern was Fred's paranoia, wondering if he suffered from some form of dementia. "Yes, I do see that. Here we are," she said as they approached the restaurant entrance. She listened for more clues as to Fred's delusional state, but other than the occasional reference to distrusting everyone at the nursing home, he seemed quick-witted and sharp—on his toes. They were ushered to their table and spent little time ordering the works of pancakes topped with plenty of berries and whipping cream. *A heart attack waiting to happen—that's the saying right?* Jewel thought. But it was not enough to deter her from diving into the stack of pancakes when they arrived.

Jewel initiated the conversation. "Tell me what kind of evidence you have on the nursing home, if you even have any, that is."

"There are too many deaths, even for a nursing home. I've watched what seem like perfectly healthy people entering the home and not long afterwards they start feeling quite poorly. I refuse to eat the food they serve, and instead I order out. Look at me—I'm in top-notch health. Well, maybe I'm not as young as I once was, but top-notch, nevertheless. I think they're poisoning the residents. Why? I don't know. But they're doing it for some reason. One can't be sure. I tried to find out, except I'm afraid if I look too suspicious, I'll be next on the chopping block—if you get my meaning. When I saw you and I got to thinking," he paused to continue eating.

He seemed to have a hearty appetite. The man also appeared quite rational, very much in touch with reality. Intrigued by his information, Jewel asked him to go on.

He started again. "You looked like a nice enough person, and I thought to myself, 'here's a girl who can help.' Besides, I'm a pretty good judge of character." He took a sip of his freshly poured coffee.

Jewel swallowed a mouthful before stating. "But I'm not sure how to proceed from this point without attracting attention to myself. Perhaps the two of us can work together—you on the inside and me on the outside. I think we'd make a good team. How does that sound?" Jewel asked Fred, who appeared more than eager to catch a killer.

"That might work, but frankly, I'm afraid for my life in that blasted place. We would have to work discreetly and be extremely cautious. I suppose it's our only hope. Besides, I don't want to see more residents taken away on a gurney to the morgue."

Jewel added. "I do understand, though frankly, I must warn you, I'm not from around here. I live in Imperial Beach. I'm only here visiting my aunt who's fallen ill. So, I'm not sure what I can do to assist. But while I'm around, I plan on pursuing the matter with the remaining time."

"Lucky for your aunt that she doesn't live at the nursing home," Fred stated. "Does she?" He looked at her inquisitively.

"No, she doesn't," Jewel responded instantly.

"What I don't understand is why, I mean, why somebody would prey on people of my age?" Fred asked. "Seriously we don't have long for this world," he remarked.

"Not sure. Did you know Iris and Ginger? They were apparently residents also."

"I knew Iris, she was a nice lady. Didn't know Ginger though. I've only been there less than six months. They both dead too?"

"Unfortunately, yes. They were my aunt's friends. She's the one who wanted me to look into the matter," Jewel acknowledged.

"I knew it! I can tell who's a snoop." Fred winked at her.

"Was I that obvious?"

"No, but I've got a keen eye for these things."

They both began to laugh at that remark, and his larger-than-life spectacles perched on his nose, he was comical too. He reminded Jewel of Columbo, a detective, who, by all appearances, did not seem very bright, but always got the job done in such a way that the criminals did not see him coming. They assumed he was too dumb to catch them, but that was his brilliance. Maybe there was some

'Colombo' in Fred? Who knows? Stranger things had transpired in her world!

Thankfully, Jewel had not detected any sign of dementia, nor psychosis. He may be paranoid for good reason. So, to Jewel, so far, he appeared quite believable.

With a smile on her face, she continued. "I think we can get along just fine. Now… regarding your safety."

He nodded, "I'm not sure how to stay alive. Who knows? Maybe I'm next to die," he admitted without qualms. "But at our age who would ever suspect a suspicious death—by whatever means they employ—poisoning possibly?"

"Maybe we should be getting some help, but I don't know anyone around these parts. My aunt or my friend Spence Walker, who happens to be a detective back home, might be able to recommend someone—somebody trustworthy that we can call upon, should things get out of control, that is? And by the way, my friend had mentioned a local detective, but the name has slipped my mind unfortunately.

"I would definitely feel better if you could arrange something," Fred gladly agreed.

"I've already put in a call to Spence but haven't heard back. After I drop you off, I'll be visiting my aunt. Perhaps she will have an idea. She may be old, but she still has all her faculties," Jewel revealed.

"Good. How about we meet up tomorrow afternoon?"

"That could work. How can I reach you without raising eyebrows? I have to be able to call you," Jewel asked.

"I have a cell phone, but rarely turn it on. My son gave it to me for Father's Day. Let me find the number. I have it written down somewhere in my wallet." He reached in his back pocket, pulling out a worn leather wallet to search through for his cell number.

"Here it is. Write this down, will you? I told them to give me an easy number to remember but I still forget. Who remembers their own phone number?" he confessed, chuckling to himself.

"I know what you mean. I've now got it written down and I'll call tomorrow with a time in the afternoon," Jewel said, as they were getting up to leave.

"Let's get going then. I'll miss my afternoon movie. They're playing a John Wayne movie, you know."

"Certainly. I'll pay and we can be out of here in a few minutes." Jewel smiled at Fred's last remark regarding his rush to watch a favorite movie.

She dropped Fred off at the front gate before heading over to the hospital to check on Aunt May's status. Jewel did not hesitate to call Professor Brown to cancel next week's scheduled appointment. It was a bit disappointing but spending quality time with May was more important and likely of greater value than revisiting her past.

The hospital seemed so somber after spending time at the restaurant. Smiling, Jewel entered May's room. "How goes the battle with the Gestapo staff?" she asked.

"If one could only get rest in this forsaken place..." May grumbled. "And be left to my own devices, I would actually get well enough to walk out of here. Did you see my doctor? He just left."

"I'm terribly sorry, but I haven't seen him. What did he say?"

"That I could go home, even though he wished I would stay a little longer. I told him that you were staying with me. Besides this place never sleeps," May complained.

"If you'd like to get ready, I'll check with the nurse to see whether we can leave the hospital."

"Good, I'd like that very much. Could you reach into the closet to fetch my clothes?"

"Of course, I can." Jewel replied, as she reached inside the closet and pulled out the clothes hanging in the small locker. "Here you go. I'm going to check with the nurse so don't hurry. I can help you dress when I return. We do have all afternoon you know."

After checking with the nurse, Jewel also made the necessary arrangements for May's discharge, signing a few documents. Upon returning to May's room, Jewel found her aunt ready—actually raring to go. On the way home, Aunt May pointed out many of the residences in Canterbury and a few historical spots to visit, should they get the chance.

Once they arrived at the house, Jewel retrieved May's small bag from the backseat, helped her out of the car and followed her inside.

"It's such a good feeling to be home again. I dearly missed my quiet house," May said, a delightful smile on her face. She could not be more pleased if she had won the lottery.

"Perhaps we can order out tonight so we can relax without worrying about cooking. How does that sound?" Jewel offered.

"An excellent idea. But first I'd like to take a nap if you don't mind," she said, looking rather exhausted.

"Why would I mind? Please, Aunt May, do not worry about me. You need to take care of yourself. I'll bring your bag into the room, shall I? You sleep the afternoon away, but first, I would like to ask you a question. Why don't I make a cup of sweet tea for us and we can sit for five minutes before you go rest?" Jewel asked while peering at May.

"Of course," May agreed, before lowering herself on the antique sofa and heavily exhaling.

After retrieving the tea and setting May's cup beside her on the end table, Jewel started speaking. "I met up with Fred Fisher this morning. He's a resident at the Canterbury Nursing Home. He would like a contact name in case things turn for the worse. Do you know any cops, or perhaps a detective we could trust?"

"I knew one, but he's long dead now. He did have a partner but I'm afraid I can't remember his name off-hand."

"That's all right. I've put in another call to Spence this morning. Perhaps he knows someone," Jewel said.

May appeared a little confused and knew she ought to get some rest. "Will he be coming here then?"

"Not sure yet. I'll call him again once you get settled into bed."

"I'm going. Don't start being bossy like those nurses, I'm still shell-shocked." May half grinned.

"I'm sorry. Of course. I just want you to get better, soon."

"I know, child, but you do realize I'm not really getting better, simply delaying the eventuality of an end."

"You know what I meant. Let's not rush things since I'm here and we're going to spend as much time together before that ill-fated day arrives." Jewel swallowed hard.

"I'll be resting. Please help yourself to whatever it is you need," she said before turning towards her bedroom.

Once the door to her room was closed, Jewel called Spence. With great relief he answered promptly.

"Spence, it's nice to finally hear your voice. Aunt May is home, and I'll be staying for a week or two. Yes, I'll tell her, but first I need a favor. Do you know a good cop or detective out here? You do? That's great! I'll take his name down—Ted Howard you said? Is he the very same one you mentioned before?" Jewel questioned.

"That's fine. Thank you." Jewel quickly wrote the name down. "Did you find out when you can come for a short visit? That's wonderful! I'll be seeing you this weekend then. Friday evening sounds great. I'll talk to you soon. Take care." She hung up with Spence but immediately called the police station to talk with Ted. Spence had mentioned that he was good, though about to retire himself. The call went to voicemail but there were no details as to when he would be in again. Jewel left her name and number and requested a callback.

The next call she made was to the professor to reschedule their meeting upon her return. He expressed his regrets regarding Jewel's aunt before hanging up.

May and Jewel took it extremely easy for the next few days. Jewel met up with Fred once, but only after she contacted Detective Ted Howard. She immediately passed on Fred's name to Ted, relaying the old man's fears that his life was in danger while staying at the nursing home. Just as they had both anticipated, Ted immediately downgraded the matter as being the rantings of a paranoid old fellow. If not for Jewel's persistence that he was quite sane, Ted would have likely dismissed their concerns entirely. Instead, Ted promised to investigate the matter should Fred ever contact him and present any valid proof of these life-threatening allegations. Jewel was not content with this, but she understood. After all, neither she nor Fred had so much as an ounce of proof to support their claim of foul play in what they believed were mysterious deaths. With or without law enforcement support, they were determined to proceed with what they had, which amounted to hunches and suspicions. Sadly, acquiring proof would likely mean there would be more upcoming deaths—a most disturbing thought to say the least—but it was the propellant they needed to keep digging.

May seemed to be in high spirits during the latter part of the week. She seemed to beam with happiness. Jewel dearly hoped for more time, even though cancer was eating away at May's body. Naturally with Spence arriving the following afternoon, they would have more to talk about—again this would fill in her time—plus, he would be an excellent diversion from May's pain management regimen. Just last evening, May had voiced that having Spence look into these untimely deaths and resolving the case before further murders could occur, gave her a strong desire to continue living, which to Jewel was a positive thing.

On Friday they both went to the small airport to pick up Spence, who was arriving at four that afternoon. When last speaking with him, he sounded relieved to have a week off. But would he have time to relax? Jewel was afraid to ask him to do more but that would not prevent Aunt May from asking. Spence would soon realize that he really did not have a choice. *Next time he'll have to take his holidays in the Bahamas*, Jewel mused. But they both knew May had so little time left and that they needed to maximize it and make the absolute best of it while they were still all together.

As Spence approached the gate, Jewel shouted, "There he is, Aunt May!" They rushed over to him. Jewel noticed that Spence still had a pronounced limp from the gunshot wound to his leg.

"Good to see you, May," Spence said. He hugged her first before approaching Jewel and with gentleness he hugged her also.

"How goes the battle?" he asked. But then regretted the question once it had left his mouth.

"I'm holding on, although I'm very happy you could take time to have an official visit," May put in with appreciation.

They left the airport and stopped for takeout—delicious rotisserie chicken with salads for supper—and quickly headed for the house. They were having so much fun belly-laughing while reminiscing at days gone by with Marcy, that it was not long before they arrived at May's residence. The pain of losing her had eased enough for the trio to go down memory lane of the good times they had shared.

Most disappointingly, but quite understandably, May grew very weary around seven so Spence and Jewel bid her goodnight. After helping her to bed, Jewel sat up with Spence for several hours. They talked about the ongoing case at home among other matters before Jewel broached the subject to assist with another investigation—Aunt May's last request.

Once Jewel had explained her concerns regarding May's suspicions, she was confident he would look into her allegations, and hopefully, point her in the right direction toward solving the mystery. Yawning several times, both retired for the night. Spence took the couch and Jewel headed to the spare bedroom. She had weird feelings about Spence, but clearly knew they were well beyond that stage. She shook them off. Jewel thought, *I'm sure he's over this. Perhaps he's from my past life, another lifetime.* Yet deep down she had deeper feelings for him than she wanted to admit.

Jewel tossed and turned the night away. At one point she nearly went in search of Spence but refused to give in to her curiosity. Morning had come soon enough. She knew that she had to make the best of their time together, so waking up early, she went to make everyone a hearty breakfast.

After breakfast, they both left Aunt May to rest while they visited the nursing home hoping to interview Fred Fisher. He was only too happy to oblige. Not wanting to raise any eyebrows, they decided to take Fred out for coffee.

Jewel felt compelled to ask. "How did the week go for you?"

"Not too bad. I'm alive, aren't I?" Fred grinned.

"That you are. Detective Walker is here for the week. We hope to get as much information gathered while he's here."

"That's great! I couldn't be happier. I have something for you also." Fred pulled out a wad of something wrapped up in tissue paper and sealed in a plastic bag. "This is last night's dinner. I've been holding onto it each night in hopes that you would come by to see me," he claimed.

"I'm sorry, Fred, but with my aunt feeling poorly, I've not been able to see you, you do understand, don't you? Now that we're here, we'll take that from you. Has anyone died this week?" Jewel asked.

"No, but they might be adding just enough to make one ill without killing them. It would raise too much suspicion if everyone dropped dead all at once, wouldn't it?" Fred shrugged.

"You could be right. We will send..." as she stared at the contents, "this out for analysis. If any trace amounts of poison are present, they will certainly find it. Now we must get you back before they find you missing." Jewel suggested while throwing a glance in Spence's direction. He nodded in agreement.

The food sample analysis results came back rather quickly and showed no traces of poison. *Maybe they only add poison at certain times to certain individuals,* Jewel wondered. *Or, perhaps this was not a case involving poison at all."*

The week flew by without any confirmation of their suspicions. Spence had to leave by Saturday night, but met with Ted Howard to catch up on their years of detective drudgery.

Aunt May had seemed much happier in their company. Perhaps their visit had helped. Jewel wondered whether May would continue feeling well or decline rapidly after they left. She promised to visit next week so she would assess her health status then.

After saying their tearful goodbyes, Spence and Jewel hopped into the taxicab they had dispatched and rode back to the airport together. Finally alone, Spence agreed to talk about the case during their flight home. They both got down to business on the case shortly after takeoff. Most passengers were seated far enough away from them to not overhear their discussion. They spoke quietly.

"Both Brock Simms and Bill Casey were formally charged with the murders of three girls and the attempted murder of Tina Miles, and the two of us." Spence briefed Jewel. "We should have him on the death of the three teens, though they're not confessing to these murders. This would be a clear conviction if we can get them to admit to their crimes. We do have enough evidence to tie them to your capture, and the attempted murder of an officer of the law," Spence pointed to his leg, "which brings a stiff penalty. They will likely spend a very long time in prison. Perhaps several consecutive life sentences, especially since Bill Casey was a police officer supposedly upholding the law. The courts will not look kindly on Casey for his part in the crimes. You are aware that you will be called to testify against the suspects. Although I empathize with May's condition, frankly I'm not sure how you will manage being in two places at the same time. You, being a key witness, the courts will summon you to testify. How are you going to deal with this?" He asked, looking rather concerned.

"I'm not too sure. I wonder whether Mrs. Miles could assist with May's care, because honestly, I can't think of anyone else I would trust to take care of her. May has made it clear she will not return to the hospital." She paused. She still had some qualms about that little problem. "But as far as the courts are concerned, yes, of course I will fulfill my duty. I also have several names I would like you to check on the database to see whether they have criminal records or pending warrants." Jewel raised a shoulder as though questioning. "Could you do this? I'm quite aware how busy you are with the upcoming trial, but it would mean a great deal to Aunt May."

The plane landed and after the usual routine at the airport, they shared a cab ride to Jewel's residence. Spence got out of the cab to hug Jewel and kissed her on the cheek. He climbed back in and left.

Being so close to Spence had stirred up many suppressed and unresolved feelings. As quickly as possible she needed to deal with these feelings since they were interfering with her ability to remain focused on the issues at hand, especially when she was in Spence's presence. Why now and with so much happening?

Sunday was spent paying a few bills online and Jewel scribbled herself a note to call the professor to confirm their appointment for noon tomorrow. She settled in for the evening. She was looking forward to meeting with him so they could resume their work together.

# Chapter 27

Spence arrived home with renewed energy to ensure the killers stayed behind bars. And now with another mystery brought forth by May, he quickly unpacked thinking he had to ensure more lives were not at risk. He despised leaving Jewel alone to deal with yet another mystery considering how ill her Aunt May had become, and yet, he was extremely busy with the courts. It was unfortunate that he could not stay longer since he rather enjoyed being near Jewel.

*She seemed different lately,* he thought. Was there a twinkle in her eye that he had once seen returning now? He could not be certain. He knew there was nothing he would not do for her, even though she would never date him again—of that he *was* certain. That ship had clearly sailed years ago after their break-up, and knowing Jewel for as long as he had, he was certain she would never entertain the idea of getting back together.

As much as he cared about her, it frustrated him to no end that Jewel's internal radar, for inexplicable reasons, always seemed to effortlessly zoom in on trouble. He resigned himself that he could not deal with other cases—especially unofficial ones not even in his own jurisdiction—while the case against Brock and Casey was ongoing.

After meeting her in Canterbury, Spence felt that having the occasional meetings together was great, but he also felt the few days together had been rather strained. He finally acknowledged to himself that he really was still hung up on Jewel, despite having tried to convince himself otherwise.

Every time they worked on something together, all he could think about was keeping her out of harm's way, and at this point, he had no means of accomplishing that. Especially with how goddamned headstrong she was, risking her own neck the way she did all the time! He would feel so much better, much more capable of doing his own work if she would just listen to him sometimes— he was an exceptionally good cop, but she still did not trust him to protect her. *I gather that's her stuff, not mine,* he thought to himself.

Years ago, he swore to serve and protect, but found he was unable to protect the one person he loved. Yes, loved! He was not ashamed to admit it, and, it had been the primary reason Spence had put distance between them years ago. Regardless he still felt compelled to be near her. Why could they not understand the dynamics of this fatal attraction they had between them? He simply could not understand why this tension existed between them, nor why he always felt so directed to do everything in his power to protect her.

Presently, another killer required his mental energy and he felt more empowered doing something in which he excelled than trying to figure this out. Women were a playing field that caused him more anguish than he was prepared to deal with.

On the other hand, he felt that he was getting close to wrapping things up with the last case, so maybe he truly should consider devoting more time to assisting May with her suspicions regarding the ongoing fatalities of her friends. It could potentially be a win-win situation that would be beneficial to all concerned: he could spend more time with Jewel and May without neither of them being the wiser.

During the investigation involving Brock and Casey, they had initially thought Brock was the trailblazer. But after numerous interrogations and interviews with various witnesses, Spence was under the impression there had to be someone else running this outfit. Or, perhaps there were many involved. This was much bigger than what he had initially thought. With a gut feeling about this, he knew he would have to outsmart a highly intelligent predator. Interestingly, Spence had noticed a heightened sensitivity within him after awaking in that hospital bed. He had chosen not to share it with anyone until he had a better idea himself as to what he was experiencing. The thing is, that since then, somehow, he knew things, or was it that his thoughts seemed clearer than before? He could not quite pin it down.

Perhaps there was something more profound about near death experiences than he had originally, and officially, thought. All he knew was that he seemed more attuned to his surroundings and 'his feelings' than ever before in his life. He was discovering that he could not turn it off, so his only option was to integrate it all somehow—something his methodological mind was having quite the challenge computing.

Regrettably, none of his leads had been successful to date. Yet he was determined to put these sick individuals behind bars with or without the mastermind.

What bothered him was that his sixth sense kept nudging him that there was some truth behind these deaths that May had brought to his attention. He had received strong hunches that somehow there was a connection between the Otay Mesa murders and the deaths of the residents in nursing homes in Canterbury, yet that seemed incredulous. Impossible. Yet he could not turn them off.

It had already been late in the evening by the time he arrived home and he desperately needed sleep. His mind was abuzz with possibilities and sleeping proved to be difficult. When sleep finally did overcome his senses, he began to dream about Jewel.

In this dream, Spence was experiencing the stirring up of his deeply suppressed feelings for Jewel. But she was there haunting his ever-sensual feelings. He felt a longing that could not be erased no matter how desperately he wanted to rid himself of the love he once felt for her. He knew full well he could not revisit his desires, those unwanted longings that continually drove him back to her.

He should have waited for Jewel to be ready to marry him when he had the chance, but that was years ago. Instead he resigned himself to protect her, to keep her away from all the violence. She was continually entangled in the life of a sleuth, regardless of his strong views against it, and this had played a huge role in his decision not to wait for her. How could he do his job as a detective, in a world of crime while also protecting her 24/7? It was an impossible endeavor, so he decided that his life was better devoting his talents to just one master.

And maybe there was more at play that prevented him from marrying her. Yes, his credibility in the eyes of his peers and the public. Being an officer of the law, how could he possibly marry a psychic? Someone who communicated with and channeled the dead—a medium. Could she not choose another profession, another career in which to help people? How many people believe in psychics, truly?

And what about *her* credibility and accuracy? Many times, he had doubted Jewel's ability to speak with the dead. He recognized that a future with Jewel would not be easy and it weighed heavily on his final decision to remain single.

The dream had amplified for him that it was all this that plagued him with constant regret. To not be with the one woman that had stirred so much passion in him was difficult. If only to protect her, he would need to stay near, especially now that she seemed more determined than ever to seek her own dangerous path through life. A life over which he would never have control. Did it have to be this way?

Always smartly dressed in a dark gray or navy suit with a white shirt, Spence had a few meetings to attend. He looked at his watch. He had one more appointment today and he would have to run if he were to make it on time. It was an important meeting involving an interview with a former acquaintance of Brock's. Very few people were willing to speak about this man, which made his investigation that much more difficult. He rushed out the door and sped to his appointment.

Driving always put him in a pensive state. Spence thought of yesterday's sleepless night. He had spent another night tossing and turning, unable to get Jewel out of his mind. His last visit with her had stirred more than he was able to bear right now. He desperately needed to focus on this case. Besides, he doubted Jewel would ever allow love into her heart again. Or would she? He was in agony again—between hope and doubt.

Spence needed to get into Brock's mind if he had any hope of understanding how this stone-cold killer, with no regard for life, functioned. He had to be fully present to pick up any subtle hints, shifts in his energy, facial expressions, body language, and nuances of any kind that would afford him a glimpse in this man's life and inside his mind. He wanted Brock to spend an eternity in a hellish prison cell, no bigger than six by six. What could have created such a monster?

He was far too tired to find the answer, but Spence did know a few facts regarding Brock. He knew that he had many classic signs of being a psychopath, although this cult fellowship was a twist that made him more unpredictable, if that were possible.

Psychopaths have many tendencies to get their pleasures—from total control over another, to watching their victim tremble and squirm in their presence, and the power to have them kneel before them—while being totally devoid of compassion and feelings. They are particularly good at grooming their victims to fulfill their every wish, but out of fear rather than devotion. Put someone like him in charge, and you have a recipe for murder. Brock had the tendencies to obsess over his insatiable desires. This sort of obsession drives the psychopath to act on any disconnected thought until he gets what he wants—usually total domination or destruction. They are usually highly intelligent, but their obsession drives them to make mistakes. And this was the opportunity Spence was waiting for: Brock's vulnerability.

Arriving at his destination in perfect timing, Spence entered the lobby of the Grand Hotel to meet with Burt Campbell. He had known Brock years ago and could indeed provide further insights as to what was really going on in his warped mind. Building a case against Brock was crucial. Spence did not want to lose sight of the fact that this man was a danger to society and needed to be incarcerated for his acts. There was no room for error. Brock could not be released from custody on a minor technicality, or worse, insufficient evidence. No, putting him away for good was the department's prime objective. Therefore, Spence would dig up every piece of evidence, follow every lead he obtained with meticulous precision, and not resting until the case was closed. He spotted Campbell at the far side of the room, sitting alone with a drink in hand. Spence made his way across the floor past a few other patrons.

"You must be Mr. Campbell," Spence asked, extending his hand to shake Burt's.

Burt Campbell rose to shake Spence's firm hand and then sat down again. He appeared to have the weight of the world on his shoulders, a telltale sign that he had serious reservations about working with the police.

"I'm very pleased you found the time to meet with me and appreciate you coming forward," Spence said, sitting across from the man.

"I daresay I almost cancelled, you know. But I knew this meeting was quite important to you, and made the effort," Burt replied. "Would you like a drink, Detective Walker?"

"No, but a coffee would be nice," Spence said. He desperately needed caffeine after last night's sleepless ordeal.

"Yes, of course. You're on duty." Burt signaled the waitress and asked her to bring a coffee for his guest. "So what information are you looking for because honestly, I haven't spent much time with Brock in the last five years if not longer."

"Any information about his behavior would be helpful. We're building a case against him," Spence paused. "So, any unusual behavior and character descriptions would assist us." Spence's gaze was riveted on Burt's face.

"Yes, I've heard. Small town and all," he paused. "Quite aware of everyone's business. Was it you that he shot then?"

"It was. And I'm determined to keep him from hurting anyone else," Spence replied.

"Don't blame you. And those poor girls, it's a dreadful business. I really don't envy your job. Now let me see. How far back do you want me to go?"

The waitress put Spence's coffee in front of him before he could answer. She left them. "Any information from the time you knew him would be useful. Go as far back as you can remember," Spence urged, sipping on the hot brew.

"Let me see. We used to chum around together, but that was ten, or fifteen years ago. We only began to spend time together in our mid-twenties while attending college. Brock had charm and charisma that drew people to him. You could say it was almost hypnotic. He wasn't easy to say no to, but things began to go weird. Like he was nice one day and the next he was so controlling to the point where you wanted to escape his clutches. He would draw great pleasure in seeing how far he could push a person. You wanted to please him of course, so you took on most dares he threw at you. Though one time I saw him kill a cat. In a fit of rage, he beat the poor creature to death. Now that disturbed me to no end. The creature had done nothing to provoke him, nothing I saw. And that was the beginning of putting distance between us. He showed no remorse for what he did either, just laughed at his prowess. I couldn't see myself spending time with someone who could destroy a life. That certainly wasn't the way my parents had raised me. But for Brock, he was a tough cookie and we always knew that." Burt swirled his whiskey and emptied the glass.

"Who are 'we'? Were there many others that hung around?" Spence asked.

"Yes, of course. There were others, but they weren't really friends of mine except for Virginia. She and I were going out at the time. It was at her insistence that I break ties with Brock, but in all honesty, I had already come to that conclusion. She said he gave her the creeps. So, I distanced myself from him, which was the best thing.

"But I ran into him once and he invited me over for a drink. I'm not even sure why I went over, I guess it was curiosity. I had hoped he had changed for the better, I suppose. But as soon as I knocked on the door, I was sorry I had gone. He seemed pleasant enough at first, and asked me to come in. He was dressed all in black with a black cape on his back. If it had been near Halloween, I wouldn't have thought much about the outfit. But it was still summer. And once I entered, I glanced in another room right across from me as I sat at the kitchen table. I had declined the beer and told him I couldn't stay, that I had only stopped to say hello. He seemed disappointed with my response. I only stayed for about ten minutes, long enough to witness some candles lit up in the next room, a circle drawn on the floor, and what looked like some type of animal skull with horns, like a goat, facing us from the opposite side of the room. It stared right at me, gave me the creeps, as though it were the devil itself. God, I couldn't wait to get out of there. It must have been some type of occult shit, I'm not sure, but it was looking like an idol of some kind. When the doorbell rang, I made my exit before I was dragged into something from hell. It was another person that used to hang around with us and I bid my farewells before rushing out."

"By any chance, do you know the new arrival's name, and perhaps their whereabouts?"

"Yes, it was Bill Casey. He arrived with another person, Lynn Williamson. She was a local girl that had left about six months later. But frankly, I'm not sure where she disappeared to."

"That's alright. Do you have an address for her?"

"She lived at the old Mason's building. It wasn't an apartment building back then, but a grand house nonetheless, and quite luxurious for its day. She lived in the attic. But after that day, I steered clear from the lot of them. I saw Brock on a few occasions but kept my distance. He seemed to dress and looked weirder over the years. There was a lot of talk about his dress and demeanor, which seemed to evolve crueler over time. So, it's no wonder people, who could help themselves, stayed away." He paused. "Well I'm afraid that's all I can share with you because any more would be hearsay, and I won't be able to help with that."

"No, you've been most helpful in building a better profile on him. So, this must have been a gradual change over the past fifteen years?"

"Yes, but people do change. We can only hope for the better, however most changes are not for the best, usually. Instead they simply get grumpier with growing years. Perhaps disgruntled at their wasted years," Burt concluded. He raised his empty glass as though considering whether to buy another whiskey.

"I should make my way back to the station. I appreciate you coming forward and all the way to Imperial Beach for this interview. I know it was quite out of your way. Have you always lived in Otay Mesa County?" Spence asked, as he and Burt stood to leave.

"Yes, I have. I wanted to leave a few times, but life's events prevented me from doing so." The two men then shook hands before Spence departed the hotel lounge. He glanced quickly at Burt and he indeed ordered another drink.

Spence knew he would have to make another trip to Otay Mesa County, although he had an uncomfortable reluctance to do so. The memories of his last experience there ran through his mind and the corresponding feelings rushed into his body like a poison entering his veins, paralyzing him with fear. He refocused.

Spence needed to find out whether there were more people involved in these abductions and murders. He needed to find a partner to work with and head out there—someone he knew was entirely trustworthy. But at this point whom could he trust?

# Chapter 28

Suddenly Jewel awoke frightened to death with her heart pounding as though it were outside her body. In the dream she was sixteen—nearly twenty years ago today—when her world had come tumbling down around her. There he was: the first boy to break her teenage heart—the young man she had dated for only a short while. He was twenty-one and much wiser than her. For Jewel, there had been an intense attraction—a one-sided affair it seemed. She thought she knew the man in her dreams from somewhere in time, but from where exactly, she could not say. If Jewel had known the sorrow that would follow their interlude, would she have taken a different path? Perhaps. The thought of that senseless pain at such a tender age was too excruciating to consider at present.

Instead she pushed aside her concerns and rose from her bed to make it to her last session with the professor before returning to Aunt May's.

Unfortunately, her previous session with the professor had not produced substantial results. Her aunt's death was imminent, yet Jewel had not received any premonitions regarding the actual day. She needed to return to Canterbury—and the sooner the better.

Unable to sleep before four AM last night, Jewel sluggishly prepared a light breakfast. Knowing that she would not have time to eat before dinner, she forced food down. Jewel looked forward to seeing Professor Brown and with this visit he may obtain some crucial answers—at least she hoped he would. She giggled at the thought of her withdrawal symptoms when she did not get her 'fix' to delve into her past, if only to resolve the growing uncertainties.

On her drive to the university, Jewel found herself contemplating last night's dream. Anthony was a dashing young man, reminding her of the most debonair man she had ever seen, more handsome than any movie star, and to her, much more charming. Their relationship did not last long, however at the time, it was one of sheer happiness. Every time she saw him, her heart would flutter like a schoolgirl. She found herself in unknown territory. Her father had not prepared her for this type of romance and what followed. Jewel secretly met with Anthony on numerous occasions. Looking back, she now realized how unwise it had been, but she needed to be near him as much as she needed the air she breathed.

Everyone remembers their first love. And those who claim they do not, have probably spent years wrestling with memories that threatened to flood their senses. There was an exception: those who married their first love and were still in love every day. How Jewel envied those who found true love with their soul mate without a devastating breakup. How truly blessed they were!

Awakening to the pain of her first heartache still haunting her memory, Jewel suspected it might be the topic of her next session with the professor. Just when she was certain she had put the whole fiasco of her youthful romance to rest, here it was revisiting her again. There seemed to be a connection to her reemerging feelings for Spence—that somehow, they had reawakened this chapter.

Jewel arrived a few minutes late and hoped that Professor Brown would not be annoyed. It was unlike her to be late for their meetings and she never wanted to miss any of her sessions. He knew that. These insecure, unsettling emotions churning her world inside out were more than she wanted to feel right now, especially after last night's disturbing dream of betrayal.

Jewel knocked gently at his door, but when there was no answer, she knocked harder. Still nothing. Perhaps the professor had not stuck around for her tardy arrival. It would serve her right for being late for her session. She tried the door handle, and to her surprise, the knob turned easily. With the door unlocked, Jewel entered but she did not find the professor inside. She scanned around for a note. There on his desk was a pink sticky note. She immediately went around the desk to read the message.

*Jewel: Went out for coffee. Will be back in a few minutes.*
*Have a seat and make yourself comfortable.*
*——Prof. Brown*

She wished she, too, had taken the time to pick up a coffee. Perhaps under hypnosis it was unwise to drink caffeine anyways. She did as she was advised and sat comfortably in her usual recliner chair. It was not long before the professor returned, entering the room with a coffee in hand. With the aroma of vanilla bean coffee floating about the quaint office, Jewel could not help longing for one.

"Good morning," the professor said when he entered the room.

"I was quite anxious to begin this morning's session," apologizing for being a few minutes late. "Though I can see you've taken advantage of the time afforded," Jewel smiled.

"Indeed," was the only word spoken that he offered before sitting down in his own well-worn, leather chair. He wore his usual gray suit with a regular tie that matched his eyes. He appeared a little disheveled from their previous meetings, however. Jewel wondered why. She was inclined to ask but decided against it. They proceeded to make small talk before beginning the session. Jewel had informed him that after this session, she would be taking a break to finish some business with her aunt.

He nodded in agreement. "We must take advantage of today then, so let's go back in time to see about your love life. Now we will begin to go back," he said before beginning the countdown.

Jewel remembered counting back and then found herself in another time, another place.

~

Meanwhile Aunt May was dealing with her own pain. Quite aware that her time on Earth was coming to an end, she promised herself that she would hang on until these murders stopped and those involved were all behind bars—even if it meant she had to do it alone. Her first order of business: to pay Fred a visit to ask a few questions regarding the goings-on over at his nursing home. *Perhaps Fred knew how her former companions had spent their last few days.*

Soon, she arrived at the Canterbury Nursing Home. Introducing herself as Jewel's aunt, Fred was only too happy to receive a visitor. He took her to the dining room to pour them coffees and helped himself to some cookies that were left out on a serving tray.

"Please sit down," Fred instructed while pointing to the chair. He placed the cookies on a napkin before pulling out a chair for May.

She gladly accepted his assistance especially since she had not the energy to stand for long. She knew she ought to be resting at home as instructed, but duty called. She was not one to lie around—waiting at death's door when something needed completing.

"Thank you. I would have come sooner. My health has not been too good of late." She waved it off like it could be shoved aside.

"Not to worry. It's a pleasure to meet you. Your niece spoke highly of you. It's unfortunate that she had to return to Imperial Beach so soon. Do you know when she'll return?"

"I haven't heard. I'm sure she will return as soon as possible." May smiled with that thought.

"Yes, of course. So, what can I do for you today?" Fred questioned, as his curiosity was running wild.

"Jewel told me that you knew Iris. I was wondering if you had any information regarding her last few days. You know, I was supposed to dine with her that day, but I wasn't feeling well so we decided to reschedule our luncheon. It would have been our last time together." Aunt May spoke, but she was quite distressed with tears beginning to form.

"So sorry for your loss," he swallowed. "But I think we should whisper." Fred pointed to one of the surveillance cameras nearest to them. "I'm sorry to disappoint you—I didn't know her all that well. But, May…, something strange is going on around here based on how many residents have died in the last few months. Were you good friends with Iris then?" Fred continued in an even quieter whisper now, almost inaudible.

May Applebee had to lip-read what he said. "I was her good friend, and I dearly miss her. I think something is up also. I wish I knew what, though. And why. Do you suspect someone in particular?" May inquired.

Fred looked around suspiciously before leaning closer to May. "I'm thinking the person in charge here has a hand in it—but I think there may be others involved also. They have the most opportunity and, motives." He whispered in such a low voice it was becoming increasingly difficult for May to hear him from across the table.

"I see. Well, opportunity I can understand, but motive is another thing. I haven't the foggiest notion why anyone would have to short-change someone with little time they have left. Now that I'm living on borrowed time, I really appreciate each day, although I must say that losing my friends has made life painfully long all at the same time," May admitted.

"You can't mean that," Fred replied, somewhat astonished.

"I'm sorry for my seemingly depressive mood. The one drive I have left is to find the SOB responsible for my friends' early deaths. So, I must somehow rid society of whoever is doing this, otherwise, he or they will go unpunished," May stated emphatically. "No one deserves to have their life taken away from them. I hope to obtain valuable information to imprison these bastards for a good long time and bring justice to my friends' memory." May sounded angry now, her cheeks flushed.

"I would like nothing better than to stop this madness myself. I'll keep a closer watch on the director and Mrs. Boucher. They stand to gain more than meets the eye," Fred added. He patted her hand while comforting May. Fred liked the spunkiness of this woman. How unfortunate they had not met before this, when life seemed much more promising. Together, they likely would have been one of those power couples that people respected and admired. But Fred had always made the best of things and his philosophy still applied now.

May suddenly felt faint. "I'm afraid this dreadful business has upset me and…," May paused. "I must be getting back," she stated, pulling her hand back to hold herself from toppling over.

"Of course. Allow me to escort you to your car," Fred replied, rising from his chair.

"No, I came by cab. I wouldn't mind an escort to the front lobby where I can call for one. Thank you, Fred." May frowned. What she needed to do, and quickly, was to lie down somewhere. It was so unlike her to feel so poorly—try as she may, she could not shake this feeling of weakness and could not regain her centeredness. Fred remarked that she was as white as a ghost.

"It would be my pleasure but are you certain you'll be all right?"

"Of course. I'm stronger than I look," May replied.

"Indeed, you are," Fred agreed, as he offered his arm.

Once both reached the front lobby, May picked up the phone, and called a cab. "That's that then. We may as well take advantage of these comfortable chairs until my cab arrives. They said it would be about ten minutes," she sighed. But it was not long before a cab pulled up to the front entrance.

"When will I see you again?" Fred questioned.

"I'm not sure. It would be nice to have you over for tea."

"I would love that. When could I call upon you?" Fred said, responding eagerly to her invitation.

"How about in a day or two?"

"Then let's make it tomorrow, that is, if this is all right with you?" Fred asked. He had enjoyed this intriguing woman's company, but he felt a strong sense of responsibility that he should begin checking up on her regularly—at least until Jewel returned.

"Most certainly. Waiting to die can be a boring business," May quipped.

"I do say, my dear, you must not become discouraged, nor be too eager to meet your Maker either."

"You're quite right and I apologize for my downcast attitude. I look forward to your visit tomorrow." May replied, taking great pleasure in having a good-looking man pay her a social call. It had been far too long since she could look forward to such an occasion.

Fred rose to escort her to the parked taxi, ensuring she was seated securely inside the vehicle.

# Chapter 29

Spence attempted to reach Jewel but was unable to do so. He would have preferred traveling to Otay Mesa County with her, although he had serious reservations of putting her in harm's way. Instead he contacted Detective Stone to ask for him to accompany him. Stone could not get away due to the ongoing pressure to resolve this seemingly difficult case, so he arranged for a trusted, fellow officer to join Spence on his assignment to question Lynn Williamson.

At 10:00 am sharp the following morning, Spence picked up Officer O'Brien. They hoped to return before nightfall. They made small talk about the case before arriving in Otay Mesa County. The officers parked in front of the woman's last known place of residence, according to the database. Spence scanned the area. With any luck Miss Williamson was still residing here. He would have called first to make an appointment with her, but there were no phone numbers registered under her name. Sending an officer from Otay Mesa police station to verify this location would have raised too much suspicion among the officers. Considering his latest experience with Bill Casey from that exact precinct, mistrust ran deep for Spence. Besides, he wanted to interview her himself. He was too invested in this case to spook their only lead.

Once at the address of Lynn Williamson, Spence had the officer remain in the car as he made his way to the front door. He knocked. There was no answer, so he rang the doorbell. Except for the frantically barking dog inside, no response came from the inhabitants. He wondered whether she might still be at work, or if she still lived at this address. He walked over towards the neighbor's property to ask around. Slowly he made his way across the street and rang the doorbell. Finally, a young woman, holding a baby came to the door.

"Yes?" She asked, apparently a little annoyed for the intrusion.

"Ma'am, my name is Detective Spence Walker." He flashed his badge. "I was wondering whether you might know your neighbor across the way?" He pointed in the direction of Lynn's townhouse.

"What of it?" She asked quite abruptly.

"We've simply come to speak with her. And I can assure you that she's not in any trouble." Spence produced a photograph of Lynn.

"I do, yes. Why do you ask?"

"We're simply seeking to ask a few routine questions, that's all. Will she be returning home any time soon?"

"Look, I don't really know her all that well, but I do see her come home at around four in the afternoon. Maybe you should come back then," she suggested, as she backed away from the door. With one hand on the inside door, she closed it to attend to her crying baby.

Spence took his cue, thanking her for her time before she closed the door on him. He walked back to the unmarked car where Officer O'Brien sat waiting for him.

As he entered the car, he said, "Well it appears we'll have to grab a coffee and some lunch. We may be here for a while."

"Sounds good. I'm already starved," O'Brien uttered.

They drove to the center of town to buy lunch at a local diner. They sat around for a few hours before they returned to Miss Williamson's residence at around two-thirty. Spence parked the car across from Lynn's dwelling, and made himself comfortable to wait until she returned home. It wasn't long before a middle-aged woman came strolling down the sidewalk to the townhouse. Stopping briefly to gather her mail, she began to rummage through her purse. She pulled out some keys and slowly opened the door. Spence took one look at his partner before they both got out of the car. He led the way towards the entrance, where the woman was closing the door behind her. Spence rang the doorbell and the dog began to bark once again. Not but a few seconds later, the door was opened to the detectives.

"Yes," the woman answered rather curtly.

"Excuse me, ma'am. Are you Lynn Williamson?" Spence asked before saying, "I'm Detective Spence Walker from Imperial Beach, and this is my partner, Officer O'Brien."

Once satisfied with their credentials, Miss Williamson invited the two inside. "A girl just can't be too careful these days," she stated to the officers.

"Yes, indeed, ma'am," O'Brien said.

The only information brought forward after meeting Lynn Williamson was that she had heard Brock's connection with some satanic cult. Besides briefly knowing Bill Casey some years ago, she would not have suspected the police's involvement. She also mentioned a possible association between the university and Brock Simms but could not elaborate further on any details.

~

May had invited Fred over to the house and was waiting for him. Nearing the appointed hour, she heard the doorbell ring. She peered through the peephole before opening the door. Satisfied she opened the door to allow Fred in. He appeared quite nervous, looking all around in a jumpy way. May closed the door behind him and asked him to be seated. She had noticed that Fred was carrying a parcel before they both sat down in the living room, where May had already set out tea with scones. Somehow, she had found the energy to bake.

"Fred, what is going on? You look as though you've just seen a ghost!" May remarked.

"I think they're at it again!" he swallowed hard. "This morning, they found Mr. Hornsby, dead." Emphasis was placed on the last word. "He was only seventy-two. I'm likely to be next," Fred mumbled in a panic, obviously disturbed by this.

"Oh my! Sorry to hear that. Did you know Mr. Hornsby?"

"We used to play cards together. But now I'm seeing a pattern," Fred flatly stated, still with fear lacing his voice.

"And what might that be?" May questioned.

"None of the victims had any living relatives. Do you see what that means?" Fred continued. He was terribly distraught.

"You might have a point because Iris McDonald was a spinster, and Ginger Ferris had been married for many years, but they never had children. Then there was Cybil Lancaster who lived at the Lodge. They never did find a single living relation either. Did Mr. Hornsby have any children?" she queried.

"Not that I'm aware of. I've only been at the nursing home for a short while. Do you see, with no living relatives, someone could easily stand to inherit their money?" Fred shook his head.

"What, their insurance money? And, who do you suspect?"

"I believe someone in charge, of course. They would have access, keeping tabs on the residents, and even the mortician could be in on it. Maybe even the staff at the home. They all have access to the lot of us. Anyone in charge could stand to gain, and the nursing home could continue receiving the pension money or insurance.

Who knows?" Fred shrugged. "But I'm on the lookout for anyone who's been spending more money than usual." He continued, sounding more paranoid than ever.

"That sounds too unbelievable. Why would anyone take a life that will likely end in a short while?" May was horrified.

"Because they may be funding some money laundering outfit, or some underground drug ring. Any motive can surely be a reason to kill, especially if money is involved. So, we should follow the money trail," Fred continued. "Have you never heard the saying, 'It's always to do with sex and money?' And, I believe this case has all the markings of 'big bucks.'"

"But how do we begin to follow the money?" May asked.

"Perhaps your niece has the answer to that question. When is she due back?"

"I'm not too sure. Although I expect not long since she mentioned she only had a few minor affairs to take care of before returning."

# Chapter 30

"Wake up, Jewel! Now you will find yourself back in the present day," he ordered. Professor Brown was clearly concerned. After snapping his fingers twice, Jewel woke up as though nothing had transpired except, she was aware that tears were streaming down her face.

"Is everything okay?" Jewel queried, looking positively puzzled.

"It is, now," he sighed heavily. "I'm not certain whether we should continue on this path," the professor said, feeling agitated.

"Of course, we should, or I may never resolve the inner issues plaguing my life. Another attempt, please?" Jewel pleaded.

"Perhaps, though we must continue much later..." As the professor finished saying this, they heard a knock at the door.

"Yes?" He called out to the visitor. A young man appeared through the doorway. "Come in," the professor said. "Jamie, how nice to see you. Jewel, this is Jamie Furrow, an associate of mine." He signaled to Jamie to enter the room.

Jamie wore a nice casual suit, no tie. He was an attractive young man. In fact, he had an uncanny resemblance to Anthony, the young man in Jewel's dream. Perhaps the reason for the dream was to announce Jamie's arrival? She would pursue the matter this evening.

Jamie spoke, offering his hand to shake Jewel's. "Nice to meet you. I've heard a little about your situation and I was wondering whether—and of course with your permission—I could follow your case? It is most fascinating and would be quite helpful to finalize my thesis. Would you mind terribly?" Jamie asked.

Jewel stood to shake Jamie's hand and as she did, she felt a warm sensation travel up her arm. She found him so alluring that she could not think straight. "Of course. That would be fine." She regretted it immediately. She had not given this any thought. On the other hand, she trusted the professor wholeheartedly, so with Jamie being an associate of his, surely, he must be credible. She needed to justify her sudden impulsivity. She dismissed her doubts, still mystified by his uncanny resemblance to Anthony—he had completely blindsided her.

Following her slip-up, Jewel advised Professor Brown that she must be leaving. She felt so out of balance, so out of sync—maybe she had not yet fully returned to her body—whatever it was, she wanted to get out of there, quickly. She was aware that she had been crying over that boy again and she was still feeling the pang of lost love. She left the men to their dialogue, relieved that her heart was no longer pounding.

"What was that all about?" She questioned her spiritual guides, as though they were truly standing outside with her—and as though a response was forthcoming. If someone had happened to be close to her, she would have appeared totally mad. And leaving a psychiatrist office would certainly prove them right. She seriously wondered if the university staff already considered her a strange duck. She also questioned the fact that if Jamie Furrow had already heard about her, then that probably meant the entire faculty had heard of her meetings with the professor.

She felt betrayed that her private information had been shared without consulting her first, and then recalled that prior to the commencement of her sessions, she had signed a waiver form wherein she granted the release of her information—which would thereafter be considered the university's property. Furthermore, she had agreed to release the university of any liability since she was agreeing to proceed with engaging in an unorthodox therapy of her own volition. *Great!* Did that allow the professor to reveal the minute details of her sessions—those she considered to be extremely private? She needed to review the waiver form once again or ask the professor for clarification.

What a strange day this had been. She was grateful to be home in her apartment, where she could finally have something to eat. Jewel ordered her meal before making a call to the local airport to book a flight for the next morning. She knew time was quite limited when it came to Aunt May's condition. After booking her flight Jewel immediately called May.

"Hello, Aunt May," Jewel chirped.

"Jewel, it is so nice to hear from you. Are you flying out to see me?" May questioned, sounding eager for another visit.

"I sure am. I'll be there by noon tomorrow. How are you feeling? Should I come out tonight instead?" Maybe she should have called Aunt May before booking a flight. *That wasn't very smart,* she thought. Then again, she hadn't been able to think straight since meeting Anthony earlier. *What was so disturbing about him,* she wondered?

"No, my dear. No rush but it will be so nice to see you again. And I've got Fred here with me so I'm quite fine."

"That's good. And I'm glad you two are getting to know one another," Jewel said. "I will be there on the 10:30 am flight and not to worry, I will catch a cab to your house," Jewel explained.

"That sounds wonderful. See you upon your arrival then," May said while hanging up the phone.

"Well that's good. Jewel will be here by noon tomorrow. She may have ideas as to how we will follow the money trail. Would you be able to come back tomorrow afternoon?" May asked Fred.

"Yes, of course I will. What time would you like me to be here?" Fred asked.

"Let's say about two in the afternoon. Does that work for you?"

"Very much so. I will be here promptly at two. I must be getting back. Oh, by the way this package contains George's last meal left on his tray. Can we get it sent to a lab, pronto? There may be traces of toxins in it," he asked May.

"I'll have it sent out tonight. Although it is getting rather late, I'm sure the couriers work all hours. Let me take care of it for you." May suggested, while putting her hand out to take the package from Fred.

"That would be excellent since I wasn't able to get my hands on the meals of the others immediately after death. This time however, I was able to sneak into George's room while the medics were present. I asked to see him before the body was removed, and that didn't seem to alarm anyone," Fred noted.

"So, if the EMS took the body straight away then how could the Home fake him 'not' dying to keep receiving his pension?" May questioned. "That scenario doesn't add up, so it must be another motive that's driving the killer. Or perhaps it's simply the two of us being paranoid? Honestly, I feel as though we are still onto something significant."

Fred stepped outside after his cab arrived in front of the house. He said his goodbyes before leaving. He truly fancied May, although he knew full well that she would not be here long. *Gees, I'm spending more time at funerals than at social functions,* he thought wistfully. He would make a trip to the funeral home. He would ask a few of his own questions all the while making it sound as though he wanted to purchase a plot for himself. He had always meant to do that anyways, and the way things are headed it may not be a bad idea after all. He could not help but chuckle at the irony.

Jewel packed her luggage with a few more outfits this time since she did not know when she would be returning. She slipped under the covers after showering. She felt exhausted from today's events and immediately fell asleep. Her dreams replayed her last session with the professor. The next morning, she woke up in tears, but why?

With little time to spare, Jewel shook off the tears, wiped her face, dressed in a hurry, and then out the door she left with suitcase in hand. She took a cab to the airport, calling Spence from the backseat.

"Spence, it's nice to catch you. I'm on my way to Canterbury. Really? Okay, so the court date will start the day after. Agreed, that is good news. Do you have any idea when I will be called to testify? Not yet, hey…, I can be reached on my cell. Will you please try to give me at least one day's notice to return to testify? Yes, thanks, and you have a good day too." Jewel hung up just as the cab pulled up at the airport. Once on the plane, Jewel was relieved a trial date had been set, and so soon. She hoped it would not last too long and that she would not be called to testify right away—she genuinely wanted to spend as much time with her aunt as possible.

It was another uneventful flight. The trip had been smooth with only a bit of wind turbulence. After catching another taxi to May's residence, Jewel fixed her hair in the rearview mirror. As the cab pulled up in front of the house, she paid her fare, and walked up the driveway pulling her suitcase behind her. The air was crisp. She loved the scenery with birds singing all around. May certainly had found a quaint little cottage with the purchase of this charming place. The smell of apple pie and cinnamon wisped by her.

Jewel rang the doorbell and stood on the stoop waiting for May to answer the door. It was not long before the door was flung open. May's delight at seeing Jewel was evident. "Welcome, my dear," she said with a huge smile adorning her lovely weathered face.

Jewel could not believe the enormous transformation in May's demeanor from when she had last seen her. Perhaps she was right, and the hospital was 'not a place to recover.'

"It's so nice to be back, Aunt May. And you look very well. Are you sure the doctors have it right? You look wonderful!" Jewel repeated. "Let me know your secret and I shall bottle it to sell," she said before she started to chuckle. She entered the house. "Is that apple pie that I smell?"

"Yes, dear. And don't worry it was one from the freezer. I have prepared a small lunch with Fred joining us for apple pie this afternoon. I hope that's all right with you?" May asked.

"Yes, by all means that sounds like the '*good old days.*' And you didn't have to put yourself out to fix a lunch. I would have been delighted to take you out, although the smell of your apple pie is divine. Thank you, Aunt May. But you have to promise me you won't be doing any more entertaining while I'm here."

"Why ever not? I've not had company in a week and, once I had some rest, I was much improved. The idea of your early return has put fire under me. I feel great," May said, a little bit more excited than her usual self.

"Now come in and please sit. We shall have a light lunch before Fred arrives. We had thought that two o'clock this afternoon would do, initially. I called him and asked him over sooner for dessert. He seems such a nice gentleman." May almost looked as though she was a schoolgirl again.

"You didn't fall for that dashingly smart-looking man by any chance, did you?" Jewel said with amusement in her voice.

"Don't be silly—at my age? That's a ridiculous notion. He's simply very nice. Besides, we get along quite well. Plus, we shouldn't forget that we both have the same interest in catching my late companions' murderer. We must do away with that lot before someone else gets murdered. Oh, too late! I almost forgot to tell you; another man died yesterday. Mr. George Hornsby. Fred came immediately after this unexpected death; shaken I might add."

"Another? That can't be! One more death?" Jewel shook her head. "Are you sure it wasn't from natural causes? It would be highly unlikely that any killer would continue to murder so soon. They would obviously be noticed, wouldn't you think?" Jewel questioned, quite amazed by May's last announcement. "I wonder whether any autopsies have been performed?" Jewel asked, thinking out loud.

They continued their conversation regarding the latest death while they ate their salad along with glazed salmon. May had already removed the pie from the oven to cool. The aroma of baked apple pie with a strong hint of cinnamon odor was notable. It brought back memories of Jewel's youth, a time when she remembered the tasty pies Aunt May baked for her and Marcy—memories that now haunted Jewel. And soon she would be faced with losing another.

Fred was expected to arrive by cab, so Jewel was on the lookout for him through the large living room window. After an intense conversation regarding Mr. Hornsby, shortly thereafter, the doorbell rang, bringing Jewel's trip down memory lane to an abrupt end. Aunt May rushed to the door, allowing Fred to enter. They both kissed on the cheek before Fred made his way to the living room.

"Good day, Fred! How are you doing?" Jewel asked.

"Just fine, thank you, and it's so lovely to see such beauties in one household," Fred complimented.

Both women blushed simultaneously with his remark.

"Have a seat, please," May said, pointing to the couch. "I will bring out the pie. Would you like some ice cream with it?"

"That would be lovely," Fred replied. "The smell of home-cooked pie was more than I bargained for. May I assist you in the kitchen?"

"Why yes, if you'd like," May said with a delightful smile.

Jewel swore she saw a little twinkle in both their eyes. What? Aunt May with a man? May was in her eighties, it seemed impossible after all these years that she would now find a man to bring back the sparkle in her eyes. Jewel imagined that love could happen at any age.

They immediately returned with the dessert in hand. May placed the tray of pies on the coffee table while Fred brought the tray with a teapot and three cups along with their saucers.

"Now eat up before it gets cold," May commented.

While eating, they discussed the relevancy of their meeting.

"Jewel, I must admit that Fred and I were wondering how we could possibly follow the money. Would you have any clues?" May asked.

"Of course, it depends on the suspects and, by the way, who *do* we suspect?" Jewel asked curiously.

May said, "We were wondering about the personnel in charge. They have access to the nursing home's clientele with possible motives in doing away with the elderly. Fred had his eye on Mrs. Boucher. The head of the Canterbury Home could have motives, not to mention the mortician. Possibly? All three seem likely candidates. If we follow the money trail and their whereabouts at the time of the murders, perhaps we can get the police involved in solving this case." May finished her piece of pie. She took a sip of tea and placed her cup down on its saucer.

By this time Fred had already devoured his portion of pie and wondered whether there were seconds.

"I should mention that Spence kept in touch with Detective Ted Howard." Jewel added to the discussion. "I'm sure Detective Howard would have the means to look into the financial details of the people in question. Though I believe we must have more evidence on each before Ted could justify prying into their business or financial affairs," Jewel suspected.

Fred acknowledged that he would dig deeper into who they were and their possible motives. He did know Mrs. Boucher was not well-liked by the residents. The owners were not known at this point, but that would be easily determined by looking up the records of ownership—Jewel agreed to look after that. The task of contacting the mortician who signed the death certificates was assigned to May since she had remembered his name—Ron Stewart.

So, with the list of specific inquiries in hand, May rose to escort Fred out the front door, wishing him well before he left. Once everything was said and done, May felt terribly tired and went to lie down.

Jewel advised that she would stay up for a bit to do some research on the owners of the nursing homes before retiring for the evening. Her research revealed that one of the owners had a connection to the university where Professor Brown worked. *Now that's an interesting connection,* Jewel thought. Despite her reservations, she recognized that like all the other leads in the case, this too, would have to be explored. She prayed Professor Brown was not involved in any criminal activities. Remaining as calm as possible, she would not permit her mind to conjure up what that would mean to her if he were—instead, she headed straight to bed.

# Chapter 31

Spence met with the District Attorney to ensure all the evidence for the prosecution was sound. They left for the courthouse during the early part of the morning just before ten. Spence looked forward to putting this whole grisly affair behind him.

After all the opening arguments the trial finally began. Spence was called to the stand. He approached the bench, was sworn in and took his seat. While seated in the old wooden chair—no doubt polished to accommodate slippery characters—he felt nervous. As soon as he identified himself, the prosecution asked Spence to first point to his assailants before recounting his traumatic encounter. Spence pointed to Philip Denver, Bradley Johnson—better known as Jeff—Brock Simms and Bill Casey.

Spence swallowed hard before describing his harrowing experience. He was in pursuit of the accomplice, Jeff, known as Mr. Bradley Johnson, Spence mentioned. Not knowing Johnson's business at Jewel Seymour's apartment, Spence followed him out of town. Up until this point all went routinely. After following Mr. Johnson for some time, Spence decided to pull him over. After approaching Johnson's vehicle, he pointed a gun at Spence. Then Johnson stepped out of the car and hit him over the head. The next thing Spence knew he was unconscious inside the trunk of the assailant's vehicle. Once Brad drove off, Spence only regained consciousness a few minutes before arriving at an abandoned house. At this point there were no opportunities for escape.

Mr. Johnson opened the trunk with a gun pointed at Spence's skull. He was ordered into the building, where he was tossed down a flight of stairs. The next thing he remembered was waking up to find Jewel Seymour chained to the basement wall. Both he and Miss Seymour planned their escape. Once out, they both made it back to town, where Officer Bill Casey joined Spence. They returned to the abandoned building only to discover that Bill Casey was also one of the perpetrators. They were part of a large network involved in the slaying of more than three girls, with the kidnapping and attempted murder of Tina Miles and that of Miss Seymour. After naming the girls who were killed, Spence mentioned that Marcy Cooper was also suspected of being murdered for unknown reasons and the investigation was still ongoing.

The judge overruled this last statement, instructing the jurors to disregard the testimony regarding Miss Cooper. At which time the court adjourned for a short recess. Spence heard the judge's gavel pound the bench before the court recessed.

Following the break, the attorneys brought up new evidence to the court—and while the judge heard arguments on both sides—it was determined that a two-week adjournment was necessary to review the new evidence.

Spence left the courthouse quite annoyed with the two-week deferment. He marched over to his office to dig deeper into the new evidence—the news that Professor James Brown from the university could be implicated in these murders came as a shock to them all.

Unfortunately, since Spence was testifying for the prosecution, he was too 'close to this case.' His superiors could not afford a prejudicial decision against their precinct, so Spence was ordered to stay away from the investigation. He therefore had to rely on Detective Stone to follow up on the new evidence related to Professor James Brown, if possible—though highly unlikely without Stone being noticed, since he was well-known throughout these parts.

However, upon his return home, Spence listened to his voicemail from Jewel. He was informed that 'he should look at the Charles Memorial Hospital parking lot security tapes to see whether they could connect Philip Denver with Marcy's murder. He should then check whether Denver had left about the same time of Marcy's untimely death.' Jewel apologized for forgetting to suggest this to him. It was only when she remembered her disturbing dream that she had pieced it all together. Spence followed this lead, but so much time had elapsed since Marcy's death that no tapes were found.

~

The following morning Jewel rose and found May had already left for the day. *How could I not have heard her?* Jewel wondered. She knew she had slept quite soundly. Researching the owners of the nursing home was tiring business but to not hear Aunt May getting ready, eating and leaving the house without Jewel being aware, was surely a first. She quickly showered and went out to confirm the new details of the case. As Jewel was getting into the car, her cell phone rang. Not wanting to miss Spence's call, she quickly answered it.

"I'm awake. What do you think I'm doing here, vacationing?" Jewel laughed at the ludicrous idea of being on holidays while a murderer was on the loose. "No, I didn't think so. What's up?" She asked, hoping for some good news. "You really have time to come to Canterbury, truly? I'm so happy to hear that! Yes, of course May wouldn't mind the extra company. But if you want me to ask her first, by all means, I can call you back as soon as I locate her. No, she simply left the house earlier than I did. And now I'm on my way to check out some information that may shed some light on this mystery case." As Jewel sat in her vehicle, the phone suddenly picked up static. Spence's voice deteriorated from that point on. "What was that, Spence? I'm sorry…," she huffed, "I can't hear you. I'll call you back as soon as I return to May's, but first I'll need to find her. I'll call you back around lunch time, alright?" There were no audible sounds on the other end of the phone, so Jewel hung up hoping Spence had heard her plan.

Aunt May paid a visit to the mortuary to find out more about her friends' untimely deaths. To her surprise May was informed that autopsies had not been performed. Was this a mistake, or the routine procedure for people presumed to have died of natural causes? According to the pathologist she met with, it was quite routine when there were no living family members pressing for answers and no reason to be suspicious of the cause of death.

She shook her head and left the mortuary. Her bed beckoned her to go home, especially having left the house so early.

When she reached her house, she felt a tingling in her arm, but dismissed it as being overtired. She went to the washroom and after taking an aspirin, May laid down. At this point it was about noon, and even though hunger was teasing her, May felt that she was beyond exhaustion. She fell asleep quickly with thoughts of how she was going to catch a murderer.

Fred could not detect anything at the nursing home either. He had not expected much since everything had been locked up tighter than Fort Knox—which begged the question—Why?

Jewel, for her part, found out that the registered owner of the nursing home was none other than Michael McKay. He was known for funding retirement homes for the elderly. Jewel found an article outlining 'how much he had given to the cause of providing homes for seniors and how he was well known as the Good Samaritan.' So, it appeared that Mr. McKay was '*Mr. nice guy.*' Who would ever suspect an upstanding citizen and philanthropist to wreak havoc in a quiet town? Perhaps this was the break they were searching for? But following the money trail had proven more difficult than the three sleuths first imagined. If this new information proved correct, it could shed light on Mr. McKay's personal and financial dealings to either eliminate him as a suspect or incriminate him.

Jewel wanted to inform May of her findings. Once she entered the house, she went to check on her aunt. She found May still asleep and knew her news would have to wait.

The phone rang. Not wanting to wake May, Jewel took the call in the living room. Spence had just booked a flight and would be leaving shortly. She attempted to warn Spence that she had not had sufficient time to ask May about the sleeping arrangements, but Spence had already hung up. Her news of Spence's arrival would have to wait also. May would be overjoyed with the reinforcement of Spence's detective skills.

As Jewel mused over her predicament, she thought she heard a noise coming from May's room. She rushed over, anxious to share all the happy news. Jewel was shocked to discover May perspiring profusely.

"Oh gosh!" Jewel exclaimed. "What happened?"

"I don't feel well," May feebly responded.

"I can see that. What's the matter? Where does it hurt?"

"I'm not sure, but I feel exhausted beyond years," May replied.

"I'm calling an ambulance straight away," Jewel said.

The ambulance did not take long to arrive. With all the commotion Jewel forgot to inform her aunt of Spence's arrival. They both reached the emergency department and May was rushed in through the side door. Jewel was instructed to sit in the waiting area while the doctors assessed May's condition. Everyone knew her condition would never improve. Jewel's greatest fear was that she might never see May alive again.

While sitting in the packed waiting room, Jewel had plenty of time to think about what was happening with May. But worrying about something one cannot change is a useless endeavor. After pushing white light around May for added protection, she decided to piece together the information she had on the case. But how could she with so little information to work with, and too many loose ends? It was good that Spence was on his way, and with that realization, Jewel left the lobby to make a quick call to him. His phone was shut off, and this could only mean he had already taken off from the airport—he was probably in the air. She instinctively left him a voice message informing him where to find them—hopefully without alarming him. She followed this message by calling Fred Fisher to inform him that May had been taken to the hospital.

After returning to the waiting room, Jewel was informed that she could see May in the intensive care. She thought it must be serious if May was placed in the ICU again. She swallowed hard and followed the nurse.

Jewel did her utmost to compose herself. "Ah, May, how are you feeling?" Jewel asked, clearly sad despite her noble attempt to present the contrary. There were machines beeping with heart rate, pulse, and blood oxygen readings making it difficult to hear May's feeble voice.

"Don't you be worrying none, my dear, just concern yourself with solving the riddle before I check out. I've not got time on my side so you must make the best of the little time and be useful in the field." Like a drill sergeant, May ordered Jewel about.

"You will be surprisingly fine when Spence comes to stay with us for a few weeks. He's already on his way."

"You didn't call him away from court because of me, did you?" May queried warily.

"Not at all. It's as good a reason as any for him to be here. In fact, he had recently called to let us know that the courts had postponed the trial for a few weeks. He has more than enough time to visit, and he is anxious to help resolve our mystery and put it to rest. Don't you think this is good news?" Jewel asked. Honestly, she knew this whole murder affair was more than May needed right now.

# Chapter 32

Spence was extremely agitated at not being able to warn Jewel about Professor Brown's possible involvement. Then again, he had no concrete evidence to support his suspicions. Without additional information—and doing so without 'infuriating' his superiors—he was better off staying far away from work to remain near Jewel.

Spence had already made reservations to fly to Canterbury that afternoon. Before leaving, he had time to pick up a few items at the house and briefly stop at the police station to check for any tangible evidence regarding the professor. He would have to be especially cautious while looking at any connection between the university and the ongoing case, disregarding his superiors' orders to 'not interfere'.

After rushing about with his last-minute errands, Spence arrived at the airport in good time. Once he landed in May's hometown, he automatically turned his phone on. Discovering Jewel was at the hospital with May, he quickly rushed to the hospital instead. He hoped he was not too late. As soon as he arrived, Spence hurried to the emergency, flashed his badge and was formerly escorted. He knew that May might not be able to wait until he got through the lineup at the front desk. Luckily, the nurse ushered him to see May without delay.

Jewel was obviously relieved to see him. They hugged one another before she quickly brought him up to speed on May's status. Apparently, the doctor said she only had days, but they could not be more specific than that. Her organs were beginning to shut down.

Before leaving the hospital, Spence had a chance to speak with May. She insisted that he stay at the house to help with the ongoing case. With a wink at Jewel, she asked if they might get closure regarding the deaths before her departure—May would then leave a happy soul. Spence assured May that he was here to help, but he was reluctant to inform her that he only had two weeks before the trial resumed. Needless to say, Spence had already testified so he was not likely going to have to restate his testimony.

Fred soon arrived while they were both leaving the hospital. The nurse allowed one more visitor but asked to keep it to a minimum to ensure May got proper rest. May did not see this as an important time to relax because, she joked, she would have the rest of time to take it easy. Jewel and Spence left Fred to visit.

Jewel unlocked the front door of May's quaint little bungalow and they both entered eager to be 'home'. Spence had insisted on picking up some chicken en route. Once he heard that the owner and director of the home was Michael McKay, he was more than suspicious. Yet once again, without more proof, they could not pursue their investigation into the man's affairs. They both knew that their evidence would have to be strong in order to charge a man of his status with multiple murder charges. After reviewing the notes that 'no' autopsies had been performed on the deceased, along with their suspicions against Mr. McKay, they both knew something was amiss.

Spence had to find a delicate way to ask Jewel what she really knew about Professor Brown. He cleared his throat before finding the correct words to ask. "So, what do you know about Professor Brown?" He blurted this out soon to regret how it sounded.

Jewel looked baffled at this. "I've known him for some time. He comes across as genuine and he treats me well. Why do you ask?" Jewel queried, quite affronted by Spence's interest.

He swallowed hard not grasping her objections. "It seems that there may be, and I assure you it is only a possibility, that Professor Brown is linked somehow to these deaths. At least there is a link through emails that Detective Stone is pursuing," he explained.

"How can that be? I have trusted him with my life. There must be a mistake because I know people and he does not come across as a killer." She paused. "Not someone like him with such an impeccable reputation. Are you sure?" Jewel was incredulous.

"Like I said, Detective Stone is following this lead so maybe you should stay clear for a while. We can follow Michael McKay."

"Let's do that. But I can't help thinking why the professor would not have kidnapped me himself, or even killed me because he had me under his direct control when he put me under hypnosis. So why not then if he was one of the perpetrators?"

Spence's eyebrow rose thinking how Jewel was under the professor's control. *If only he personally had that kind of control over her?* he reflected. "At the moment I can't answer that. Though you do make a compelling argument." Spence had to agree.

Their discussion drove them to stay up later than they expected. Jewel did not think too long about the professor's possible involvement before falling into a deep sleep.

As she was sleeping, Jewel found herself standing at a beautiful resort overlooking a wonderful beach, when a man appeared. She recognized him as Michael McKay. At that moment, a fog rolled in, sweeping over her feet initially before reaching her waist. She was fearing for her life. Mr. McKay walked up to her and laughed in her face. The laugh was so cynical that shivers crawled up and down her spine. She immediately woke up with a freezing feeling as though someone had left the window open, and a cold breeze swept over her. She rose to get another blanket but noticed that her window was indeed open. Jewel shivered and thought of joining Spence to warm up but thought twice about that decision. Instead she closed the window. *Why was it open?* she wondered. Something did not seem right. She armed herself with a curtain rod left in the closet and quietly went to investigate the rest of the house. She would go to Spence now, after all. Could an intruder have come in through the open window? It seemed unlikely. Jewel slowly crept into the living room where Spence was sleeping on the sofa.

He woke instantly curious to know why she was still up—and holding a rod in her hands. Was she so angry with him about accusing Professor Brown of any involvement that she was about to strike him?

"I thought I heard something, or maybe it's my imagination going wild, I'm not sure. My window was left open. Did you open it?" Jewel asked, desperately holding her racing thoughts together.

"Not me, but then who? Let me look around. Stay here," he ordered.

After checking out the whole house, and finding no one, Spence returned to the living room. He sat on the sofa.

"I swear I did not leave that window open," Jewel stated flatly. She shrugged in exasperation.

"There are no intruders. Are you alright?"

"No, not exactly. My only living relative—except she's really not my relation, and yet, May has raised me to be the woman I am today—is about to die. So, not really, no! I can't sleep without having dreams that haunt me and I woke up with shivers that cooled me down like an ice cube. I'm not feeling okay." Jewel said, while forcing back her tears. She knew that if they started to flow, they may never stop.

"I'm sorry that wasn't what I meant…" he hesitated, unsure of himself, "to upset you. Come and sit with me. I will do my best to warm you. Please?" He waved his hand for her to join him on the sofa. "I'm not an expert on these matters but I do know you've been through a lot these past months. Please let me help you." He wrapped his arm around her shoulder.

"You already have, and I really appreciate that you came out to see us." Jewel could feel the compassion he was displaying on her behalf. And, she could sense the renewed attraction between them intensifying—something she feared.

"We will catch this guy, I promise you," Spence reassured her, sounding determined as ever.

Jewel confessed, "My dream was of Mr. McKay. His sinister laughter made my skin crawl. And instantly I awoke to the freezing air from the open window," she shivered again. "With this particular dream I believe we are on to something big. We've got to find the paper trail linking him to these deaths. I can't imagine how they are murdering them. With no autopsies being performed on them, it's assumed that all evidence went to their graves." Jewel heavily sighed.

Spence held out his hand for her to lay her head on his shoulder. "Just relax with me," he insisted.

Without thought, Jewel complied. She noticed how nice his cologne was and reveled in the scent, breathing it in like there would be no tomorrow. In a way she hoped there would not be.

Once they were both curled up together on the couch, Spence spoke again. "If we can find anything at all that links Michael McKay to these deaths, we can exhume the bodies and look closer into their cause of death. In the morning we will find the link, alright?" Spence assured Jewel before they both fell asleep.

The sun rose through the living room window. Jewel watched as Spence slept. Everything seemed so perfect, so natural. There they were—arms wrapped around each other—he looked peaceful. She had not seen this side of him in a long time. He gave her the comfort and sense of security she had not had since her father had passed away, after which she felt totally alone in the world. If not for Marcy, and of course, Aunt May, she would have been totally alone.

She had grown close to Spence but maybe for all the wrong reasons. Why shouldn't she have this intimacy? They may not be passionately in love with one another—at least he was not—but they were there for one another, like companions. Was that so wrong? Is that not what some people do? Yet, Jewel knew somehow that their beliefs were so very different that any hope of surrendering to love with this man would be impossible, if not foolish. He was a cop, a detective with a reputation to uphold. She was a psychic who sees people that go bump in the night. How could two very opposing forces ever make a go of it? No, it was clear to her that she must remain single unless somehow the right man would come along.

Spence woke at that moment, watching Jewel as she gazed at the sunrise. *She looked distant, as though she was thinking of being somewhere else,* he thought. With a warm smile on his face, Spence spoke—his voice a little low, but manly. "Good morning. How did you sleep?"

"Just fine," Jewel replied without further hesitation regarding their nearness.

"Not scared, or cold any longer?" he asked, grinning.

"No, and I can't thank you enough. I see a super-busy day ahead of us, so we've got to get ready quickly," Jewel managed to say, avoiding any further eye contact with this enticing man while in this very intimate position.

"Sure, but we should call the hospital to see how May got through the night?" Spence asked.

"Yes, of course we must, that was my first thought," Jewel lied. "I'm sure the hospital would have called us though." She rang the hospital, and once given the 'all okay' from the unit clerk, Jewel left a message with her for May.

As they prepared to leave, they purposely made efforts not to get in each other's way, but that was not working very well. They seemed to be bumping into each other in awkward moments in the single bathroom. There were a lot of "oops-sorry" as they navigated their otherwise normal morning routines.

They left the house in good time and went for breakfast. It was only really sinking in for Jewel just how upset she was that Professor Brown might be involved. Spence called Detective Stone for further updates and also to do a background check on Michael McKay. Spence also placed a call to his longtime friend, Detective Howard, and asked him to run a financial history on McKay.

# Chapter 33

On their way to the hospital, Spence received a call from Detective Howard. He had discovered many inconsistencies with Michael McKay's financial history, far too many discrepancies to be legitimate. Spence asked to see him once they were done at the hospital. After their visit with May—and giving her a few updates to keep her happy—they both set off to see Detective Ted Howard.

They were gladly ushered inside Ted's residence and Spence introduced Jewel to his associate. Ted offered coffee and they sat down. With paperwork laid out in front of him, Spence could see that he was staring at the motive for killing the elderly.

"It appears that May was on to something significant, huge in fact." Spence motioned with his hands spread far apart in illustration.

"But in this case, how do we proceed?" Jewel demanded.

Apparently working for years in the local district, Ted Howard knew a judge by the name of Sam Dumont. Howard felt he could easily persuade the judge to act on this information and open a case against Michael McKay.

Judge Dumont was informed that all but two bodies, George Hornsby and Cybil Lancaster, were cremated even though the deceased had never signed any documentation expressing such requests. This alone angered the judge and before long he ordered the bodies exhumed for further analysis. Judge Dumont immediately called the mortuary to stop any additional cremations until further notice. A police car was dispatched to the mortician's office to enforce this order. The body of George Hornsby was just about to be cremated when the officer arrived. A pathologist from out of town was brought in to investigate the deaths with a screening that would make the FBI look incompetent.

The results did not take long to arrive. George had died from higher than normal levels of potassium in his blood, evidently injected into his armpit. One could only wonder whether the others had died similarly. The second body would be also going under the microscope to determine the cause of death.

Detective Stone returned Spence's call with information that someone at the university was implicated in the deaths of the young girls, and that they were now focused on Professor Brown and his assistant, Jamie Furrow.

It hadn't taken long for the department to determine that his assistant had access to Professor Brown's email account. It was established that Furrow was able to use the account while the professor was preoccupied with appointments or lectures. Furrow was sending out emails not only to Bill Casey, but also to Michael McKay. Had Spence not given McKay's name to Detective Stone, he would have overlooked these emails, focusing solely on the court case of Bill Casey and Brock Simms. Even with this new evidence, the police would never have suspected Furrow's emails sent to, of all people, a police officer being anything other than innocent communication. And Stone was grateful that Spence had interviewed Miss Williamson to ascertain the involvement with the university. As it turned out there was no evidence to support that Professor Brown was associated with any wrongdoing, except perhaps, allowing access to his email account.

~

The evidence against Mr. McKay was overwhelming. Once Cybil Lancaster's remarkably preserved body was exhumed, the pathologist discovered puncture marks in her armpits as well and small traces of potassium, the same substance found in George Hornsby's remains. The judge ordered Michael McKay's arrest. Spence could not be more delighted with his capture and rushed over to inform Jewel.

Jewel returned to the hospital to give May the good news, but May's health had deteriorated greatly. Jewel stifled a gasp. She made efforts to whisper to Aunt May that they had succeeded in making an arrest regarding the deaths of her companions. May feebly attempted a smile. The nurse entered to change her IV line.

Jewel was warned that May would not likely make it through another night, but an hour later, May had regained her strength to speak with Jewel. May thanked her and Spence for all their hard work in solving the case.

Fred Fisher also arrived to visit, but with the nurse on 'Gestapo' watch, she steered Fred to wait until Jewel had finished her visit. Once Jewel left in tears, Fred was permitted to say his goodbyes. He left the room with a heavy heart. At his age he knew that losing loved ones was something that occurred frequently, but he had grown so fond of May that this seemed too much—even for him.

Jewel stood waiting for Fred to inform him that he could sleep soundly now that the police had arrested the owner of the nursing home. Fred thanked Jewel for all her devoted support, promising to stay in touch, and she agreed to do the same. Once Spence arrived, he too was permitted to see May.

"Spence, my boy, please close the door." May's voice was weak, though she knew she had to say what was on her mind. In fact, nothing was going to stop her, unless the good Lord would take her at this very moment.

"Spence, I want you to promise me that you will take good care of Jewel. She needs someone to help her and I can assure you that she loves you, but don't tell her I said so." She winked. "You must find a way to tell her how you feel, and not take no for an answer. Be strong. You will see how right she is for you. Promise me you will do whatever you can to keep that promise." May's words were fading.

He nodded. "I don't think she feels for me in the same way that I feel for her. I have watched her carefully and I can assure you that she will not give me the time of day." He swallowed hard. "But I must also tell you how much your love, support, and kindness has been a constant presence in my life. I just wanted to thank you, May." Spence was near shedding tears. For a man not easily moved to tears, this moment was precious indeed.

May could see how much he loved her, and gently smiled at Spence before passing in 'the world of the departed.' Spence kissed her forehead before exiting the room.

With a huge lump in his throat, Spence cleared it before speaking. "She's gone. You might want to go in to see her one last time."

Jewel pushed back her tears. Both she and Fred re-entered the room to sit with her when a nurse soon entered to declare the time of death.

~

May's funeral was set for the following Tuesday in Imperial Beach and she would be buried next to Marcy and Gisele Cooper. With so many of her friends already in the afterlife, very few came to the service. Jewel, Spence and Fred stood proudly together. Professor Brown attended but kept his distance. Jewel noticed him midpoint through the service. After the minister said the eulogy, the coffin was lowered in the ground and once again a sense of loneliness overwhelmed Jewel. She threw a pink rose on top as the coffin slowly lowered to the earthly realms, and with luck to the heavenly kingdom as well.

"What now?" Jewel whispered to May, while she wiped her eyes. It was then that Jewel witnessed May's spirit rising from the ground as though she had risen from the dead. Jewel immediately gasped and glanced around to see whether anyone else had witnessed this rare event. No one was reacting. Following this feat May approached Jewel, whispered in her ear—"Spence will be there for you and you won't be alone." And with that last pronouncement May disappeared into the light toward the setting sun. Jewel blinked before turning to take Spence's arm for support. He seemed happy she had.

Jewel was filled with emotion that was difficult to resolve. After the funeral, and seeing Professor Brown standing there, alone, she approached him. She asked whether he would make time to see her this week, preferably as early as possible. He was very accommodating and scheduled her in for tomorrow.

Jewel returned home with Spence, but not before dropping Fred Fisher off at the airport. He was thinking of moving to be close to Jewel, as he felt a special bond with her and would not take no for an answer. Jewel was thrilled at this prospect.

Spence had stayed the night at Jewel's apartment to ensure she was all right. They slept in the same bed for the first time in years, holding each other. Being a man of honor, Spence did not take advantage of Jewel's vulnerability. Jewel's intoxicating perfume had not gone unnoticed and Spence tossed and turned for the better part of the night.

The next day Jewel had an appointment with Professor Brown. After breakfast Spence dropped Jewel off at the university, informing her that when she was ready, all she had to do was call and he would pick her up again. With that reassurance she climbed the steps of the university, disappearing through the large double doors.

The professor was extremely sensitive about Jewel's feelings. "Are you sure you would like to resume these sessions so soon after the death of your aunt?" he questioned. "I just find it very curious that death has been all around you and still you choose to focus on love," he stated, knowing how intrigued he'd become by this woman.

"I'm quite sure the distraction will be good for me. I had another encounter with a spirit, and even though it felt empowering, I'd really like to get more information on this experience. So please do continue," Jewel repeated, defending her position.

Satisfied, he said, "Let us begin then. Once we get the answer to your question—and you do understand that this method is not an exact science—we will move on. There are no guarantees where you will go. So, are you comfortable with this procedure?"

"Yes, most certainly," Jewel casually replied.

"Now that you are quite comfortable, your eyes are becoming heavy. So much so that your eyelids are drooping while you chase sleep. Your mind slows and is numbed to the outside world. There's a staircase directly ahead of you and you willingly approach it. Now step down the first step, then the second and third as you go farther back in time. Continue down the fourth, fifth, sixth, and seventh steps. Carry on downward to the eighth, ninth, and finally the tenth, reaching the bottom where a hallway of time awaits your review. Are you there?"

No reply came forth at first. Then Jewel slowly nodded.

"Before going too far back who was the spirit you saw?"

"It was at the graveyard that Aunt May rose to greet me to say goodbye." Jewel said in awe. "Initially and very doubtful of May's presence, and yet, she was there for me," Jewel said emotionally.

"I sympathize." Seeing Jewel relaxing once again, he pushed on. "Let's proceed then. You're going back in time. Do you see where you are?" Professor enquired.

"Yes," Jewel's monotone voice responded.

"What do you see?" Professor questioned.

"I'm in a large hall—looks like a mansion," Jewel answered the questions with a very different voice, a cheerful voice.

"Do you know what time period?" he prompted.

"By the looks of the current fashion, I believe it's the eighteen century. It's the turn of the century. A festive time for the upcoming new century with many events underway!" Jewel exclaimed excitedly, beaming a smile. "Yes, it's 1799 and I am Katherin. My mother is Lady Constance Hampton, or whom I call Mummy." Jewel replied to the professor as though she had no other choice. Inexplicably her speech had ultimately changed to a youthful voice.

"That's nice," Professor commented. "Now I want you to relax, breathe in and slowly exhale. That's better. You're doing great. Can you tell me more?"

"I am in England. I live a life of riches that I'm happily living with my family. My father is a gentleman who has been blessed with a good existence." Jewel continued in a juvenile voice.

"What else can you see?"

"I am sixteen, just turned." Jewel said while she attempted a half grin. "I am quite content in a comfortable home with sisters and a brother. I cannot see Mummy though. I am somehow aware that there is news about a marriage." Jewel voice changed from gleeful to disconcerting.

The professor cut in. "Are you all right? Your breathing is becoming erratic once more."

"I'm fine," Jewel sounded in high spirits though wary.

"Do you want to find out the nature of the marriage?"

"I am headed towards Father standing on the far side of the ballroom. I am livid with him. I demand to know how he could do that to me—accept a marriage proposal without so much as a word spoken between us in this regard. I am terribly upset!"

"Father informs me that I need to realize the benefit of this marriage and how it will be very beneficial to my entire family. Father declares that the 'gentleman's' good standing is impeccable and that he is very wealthy, generous and kind in nature."

"I repeat that I cannot marry that man! That I will not marry someone I know naught. I am terribly angry and demand to know why he did not discuss this beforehand." Jewel pauses.

"Oh my! I am currently tearful. Tears flow down my face."

Professor Brown saw that Jewel was crying. He had forgotten to give her tissues before the session began. Too late! Now he could not give her any or she would be startled. Professor Brown gave Jewel some suggestions. "Just relax. You are safe. If you want to, you can just watch from above and tell me all about it."

"It seems Katherin is being forced in a marriage that repulses her. She doesn't understand why her father is demanding this of her. The man is at least twice her age. I don't think she has a mother, not present at the ball. At least, I'm not seeing her anywhere. No. I don't get the feeling she has a mother. She is trying to figure out a way to get out of this mess. Oh! And she's very smart. Oh wow! She's stubborn and this man is going to get more than he bargained for, I think... I... think he's a king or something..."

The professor reached for his phone and quietly called his secretary. "Jane, can you reschedule my afternoon appointments? I'm going to be here for a while..."

~

# About the Author

Born in late winter on a rural road in a half-ton truck during a March snow blizzard in northern Ontario—came the announcement of a small bundle of joy known as Marie Jean. It is not surprising that she still resents the cold to this day. The frantic parents were on their way to the local hospital in a nearby town when they were forced to pull over to the side of the road to deliver their third child. The little baby girl was born in the wee hours of the morning with her father assisting her mother to give birth, using only a jackknife to cut the umbilical cord while the snowstorm raged overhead. To her parent's great relief, the baby cried her own storm and loudly protested the cold weather as they continued to the hospital.

These events had been retold countless times by her loving father and the catalyst that brought Marie Jean Davis forever closer to him. His humorous accounts helped the author begin the long career of writing these deeply moving stories. "With pleasure, I wish you happy 'tales.'"

# Acknowledgment

Many thanks to Roxane, who did the first edit of this book. Many more thanks go out to my good friend, Linda McRae, and also Connie Auger, who both tirelessly worked reading the many revisions on these books. You helped give them style, consistency and with great efforts, you both helped transform this book into a work of art. I thank you for your ongoing support and patience while this and many other books went from the author's feverish mind to the penned outline, and then into a work of fiction interlaced with memories of the author's past and her past lives as well. I would also like to thank my readers, for your ongoing patience and your enthusiasm for the Jewel Seymour Saga, journeying together to the next anticipated series through the pages of history. There are so many people involved in getting this series out to you from my heart to yours.

~~~~~~~~~~~~~~~Happy trails~~~~~~~~~~~~~~~

The next book in this series Volume 2—Revised and released in December 2021

## CRUEL PROVIDENCE!

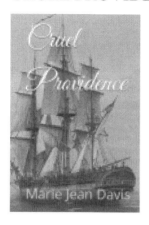

Manufactured by Amazon.ca
Bolton, ON